Praise for *Terry Dactyl*

"The historical novel on acid. Terry's existence—between protesting George Floyd's murder, and chatting about a new cruising app called Sniffies—creates a recognition of social absurdity that Mattilda elevates with her iconoclastic, stylish beauty into a work that has as much to say about vulnerability as it does about trees, and about time itself. This is a book about consciousness, art, and 'getting ready' to be part of a world that will never be ready for you." —**Sarah Schulman,** author of *The Fantasy and Necessity of Solidarity*

"*Terry Dactyl* is the realest fiction I've read in a long time. It's the exact sort of novel we need at this (or any) historical juncture: hilarious, moving, and radically political. The writing sparkles. Sycamore has excelled herself and that's saying something." —**Isabel Waidner,** author of *Corey Fah Does Social Mobility*

"Expansive and confidential, nostalgic and hopeful, *Terry Dactyl* follows its singular, indelible heroine and her search for meaning and community over the span of several decades, from growing up in the AIDS crisis to the club and art scenes of the 1990s to the isolation of the early COVID pandemic, all through the voice of Sycamore's piercing, mesmerizing prose. You won't be able to put it down."
—**Lisa Ko,** author of *Memory Piece*

"*Terry Dactyl* made me cry and made me laugh out loud. It has all the pain and joy, struggle and delight of the lives of those who color outside the lines. It's a book about family and friendship and love and knowing when and how to change your life." —**McKenzie Wark,** author of *Love and Money, Sex and Death*

Also by Mattilda Bernstein Sycamore

Touching the Art
The Freezer Door
Sketchtasy
The End of San Francisco
So Many Ways to Sleep Badly
Pulling Taffy

AS EDITOR

*Between Certain Death and a Possible Future:
Queer Writing on Growing Up with the AIDS Crisis*
*Why Are Faggots So Afraid of Faggots?: Flaming Challenges to
Masculinity, Objectification, and the Desire to Conform*
Nobody Passes: Rejecting the Rules of Gender and Conformity
That's Revolting!: Queer Strategies for Resisting Assimilation
Dangerous Families: Queer Writing on Surviving
Tricks and Treats: Sex Workers Write About Their Clients

TERRY DACTYL

Mattilda Bernstein Sycamore

COFFEE HOUSE PRESS
Minneapolis
2025

Copyright © 2025 Mattilda Bernstein Sycamore
Cover design by Sarah Schulte
Book design by Rachel Holscher
Author photo © Dorothy Edwards

Coffee House Press books are available to the trade through our primary distributor, Consortium Book Sales & Distribution, cbsd.com or (800) 283-3572. For personal orders, catalogs, or other information, write to info@coffeehousepress.org.

All rights reserved. No part of this book may be used or reproduced in any manner for the purpose of training artificial intelligence technologies or systems.

Coffee House Press is a nonprofit literary publishing house. Support from private foundations, corporate giving programs, government programs, and generous individuals helps make the publication of our books possible. We gratefully acknowledge their support in detail in the back of this book.

LIBRARY OF CONGRESS CATALOGING-IN-PUBLICATION DATA

Names: Sycamore, Mattilda Bernstein, author.
Title: Terry Dactyl / Mattilda Bernstein Sycamore.
Description: Minneapolis : Coffee House Press, 2025.
Identifiers: LCCN 2025019123 (print) | LCCN 2025019124 (ebook) |
    ISBN 9781566897419 (paperback) | ISBN 9781566897426 (epub)
Subjects: LCGFT: Queer fiction. | Bildungsromans. | Novels.
Classification: LCC PS3619.Y33 T47 2025 (print) | LCC PS3619.Y33
    (ebook) | DDC 813/.6—dc23/eng/20250530
LC record available at https://lccn.loc.gov/2025019123
LC ebook record available at https://lccn.loc.gov/2025019124

PRINTED IN THE UNITED STATES OF AMERICA

32 31 30 29 28 27 26 25   1 2 3 4 5 6 7 8

For JoAnne, 1974–1995

For Chrissie Contagious, 1974–2010

For David Wojnarowicz, 1954–1992

The first time I met Sid she was on the dance floor in a silver and gold tube dress pulled over her head except it wasn't just a dress because the fabric went on and on and somehow she knew the exact spot on the dance floor where the light would shine right on her or that's how it felt when she was writhing inside this tube of fabric, pulling it up and down, a hand out and a hand in, and then her face exposed in harsh white makeup and black lipstick with long glittering eyelashes and then she rolled onto the floor, she was crawling or more like bending but also she was completely still in the bouncing lights and all this was happening on a crowded dance floor at the Limelight while I was sipping my cocktail and I didn't know what I was seeing I mean it felt like this went on forever, how many songs, it was like there wasn't even music anymore just my body inside the fabric peeking out and then she pulled the dress up around her neck like a huge elegant collar, and underneath she was wearing a gold bodysuit with a silver metallic skirt that flared out, with ballet slippers also painted gold and she walked right up to me and said what did you think.

And I had no idea how she even saw me but I must have mumbled something because then she took my hand and said let's go upstairs, honey, and I thought we were going to the balcony but we went up the stairs in the back, and at the top she kissed the door person on both cheeks and then we went inside.

And there was a whole other dance floor there, the club inside the club, and she guided me over to the bar and said: I can't believe she's gone.

And then she said it again: I can't believe she's gone.

And then she looked up at me and started laughing—oh honey, she said, I totally thought, I totally thought.

And then she just stopped right there. I didn't know if she thought I was someone else, or if she thought—I really just didn't know.

She said what are you drinking, honey, but she didn't wait for my answer she just ordered two vodka sours with grenadine, I loved the color and after I took one sip I knew this would be my drink from then on. She poured some coke out on a coaster and then handed me a straw, and I made sure just to snort half but she motioned her hand like you take the rest, and when I was done she handed me a big flat round pill and I swallowed it with the vodka sour.

I was a little worried because I was already a bit coked up and alcohol and coke mess with ecstasy but I definitely knew not to turn down free drugs, I mean wasn't this what was supposed to happen in New York?

Sid, she said. Sid Sidereal.

Terry, I said. Terry Dactyl.

And she touched my back, and said: Where are your wings?

I could feel them right then. It was the way she touched me. Like she was drawing my wings on.

One by one, the others came upstairs and took their magic pills—I didn't know anyone yet, but when they saw me with Sid it was like we were old friends.

Sid was so high that her eyes would roll back whenever she wasn't speaking, and I was ready to go there. Jaysun Jaysin kept petting her coat like it would take her to heaven or maybe she was already in heaven. Bleached curly hair with dark roots, eyebrows dyed green, and she was wearing a big ratty faux-fur coat and maybe nothing on underneath and she touched my nose and said: Twins. I looked at her nose, and noticed her gold septum ring did match my silver one, and everything in her eyes. And then String Bean arrived in clown makeup and ruffles, platforms that made her so tall that everyone had to look up to her. And CleoPatrick, with a giant red Afro and tattered ball gown. And then Tara and Mielle, in matching suits and bleached hair with spit curls like Jazz Age style-dyke twins.

And eventually Sid said: Is everyone ready? And we all went downstairs to the coat check and Sid picked up a box with her coat, and then we went outside and jumped in two cabs—I didn't usually take cabs in New York because I was still in love with the subway but here I was with Sid, Jaysun, and Cleo, all of us squished together in the backseat and Sid said Christopher Street Pier and then soon enough we were there, one cab and then the other like we were in tandem.

And I'll be honest here and say that I hadn't even been to the piers before, I mean I saw *Paris Is Burning* in high school when it played at the Egyptian, and then of course everyone started lip-syncing to Madonna and practicing those moves, but that was about all. It was late, and I didn't see anyone voguing, but there was music, and just as we started walking out onto the pier this queen ran up behind us and said Esme!

And Sid turned, and this queen said girl, I thought you were dead.

And Sid said: I thought I was dead too.

And this queen said: Oh honey I've missed you and your messy makeup.

And Sid said: My messy makeup can't compare to you.

And then she put her box down, and opened her arms, and the two of them were jumping up and down and Sid said oh Monique. And right about then I started to feel this pounding inside and I looked around to see if everyone else was feeling it too, and Monique said so are these your children or did someone get lost on the way to the circus.

Monique was ready to read each one of us, and we just stood there in the way it takes a while to react when the X is really kicking in and when Monique got to me she said girl, you're as tall as me and you've got them tranny shoulders so why the freakshow makeup—and it felt like I'd been waiting for someone to say tranny shoulders all my life, yes, what was I doing wasting my time with the dead white men of the Core Curriculum when I could be so alive right here with tranny shoulders the air on my skin so much air and that current going through my body my eyes yes my eyes and lips yes lips and tongue, and there it was, language, when I said: Takes one to know one.

And Monique shrieked, and held out her hand, and I got on my knees and kissed it, and she said oh honey I'm not a lezzbian but I do like the attention. And then when she was done clocking all our outfits, she said: So what's in the box.

And Sid said JoJo.

And Monique gasped, and stepped back, and she was so dramatic about it that at first I didn't realize what was happening, but then she and Sid hugged again, and this time there were tears, and I got a chill up my back even though it wasn't cold, not really, was it, I mean a second ago I was sweating and now I was cold and I knew this X was going to be good but also I felt like this wasn't what I was supposed to be feeling, even if I could tell we were all feeling it, and maybe that was the point.

And Sid said I came here to tell Estella, and Monique said she's with a date. And Sid said JoJo wanted her ashes in the river.

And Monique said that bitch stole a hundred dollars from me, twice, and then paused, and said: Not that I hold it against her.

And Sid said could you tell Estella for me. And Monique said what's in it for me?

And Sid pressed something into her hand, and Monique held a baggy of coke up to the light and said oh honey you know me, you know me too well, and then she kissed her on both cheeks and we were off.

And when I say we were off, it wasn't exactly runway it was just the only way to walk, all together now, walk, and at this point my eyes were rolling back and I was licking my lips and holding someone's hand, feeling that clamminess, we were all bodies and wind and the cars going by—me and Jaysun, String Bean and Cleo, Sid and TaraMielle—they went by one name together I didn't get it the first time but I got it now.

We walked down the West Side Highway until we got to another pier, I don't know how long we walked and I don't know which way because I've never found that pier again or maybe I found it but it didn't look the same so all I know is when we got there it was just us, just us in the sky, the sky and the air, the sky in the air in my body inside this coat and we walked out to the middle of the pier, and Sid opened the box, and I'd seen this before, the ashes in a box like this or a big glass bottle or a beautiful urn or sometimes just a bowl so you could touch with your fingers, yes there were chunks of bone but on ecstasy it felt like I was part of this ash, this water, this bone, this air, the sky, this breath, it was all of us.

Sid handed out paper cups and maybe I was thirsty but the cups were for the ashes, each of us filled one up and we walked out to the end of the pier, the thing about the Hudson is it's always wider than you think and you're looking out at the skyline but it's Jersey. The lights, I said, look at all the lights and everyone nodded their heads, we were there, in the lights, I could feel it.

And Sid said before we get this party started, I want everyone to know one thing, and we all turned to face her, and she said: Don't ever call me Esme, okay? Sid, Siddhartha, Sadie, CeCe my Playmate . . .

And Jaysun said: Come out and play with me.

And Cleo said: Do you know what that bitch said to me? She said . . . No, never mind.

And Jaysun said: What.

And Cleo said: No, no, I don't even want to say it . . . Okay, she said: You look better as a boy.

And we all gasped. And then String Bean hurled her cup of ashes way out into the water just like that, and then she did some kind of om shanti thing, blessed be, she kept saying blessed be blessed be blessed be, and I definitely didn't believe in any kind of blessing but my eyes were open wide. Cleo said JoJo's the bitch who taught me to walk, and she turned to show us, and so we all turned and there it was, New York, New York—New York, New York and JoJo I mean Cleo was walking with New York, she was walking with New York but leaning to each side because New York was heavy in those big platforms that weren't tapered so they looked kind of dangerous and right then I realized I needed to get the ones like String Bean's with the wedding-cake effect, and when Cleo turned she almost tripped but what was wrong with falling, we were all falling another way to fly and some of the ashes flew out of her cup and when she got to us she said see, I still don't know how to walk, and we can all blame JoJo. And you could really see the glitter in her eyes—I tried to hear the ashes land but what do ashes sound like, just the water and the cars and the music, I mean it was the sound of the water against the piers or maybe metal slamming a buoy but it was music now.

TaraMielle sat down on the ground and we sat down with them and that's when Jaysun started crying and Sid put her arms around her and then we became one big mass of breath and oh and oh and ohhhhhhhhhhhhhhhhhh and I wanted to say this is the best way to celebrate death. But I couldn't say that, could I? And just as I was thinking how did we even get here, when we were at the Limelight, suddenly it was like we were at the Limelight again because Sid pulled the tube dress over her head and down to the ground, there was so much fabric she was in the tube and I realized that earlier was a rehearsal because here it was again one hand out of the fabric toward heaven, and one foot out of the bottom toward the water beneath the pier and the way she could roll over herself, twisting around I mean everything was fluid and brokenness and this was a dance for death, I knew it now.

And then String Bean started waving her arms and Cleo was twirling around and around and then I threw my ashes into the air and they fell down on us as Sid was pulling one arm in and then pushing one arm through, like each part of her body wasn't connected to anything, just floating on its own, her face peeking out, just one of those gold eyelashes and then back into the fabric, it was like we were all in the fabric we were inside we were inside we were inside we were inside-out.

In ninth grade, we had an AIDS awareness assembly and I was prepared. My mothers were dykes and most of their friends were fags who had been partying at our house for my whole childhood and now they were dying, one by one they were dying I mean one day they would be dancing with that disco ball and the mirrored walls in the living room and then we'd be at a memorial at the park or the Arboretum or at someone's apartment where I'd never been before.

When I was five, my grandmother died of brain cancer, but I'd only met her once when we flew out from Seattle to visit her, and when we were getting ready to make the trip from Boston to Nantucket my mothers said let's play dress-up. I already knew they weren't going to let me wear my favorite pink dress because they wouldn't let me bring it, and they said I couldn't even wear my hair in pigtails, not until we got home, so I watched them get dressed instead. They were wearing wigs and makeup that made them look kind of like *Charlie's Angels* and I knew Eileen didn't really like that show but we watched it every week at Jack and Rudy's and all the queens were obsessed. Eileen and Paula looked at each other and then at me and said isn't this fun but I could tell they were tense. When we got to my grandmother's house, she didn't look scary like I'd expected she just looked like an old lady who pinched my cheeks and said my my isn't he a beauty, just look at those curls.

I was focused on the glass panda sitting on the table in the entryway, I'd always loved pandas and my grandmother noticed and said Melody, please wrap this up for my grandson, isn't he a prize, and she took my head in her hands and said oh, let me get a good look at you again, my my isn't he magnificent.

That panda is the one thing I have of hers—a clear glass paperweight with those dark panda eyes, and pink and red and blue flowers growing inside its belly, it looks like there's water in there too but I guess it's just glass. I still love that panda, the feeling of its weight in my hands, but now I know we were visiting my grandmother to prove that her dyke daughter was worthy of an inheritance, I was the proof that she had finally done something right. We got the inheritance, which paid for us to move out of the Biltmore and into our new house on 12th right by Volunteer Park and when I had an asthma attack on the first night and had to go to the hospital we moved back into the Biltmore while all the carpets were torn out, the floors stained, and the walls bleached and repainted and the windows replaced and I even got to choose the colors for my bedroom walls—bubblegum pink, with lavender trim—so when we got back a few months later it was a whole new place.

So my grandmother was the first person I knew who died, even though I didn't really know her, but she was the only grandparent I ever met—my grandfather died before I was born, and I never met my other grandparents because they kicked Paula out of the house when she was sixteen after she got caught making out with her friend in bed and that was the end, just like that, when I was little I didn't understand how parents could be so mean when they were supposed to take care of you, and probably I didn't understand death either, but when my mothers' friends started dying in the '80s I understood more.

There were no platitudes about heaven or a better place or anything like that, they just got really skinny and their eyes got scared and then they were gone, like Peter who was standing on the card table in his gold platforms and gold pants with matching gold bomber jacket unzipped to show off his muscly chest, holding the disco ball and saying I'm Atlas, I'm Atlas, and Paula who was DJing said Peter get down. And then I heard he was in the hospital, he had thrush and pneumonia and maybe shingles, I would hear the words and look them up in the dictionary I mean I knew what pneumonia was but I didn't know why.

So I was ten or eleven when it all started, and then it didn't stop.

They kept dancing, though, and I kept coming down from my bedroom in the early hours of the morning to sit on the sofa and cuddle with these dancing queens and their cocktails and pills and visits to the bathroom to powder their noses. My mothers gave me my own cabinet full of potions in the kitchen so I could join everyone, and I would make elixirs out of pomegranate juice and St. John's wort tincture or damiana and kava kava and lemon balm and lemon juice, and I would sip my potions in sparkling plastic cocktail glasses with all these queens dancing in the living room while Paula reigned from her DJ table, hair dyed and spiked out or permed and asymmetrical, makeup in bright colors forming shapes across her face or swirls and curls around her trademark cat eyes. When I was a kid I thought Paula was the rich one because every day she came home with a new hairstyle and some wild shiny outfit, but that was just because she was the receptionist at the hair salon so she was the in-house hair model, and after work she would stop at Chicken Soup or Value Village, and Eileen might have looked plain in her burlap or denim or cotton jumpsuits, dark curly hair pinned back with barrettes, but everything was Liz Claiborne and she shopped at the Bon although it didn't seem like anyone noticed the difference in those spinning lights with Paula playing Donna Summer or Nina Hagen or ESG or Kraftwerk I mean everything felt like magic except when someone suddenly looked sad on the sofa all alone staring at the lights and I would go over and we would stare at the lights together.

 I still remember the first time some girl at school said everyone had a mother and a father, not two mothers, and when I asked my mothers about this Paula just laughed and said oh honey that's nonsense, you have two mothers and a whole roomful of fathers, don't you. So when I was little my fathers would hold me in their arms and tickle me and lift me up to the spinning lights and I would get giddy until I fell asleep on the sofa and someone would carry me up to my bedroom and I would sleep for the rest of the night. When I got older I would go to bed like usual, but as soon as I heard the music I would run downstairs in my favorite silky robe and a tiara, and everyone would call me their little princess, so I was a princess among queens.

 Technically maybe they were my fathers, even the ones who didn't seem like men at all, they were somewhere in between or beyond but that's how my mothers got pregnant, it was their sperm in the turkey baster—did all those queens get together for a sex party first, or maybe just one by one jerking off in the bathroom, of course it wasn't just one time I mean the details of the story changed but what didn't change was that all the sperm was mixed together so if this worked out then no one would ever know who the father was.

When I was little, my mothers told me they both got pregnant together, no men involved, but once I realized half of me couldn't have come from one mother and half from the other they told me it was Eileen who gave birth to me but they were both my mothers and I could tell they were nervous about this but I was relieved because I thought they were going to say Paula, there was something about our connection that felt more physical, but once I realized it wasn't her this kind of balanced things out.

So by ninth grade it already felt like all my friends were dying, like this had been going on forever and it would never stop, and I know they were my mothers' friends but I grew up with them way more than with other kids. I didn't understand kids, so I would climb trees, I liked the way you had to really focus to get somewhere but once you were there you didn't have to focus at all, and at the AIDS awareness assembly I thought we would all share stories of friends we'd lost, so I was surprised when it was just about which bodily fluids contained HIV and how we were all at risk so here's how to put a condom on a banana and I knew all that, I mean there were condoms and pamphlets about safe sex all over our house. But at school everyone laughed at the banana and then their questions were weird like can you get AIDS from kissing someone on the cheek or what if you cut yourself and no one was around and you only had a dirty sock to wipe it off, could you get AIDS from a dirty sock that really really smelled and then someone said I feel sorry for the AIDS victims but it isn't their fault, and that's when I raised my hand.

I said I have something to share, and the teachers nodded, and I took out a list that I'd prepared ahead of time because I didn't want to get nervous and forget anyone. I started with Peter, and how he used to shake the tambourine—he would run all over the house singing shake shake shake and I would run after him. And Marty, who used to cut my hair at home because of my asthma so I didn't even have to go to the salon we would do it in the kitchen and he specialized in curly hair so he always got it right. And then his boyfriend Tommy who didn't look sick but then I started seeing the sores on his neck and wrists and back, my mothers said they weren't always painful but they really did look like they hurt. A lot of my mothers' friends had the sores, some of them would try to cover them up with makeup but you could still see. Like Cammy who taught me the eyebrow trick and the secret ways to do contour and how to always use lip liner if you wanted your lips to stay that way. Or Ansel who used to wear the prettiest dresses and hold her hand like a microphone and do these elaborate dance numbers while I would try to learn the moves but I just couldn't keep up.

I wanted to say more, but the bell was ringing so I looked up to see if it was okay to keep going and the first thing I noticed was that everyone was completely quiet, I mean not even the boys in the back were making jokes anymore, and as soon as I stopped I could tell there were kids who were about to cry or maybe they were already crying and the teachers looked shocked too, especially the PE teacher who everyone said was gay, so she must not have been gay or why would she have been shocked, and I didn't know what to do so then I stopped talking.

There are two types of galleries—the ones that need to sell art in order to stay open, and the ones that don't. For twenty-three years now, I've worked at Sabine Roth—when she opened the gallery in the '60s, she changed her name, so no one would know she was a Rothschild. So everyone knows her as the Rothschild who changed her name.

But here's the thing with Sabine—maybe that was her strategy all along, back when Soho was something new—it was definitely a way to get people to remember you. Sabine always has a few tricks up her sleeve, as she likes to say. But, trust me, there are two types of galleries, and Sabine Roth doesn't need to make money in order to stay open.

I was not meant to be in the art world, not at all. But for twenty-three years I've picked up that phone and said Sabine Roth. Sabine Roth. Sabine Roth. It's like I'm her.

It all started one fateful night in 1997 when I decided to take a second hit of X at 11:00 a.m. When you're the dealer, you can make these types of choices. I wasn't dealing X but I could always trade. So, needless to say, when Twilo kicked me out at noon I was walking on those pink platforms like there was nothing beneath me except air.

There are two types of club kids—the ones who need a group to go out, and the ones that don't. So let's just say I didn't need anyone. Not anymore.

But I did need the drugs—there are two types of club kids, the ones who need the drugs, and the ones who really need the drugs, and, trust me, I really needed the drugs.

So I was taking the long route home, drenched in everyone's jealous stares. I don't know how the hell I decided to walk through Soho, except, like I said, I was flying. Tourists were taking snapshots of me because they were looking for excitement and they weren't going to find it in Soho, that was for sure. But then I showed up.

Usually I liked to walk through Soho at night, when everything was closed and I could look in without anyone looking out—I didn't need to go inside to know what was inside. But this was daylight, and when I got to Sabine Roth I saw that everything inside was pink. Did I mention I was wearing all pink? Magenta, to be exact.

I went in. There were these fabric sculptures in the middle—giant creatures with cunts, and just when I was thinking about sticking my fingers inside and what would the fabric feel like, that's when this woman with a perfect gray bob came out in a power suit—a pink cravat tied at her neck, and some kind of sculptural earrings, also pink—but everything else was black. And she held out her hand and said Sabine. Sabine Roth.

I had no idea what she was talking about—I was too busy thinking about how warm her fingers felt, studying the blue lines in her hands against the magenta of my hands, I mean I'd painted my whole body magenta, including my face, but then I realized what I was doing and I looked up.

Cold hands, warm heart, Sabine said. And your name?

Terry, I said. Terry Dactyl.

Follow me, Terry, she said, so I followed. She motioned toward a chair in her office in the back, and I wasn't sure whether I wanted to sit down but when I did I realized how soft it was. Velvet. This must be why I was there. I mean I needed to rest my legs, didn't I. Why didn't I come here more often.

Terry, she said, that's right, make yourself comfortable. When you're ready, tell me about art. What moves you.

Tell me about art, I said. And I looked her in the eyes. She didn't look away. I'm not sure whether she could actually see my eyes because of all the makeup, and those double eyelashes getting in the way, but I could tell she liked eye contact.

What does art mean to you, she asked.

It was nice to sit down—this was the right decision, I could feel myself sinking into the chair. The phone rang. Sabine picked it up. Cancel my appointments, she said. And she put the phone back down.

I love that sound, I said, how it echoes off the walls but also it's inside. And Sabine said yes.

I was looking at her eyes, wondering if she was on drugs too—she seemed nervous now and I wanted to comfort her so I said I want you to know, Sabine, everything in this room is exactly the way it should be—the temperature.

And Sabine said yes.
The lighting.
And Sabine said yes.
The walls.
And Sabine said yes. Tell me about the walls.

But then I looked at the walls again and realized that all that white was oppressive. I don't know if I can handle it, I said. I don't know if there's enough feeling. Do you know what I mean?

And she nodded.

Why aren't the walls pink, I asked.

Good question, Sabine said. Your outfit. I can't believe it.

I can't believe it either.

Does Veronica have all your information.

When she said Veronica I was thinking about Angelica Kitchen—carrot juice, that's what I needed. Carrot juice with ginger, and a shot of wheatgrass. Maybe I could pick up one of those Odwalla juices on the way, the one with strawberries, vitamin C, to bring up the colors. Strawberry C Monster, yes, that's what I needed.

Strawberry C Monster, I said, and I made a big movement with my lips, felt all the glitter I'd attached with Spirit Gum but how long ago was that? I needed to check my makeup. Do you mind if I use the bathroom, I asked.

The phone rang again and Sabine said Veronica? And I thought she was ordering the juice.

Veronica, she said, I found the one. No more applications.

So I got the job. Even though I wasn't applying for it. I already had one job, and that involved going out every night. But honestly it was barely paying the bills. Because of all the money going up my nose. So when Sabine called me a week later and somehow I actually answered the phone and we went over the job offer—salary, health benefits, I mean that's not something you have when you're a drug dealer.

The first two weeks, when Veronica was still working, were about training. We took out the art in the back—piece by piece, they explained the details and technique and inspiration. I retained none of this information. Sabine asked me for my opinions, and I gave her some coked-out nonsense, and she nodded her head. I didn't think this would last more than two weeks, but then I got my first paycheck and I was still there.

Sabine had rules, but they were easy enough to follow. For example, when answering the phone, never say how may I help you. Just say: Sabine Roth.

If someone thinks you're Sabine, never transfer the call. Always ask who it is first.

But if someone says can I speak with Sabine, always transfer the call right away.

Never approach anyone in the gallery unless they approach you first.

Never offer a price list unless they ask for it.

There were even some rules that I liked. Sabine said: Never assume anything—collectors are idiosyncratic, you can't tell by how they dress. Never look at their shoes, only their eyes. If someone asks to use the bathroom, it's theirs. Never follow anyone, not unless they ask you to. If there's a problem, call 911.

911, I asked, are you sure?

Call me first, Sabine said.

But here's the thing—other than those rules, I could do anything. She hired me because of the way I looked, right? I was floating in the sky on two hits of ecstasy and who knows how much K, not to mention a few bumps of coke and the pot I smoked outside Twilo, and then I walked into the gallery in a magenta '80s prom dress that I'd found at Goodwill, with wings coated in glitter and made of trash, and that giant pink wig that was a bouffant at the top and a mullet at the bottom, with the longest silver and gold eyelashes curling both up and down. And Sabine was enthralled.

And then, once I started working at the gallery, she loved it when my friends would show up. They would show up to pick up a bag of coke and head right to the bathroom. So I had two jobs at once. And Sabine loved it. I don't know if she knew about the second job, but she definitely loved every single mess that came in to pick up their nose candy, now that I had regular day hours.

I still remember when I showed up to work on that first day, and trust me I was rushing to get there by 10:00 a.m., I mean of course I'd stayed up all night just to make sure so I was proud of myself when I walked in like thirty seconds early, and Sabine was in the back of the gallery just staring at that door. At first I thought she was clocking my outfit, I mean I wasn't wearing wings this time, or platforms, or body paint, but I did look good. Although when I smiled and said hello and headed to the bathroom to make sure I didn't look too coked out, Sabine stopped me, and said Terry.

Sabine, I said. And I waited.

Terry, she said, I want you to know that I'm dedicated to you. If you're dedicated to me. But I want you to know. I do not tolerate tardiness.

So I knew what I had to do.

When I went into her office, there were two glasses of champagne on the desk. Crystal glasses, with gold etching. You could hear the crystal with our toast, that delicate ring. To a new era, Sabine said. This is us, it's our era.

Champagne at 10:00 a.m.? I was ready.

When I started working for Sabine I didn't know about the art world, but I did know about clubs so when she asked me to curate a show I called it Club Kid Diaspora. This was in 1998, when people were getting arrested for the same things they'd always done and everything was shutting down and opening up and shutting down and the club kids who were left were banished to some corner of the room I mean we were still there but we were not important unless we were totally polished and on someone's payroll.

So Club Kid Diaspora started with me and Jaysun going over to Domsey's and picking up bag after bag of anything that drew our attention—ratty dolls, outdated toys, any dress on the ninety-nine cent rack, children's clothing, hair brushes and combs, stuffed animals, broken necklaces, bobby pins, electrical cords, anything bright and plastic, shiny or ruined, and then we just stapled it all to the walls, glued it, whatever worked—everything that was discounted and anything that would stick, we stuck it there.

Needless to say we were coked out to the max, and once we established the right rhythm of bumps I asked Jaysun to DJ.

Bitch I'm not a DJ, she said, but I could tell by the way she pulled her head back that she was already excited. She'd been spinning records since I met her—I would watch her taking one track and stretching it out for a whole hour. Actually, I wouldn't watch, because she would say close your eyes, and then I would listen to the endless back-and-forth that felt like meditation, medication, devastation, liberation, confiscation, and what I mean is the words would stretch out broken and warped the beats distorted and sharp and deeper and faster and then slow and almost unrecognizable until you were back in the song again, as it was intended, but not yet, because just when you started to relax and think oh, then it broke up again.

This was back when Jaysun only had one turntable, and maybe five or ten records—it was a few years before she pulled it together to get a second turntable and a mixer, I mean her priority was always to make sure she had a hit of X to take before she left the house, so when she walked into the club her eyes were already rolling back, and it was just her in that coat. At first it was the same coat every time, but then she started collecting them—the messier the coat the better—I remember when I went over her apartment, I mean it wasn't an apartment it was a room barely bigger than the tiny mattress she slept on, if she ever slept, and then a clothes rack that was filled with nothing but coats, probably fifty of them, way too many to fit on the hangers so then they were piled up on top above the door which was lower than the ceiling, I mean there was a gap. And then she had her briefs freshly bleached and hanging to dry on clotheslines—they were your standard tighty-whities but Jaysun covered up Hanes or Jockey or whatever with rhinestones that spelled out JAYSUN on the front and JAYSIN on the back, that's why she had to hand wash them.

She called that place the faggot brothel with all the queens living there in these tiny compartments with plywood doors and a Master lock on the handle instead of a doorknob, so if anyone went too long without paying the rent the landlord would just cut the lock and take everything, that's what Jaysun said, although I don't remember that ever happening, but it's not like I was there all the time.

At the clubs Jaysun would walk back and forth on the dance floor all night in one of those coats, like she was in a trance. When she was really feeling it she would throw the coat on the floor and just walk around in her undies, that's all she ever wore. With her platforms, of course, and her hair that kept getting more and more elaborate, those curls bleached and shaved and dyed every combination of colors. Yes, she was looking for something in the lights, and if you were there with her then you were in the lights too. But her secret was the way she could spin—it was all that focus she devoted to a single track, the way the smallest shift could create the wildest distortion and I would just lie there in a K-hole even if I wasn't in a K-hole it was the way she stretched out those tracks—even when Cleo got Jaysun out of the faggot brothel because she needed a new roommate on Avenue D, and they called their place D-viance—even then, Cleo made her spin her records in her room because she said she couldn't deal with all that repetition, it was giving her a headache.

Out of all of us, Cleo was the one who was the most together—even when she was falling apart, she had it together. I mean I had it together too, but that was just because I had Sid, and once she was gone I was spinning so far out of control you couldn't even have put me on that record player, and when I got the job at the gallery I had to do more coke to make sure I was alert and I had no idea what I was doing but I did know that Sabine wanted something from me that had something to do with the actual me, that was the important part. Otherwise why wouldn't she have hired someone sleek like Veronica. Now of course I know she was funding Veronica's new gallery, so she could have it both ways, but at the time all I knew was she wanted me to do a show. And I had no idea this was not how things worked, you would not start a job as a gallery assistant and then suddenly be curating your own show, but I guess because I had no idea, that was why Sabine wanted it I mean I might not have known what I was doing but Sabine sure did.

When I asked Jaysun to DJ I was already thinking about Cleo because she worked at the neon factory and she always said she wanted to do something more with those lights, I mean of course she made the D-viance sign in her living room that you could see from the street, but something more. So as soon as I knew Jaysun was involved I asked Cleo if she wanted to make some pieces for the show, even if we weren't really talking at that point she didn't pause for a second, she just said how many, that was her only question, and then I went back to Sabine and she said they had sixteen outlets in the gallery because they'd done video installations before, so how did that sound, and Cleo just said girl, I can't believe this is finally happening.

She was an art school dropout—Parsons, not FIT, and she went to the upstate version of School of the Arts for high school so the point is that she was thinking about art from the beginning. Her parents were ready to support her, but they weren't as happy about her faggot ass, that's what she said—they were white Christians living upstate who'd adopted this Black child out of the kindness of their hearts, and they were actually kind, according to Cleo, but they couldn't handle the whole package, and after a while she got tired of dressing like a man to get on the train to go visit them so she went as herself and it didn't go over well. That's when she dropped out of Parsons and got the job and got on hormones, or got the job and got on hormones and then dropped out, I'm not sure which way it went.

Pretty much everyone had a dramatic story about their parents, I mean Jaysun's parents kicked her out when she was fifteen. Her father waved a gun in her face and said: I've killed the enemy before and I can kill the enemy again—he was in the military, and then he became a cop, so he knew what he was saying. Jaysun took the bus to Port Authority with a few hundred dollars and two suitcases she could barely carry although she could wheel them over to Times Square like any other legendary child but pretty soon she got rid of the suitcases and got a backpack and for a few years she was a Times Square regular, as she said.

God bless the chickenhawks of Times Square, she would say to me sometimes at the Regal Diner or Odessa or one of our late-night recovery spots. God bless the chickenhawks of Times Square. And then she would sigh dramatically and roll her eyes up to the ceiling.

They would pick her up on the street and take her back to their hotels, and say WHERE ARE YOU FROM?

And she would say honey, I'm from Jersey.

But where are you originally from, they would ask.

So she started making shit up—India was what they wanted, so she gave them India. Do you speak Indian, they would ask.

Once in a while she would say Sri Lanka to test their geography skills, but that usually got to be too much for these tricks because, as Jaysun would say, they just wanted their dark meat—they'd tried fried chicken, they'd tried chicken enchiladas, and now they wanted their tikka masala.

By the time I met her she was already a club child—she had found her place on the dance floor and she would walk back and forth all night. She wasn't that coordinated, but she was dedicated, and once you do something enough then it kind of becomes your personality.

But back to Club Kid Diaspora.

Cleo's first piece was *No More White Cube* and it went like this:

NO   MORE

WHITE   CUBE

It was, of course, an exact cube, and first it would flash "NO MORE" then "NO WHITE" then "NO CUBE" and then "NO MORE WHITE CUBE." Purple lights.

Sabine came in when we were testing it out, and she clapped her hands. Wait until Bruce Nauman sees this, she said, and I had no idea who Bruce Nauman was, but I could tell she was excited, and that's what mattered.

Let's install this on the outside of the gallery, she said, don't you think. And Cleo raised her eyebrows and looked at me like who is this bitch. But in the best way.

Then Sabine looked over at the mess on the walls, and she said tell me about this. I can't remember what the hell I said, but I guess I convinced her because she said excess instead of understatement, I see. And then she suggested making blackout curtains to block out all the light from the street, so we could have a sealed environment. A palate cleanse, she said.

And then it was her idea to keep all the lights off in the gallery except the neon—an immersive installation. So Sabine wasn't as straightlaced as some people thought, but she did look the part.

Then Cleo made the rest:

First came the ghouls of the art world, or a few of them, anyway:

LEO CASTELLI IS DEAD
LARRY GAGOSIAN IS DEAD
JEFFREY DEITCH IS DEAD
PAULA COOPER IS DEAD
KEITH HARING IS DEAD
JEFF KOONS IS DEAD

Of course, Keith Haring was the only one who was actually dead.

And then came a taste of fashion, a hint of club drama, and an ode to politics, all wrapped up together:

DONNA KARAN IS DEAD
PETER GATIEN IS DEAD
SUSANNE BARTSCH IS DEAD
MICHAEL ALIG IS DEAD
ED KOCH IS DEAD
JAMES BROWN IS DEAD
RUDY GIULIANI IS DEAD
GIANNI VERSACE IS DEAD
CLEOPATRICK IS UNDEAD

Of course, only Versace was actually dead, but who couldn't use a little positive thinking? And the prize for the back wall, which was my favorite and my favorite forever:

Art is not dead
Art is   dead
Art is not
Art

That one she set so that at times it would just say

Art
Art
Art

And at times it would just say

    dead
    dead
Art
Art

And sometimes it would just say

    dead

There were a lot of other variations along the way, but what really created the scene, remember, was how the neon would reflect off everything on the walls, and, yes, we got a disco ball, and then Jaysun was DJing right in front of Art is not dead or Art is dead or Art is not Art, and I still remember how she started opening night with It's not . . . oh oh oh oh oh oh ver. . . . It's not . . . It's not . . . It's not . . . It's not . . . It's not . . . It's not . . . It's not . . . It's not . . . It's not . . . It's not . . . It's not . . . oh oh oh oh oh oh ver.

Mixed with Wake up . . . Wake up . . . Wake up . . . Go to sleep . . . oh oh oh oh oh oh ver. . . . It's not . . . It's not . . . It's not . . . It's not . . . oh oh oh oh oh oh ver. But then the bitch track was when she played "James Brown Is Dead," and I swear that song was playing at the Limelight on the night we met seven years before, but anyway the crowd at Club Kid Diaspora went wild because at that point "James Brown Is Dead" was a classic, and the crowd was basically just people I'd flyered at the clubs like I was promoting a night, even though it started at 6:00 p.m., but 6:00 p.m. for breakfast, right? Especially with all that free wine, although that did run out fast. Of course there were people who asked me for a bag or two, and I was prepared, but I'm not sure if there were any art people there at all.

Michael Musto was there, though, and of course we'd all grown up with her column, I mean I used to get the *Village Voice* every week at Bailey/Coy in high school, and "La Dolce Musto" was where I first got the gossip about downtown club culture, all the way in Seattle. I mean aside from all the queens I'd grown up with, but anyway Michael Musto didn't write about the show. No one did.

But Sabine seemed entertained, and people would trickle in during the week and then a little more on weekends, and it kind of felt like they'd stumbled into the wrong club, which was exactly what it was supposed to feel like, with Jaysun DJing all day—yes, I got her to do that, I mean Sabine paid her and I gave her a bag of coke at the beginning of every set, and Sabine bought *No More White Cube* and *Art Is Not Dead* from Cleo on opening night so Club Kid Diaspora felt like a success for the four of us, anyway.

And Michael Musto kept coming to the show, and we would wave at each other, and trust me I would count down the days until Wednesday.

But still no column.

Except then, just when I'd given up, there it was, and it was everything.

"Terry Dactyl, resplendent in . . . well, what isn't she in, since she hasn't repeated an outfit the whole month."

And, "If you can't remember what happened to all that junk you lost in the sofa—all those naked Barbies, the leftover tinsel from last Christmas, the missing bristles from your treasured hairbrush, that slippery bottle of lube, your french poodle's favorite chew toy—it's all right here at Sabine Roth, stuck to the walls, as if we didn't already know minimalism was outdated."

And, "Jaysun Jaysin reinvents the wheel—the turntable wheel."

And, the finale—"CleoPatrick may be undead for now, but just wait until Larry Gagosian and Susanne Bartsch see this show."

When I handed the article to Sabine, she looked it over and let out this hum that was a cross between a gasp and a sigh—more subtle, of course, but it really did feel like a gasp to me because I was holding my breath.

Congratulations, she said, and then she read it again. You did this on your own, she said. I'm extending the show. The closing party will be a reopening.

And that was the party where the whole art world showed up.

If I try to think of a time before everyone started dying, I realize I can't, not really. Because once the dying started it felt like there was no before. Maybe waking up and going downstairs and finding my mothers' friends passed out on the sofas or still chatting in drugged-out fervor, and feeling this excitement there, and then someone would get up and ask me if I needed anything. Sometimes it was someone I knew, and sometimes it wasn't. Sometimes their eyes were in this world and sometimes they were somewhere else, and I loved this adventure, all of us together in the house making something special.

Yes, there would be the times when I would find Paula slumped over on the kitchen table with the open bottle of gin, but when she saw me she would give me a big hug and tell me how much she loved me, and then she would go downstairs, and when she came back up it felt like a magic trick the way she entered the kitchen renewed. Yes, it was the drugs, but I didn't realize that then, I just noticed that suddenly her makeup was fresh and every strand of hair was in place and her eyes were alive again.

But then it started happening every day, I would come downstairs in the morning to get my breakfast ready before school and Paula would be slumped over the kitchen table or sometimes she was awake and I could tell she'd been sobbing for a long time. It's too much, she would say, isn't it too much, and I would hold her. But still I felt a kind of joy there, like I was taking care of my mother and this made me proud. Then she would go downstairs to pull herself together, and when she came back up I would bounce off that energy.

So if there's a before and after, I guess it's before and after rehab—six months for Paula at this posh place in Malibu, and that's when I realized we really had money. I mean I knew things changed after the inheritance, I knew I went to private school, I knew Eileen quit her job and went to grad school for social work, I knew we lived in a big house and we renovated it because of my allergies, but I was five when we moved in so I was just worried I would miss everyone at the Biltmore, even though my mothers said we could visit anytime, it was just down the hill.

And our house felt so different than the houses of my classmates, where they had a housekeeper and sometimes a nanny, and there was a specific place for everything, you would sit down for dinner and you were supposed to have your fork on one side, and your knife on the other, or something like that, whereas at our house the kitchen table was always filled with bottles of nail polish and hairspray and piles of magazines, maybe a liquor bottle or two, the mail, groceries that hadn't made it into the cabinets, and a rotating cast of stuffed animals. Henry the Hippo, I would say, are you ready for dinner, and Paula would say isn't Wilma the Wombat joining us tonight, and I would run and get her.

But really what changed when Paula went to rehab was that she would call and say honey I'm sorry I left you in danger—usually she would be crying and I would want to hold her, but honestly I had no idea what she was talking about. Because I never felt in danger.

Or she would say Terry, I'm sorry for relying on you, and I guess she meant I shouldn't have been the one comforting her because she was the mother and I was the child, but it helped with my grief too. Because I didn't even know it was mine.

It's not like Eileen wasn't partying too, but I guess I never found her slumped over the kitchen table. On our first night alone, when we sat down for dinner she brought out a bottle of wine and asked me if I wanted a glass. She'd never asked me that before, and I didn't really like wine, but I was in high school now so I said sure, and I sipped it slowly over the course of the meal while she drank the rest of the bottle, and then when I went upstairs to study I liked that warm feeling in my head.

Everything was a problem for Paula now but before it wasn't, and I was confused about this but also I wondered if they were going to talk about how everyone was dying and there was no rehab for that. So if there was a before and after, maybe it was after I started doing drugs, which was before Paula went to rehab, I mean I started smoking pot with Claire when she first started coming over on Friday nights, and we would smoke on my balcony and then stumble down the stairs to raid the kitchen, and one time Eileen and Paula were in there and they caught it right away, Eileen said are you kids high?

And we couldn't stop laughing. And they were laughing with us. And Claire couldn't believe my mothers would just laugh at something like that because her parents would've killed her, that's what she said, I mean the only reason they let her stay over was that Friday night was their night out so now they didn't need to worry and Claire told them her friend Terry was helping her with school and they always said she was more alert when she came home, not all groggy like usual so I must be a good influence.

Claire's parents were the type of Christians who warned her about sinners and the apocalypse, so obviously they didn't really know about me, that's for sure. And my mothers were happy to let her sleep over, they said they didn't believe in those rules about boys and girls, or whatever, and I could tell they were thrilled when they realized we were more than friends because they thought this would make me straight and I know that sounds weird because I'd been dressing up with them since I was a toddler and it's not like any of their friends were straight but that's what it felt like, I mean they said they wanted to make sure we were using protection, there was HIV to worry about but also there was pregnancy and I said gross, it's not like that, we don't take off our clothes.

Besides, I said, I'm a dyke, and Eileen said Terry, that's just not possible.

Of course they weren't the only ones that didn't think it was possible, but I didn't understand why they didn't understand—when people say nature or nurture, I just think nurture nurture nurture, I mean if anyone made me a dyke it was them, right?

When Claire asked me if I wanted to do crystal, I told her I didn't want to end up mumbling to myself on the street or pounding my head against the wall, but she said you just need to smoke a lot of pot to come down, and I already liked smoking a lot of pot so I said sure. And when I did that first tiny line my nose burned so badly I was throwing cold water on my face for fifteen minutes while Claire was kissing my neck and saying it's okay, I'm sorry, it's okay. But once the burning stopped I felt so good that I couldn't stop laughing, yes there was the pot we'd already smoked but also it was like I was on the ceiling, and then when we went outside there was nothing but sky.

So it became our secret—Claire would come over on Friday nights and we would do crystal and explore the park and climb trees and if it wasn't too wet we would lie in the grass and look up at the clouds blowing by, the moon, and even if there weren't any stars we were stars, the trees were stars, everything going flash flash in the dark all that light inside and one time when we were falling on one another on my favorite cedar tree, catching and falling, catch me now, we realized it wasn't just us I mean we were right in the middle of the cruising area and of course I knew about the cruising but I didn't know that's where it happened.

So we found our own spots, like underneath the monkey puzzle tree with the branches hanging down and we could almost swing in there, or even better the spruce that went all the way to the ground and once you pushed your way through you had your own little house inside although then we noticed the fags were cruising by the bathroom too so we would watch them from inside our tree and try to figure it out, sometimes I thought I saw one of my mothers' friends and I wanted to run out and yell girl what are you doing out here in the park on a night like this, which is what I thought they would ask me, but instead I just said shh to Claire because it wasn't like we weren't supposed to be there but it kind of felt that way I mean technically the park was closed but did anyone pay attention to that, it was practically my backyard.

Eventually we settled into my favorite sequoias on the other side of the park, the ones with trunks so wide and all that thick bark like cork and sometimes there was a ledge formed by a branch that had broken off and you could stand up on the ledge like you were another branch and all that texture, feel it on your hands your back your head your legs your lips all the sensations blurring into the sky until our hands got numb and then we'd play a game where we'd chew on each other's fingertips and say can you feel this, can you feel this—how about this? And then sucking on each other's fingers taking as much of the hand inside your mouth as you could until you were choking and then we were kissing again.

And then sometimes there would be music, some queen with a boombox or someone's car radio, and if they looked friendly we'd come out and dance and they'd be like where did you girls come from we'd say we're always here what about you and we were sweating even when we were cold and of course it was the drugs but also desire and then there was the stillness, how it would start inside and then expand out, tumbling into bed in our clothes and passing out in a haze or unable to fall asleep but either way holding each other as late as possible, maybe going out on the balcony at sunrise if we did too much but mostly just lying in bed until we couldn't stand it any longer and then Claire would take the bus home and I would do more crystal and study until the afterhours began, the crystal really helped with my schoolwork, even Algebra and Biology would go zoom zoom zoom I'd just keep going until I was done and then I'd head downstairs to celebrate.

Since it was okay that I smoked pot I would smoke as much as possible on my balcony first so when I was messy it would just look like pot because even before there was a problem, I mean before there was a problem for Paula, which Eileen said was a problem for the family, even before that I knew there were some kinds of messy that were okay, like laughing in the living room with all the lights spinning round and Eileen waving to me from the endless purple sofa, Paula playing one of my favorite songs which was any song at this point I knew them all and I knew nothing, twirling around on that dance floor and Paula would yell out hey Terry hey Terry and when I looked over she'd say you're turning out to be quite a dancer, and one of the queens would say girl you're flying and someone else would pull Eileen off that sofa and she would say oh my I'm high as a kite and we would twirl together, she'd look me in the eyes and it was like I was five I was ten I was fifteen I was a hundred and fifty I mean we were mother and daughter but also sisters or party girls shaking out our hair, that's right, I'm high as a kite, floating way, way, way up there with nothing but that string and that's when Paula would give us the extended mix of "I Feel Love" or "Girls Just Wanna Have Fun" and someone would be shaking a tambourine or blowing a whistle or blowing kisses or we'd all hold hands on the dance floor and twirl together, spinning against one another, our bodies together in motion in commotion in grace in clumsy ridiculous glee it all felt so good watching those mirrors like I was floating but also like everyone was holding me.

So when Paula went to rehab I figured there wasn't going to be an afterhours because who would be the DJ and what did this mean about the future. I wanted to say something about how I would miss all the parties but I knew I shouldn't. Claire came over on Friday night like usual, and Eileen went out to the bars all tipsy, so maybe this would be our new routine except Claire always had to be back home on Saturday and what would I do after I finished studying, I mean who would I dance with—now I didn't want the weekend to end, I would be in French class just thinking oh I wish I could be high all the time, but look what happened to Paula, all by herself at that rehab and it was way too soon to send me there so I would only do drugs on weekends, that was my plan. I would keep studying hard and impressing all my teachers, especially French and English and History because that's what I loved but I was starting to think I loved drugs more. Especially when I would doze off in class and I'd always had energy before, all the thoughts in my head racing around and I was just trying not to answer the questions too fast so everyone wouldn't hate me but now I didn't care as much about the questions or the answers or what anyone thought and I knew I was supposed to care more because of college but I just kept thinking about that burning feeling in my nose, I wanted to feel that again but I didn't want to go to rehab so I started snorting NoDoz and Vivarin in the bathroom at school because those weren't drugs, right, it was just like drinking coffee, but faster.

Then Paula started calling, and crying on the phone, and saying you would not believe these rich bitches, it's like they've never seen a dyke before—why did I do this to myself, it's so fucking embarrassing. Just the detox alone, she said, no one should have to go through that—I was screaming to high fucking heaven, I was cursing everyone out, I had the shakes, I couldn't control my emotions, my skin was all clammy there was nothing that could possibly help me nothing except a fucking drink or a line or just go ahead and shoot me up just shoot me up I never shot drugs but I would have shot drugs right there, anything to get past that feeling like I was going to die but I wasn't dying, that's what I kept telling myself, Paula, you're not dying, this is what it feels like to be alive, but why, Paula, why—and I could tell Eileen was nervous about letting me hear everything but Paula said she didn't want to hide it, that was the problem, the hiding—you don't need to hide anything from us, she would say to me, and then she'd take a deep breath and start crying again.

She would call us every night right after dinner with updates, and slowly you could tell things were getting better—I still hate these rich bitches, she would say, but I'm getting used to going on walks with them and hearing their stories. She would tell us about all the weird plants they had on the grounds of the rehab place, how she was practicing her patience by trying to touch the cactuses, you had to do it really carefully and then you wouldn't get hurt, sometimes you had to try from five or six or ten different angles and it could be frustrating but once you figured it out it was the best high—I shouldn't use that word, she would say, should I—I'm learning how to take things really slow, one day at a time, like they say here, I'm taking it one day at a time. She talked about when she was living in a squat in Pioneer Square when she was eighteen and a pipe burst and flooded the whole building and she practically drowned, and the time she got arrested for turning tricks but she wasn't turning tricks she was just waiting for drugs—how much time in my life have I spent waiting for drugs, and the rest of the time drinking, she said, if only I could get all that time back, and then Eileen took the call downstairs.

Then one night when Eileen and I sat down for dinner I noticed there wasn't any wine, but I didn't say anything because the wine wasn't really for me and I could tell Eileen was kind of jittery with just a glass of water. And then at some point she took a deep breath and said there's something I want to tell you. She said I think I have a problem too. With alcohol. And other things. She said she was going to start going to meetings, AA—Alcoholics Anonymous. Just to see what it's like. She thought it might help to be around other people who have the same problem.

She said she had an idea—she wanted to pour all the alcohol out into the sink—it wasn't just Paula, she needed a fresh start too. Would that be okay, she asked—could we do that together, just the two of us, and I said of course. There was a lot of alcohol to pour out and I wondered if maybe we should just give it to someone but I didn't say that, I kept pouring it into the sink, so many different kinds of liquor the smell made me nauseous.

That's when I started to worry Eileen would worry about me, but she became so preoccupied with her own addictions that she didn't notice mine at all. She had a busy schedule with all her AA meetings and then socializing after the meetings to get a new friend group started, that's what she said, she needed a healthy friend group, and then there were meetings with her sponsor who said she should take a more active role right away, so then she became the secretary of one meeting or was it the treasurer and then there were all the workbooks but also all the work she was doing to build her private practice. Any time you need me, she said, just let me know, you're always my top priority—you know that, right?

I'd always had privacy in the house, since I lived upstairs and my mothers lived in the basement, and we had an agreement that we would only go into each other's rooms with permission, and of course that wasn't just for me it was so they could hide their own messiness in their Den of Iniquity, which is what they called their basement hideaway which stretched across the whole floor, with the king-sized four-poster bed and the psychedelic floral wallpaper and corduroy sofas, the ceiling a mosaic of glass and mirrors reflecting off the chandelier with those bulbs that looked like candles so everything in the room was a burst of color and shadow.

I met Claire when I started hanging out with the queer kids at the Broadway Market, or I wasn't really hanging out with them yet I was just sitting near them to figure everything out. After school I'd get a juice at the Gravity Bar, and then sit at a table in the mall and study there, and then eventually the queer kids started talking to me, and one day this goth girl with bleached hair and a nose ring came over to ask me about my juice and that was Claire.

I was drinking cucumber and beet juice with a double shot of wheatgrass and too much ginger, which was making me sweat, but I don't think I mentioned the sweat.

That's cool, she said, are you like vegan, or something?

Yeah, I said.

That's cool, she said, how long have you been vegan?

Since I was seven.

Are you a girl or a boy, she said, but not in a mean way.

I'm a girl, I said, but not everyone believes me.

That's cool, she said, I'm bisexual. Wanna go on a walk?

Sure, I said, even though I'd just gotten there.

That's how it started, and then we'd get together every day after school for the whole year, we were fourteen and then when summer came around we were fifteen and Claire was going to her grandmother's in Ohio—her parents always made her go—that'll keep you out of trouble, they said. We couldn't even talk on the phone, she said it was too risky. I didn't even have her number at home in West Seattle, she would just show up every day to meet me at the Broadway Market so I could get my juice, and then we would walk back and forth down Broadway like everyone did, and then over to the park before she went back to the Christians, that's what she said when she would kiss me goodbye, I have to go back to the Christians.

I was already thinking about what would happen when we graduated high school, because Claire said she wasn't going to college, she didn't need that shit, and I was kind of jealous because I was addicted to school. I thought about my mothers, how Paula was a high-school dropout and Eileen went to Smith, and they met on the dance floor at Shelley's Leg and that was that. And maybe that was like me and Claire, although we didn't meet on the dance floor and I definitely wasn't going to Smith. But our connection happened right away and it meant always, so we were like Paula and Eileen except we were getting started earlier—we had so much time to plan for the future.

But actually we didn't have time to plan, because after Claire left for the summer I never heard from her again.

I don't know how they match you with a college roommate, but my roommate at Columbia taught me to pour coke into the bowl when we smoked pot, and that changed everything. Jacques was French-Algerian but he spoke with a British accent except when he got high, and then he spoke so fast, back and forth between French and English—he liked to tell me his family secrets, and even though I wanted to be fluent in French I wasn't there yet, so I'm sure I missed a lot. But his favorite thing to say was that his family got out of Algeria just in time, and then he would laugh oh he would laugh, and I would laugh with him even though I didn't know what we were laughing about, not exactly, but eventually I realized his family fled Algeria just before the revolution, and they took a lot with them—they robbed the country blind, he would say, and then he'd say it again the way he liked to repeat his favorite phrases, he would pick them up from someone else and make them his, like when he started saying okay cool all the time, okay cool—and then I realized he got that from me, which was hilarious because I didn't even realize that was something I said.

Anyway, his family's wealth came from fleeing Algeria with everything they could take, and even though this was before he was born he wanted to make it clear that this was not something he was in favor of—they took half the country with them, he would say, before handing me the bowl to smoke more pot laced with coke and then we'd go out for falafel—it's fala-fell, he said, with the emphasis on the second syllable, but when I ordered that way people would speak to me in Arabic and I would get confused, so I went back to the American version when I wasn't with Jacques. He would also correct my French, which was helpful, and he wanted me to correct his English too, but I didn't really feel comfortable doing that.

Somehow Jacques already had a whole group of friends at Columbia, he never explained how they met it was just like they were all European so somehow they knew one another. He called them Eurotrash, and as far as I could tell there were two different kinds—the ones who wore sleek black designer clothes and chain-smoked and kissed each other on both cheeks, like Jacques, and the ones who looked like they could have been in *Dead Poets Society*—some Eurotrash even wore baseball caps and cowboy boots, more American than Americans—but they all hung out together, drinking in the middle of the day, and everyone knew they had the best drugs. A few weeks into the semester, when I was trying out my first club outfits and figuring out my hair, which I was twisting into all these wild shapes with silver clips and rubber bands and bobby pins and barrettes, as many as possible, and Jacques announced that his parents had bought him a brownstone, so he would be moving out pretty soon, but not to worry, I could come over anytime, and who needed a roommate anyway—now I would have my own space.

He was right—I didn't need a roommate, but I did need friends, so sometimes I went over to Jacques's house filled with all the Eurotrash who'd moved in, sitting around with their cocktails at any time of the day and they were friendly enough but I just didn't feel like I belonged, unless I was practicing my French or picking up drugs. I did learn about Edmond Jabès from Jacques, and I kind of became obsessed with *The Book of Questions*. Every sentence was a question, leading to another question, and I didn't understand it all but I knew I wasn't supposed to look at the translation if I wanted to become fluent so I would just sit with the gaps between the sentences, and Jacques said yes, yes, that's exactly how you're supposed to read it, it's a dialogue of the word, in the word.

Once Jacques left, I spent most of my time studying when I wasn't getting ready to go to the Limelight, and I guess it was Thanksgiving break when I was kind of lonely and Jacques called to invite me to a party because he wasn't going home either—neither were most of the Eurotrash, it was too short a break for a trip back to Europe, and I wasn't going home because I didn't believe in Thanksgiving, and neither did my mothers, so I went to the party.

I didn't really drink because I liked drugs better, but these Eurotrash were lushes so I was gulping down shots like I was some kind of expert and this one super-preppy guy wearing a blazer and a Polo shirt got really excited about talking to me. He wanted to know how I learned to do my makeup and was that my real hair and how did I get it so many colors and was it naturally curly and how long was it if I let it down and how did I decide which parts to braid and which parts to pull up and where did I get all those hair clips and what kind of hair products did I use and how many earrings did I have and did they hurt and what about the septum piercing, was that more or less painful and what did I call this style and when he asked what I was reading I said Edmond Jabès, and his whole face lit up and he started quoting Jabès in French—Jabès is my hero, he said, not many people know about Jabès here but back at home it is different and did I know that Jabès had just died at the beginning of the year.

Have you been to Paris, he asked, before I could respond—so I told him about my trip with my mothers the summer after junior year of high school and how I wanted to sip absinthe on the Left Bank like Sartre but my mothers were sober and he said oh, I have absinthe, come down to my room, so I went down with him but he couldn't find the absinthe, maybe someone took it upstairs, but he mixed me a drink with a bunch of things from the cabinet, something fruity and really strong and then he went to get his favorite Jabès book, which hadn't been translated into English and I sat down on the bed because it was the closest place, and he was standing and reading from his favorite book and I was having trouble focusing but he was getting more and more animated like he was giving a lecture, hitting the book against his leg or his chest in between quotes and I was trying to focus but getting lost and at a certain point I fell back onto the bed like a doll, it happened so fast that for a moment I didn't realize he was on top of me I just froze. I was trying to figure out what was going on but I still couldn't focus I didn't know what was happening maybe I was saying something and then he pushed a pillow over my face, a down pillow I could tell and I was allergic to down so I tried not to breathe.

I don't need to tell you the rest because we all know the rest. So I'll tell you about the next day. But the next day, I was still in his bed. I was so hungover I could barely move but it wasn't just that it was like my head wouldn't move there was nothing inside it was off. And then there was my body, why. I knew I needed to get up but it took a really long time. I don't know how long because I lost something. I lost. I lost. Something. There are gaps, and maybe I don't want them back.

Let's just say I made it back to my dorm, passed out in bed and then woke up in the middle of the night and I was in a panic. Was there someone in my room. There was someone in my room. Was there someone in my room. I tried to stay as still as possible, and I didn't hear anything, there really weren't any noises at all and maybe that was the problem so I rushed out of bed with the sheet wrapped around me and turned on all the lights. No one there. I made it to the shower, but I forgot to turn on the water before I sat down on the floor and passed out. Or maybe it was better that I didn't turn it on, because I passed out on the floor of the shower. When I woke up, I took a hot shower, and a cold shower, and a hot shower, and then a cold shower, until my skin got all wrinkly.

Don't be dramatic, I said to myself, but this was dramatic, wasn't this dramatic?

What.

Don't say it.

Who are you.

Terry Dactyl.

Where are you.

This is my dorm.

Why are you here.

I don't know.

Who are you.

Terry Dactyl.

How did you get here.

I flew.

That made me laugh. Because I was Terry Dactyl, and I flew to New York. I spread my wings, and I flew, that's how I got here.

Terry Dactyl, I said, have you seen my wings? I got out of the shower, dried myself off, went back to my room and I put on my wings. They were behind me, I spread them out. Terry, I asked, where'd you get those wings? Oh, it was after Halloween, everything was on sale, I combined angel with bumblebee and fairy princess, made the edges sharper with packing tape, spray-painted the wings silver for angel and gold for bumblebee, and bronze for fairy princess, started gluing shiny things all over, I wasn't done yet.

I put on my wings and looked in the mirror—pointy shoulders and collarbones and wings—Terry Dactyl, it's time to get dressed. But what to wear. Maybe the furry fuchsia dress under the clear raincoat, cut off the bottom of the coat and wrap it around my neck as a collar, yes, that's a start.

Googly eyes, that's what I needed. I started gluing them to my face with spirit gum, spreading them out on my cheeks, up my forehead with my hair pulled all the way back, all my favorite clips and barrettes. Silver eyelashes. Painted spirit gum over my lips and then kissed a whole jar of glitter so it would stick there in so many layers a sculpture on my lips.

Terry Dactyl, this is good.

Wrapped an iridescent plastic jump rope around my waist. Then another, and another. Thank you, dollar store.

I didn't have platforms yet so my boots would have to do. Just paint the glitter on. Push the layered shimmery skirt underneath the dress, yes, that's the way to do it, layers always work.

What to do with my hair, is it done?

More braids. Terry, there's a lot of hair, all these curls but who would know.

Who wouldn't know.

Oh, those dangly fish earrings. Yes, the dangly fish. Four in each ear. Mirror, mirror, on the wall—who's the dangliest fish of all?

Yes, the way the earrings hit one another, fish in the sea.

Terry Dactyl, with the googly eye face, are you ready?

Let's go.

You can't fight dementia with logic, that's for sure—I mean maybe you can't fight anything with logic, but you definitely can't fight dementia. That's what I learned from taking care of Rudy. My shift was twelve to six every day in the summer after I graduated from high school, and I volunteered because I knew my mothers needed help finding twenty-four-hour care and that was the hardest shift to fill, and actually it worked perfectly for me because I was trying not to do too many drugs before Columbia, and getting somewhere by noon in the summer meant I couldn't do too much the night before.

Dementia means he might not know who you are. This doesn't matter. Just play the game. So every day we played. One day I might be his sister, the next day we were both sisters, the day after that I was his aunt Trudy—once I was even Marilyn Monroe.

Dementia means they lead and you follow. Don't try to bring them back to reality. It's too late for reality. Reality just means death, and no one wants to think about that, not when they have dementia.

Dementia means the sun is too bright oh it's too bright why is it so bright, but actually it's cloudy outside. Close all the blinds anyway. Maybe you need to dim the lights too.

Dementia means we're in this together. It doesn't matter what it is, we're in it together. Is someone out to get me. No is not enough. Maybe someone's out to get both of us. Try it. Do you see what I mean? Now we're in this together.

One day I came over, and Rudy was running around the room naked and screaming ca-caw, ca-caw. So I took off my clothes and joined in. Ca-caw, ca-caw, we both flew around the room.

And then Rudy said Terry, what's going on, are you trying to seduce me.

So then we got dressed.

Maybe the worst time was when I came over, and Rudy was in the bathtub, smeared in shit. I don't have to tell you how it smelled.

I'm pregnant, Rudy said, can you help.

I can help, I said, but first we have to run the bath. For the delivery. Can we practice our deep breathing?

We practiced our deep breathing. It was hard with that smell, but death is hard.

I ran the bath. It filled up faster than I thought, and then Rudy gasped, and said something smells like shit. So we drained the bath, and then she took a shower, and I washed her off, and then I helped her get dressed.

This was when it was hard for her to get dressed alone, but she didn't seem to have trouble taking off her clothes. Of course she was all skin and bones, skin and bones and bruises and cuts and lesions and it was scary to see her that way but also I already knew, so it wasn't scary, and sometimes she was so weak it was hard for her to even stand up so she would just lie in bed mumbling with her eyes drifting off. But then suddenly she'd be jumping up and down. Where the hell did she get all that energy, I wondered. But that's death. Sometimes there's a lot of energy.

It was hard to tell what was real and what wasn't, I mean did she really think I was Marilyn Monroe that one day, I don't look anything like Marilyn Monroe—I'm like the opposite. Did Rudy just want to play, or was she so far gone that she could only play?

What matters is that we played. And I'd always loved playing with Rudy, ever since I was a kid. She was my favorite. Going to her apartment just down the hall from us to watch *Charlie's Angels*, I loved looking at all her wigs and how we'd play dress-up, and she'd tell me I could be a supermodel but I was smarter than that, wasn't I.

Charlie's Angels was the magic trick. It worked every time. *Charlie's Angels* brought Rudy back. Then she remembered. She would tell me how, when I was two or three or four years old, we'd come over and sit on her sofa—yes, the same gold sofa where we are now, she would say—it's a little worn out, maybe I should replace it, but it's so comfortable, isn't it.

We were neighbors, she would say—do you remember?

I remember.

When you were two you were this big, do you remember?

How big?

This big, Terry, you were this big, like a beautiful porcelain doll. I wanted to do your hair, but your mothers said you were too young for product. But I wanted to do your hair. All those curls—look, Terry, those curls.

You can do my hair now.

And Rudy's face would light up and she would run into the bathroom and come out with all her products but I had to tell her no, not that, I'm allergic. Let's just use the brush.

But Terry, how will we make it last?

It doesn't have to last, because we can do it again.

So she would take the curler brush, and smooth out my hair, she would twist the brush this way and that way, and then she would get out the paddle brush. Maybe a comb.

How about barrettes, she would say.

I love barrettes.

She would put barrettes in my hair—oh, sweetheart, I wish I could bring out Miss Clairol, but I know you're allergic.

Rudy, it looks so good now, I would say, and she would say really? Really.

Really it didn't look good, but it felt good. And then Rudy and I would sit there on the sofa, holding hands. Everything was quiet except the TV.

The saddest part was when she would talk about Jack—he left me, she said, why did he leave me? He left me here to die alone in this prison.

Jack left for New York when he got his diagnosis because he said he didn't want to die in this godforsaken town where it was always winter even though it never snowed or if it did it didn't stick and no one could even make a decent martini and Rudy didn't want to go with him, but I didn't say that, I said I don't know why Jack left you, Rudy, but I'm here with you now, in this prison.

Everything in the apartment was still in the same place as when Jack left, all the gold-framed mirrors and the doilies on the brass-and-glass end tables and frilly this and that covering every surface. I don't know why he left you, I would say, but I'm here with you in this prison, we can die together.

But Terry, I don't want you to die.

Okay, then I won't die.

And then we would hold hands again and watch *Charlie's Angels*.

One day near the end, when I got to her place she asked me to close my eyes before opening the door, so I did, and when I opened my eyes she was wearing her beehive—with pearls, and matching earrings, and a sequined gown. And her furry slippers. Her face was done, but she'd confused the lipstick with the eyeshadow, so her eyes were red, and her lips were blue, and she looked amazing.

Guess who, she asked.

Marilyn Monroe?

Don't flatter me, she said. It's Peggy Lee.

And there she was on the stereo, "Is That All There Is?"

And we danced, oh how we danced. Then suddenly Rudy stopped and looked at me and said who the fuck are you?

It's Terry, I said, and nothing registered.

Terry, I said again—Paula and Eileen's kid. And then her eyes lit up. Terry, she said, how on earth . . . How on earth did you get so big? Terry Dactyl, she said. You're my favorite big bird.

So that's how I got my name.

Terry, she said, I can't believe it, after all these years—we are going to have so much fun together.

And we did, we really did.

There are two kinds of club children—the ones who smoke pot and the ones who don't, and luckily Sid was one who smoked pot because when we got to her apartment I was so high on X I could barely speak I mean each time we walked up another flight of stairs I was getting higher and when she opened the door to the roof it was like we were walking out into the sky with all the buildings—hello World Trade Center, hello Chrysler Building, hello to all the cars on First Avenue all the windows all the rooftops all the glittering night lights and the thing about pot is that it's the perfect thing to do the day after X because it brings it back but if you do it while you're still flying then you're on the swing set when it gets to the top, and the swing flips all the way over and above, stretching out, and then you just stay up there.

But Sid was ready to go back downstairs so we went into her apartment on the top floor yes the top floor but you couldn't see out and inside everything was red—red sofa, red brick, red curtains, red walls covered in Polaroids, so many Polaroids, was Sid in every one, there were so many Polaroids.

I still had the googly eyes all over my face, keeping me company with that rustling sound every time I moved around, my glittery lashes and lips yes I've got my eyes on you. My eyes on me. And Sid had her eyes on me now, that was the best part. The diagonally upward and back. The feet on the ground and head stretching up, up, the current in the air, the air, the air, the air and me, the air in me, yes, that moist spongy texture, oh, Sid's hand, the texture of her fingers, squeezing, we were squeezing hands.

Are you okay, she said.

Oh, I'm . . . I'm . . .

I was trying to figure it out, and she said you're really feeling the X, aren't you.

I was really feeling it, her hand, and she said should we put on music, and then there were beats, clicks, and chirps and I was thinking about the dolphin stuffed animal I had as a kid, it was almost as big as me and I would hug it in bed.

Your dolphin, Sid asked, but how did she know. Maybe I said something.

The sounds it makes, the chirps and clicks. Is it in the music.

Honey, she said, you're really high—I'm kind of jealous. I don't know if I can get that high anymore.

And she put her hand on my hand, were we about to kiss, yes all that moisture and spit, tongue into the lines between her teeth, gums and moaning, was that me or her, the corners of the lips, the sides of the cheek and ears, salty, back to lips, bounce, bounce, pucker, bounce, pucker, bounce, tongue outside of mouth, glitter going everywhere, pucker bounce bounce the clicks and clanks and chirps and cranks and chanks and slurps and burps and banks rank-a-dank dank-clanks franks, shertranks, granks branks bankcrank rank-a-dank crank-tank-a-mank and bounce, pucker, bounce, pucker, tongue into temperature, oh, neck, oh, that shivery feeling and eyes, open, hers are closed, lashes, I'm kissing the lashes and eyes and forehead, oh, this feels so good, more spit please and those chirps and clicks, oh.

Then Sid pulled back and reached for my hand, all that sponginess, a pulse, me and her, this red, where am I, red curtains red walls Polaroids and red red.

Terry, she said, I have something to tell you. It's kind of a big deal.

I'm sorry about the glitter on your face.

Honey, it's fine. I love glitter. You know that.

And all the eyes—are they okay? Are they getting in the way? Should I take off my wings?

You can take them off or keep them on, whichever feels more comfortable.

Okay, maybe I'll keep them on. I'll keep them on so I can keep flying. Can I tell you about my dolphin?

Yes, but first I have something to tell you. It's important. Is that okay? I have to tell you before we go any further.

Okay, I said.

She kissed me on the lips again, pucker and bounce, and then she looked at me, and I looked at her, and she said I'm HIV-positive. I have AIDS. And I want you to know that we will never do anything unsafe.

We will use dental dams, finger cots, condoms on dildos, condoms on everything, everything will be safe. I don't mean to be getting ahead of myself, I just want you to know beforehand. We don't have to do any of that. I just want you to know, just in case. I will never put you in danger. We will be entirely safe. I just want you to know.

Okay, I said. It's okay. I love you.

I didn't mean to say it but there I said it and now she looked shocked. Maybe I looked shocked? All that quivering inside.

It's okay, she said. We can let the ecstasy talk. I'm okay with that. There are all kinds of love and I want to embrace them. I just wish I could be as high as you. Did you eat today?

Today, I asked. I don't know what day it is. Maybe yesterday? Or the day before.

I wish I had something to offer you, but all I have is tea.

Tea, yes.

Red Zinger?

Yes, that color, yes.

We sipped the Red Zinger in red mugs on the red sofa with the red walls and I told her about my dolphin, the chirps and clicks and Sid put her hand in my lap, and I held it there, we were dolphins in our hands.

I knew you were kinky, Sid said—let's do that sometime, let's play with our dolphins.

I couldn't keep myself from smiling, smiling like a little kid, and leaning into Sid. I'm a little kid, with Sid, I kept thinking, that rhymes, I could be a kid with Sid and this was going to be so much fun.

Sid was a junkie with rules. She would never shoot heroin more than once a week, she said that way she wouldn't be an addict. But sometimes, she said, I just need a heroin vacation. And that's when she would lie in bed all day, watching the patterns in her head and going on that journey. Sometimes I would lie in bed with her like that, she was asleep but so awake, every sensation in her body I could feel through mine.

What do you see, I would ask, and she would tell me. But then I would go out to face the world because I knew she wanted that vacation.

Heroin was the one drug Sid shot up, the one that was kind of a secret, something she did in privacy. She told me she would never let me see her shooting up, and I couldn't live with her if I was shooting drugs—she'd already had a junkie girlfriend, and look where that got her—and that was fine with me because I was afraid of needles anyway, and the one time I snorted heroin it felt like I was dead inside so I definitely didn't need any more of that.

Sid had a calendar on the wall, and for every day she would mark the drugs she did—maybe Monday would say HV for heroin vacation, and then Tuesday might say C K, for coke and K, and then Wednesday might say C V C C X, because she did a lot of coke that night, with Valium and then ecstasy, but a lower-case x meant Xanax, and then she might mark a bunch of days with NO H ahead of time. Sid knew how to fly, I think that's why she loved heroin so much, because it kept her grounded to stay there in that bed for a while and I was afraid of all that stillness but I didn't say anything because I knew it was her time to rest, and we all needed rest, didn't we.

Is it stupid to say she was my heroine? I mean I needed her. I needed her for everything. And I wasn't the only one. Our whole little crew—there was something she gave us, how she walked into the room like there was no one there. No one. No one was there. She would just set herself up for whatever she had decided, she would make that room into her own. There could be hundreds of people dancing into oblivion, but the room was hers. And if you were there with her, that room was yours too.

Sid taught me everything. Everything.

How to walk outside like no one can touch you.

And then they can't.

Okay, okay, they can, but when you walk outside like no one can touch you, they might not know it.

There are two kinds of club kids—the ones who know how to sew and the ones who don't. My outfits were made from staples and safety pins and everything ripped and stuck together and of course there was a glamour to this, it was my look, but everything Sid made was flawless. She would scour the thrift stores like the rest of us, but she was looking for the raw materials, the fabric for her creations. Or sometimes a pattern to copy, and then she would search the Garment District for all the shimmery fabrics to make the tightest outfits that still somehow looked spacious, she said she wanted the fabric touching her skin to feel like another skin.

Her apartment was technically a two bedroom, but the second bedroom, which was tiny, more like a walk-in closet, it was filled with all her creations hanging on a clothes bar on one side, or in built-in drawers above or below, and her sewing machines on the other side. A mirror on the door so you could try everything on. This was the only room that wasn't red, it was gold, so the walls shimmered like another fabric.

When I moved in with Sid I offered to split the rent and she said sure, honey, but my rent is only $490 because I've been here since 1980 and it's rent-controlled and we can split everything, sure, but what I really need is someone to help me with business at the clubs, do you want to help with that. And I said of course, so she taught me the rules.

Only sell to someone you know or someone who knows someone you know.

If some random person comes up to ask where to find drugs, you have no idea. Unless they're working a look that's off the charts.

Never leave any of the merchandise at the coat check because it will be gone. Who wouldn't take it? It's not like you're going to call management.

Never give anyone change. That's the bartender's job. When someone hands you a twenty, you give them a bag. If they hand you a fifty, you give them two.

We only sell twenties at the club—we can sell them as many as they want, but if they ask for a bulk discount then they need to come over to the house ahead of time.

Sid kept all the drugs in a safe inside a nightstand by the bed. It was compact, but very very heavy. All the baggies had glittery hearts on them, which was Sid's trademark. She made my business accessories—a string of pockets that I could tie around my waist for easy access to store money and drugs under all my other layers, plus a little lipstick or eyeliner for a refresher, and then a pair of bloomers I'd wear under everything and that's where the baggies would go, flat against my body in five pockets on each side. Take a few out and put them in the other pockets if you want easier access, but never leave more than three or four in those pockets because they're more exposed. If someone catches you with three or four bags, they could just be yours to party with, but more than that, probably not.

The bathroom is your hallowed ground, the stall is where you can arrange and rearrange everything. It's also a great place to make the transaction. Always tip the bathroom attendant and the coat check, they are your best friends.

Always be generous with your stash because that will get you more business. Sharing is caring.

Oh, and never tell anyone your source. Don't let them trick you into revealing this by asking how you know it's pure. Nothing is pure, honey.

But maybe I'm getting ahead of myself. Although I guess that makes sense because I was definitely getting ahead of myself then—I mean three days after I slept with Sid, I hadn't left—we kept ordering food in, and her regulars would stop by to make their purchases while I hid in the bedroom, and at a certain point I had to tell her that I didn't want to go back to my place. And she said fine, don't go back, I like having you here.

We were coked out and I was wearing a jumpsuit she'd made for me out of this amazing purple silky fabric—I couldn't really borrow her clothes because she was five foot two and everything she wore was skintight, so she was making me things. She even had this purple faux fur coat with magenta trim that she was going to cut up to make something with but she said wait, try this on, and it looked incredible, I mean that became my favorite coat, it was like a trademark.

Eventually Sid said so, should we go get your stuff? Just like that. I didn't even have to tell her what happened.

So she called Jorge and Miguel—we grew up together, she said, they're the ones who are going to take care of me when I die—don't say I'm morbid, I know I'm morbid but it's just the truth and they own a moving company, just a little one, just the two of them, you don't even have to go inside, just give me the key and then I'll ask them to handle everything—how much stuff do you have? Just clothes and books, a coffee maker, and a boombox—what are you, a student? Wait, wait, don't tell me how old you are, whatever you do, don't tell me how old you are.

So then we went up there together to meet Jorge and Miguel—they were muscleboys in tight jeans and white T-shirts even though it was December, hair cut close to the scalp and they could have passed as brothers the way they matched except they swished in all the best ways and puckered their lips to kiss us hello and they hugged and squeezed me even though we'd never met and then Sid said okay girls, we'll meet you at Tom's Diner, okay.

Tom's Restaurant, I said—Suzanne Vega changed the name for the song. And everyone thought that was hilarious, that the actual place Suzanne Vega wrote the song about was right around the corner, and Sid had never been there, and even if you didn't like Suzanne Vega, or the song, when someone stole it and made a remix, and then instead of suing them, she released the remix on her own album, I mean everyone loved that.

But anyway we went over there but did we really want to go inside, it was too early for a diner I mean this was right in the middle of the day and we weren't in the mood, not at the moment, so we walked around the block and got falafel and I was thinking about when I first got here and this was New York for me, and yes I sat in Tom's

Restaurant like everyone else, hoping I would see Suzanne Vega, but why, I mean I liked her music in high school but that already felt like so long ago, and before we knew it Jorge and Miguel were there in the van. Jorge got out and opened up the back doors, and we jumped in and everything was neatly arranged in boxes, I'd told them to throw it all in garbage bags but they were like no girl we're professionals, don't worry, it's not a problem, Sid's family, and in the van we did more coke, passing around the vial before heading downtown and then we were back at Sid's, just like that.

The hard part was that I had to tell my mothers I wasn't going back, I mean this was just before winter break so I figured I better call them to tell them beforehand, but the problem was that I couldn't say it, I just couldn't say why.

What do you mean you can't go back, Eileen asked.

I just can't, I said, it's not what I want right now, I need to be on my own—I found an apartment, I have a job.

You what, Paula asked—you found an apartment already, you have a job?

And Eileen said Terry, what on earth is going on?

And Paula said we need to talk this over first.

And I said I just can't go back.

Terry, Eileen said, you need to tell us what's going on—we know you haven't been stimulated by your classes, but that will change. The first semester is always the hardest. You'll get used to it.

I can't get used to it, I said, I can't.

What do you mean you can't, Paula said, isn't this what you've worked your whole life for?

I know, I said, but it's not what I want now.

Paula, Eileen said, what are we going to do about this?

And I said I can't talk right now, I just wanted to let you know before I come home.

And Eileen said you found an apartment already, you have a job, you can't just leave that to come home, can you, and she hung up.

Was Paula still there. I don't know because then I hung up the phone.

So I didn't go to Seattle for winter break. I wrote them a letter telling them everything except the actual reason, I mean it was true that I hated my classes, true that I felt like Columbia was squashing my creativity, true that I wanted to live in a queer world like the one I'd grown up in, they could understand that, couldn't they, true that I needed to explore New York on my own, to expand the possibilities for my life rather than accepting everything that was predetermined, true that this didn't mean I couldn't go back to school in the future, it just wasn't for me now.

But I didn't tell them the rest. The real reason. I just couldn't.

I guess my letter worked, because they called right when they got it and said Terry, it's so great to hear your voice, do you need anything?

They wanted to come visit—was that okay, could they visit me sometime soon, whenever I was ready?

They came to visit in February—they wanted to meet Sid, they thought it would be fun to go out with the four of us. So we went to Angelica Kitchen. Of course there was a line, and we were waiting outside together in the cold and smiling at one another and chatting and I was looking at them and thinking how strange that these were my mothers. It wasn't a bad feeling, it was just kind of surreal to be with them at Angelica's, standing out in the snow and waiting for a table, all of us on our best behavior.

I'd only had one real argument with my mothers before and that was when Paula got home from rehab and told us she'd started eating chicken and fish, that it was helping with her cravings, and would it be okay if she cooked that at home, and I just lost it. Because we'd gone vegan together, they'd taught me the horrors of factory farming, they'd made fun of anyone who talked about responsible slaughter, they were repulsed by all forms of animal cruelty, they helped me to find vegan shoes, they taught me how to balance every meal so that I got enough of every nutrient, how to supplement my diet when I needed to, and it felt like they were taking all of this away. So, like I said, I lost it. I told them I would move out if they brought meat into the house, there was no way I would live there if they were eating meat.

And they backed down right away—we totally understand your concerns, Eileen said, like this was a business meeting—and we will only eat meat outside of the house, we will respect your wishes. And even though they backed down, I couldn't believe that Eileen was changing her values too, just like that, I mean was that really what it meant to be sober?

Of course I was fifteen—everything was clearer then, I know this now, but also I know that the only rule I gave to Sid was that we couldn't have meat in the house, and she said yes, of course, honey, I'd be happy to do that for you. And then I asked if we could clean out the refrigerator together, because whenever I opened it I just saw a moldy loaf of bread, a few nearly empty jars of expired mustard and jam, bottles of chili sauce and fish sauce, a jar of pickle juice without the pickles, and then a carton of milk that must have expired a million years ago, not to mention a bunch of to-go containers that I didn't dare open, and she said oh, I've been meaning to do that for a while, so then she just opened the refrigerator door and threw everything in a garbage bag, and then scrubbed the shelves, and that was that.

Like most club kids, Sid didn't really cook anything, and neither did I at this point, but I knew my mothers would want to see the apartment so before their visit Sid and I went over to Prana and bought a bunch of bulk foods—beans and grains and nuts—and then I arranged them carefully in mason jars like my mothers did, next to bottles of apple cider vinegar and olive oil and tamari. We also got tempeh and miso, tahini and vegetables and soy milk and a few juices so the refrigerator wasn't totally empty.

At Angelica Kitchen we ordered all my favorite appetizers—Angelica's cornbread, walnut-lentil pâté, the pickle plate, the ruby kraut, and the norimaki to split. My mothers couldn't believe the cornbread, which was exactly my response when Sid first took me there—you bite into it, and you're like what the fuck is this, because there's rice, and tahini, and at first you're confused but then you can't think about anything else. So anyway the dinner was amazing, and everything went so smoothly—it was a little strange because maybe my mothers were turning into normal lesbians, I mean now that Paula was getting a degree in public relations and she wasn't working a different hairstyle every week, and Eileen was really starting to look like a therapist, and Sid and I were total freaks, but they complimented us on everything—they loved Sid's blue metallic eyelashes and my shimmering magenta and green eyeshadow spreading onto my cheeks, and all my new geometric earrings poking out in all directions in between the silver hoops—so it wasn't like they were completely normal.

They were in New York for a week, staying uptown, so I would meet them at their hotel and then we would go out for lunch—they'd done research, so they found these great vegan places that I wouldn't have known about otherwise, like the Candle Café, which was on the Upper East Side near their hotel, and then HanGawi, the vegetarian Korean restaurant in Midtown, with the most amazing squash soup and fresh almond milk. Then we went to MOMA, the Whitney, and the Guggenheim, and even to the top of the Empire State Building, all the things I would never do otherwise, but it was kind of fun to be a tourist in New York with my mothers, we hadn't done that before.

They wanted to visit my work—I'd told them I was working at A Different Light, the gay bookstore, but that I'd taken time off for their visit and so it would be weird to go into the store with them, wouldn't it, so they went on their own and they were impressed, Paula said everyone was so friendly to us there, it felt like family, didn't it.

And then on their last night I decided to make dinner, so I made the pomegranate tempeh that was my favorite from childhood, with a miso vegetable soup and millet cooked with carrot juice like they did it at Angelica Kitchen, and shredded steamed kale with tahini dressing, and when my mothers arrived Eileen said oh, all this red, it's like we're all in the womb together, and Paula said oh Eileen, and it was like I was home. I mean I was home, but it was like we were all home together.

And maybe the best part was how they asked all these questions about Sid's photos, because I had to catch Sid at the exact right moment to get any information or else she would just say oh, that one, I'll tell you later, and that would be it. So when they asked about the one black-and-white photo that was framed in the corner of our bedroom, and

Sid said oh, that's my Warhol, and everyone laughed like we weren't sure if she meant really, but I think she meant really.

That was when she still had her hair, which was even curlier than mine, so I knew it was from before she moved into this apartment, because that's when she shaved her head—she said that's when I was finally ready to be me. So I guess the Warhol must have been when she was in her late teens, and the only other photos from that far back were with Jorge and Miguel on the piers, sunbathing, I would stare at those photos all the time, like I was looking at something I wasn't supposed to see.

And when my mothers asked questions, I found out that one whole wall of photos in the living room was all at Danceteria, in three different locations, and then a few at Studio 54, and my mothers were like is that Area? And is that? But I didn't catch all the names—they knew more about this history than I did because of all their friends who would take the redeye to New York to party for the weekend. But when I looked at all the photos, I always focused on Margarita, who was Sid's junkie ex, and how happy they looked together, the two of them with their freshly shaved heads and big gold hoop earrings, matching curvy bodies and tight dresses, looking out at the camera with all that lipstick and eyeliner.

There were photos of Sid during her Siddhartha period with String Bean at the Palladium, where they both look like Hare Krishnas, and then photos of TaraMielle dressed as Siamese twins in outfits made by Sid, and then a few where the three of them were dressed as triplets in identical geisha makeup at the Roxy, and then there were all the photos of Sid during her dayglo wig period in the early days of the Limelight, when she and Cleo would go out in wigs that were the same color, and there was even one photo where they were wearing matching Afros, and then one where Sid, Cleo, and Jaysun were all wearing purple bobs, which I think was when Jaysun first arrived.

But my favorites were all the photos of Sid dancing, the camera catching her in motion, the body curling in and out, the bending and the collapse, the flipping out of control but always back to gravity and that's how I found her, right, and still every time I saw her dancing it was like something brand new the way everyone was trying to be high up above in our platforms but Sid would show up in ballet slippers and melt into the floor.

So when I took my mothers back to their hotel in a cab they said they were proud of me, they could tell that Sid really loved me, it was beautiful to see, and they had a little gift for me, just something to help with my settling in, and they gave me a check for $2,000, which I deposited at the ATM on my way home because I didn't want to lose it.

But then a week or two after my mothers got home, they called to say they were worried about me.

Don't take this the wrong way, Eileen said, but is it okay if we tell you something in confidence.

I didn't say yes or no, but then Paula said it's about Sid, we were noticing some of her movements, and to be perfectly honest we were a little worried that she might be using heroin.

What, I said, like I was shocked, and I was shocked, because Sid wasn't on heroin when they were there, and both times we'd gotten together she was totally composed, I mean maybe she'd taken a Valium or some Xanax or a few bumps of coke, but that was all. And I'd been doing the exact same thing. What was it about Sid that they noticed?

Anyway, I acted totally offended, and said I have no idea what you're talking about, and they backed off and said maybe they misinterpreted, they just wanted to bring this up, just to make sure I was safe, and it was that word that freaked me out. Because we were totally safe, and Sid was the one who was concerned about me. She'd already taken me to get an HIV test, she'd come with me to get my results.

Honey, Sid was already saying, you have to be ready for after I'm gone, you have to have a plan. And I didn't have a plan at all—she seemed totally healthy, she was always doing yoga and practicing dance routines and her body was all muscle, whereas I was all skin and bones. I would try to cheer her up, and say it's possible they'd find a cure, and she would just laugh—honey, she said, I'm not taking that shit, you know it kills you faster, I've got my own medicine, but it's not going to save me and neither are you.

So when my mothers said they were concerned that Sid might be using heroin, that's when I knew I could never tell them she was positive. Even though they were the ones who would understand the most. They were trying to support me, but they fucked up, and I didn't know how to tell them.

When New York went into lockdown, Sabine called me up and said Terry, art must not die.

So I knew she had a plan. And I was ready.

She'd already stopped coming into work because she was in a high-risk group, she didn't say which one but I knew she had to be in her eighties, she never discussed her age but there was that one time when I told her Eileen had gone to Smith, and she said that's my alma mater, what years, and when I said sometime in the '60s she said oh she's just a baby and smiled stiffly in that way that you could never quite read. Twenty years later and she still had posture so upright it looked painful, her hair and makeup were still the same, the tailored clothes subtly updated to make her visible in that way that was also invisible, and her eyes were as sharp as ever. Now she always wore a silk scarf around her neck for a flash of color or a pattern to set off the black, and maybe this was also to cover her wrinkles but mostly she just looked more and more aristocratic, and if she'd ever had plastic surgery it was the kind designed to look like she'd never had plastic surgery.

So now I was working in the gallery alone but of course Sabine would call me every day exactly at 10:00 a.m. to make sure I was there, and I would forward her all financial or media inquiries, so we basically had the same division of labor, it's just that we weren't in the same space. Except when she would come in to look for something, or to choose pieces, but she would do that in the morning before I arrived.

So when she said art must not die, she meant that even if the gallery had to close she wanted me to come in every day and work like usual, to arrange displays in the windows and answer the phone and take care of anything else and honestly I was totally fine with that because I needed a routine to get me out of my apartment, to stop thinking about the coughing downstairs or next door, to stop worrying about who I was going to encounter in the hallway and whether they would be wearing a mask, and if they were wearing a mask would it be pulled down from their nose, I needed to stop thinking about everyone dying in nursing homes and assisted living or everyone trapped on cruise ships or all the yuppie joggers exhaling all that spit on everyone, not to mention the dog walkers, had there always been this many dog walkers, I mean they must've been there before but it felt like there was a sudden surge in clueless assholes taking up the sidewalk and you didn't want to go full New York and push your way by, right, because you had to keep that six-foot distance, which of course was impossible, especially in the crosswalks, I mean have you ever been in a crosswalk in New York, try one foot of distance, and then there were all the shiny happy couples suddenly in love in public, holding each other tight or stopping to make out in some random spot that wasn't romantic at all, just to say we have this and you don't.

When I was a kid I always wanted to go on a cruise, I loved the idea of being out there in the middle of the ocean on a boat that was its own world but my mothers said no, it's not like *Love Boat,* it's one of the most destructive industries in the world, those ships kill so many sea creatures and then there's all the pollution from the fuel, not to mention the substandard living conditions of the people working on board, it's practically modern-day slavery—and then there's the food, you don't even want to know what they serve, it's just awful. So they took me down to the pier where the cruise ships were docked, and right away I started coughing from all that pollution, and after that I didn't want to go on a cruise.

So when the story broke about everyone trapped on that first cruise ship I just kept thinking about all that coughing, everyone in their rooms, coughing, the ventilation for each room connected to the next, and how there was no way to open the windows so even if people could see out they couldn't let that air in and they knew that people were dying on board and who would be next.

But Sabine was prepared. She'd already installed the best air filtration system in the gallery, and made sure there was an endless stash of N95 masks, nitrile gloves, and alcohol wipes in the back closet as soon as the news broke, and she told me she didn't want me to use any mask twice, she had plenty more where those came from, don't listen to what they're saying on the news about a shortage, there's no shortage, take as many as you need, don't use them more than once, I want you to be safe.

I tried not to think about the outbreak at that first assisted living facility in Kirkland so close to Seattle, people were dying inside and no one could visit, no one could save them, families were gathered outside to wave to their loved ones through the glass, I kept staring at the photos of those vulnerable people looking out in shock, wanting to smash the windows so they could get away, but where would they go, and did I know anyone in Kirkland, I mean I definitely knew people who grew up in Kirkland, and now this was the epicenter, all these people dying inside a place called Life Care.

Kirkland, I kept thinking, do I know anyone in Kirkland. I called my mothers. They said Terry, we're doing okay. We're taking all the necessary precautions. When was that, it already felt like so long ago the way time broke open and closed, open and closed, and you had to figure out how to do the things you'd always done, but with all the risks that before weren't risks, I mean like laundry, which was always a hassle for me because of toxic detergents and poisonous fabric softeners, so I'd always stuck my head into each machine to see which smelled tolerable but now I would just throw everything into whichever machine was open and then run outside to wait in the cold with the smokers and how much spit was in their smoke, could we get the coronavirus from smoke, that's what I was wondering.

Sid and I always did laundry at Cosmo's because it was right around the corner but every machine there was toxic so once I discovered JJ's that was my spot because they had the machines where you could put detergent in the prewash and the wash, and that really helped wash everything away, and also you could leave your laundry in the machine and go home to wait without worrying someone was going to steal it but now I didn't want to go home to wait because then I would have to walk past all those coughing doorways in my building again, it was easier when I was leaving because I could look out my peephole to make sure no one was there and listen carefully for any sounds but going back I didn't have a choice so I thought of walking over to Tompkins but too many people, right, although I was spending more time on the hill but then they started locking that part of the park, why were they locking it when we needed air and I already had my route to work to avoid the tourists and the students and the shoppers, obviously stay away from St. Mark's or Broadway or Prince, I mean I had to take Prince or Spring but just for a moment, but then Ninth felt too risky and forget about Sixth or Seventh and I didn't want to walk past the precinct on Fifth, and Fourth could get crowded so then I was on Third but then the street gets skinny so you're turning to the side to let the other person go and I never realized before that when I turn to the side I always turn toward the other person, so now I had to retrain my body and maybe the bigger streets were better especially when everyone was walking in the same direction but then boom that could change in a second and suddenly you'd be faced with all those breathing bodies and, yes, laundry was just a few blocks away but suddenly going anywhere felt like an obstacle course and I couldn't even make basic decisions like did I want to go into East Village Organic to get soup and sit in front of JJ's on one of the plastic chairs, at least they had chairs outside, okay, I'll just run into East Village Organic for a second and get that soup, no bread, thank you, but then I wasn't sure about sipping the soup right from the container like I usually did and I got so stressed out about what to do that I ended up leaving it on the street for someone.

Of course I thought about dropping off my laundry or sending it out, but then what if they used fabric softener without telling me I mean then I wouldn't be able to breathe and speaking of breathing someone would be breathing on all my clothes and what about those respiratory droplets and I didn't want to turn into some shut-in but anyway once I got to the gallery I didn't think about laundry, and I wasn't at home scrolling through headlines to see what Trump had just said about injecting bleach or everyone hailing Anthony Fauci for doing what, nothing, absolutely nothing, but everyone said that without him there wouldn't be anyone with any sense left but what kind of sense I mean wasn't this the same Anthony Fauci who was responsible for so many AIDS deaths, how many thousands of dead bodies piling up before he came to his senses and now we were supposed to think he was a hero but luckily we didn't even have the internet at the gallery because Sabine thought it was a terrible distraction and I had enough of the internet at home anyway, I was perfectly fine with going into the gallery and continuing to work even though we were closed, at the gallery I didn't need to think about social distancing quarantine lockdown isolation testing surveillance shelter in place or whatever was coming next, I could just close the doors and try to focus on art.

Time was slippery and we'd all fallen in—nothing temporary felt temporary anymore, I mean it already felt like so long ago when I went to ecstatic dance, I didn't know if I should go but then I went, I was thinking about how this was a lung infection we were all trying to avoid, but was anyone breathing, and every store was out of vitamin C but at least this felt comforting because everyone wasn't just trying to kill kill kill the virus and could we build immunity together, but the last time I went to ecstatic dance, before everything closed, and yes, it was a lot less crowded than usual, but there was breath and it was our bodies in that room and touch, the falling into one another the softness the flickering inside.

In the circle afterward, someone said: I don't come here to dance, I come here for your shares in the circle, you should record those for NPR.

But what did I say? Something about how I start in one place, a place of how is this possible? To be in this room with these other bodies, to make room. When I'm on that dance floor, moving in and out, and when it all blends, the spaces we make together.

No, it wasn't that—something about fluidity, how my body can move in ways that aren't possible elsewhere, and how to make that possible everywhere, how outside no one moves like this, because they're too afraid.

But now we were all afraid.

I kept imagining my mothers, waving through sealed glass, I mean what if they needed assisted living?

What if I needed assisted living.

But actually it was a rehab center, Life Care, some of those people were supposed to get out in a few weeks. They were just there to get better.

Wuhan was the epicenter. Seattle was the epicenter. New York was the epicenter. Italy was the epicenter. Everywhere was the epicenter. I didn't need any more epicenters.

Someone posted a photo of a tulip on Facebook, and I started crying. No, I wasn't prepared, but Sabine was.

So I would turn my head from anyone on the stairs in my building, I would dodge the joggers and dog-walkers, not to mention all the suddenly sneezing kids, the moms so close to them, shouldn't they be keeping their six feet from one another oh right they lived together, that's what families do, at least they were shorter than me and I had my N95 but did it really work, it certainly hurt my neck and pulled my hair and when I took it off there were always red marks, the headache growing, but still I felt better going into the gallery than staying in my apartment, that was for sure.

I was so glad I lived alone but also I was sad that I lived alone, I mean after so many years without drugs without clubs without the ways I'd found intimacy before I'd finally figured out a way through ecstatic dance and I was experimenting with contact improv and trying to think of more movement practices where I could create intimacy with strangers or almost-strangers so my body could breathe the everyday, walking around the city in search of the city, like you're watching the pigeons to see what they're pecking at, and it's a package of hazelnut cacao nib granola, but suddenly any mundane interaction could lead to death, right, the hospitals were filling up the bodies were piling up, there was that nursing home in New Jersey with thirty-five corpses in the back, they were trying to hide the dead and was that what a nursing home was for, I didn't want to be discarded like that, no one does.

Like Mona Foot, who went to the hospital because she was having trouble breathing and they said it was just a mild case of COVID so she should go home. She went home and died three days later.

Mona Foot was my neighbor, I used to see her in the East Village all the time. I know she didn't like to be called Mona when she was out of drag because she and Cleo had a run-in about it, even though Cleo was just trying to compliment her show and Mona went off on her, so after that Cleo and Jaysun refused to go to *Star Search* even though before then they'd been groupies, and I stopped going too, until Cleo and Jaysun dropped me, but that's a different story.

So many drag queens turn into evil bitches once the makeup is done, but Mona was an evil bitch until she was in drag and obviously I'm a fan of the universal feminine so I'll stick to Mona because it's when she was Mona that she would actually acknowledge me. She was regal in her Wonder Woman outfit, presiding over *Star Search* like the Amazon we were all waiting for, I mean sometimes someone called me an Amazon although I was no match for Mona Foot with her gold bracelets but the hospital turned Wonder Woman away, just like that, she wasn't even in drag, just this muscular Black queen who couldn't breathe and they sent her home, she was only fifty, just three years older than me, she was HIV positive and they didn't think she needed help, or she wasn't a priority, and was this because she looked fit to them or was it because she was Black, they sent her home and that's when she died, they killed her, the hospital, that's what I thought, they killed her just like that and if our Wonder Woman could die that fast then anyone could so I kept my N95 on I sanitized the doorknobs after I touched them I washed my hands before I put on gloves and I washed them after because I had plenty of health problems already and I didn't want to end up at the hospital, gasping for breath, I mean I'd had asthma as a kid and I didn't want to know what that was like again.

Time spread out in the gallery, so instead of thinking about the present I would get obsessed about the most random thing from my past, thinking about it from all different angles, staring into space which meant staring into my head and down that tunnel of memory and this was so much better than staying in my apartment. Especially without anyone else in the gallery, I mean I didn't even have to wear my mask, I could do some dance moves on my own, using the walls to support me like someone at ecstatic dance, rolling around so my body could make different shapes because without touch my brain couldn't slow down so that's what I was trying to replicate, I wanted a community of gestures and yes this was too much to ask so now I was trying to soften with those white walls.

Everything was spinning but at least I didn't feel so trapped, not in the same way, especially when I had window displays to prepare and all this filtered air, and then I remembered Cleo's piece from Club Kid Diaspora, which Sabine bought for herself and it was in storage in the back, and I asked Sabine if we should put it up outside and she said Terry, yes, what a magnificent idea.

So Raul came over to install it, and I gave him an N95 and he was so grateful but then I couldn't see his smile anymore, we were smiling inside masks and yes you could see it in the eyes but mostly just fear, everywhere, that's what I saw but Raul bolted the art to the outside of the gallery and connected the wires and then it was ready, it was ready to flash at us once again:

Art is not dead
Art is   dead
Art is not
Art

It was like Club Kid Diaspora but flashing outside above the doorway instead of inside, we were all inside-out and it got a lot of attention—it's not like anyone remembered it from 20 years ago, now it was brand-new and there were photos all over the place and people were coming just to look in the gallery window, especially after the story in *Hyperallergic* and then the one in *ARTnews,* I mean the headline was already there in the title of the piece and now everyone wanted to buy art, they wanted to support the gallery during these tough times, it was an independent business, and Sabine said yes she was closing the gallery but she was not boarding up the windows so there would still be exhibits, she was not afraid of the people the people needed art so the lights would be on all night and art must not die even if so many people actually were dying, right, I mean collectors still had plenty of money and what was the point of all this I mean it did keep me busy. Although of course then I couldn't help thinking about that first show when all the walls were covered in everything Jaysun and I dragged over from Domsey's and now they were back to basic white, I mean they'd been basic white ever since I stopped doing drugs and how long ago was that—fifteen years?

Cleo became an art star after the show sold out—everything except CLEOPATRICK IS UNDEAD, which she wanted for herself anyway. Then she started getting commissions—TOKYO IS DEAD for a nightclub in Nagoya, and then PARIS IS DEAD for a Dior show, and then the biggest one was VEGAS IS DEAD—each letter was 45 feet tall, the same height as the letters on the Hollywood sign and the same font too, so VEGAS looked just like HOLLYWOOD and then IS DEAD was in flashing red red red, Vegas is dead, she rented an old airplane hangar to make everything, and even though the casino never actually got built and who knows where those letters ended up, Cleo still got paid, I mean she made so much money off that one commission that she bought a condo with cash, and that's when I really started to understand how the art world worked. It wasn't necessarily what you sold in the show, but what happened afterward. Cleo opened her own neon factory and of course it was called NEON IS DEAD, the sign for the factory an advertisement for more signs, and then she was there all day doing coke with her newly-hired assistants.

Then Jaysun started getting DJ gigs—first it was private parties for all the awful art people, I mean I'd never seen so much Botox in one room before and was everyone wearing the same outfit but they loved her music, these art people, that was for sure, not at the clubs where the beats were too irregular but at these private parties and there was this one guy who looked like Brad Pitt, I mean that's what Jaysun said but maybe it was just the eyebrows, eyebrows and cocaine and he was obsessed with Jaysun's underwear even though he was straight, or that's what he said, and it turned out he was a music rep so then Jaysun started getting flown around the world to do shows in Goa and Lisbon and Mexico City and Ibiza and London and Berlin and then she was mostly living with Brad so I wasn't seeing her as much, now that she was DJSun or DJSin, depending on her mood.

So Sabine and I were a team, because I would find the talent and then she would create the machine, and after Club Kid Diaspora every mess at the clubs wanted me to show their work and I had to figure out who could actually make something interesting and who was just your average cokehead—not that I had anything against cokeheads, of course, like Govinda, who made the glass ice stalactites hanging from the ceiling like you were inside a chandelier a cave of glass and then every high-end restaurant with a high ceiling wanted one; or Miss Martine, who made the giant ruby slippers that were shattered on the mirrored floor for *There's no place like home, there's no place like home, there's no place.* So I would organize the shows, and Sabine did the interviews, I didn't want the spotlight because my spotlight was still walking into the club, that's what I wanted, those were my lights.

For the first five or six years working at the gallery I never went to sleep until the evening, I mean I figured out a routine—when I was done with work I would go over to Souen for dinner, starting with the mu tea and the miso soup, then the cornbread that wasn't as mysterious as Angelica's but it was still crunchy and chewy at the same time and oh, that apple butter spread and the kinpira and then maybe I'd get the vegetable kuzu stew with tempeh or the futomaki, or one of the specials, and that's what would calm me down enough to go home and take a bath and a few Xanax or Valium or Ambien or whatever, and get in bed. But I never could sleep for more than four hours, so then I'd get up and do more coke and get ready to go out, and then after the clubs maybe there would be a few hours in the early morning to lie in bed and drift away but I didn't take any pills then, I would just float up to the ceiling and down, down, watching the colors or playing TV in my head until it was time to get ready for work and by then I was so coked out I would walk into the gallery like every step was runway, like this was the after-after-hours and I was ready.

Sabine loved that energy, and all my customers showing up to pick up their goods, so we were in this vortex like that for five or six or more like seven or eight years, right, and I think what kept me alive was that on Sunday night, after I got home from wherever, I would take a bunch of pills, and I would sleep through Monday and wake up sometime on Tuesday completely strung out, I mean totally destroyed, but then I'd do a few bumps or smoke some pot laced with coke and head over to Angelica Kitchen to refresh, so I guess that was another thing that kept me alive, I never stopped eating, I mean I would go for twenty-four hours without eating a thing, especially when the X was good, just juice or candy or tea but other than that I never lost my appetite, even when I was totally coked out and it was the middle of the night I would head over to Veselka for sweet potato pierogies or Odessa for mushroom barley soup and dolmas, or 7A for steamed vegetables and tofu with brown rice and carrot tahini dressing, and maybe the key was all the pot I was still smoking so I still loved eating and those late-night/early-morning moments with Jaysun once everyone else went to bed.

So that was my New York for all those years, the nights that lasted forever, but the problem was that after a while it was a routine just like any other and after 9/11, everything changed, as they say, and what changed for me was that I really started to hate New York, I mean it was already Giuliani's wasteland but now there was this explosion of patriotic fervor, suddenly everyone and everything was draped in the stars and stripes and before 9/11 those I Love New York T-shirts were already beyond tired but now they meant let's bomb the world. The whole country was saying I Love New York and that's when I knew it was over. It was done. But I was still there. We all were. And now here we were, nineteen years later, with this new pandemic the rich people were fleeing while the poor people were stuck, and then there were the people like me who were in between who were suddenly saying things like I could never leave New York, no matter how bad it gets we stick together, the real New Yorkers, this is our only home, I could never live anywhere else, we need to stick together, and it kind of felt like that same kind of patriotism and I guess that's when I realized I needed to get out.

Sid was always cold in bed and I was always hot, so the first time she got really sick I didn't realize all the heat was coming from her because she had all the covers and I just had my own sheet, that's how we always slept but she was drenched in sweat and still so cold she was shaking and I'd never seen her like that. Sid, I said, do you have a fever, and I went into the bathroom to look for a thermometer, did we have a thermometer, I finally found one and her fever was 105, was that actually possible, and she was totally delirious but I knew what I was supposed to do so I called Jorge and Miguel and they came over right away and Sid was saying no, not the hospital, but they said Sid, we have to, your fever's too high, and she kept saying I don't want Terry to see me this way, even though I was right there but when Sid went in the other room Jorge said honey I think you should stay here, trust me.

So I stayed home and Sid went to St. Vincent's, they admitted her with PCP pneumonia, too weak to walk, and Jorge would call me every day with updates, she was getting better, no, she didn't want me to visit, and then she came home and stayed in bed for a week and after that she said she was fine. We went back to the usual schedule of clubs and drugs and Sid was making her outfits in sixes now, she said six outfits for six days, like six was her magic number because that's how long it took for her to get out of the hospital but also she said it was about the shape, just look at that shape, and I was thinking eight would make more sense, right, because of infinity, but then I looked closer and there was something about the slide of the six that made more sense, I mean it was faster.

I already had four pairs of the bloomers to hide the drugs, but she made me two more, and then three more of those strings of pockets, different colors for each one so now I had six of those too, and of course I thought about 666 and she said no, it's not like that, honey, it's six for sexy, and then she made a six on my face with her tongue, starting with the forehead and then over to my cheek and down to my chin and then up to the other cheek, over my nose, across my lips, and into my mouth, and then it was my turn to try it on her, she was right, so then that became our refrain, six for sexy, and it worked everywhere—

back, tits, thighs, belly, ass, armpits, cunt, six for sexy, yes, Sid was planning for her death but she was planning for our life together too and do you see how I loved her.

Sid said okay, now we have to get you on the lease—you could just keep sending money orders to the landlord in my name after I die, but that might get sketchy after a while so why don't I write to the landlord now, and tell him I have a new roommate, and see if he accepts you.

We'd already been sending in two checks for years, or actually a check from me and a money order from her, and they'd been depositing both, so legally I had the right to live there but Sid said that wasn't enough, we needed to make sure. She'd only met this landlord once because he'd bought the building from the old landlord, but she figured it was worth a try because if it didn't work then we could always go with the other strategy, right? So anyway we sent in the note, and someone from the office actually said yes, and when we got the paperwork it looked like that was settled.

Then Sid started asking me what I wanted when she died, and I said I don't want you to die. And she said honey, that's not on the list. The apartment's yours, but what else do you want. She kept asking until finally I said okay, how about the photos. And she said I can't give you all the photos, which ones do you want the most? And I said the ones of you dancing. So those were mine, and then she started calling everyone who was still alive to see if they wanted the photos they were in, and that was one list, the photo list, tacked to the refrigerator, it kept growing.

Then she asked me if I wanted the furniture, and I said not if someone else wants it, and she said what about the bed? I said I guess I should keep the bed. And the kitchen table?

I thought about the kitchen table, which wasn't in the kitchen because there wasn't enough room but it was a red Formica table from the '50s with rounded chrome edges and matching chrome chairs with red cushions, but I thought that if I kept the table then it would just make me think of Sid, right, every time I sat there drinking tea or eating my morning oats which were the only thing I cooked anymore. I would just bring the oat groats to a boil before bed if there was bed, and then add some powdered cinnamon and a hint of nutmeg, and then close the lid and turn off the heat, and then they were ready whenever I got up or remembered. I loved those oats, and so did Sid, she really loved those oats.

But the table, I was worried about the table—I could keep the red coffee mugs in the cabinet if I couldn't deal with looking at them, right, but not the table, so I said no thanks, and then Jorge and Miguel got the table, and all the antiques, which was a relief because could I really stand to look at those antiques after Sid was dead, the way she polished the wood to keep everything shiny, no, that would be too hard. So I guess I'm saying I was starting to realize that Sid was actually going to die, and maybe that was the point of making these lists with me.

Cleo asked for the sofa, Jaysun asked for the curtains and the stereo, TaraMielle asked for the sewing machines and fabric, Jorge and Miguel asked for the Warhol, and that made sense since they knew Sid then. And that's how it went, for days on end, until Sid would remember something else and then she needed to know who wanted it.

What about money, she asked, I might have some cash. And we both agreed that should go to Jaysun, she's the one who needed the money the most, and any leftover ecstasy since Sid always bought ecstasy a hundred hits at a time to store in the safe—it cost her $500 for a hundred pills, so just five dollars a pill—so she'd give that X away on special occasions because she said X should be free because it makes us free.

And then there was Dominic, our connection to the world of commerce—I don't know what Sid said to Dominic, but the next time he came over he said so you're the boss now, and I tried not to look surprised. You couldn't lose Dominic because he showed up right on time, and he always had the goods, you didn't even need to count the bags because he would never cheat you, he was loyal that way. And he did the custom touches like the baggies with hearts on them, and the blue glass vials, and he didn't even charge extra.

The one thing you had to do every time, though, was open up the package, glance at everything neatly arranged in its place, and pull out a vial or bag and pour some out on the mirror, hand Dominic a straw and do a few lines together. That was to test the merchandise. He'd never cheated before but you had to make sure, and yes he was sober but this was business so it didn't count. Usually he'd leave as soon as you'd acknowledged everything was okay, but sometimes you had to entertain him, it was a job with its hassles like any other.

Yes, Sid was planning for her death, but otherwise she seemed better than ever, like it was cheering her up to settle everything, and one day she asked me how long it had been since we'd heard from String Bean and I couldn't remember, so she said let's go check on her, she isn't answering my calls and hasn't it been a while, so we took a cab to String Bean's place and we were ringing the bell but no one was answering, and then Sid recognized one of her neighbors, and she said Ella, how are you, and Ella said same-old same-old.

Ella, Sid said, have you seen Jerome, and Ella looked worried.

Sid said is something wrong.

Ella said what, you haven't heard.

And Sid said heard what.

Suicide, Ella said, and Sid opened her mouth like she was going to say something but nothing was coming out, she was just frozen in that position with her hand over her mouth.

I'm sorry, Ella said, and she went inside.

I was trying not to cry because I wanted to be there for Sid, I mean String Bean was my friend but she wasn't my sister, and Sid had known her almost as long as she'd known Jorge and Miguel, and I said Sid, are you okay, even though obviously she wasn't okay, she just stood there with her mouth open until she started shaking, first her head and then her lips and face were moving into all these uncomfortable expressions, involuntary and primal and lost, totally lost, and then I thought of it, I said let's walk to the piers.

She looked up like she'd just noticed me, and her whole body started shaking almost like a seizure although I'd never seen a seizure and then suddenly everything stopped, and she said yes, Terry, we might as well walk to the piers.

It was that time of day when everything gets beautiful, too beautiful for this, and I reached out my hand, and we walked down the cobblestones I always loved in this part of the Meatpacking District, even if I didn't like thinking about the meatpacking and maybe it was about the sky, how there's more of it over there, or there was more of it, but then Sid stopped, threw her hands up in the air and just started shrieking, until someone leaned out their window and said shut the fuck up, and Sid said you shut the fuck up, and whoever was yelling slammed their window shut.

That fucking bitch, Sid said, that fucking bitch left me. She looked over at me and said: We were supposed to die together. And she left me. Couldn't she at least have told me first.

That's when she pulled me in the other direction, and we headed to 14th Street, and walked all the way home. We did some coke, got dressed, took a hit of X, and went out. We didn't usually do X before we left the house but this felt different, it was like we were Jaysun, walking back and forth with our eyes on something elsewhere, and was this freedom I mean that's what I was thinking after the K, but then I realized I just needed more pot, Sid taught me how to manage everything with drugs—don't ever crash, she said, just glide. And I was gliding, right, I was gliding.

You have to be ready, Sid kept saying, and of course she meant ready for her death. But I wasn't ready when she planned her memorial, she asked for advice but I wasn't ready. I wasn't ready when she made the invitations. I wasn't ready when we headed over to Jorge and Miguel's house in the Bronx so she could show me the bed in their guestroom where she was going to die. She said she wasn't going to die in our bed because of Margarita—I don't want to put you through that, she said, and I said what do you mean, didn't Margarita die of an overdose, and she said how do you think I'm going to die—honey, I'm taking myself to heaven so they can slam those doors in my face—and I liked the way she was laughing so I didn't ask any more questions. It did look comfortable in that guestroom with all those fluffy pillows and the gold brocade bedspread, but I wasn't ready. She kept saying we'll go there together, okay, just don't take me to the hospital, I don't want to die in the hospital, and I wasn't ready.

I wasn't ready when she said this has been the best four years of my life, but it hadn't quite been four years yet so I felt a little optimistic. I wasn't ready when she started losing weight because nothing would really go down except my oats, she still liked my oats although she was shitting everything out. I wasn't ready when she started lying in bed all day because she said she didn't have energy, she didn't feel like going out, but I should go, she needed time alone. I wasn't ready when she stopped marking the letters on the 1995 wall calendar because now I guess it would just say H H H H H H H H H H H H H H H since her heroin vacation was stretching on and on. I wasn't ready when she said she wasn't hungry, and I would go out and buy her favorite pastries from the Globe, Angelica's cheesecake, and even the Sicilian cheesecake from Veniero's, just so she would eat something, and she would eat the cakes, but then she would shit everything out.

But one day when I went out to get more oats and Prana was out of whole oats so I decided to walk all the way over to Integral Yoga, why not, it was a nice day, and it's not like I was going to eat rolled oats, they were rancid, that's what my mothers told me as a kid, so I went over to Integral Yoga for the oat groats, and more Red Zinger, might as well get a bunch of Red Zinger, and oh it was the time of day when the deli went on sale and I loved their curried TVP, yes, they still had some, and then I wandered around the store and ended up with essential oils and natural sponges and a bunch of other things and I stopped by the Center to get the free papers, I hadn't read the papers in a while, and when I got back home the music was on and it felt like I hadn't heard music in a while, not at home because Sid was always in bed, and this was that Danny Tenaglia mix from Portugal, or no, it wasn't Danny mixing it was someone else but it was Danny's mix of "So Get Up," which was Sid's favorite track, she was doing her makeup and that's when I realized something about how makeup hides everything, I mean not that I hadn't realized that before so I guess I mean how I didn't even realize String Bean was positive, she was just this tall skinny queen in clown outfits and om shanti who said her ankles went up to her hips, look, look—you could joke about it, you could make it wilder, you could go out and turn it out and no one would know.

So Sid was making these outfits with ruffles, big giant ruffles that had some kind of underwire, I mean she was making them before but now she was making them again. Try this on, she said, and she went over to the CD player to rewind several tracks, and it was DJ Vibe, right, the DJ for this mix and the coke was out on the mirror so I did a line and then I put on the dress or it wasn't a dress but what was it, like you would open your arms and you were an accordion, front and back, everything would open up and I thought of a starfish, yes, it was a starfish tunic ruffle dress.

Everyone's coming over, she said, and I said okay, and started my makeup. We had plenty of time before Jaysun, Cleo, and TaraMielle arrived, plenty of time to do more coke, and Sid said she made all our outfits—she'd already measured us a while back. We didn't usually do the matching thing, not really, but this was different because when was the last time Sid went out, so everyone was excited. This is the best thing ever, Cleo said, when she tried on her dress, and Jaysun said what would people think when she was wearing so much clothing, and TaraMielle had one that joined them together at the waist, and we all spread out in the living room for a photo shoot we were like paper lanterns, if paper lanterns were made of starfish polyester, gold mixed with red blending into pink and tan, but the overall effect was shine, shine on, shine on you paper lanterns, and now it was Junior's mix with the air raid sirens, yes, tonight was the Sound Factory but first we were stopping at the Tunnel so everyone could see our outfits.

And the Tunnel was my favorite because of the bathroom, I mean the crowd was whatever although I always made the most money there, but the bathroom with no borders and the DJ booth right in the middle, we were all in that bathroom spinning around the lights in our eyes and Sid was rolling on the floor, into a backbend, and then flipping her legs right up into the air and people were cheering and had I ever seen her do that before, had I ever, and then I went to the floor too, it was my first time feeling that softness, I mean the floor was hard but the softness in my body, it's where I wanted to live but then Cleo and Jaysun had to pull me up because I was wearing platforms and Sid was doing figure eights then a Z-pattern jigsaw homeostasis water fountain twist-and-spin wring-it-out bounce-and-shout rope-swing windstorm back to the floor and up, up, and then we were all suddenly doing runway together the sound of the accordion the almost falling down the clank clank of the jump rope beats X, X . . . ten ten tens across the board, X, X, X-trava-gaza, and were they even playing that song but we were up and down the bounce and frown flounce town we were jumping in and out of each other's eyes, and then Jaysun and Cleo to the walls, were there walls, TaraMielle joined at the hip like a giant fan and I remembered my arms, out and in and Sid and I were leaning against one another and the lights, everything into our eyes, take it in, take it in, take it all in, the swing and sway, I was watching Sid for the way she would turn so I could turn with her the spin of the fabric and we were starfish, one two three four five or six of us depending on how you counted, how many arms for stars, reaching, touching, pulsing, grasping, glowing in the night lights I swear I could see the sky we were up there with the stars and did we even get to the Sound Factory.

I just remember waking up and Sid was saying I'm sorry, I'm sorry, and everything smelled like shit and it took me a moment to realize what had happened and I said Sid, don't worry about it, it's okay.

She was in the corner of the room holding a blanket around her like a little kid and saying I'm sorry, I didn't mean to, and I said of course you didn't mean to, don't worry about it, I'll take care of everything, so then I got up, and went in the other room for a garbage bag for laundry, came back in and Sid was sitting on the floor and I said Sid, do you want to take a shower.

She said I don't want to put you through this—but why was she thinking about me, I wasn't innocent—I'd grown up with everyone dying, I'd taken care of people before, but I didn't say that because I'd never told her.

Then she said: It wasn't me. And that's when I knew this was bad, but I was trying to stay collected. Okay, I said, do you want me to run your bath?

But we didn't have a bath, we just had a shower.

I'm not a little kid, Sid said, and her voice had changed back.

Terry, she said, I don't want to be like Margarita.

Margarita had died in that bed. Our bed. That's where Margarita had died. Or maybe it wasn't the same bed, I'd never asked, but it was the bed that was there in our room before I was there. They'd woken up one night, but Margarita didn't wake up. It was just like that. Sid hated her for it. It's what made her so regimented about heroin, because that's what killed Margarita, that's why she couldn't get out of that bed. But now Sid was in that bed most of the time, right, so it made sense, what she was afraid of.

Sid looked over at me like a little kid again, her lips forming a little girl's frown and she said Terry, I'm scared. And then she was crying. Is it possible that I'd never seen her cry before, I mean she was crying and I was holding her, her head against my chest she was so small now I was rubbing her head and she was crying I could feel her ribs she was so small she used to be so strong and now she was wasting away, that's what was happening, for the first time I said it in my head I was holding her and thinking maybe we needed pot or a few bumps or some oats but also I was thinking this is it.

After Sid died, I couldn't stop crying. I stayed in bed for days like maybe I could feel her there but I couldn't stop crying. I thought about a heroin vacation but that wasn't me that was Sid and I couldn't stop crying. I couldn't stop I couldn't stop so I called my mothers.

Eileen answered the phone, and I was still crying. Terry, she said, what's wrong, and I couldn't stop crying.

Finally I said Sssss but I couldn't say her name, and then I tried again, when Paula was on the phone too and she said is it Sid, is it something about Sid, and I couldn't stop crying.

And Eileen said oh honey, oh honey, we're so sorry, and I couldn't stop crying.

Finally I said Sid's gone, she's gone, and I couldn't stop crying. I said I don't think I can talk right now, I just wanted to . . . And then I couldn't stop crying.

Oh honey, Eileen said, let it all out, just let it out.

And Paula said we're here for you, we're here for you whenever you need us.

And I got off the phone and took a deep breath. And I did a few lines, which is what Sid would've wanted me to do, and then I was ready.

Jorge and Miguel came over for the furniture, and they gave me the best hugs, and asked if I needed anything, and once they'd taken the furniture away I realized I needed furniture. They came back and we were doing lines because we all knew this was what Sid would have wanted, we were talking about painting the apartment, did I want something different, and Jaysun came over for the curtains and the stereo, and she asked if this was okay, are you sure you don't need the curtains, and we did more coke and gave her the extra cash and extra X and she said really, are you sure, and we said it's what Sid wanted and when I hugged her she kissed me on both cheeks and then on the lips three times but after she left I realized maybe I'd made a mistake about the curtains because now I could see into everyone's apartments and what could they see in here.

TaraMielle came over for the sewing machines and the fabric, and Sid's clothes, and we did more coke and decided to paint the apartment right then, Jorge and Miguel knew where to get paint, they said Sid told them to change everything, so they asked me what I thought about a pink-and-green paisley comforter, and pale green sheets and towels, they were on sale, a major sale, so they brought them over—what, are you serious?

They were serious. They'd already washed everything, unscented detergent, and I said how did you know?

Sid told us, they said, she didn't want you to be stuck with any memories you didn't want, she said once I'm gone I'm gone, and we did more coke. They said what do you think about mid-century modern furniture, we found some laminate dressers, a table and chairs, great colors, everything's in good shape, are you interested.

I was interested, yes, I was interested. So we did more coke and took all the photos down, and Jorge put them in envelopes that were already labeled for everyone, and it was eerie to see the imprints on the walls where the photos used to be, so we washed the walls while I decided on the colors. Maybe yellow for the bedroom, would yellow be good for the bedroom?

Hey what's cooking, Miguel said—like the kitchen's in bed with you.

Yes, yes, like the kitchen's in bed with me—and then maybe a pale blue with the brick in the living room, what do you think, or, wait, green, yes, mint green, and then orange for the sewing room I mean walk-in closet, and maybe lavender for the kitchen and pink for the bathroom?

Miguel said that sounds like a sherbet factory, and I gave Jorge some money for paint, they said we'll bring the furniture for you to look at when we get back, and then I was talking to TaraMielle about how weird it was without the curtains, wasn't it weird, I mean we could see down to the courtyard, whose courtyard was that, and Mielle said let's look at the fabric, I think I saw some blackout fabric, and she was right, there was plenty of blackout fabric, a whole roll, and Sid had the right kind of sewing machine to make curtains, now we just needed to figure out what would go on top and Tara said let's stay up and go to the Garment District and pick something out, so we did more coke.

Then we smoked pot, Sid would've wanted us to smoke pot, we stayed inside and blew it out the windows because now the windows were right there but they were kind of gross, and when we tried cleaning them it looked worse because then you could just see all the grit on the outside more clearly and I made Red Zinger, and we all sat on the floor with the red mugs, talking about our plans for the apartment, should we change the red bulbs, yes, we should change the red bulbs, and we moved everything into the closet or to the center of the living room, there wasn't that much left just mostly my clothes and what I was keeping of Sid's, plus the bed and end table with the safe it was like we were a team and this was what Sid wanted, she said get everything done, get everything done fast, before the memorial, and the memorial was on Wednesday because of course it was at Disco 2000 so we had two days, and then Jorge and Miguel were back with the paint and overalls, they had extra overalls and drop cloths and ladders and they'd already gotten the light bulbs because they said we needed more light for painting, right?

So then we did more coke and I couldn't find my boombox so we went with the sounds of the brushes, the rollers and plastic and more coke and the primer dried so fast in the bathroom it was good primer it actually covered the red except where there were cracks so now the bathroom was ready for the first coat of paint, and then the kitchen, and then everywhere else, we were doing this so fast we got one coat over everything we were laughing and dancing to the music in our bodies and sure the paint didn't look perfect because we didn't use tape we just covered the trim and Jorge said she would fix everything afterward, no problem, don't even worry about it, and we did more coke, and went to the roof to smoke some pot, the air felt good I could look at the Chrysler Building all night, we decided to go to Odessa before doing a second coat and we all went down in our overalls, now we were a team and once we got outside I thought maybe Veselka sounded better, did Veselka sound better, so we went over to Veselka I said my treat, it's my treat, and I got the sweet potato pierogies and lentil soup and chamomile tea, and I tried not to pay attention to what everyone else was eating, yes, more hot water for tea, please, and then we went back and the paint was dry so we did more coke, it's a good thing I had plenty of coke, maybe it was seven or eight in the morning and we were done with the paint, and Jorge and Miguel said wait, we forgot the furniture, and they went downstairs and brought up all this wacky furniture made of strange laminates—green dressers with orange drawers, a powder blue Formica table with a pattern that looked like stars, were those stars, and then purple chairs that didn't match but the color really set off the blue and yes, this really was the sherbet factory, Miguel was right, from now on this will be the Sherbet Factory, I said, welcome to the Sherbet Factory, we serve all flavors.

And Jorge was already pulling down the red shower curtain because she'd brought a new one with lips all over it—big lips, small lips, open lips and closed, lips with teeth and lips without but otherwise it was clear, that would be good to bring more light into the shower and I was beginning to think that Sid planned all of this, she must have planned it, right, she was helping me with the future but I didn't say that, I just said everything looks amazing, this is incredible, thank you, and Jorge and Miguel said we're family, anytime you need anything just call, but we better go now so we can make ourselves pretty before work—and they really gave the best hugs, they always gave the best hugs and when they left I poured some coke in with the pot and smoked some more with TaraMielle and then they said what do you think of doing a hit of X, they had an extra hit if I wanted it, and wouldn't it be fun to do X and wander around the Garment District, the train came so fast we actually arrived before the X hit, we still had the overalls on, covered in paint, we decided this was our new look, so comfortable, but then the X hit hard in this one fabric store so we spent a lot of time touching the faux-fur and someone kept saying can I help you, and we didn't know what to do so we left.

Then Mielle spotted it—purple and green paisley, no way, it would look so good with the comforter, but what about the rest, should we do that everywhere or maybe just the bedroom, and then Tara came over with butterflies, magenta and green and yellow and orange and blue and golden butterflies, yes, you're giving me butterflies oh yes oh yes oh yes, and then when we got outside we were so excited about the light, yes, the light, but should we stop at Madras Mahal for uttapam, I love their uttapam, and TaraMielle said are you really hungry, no, I guess I wasn't hungry, not yet, but this was my favorite vegetarian Indian restaurant and I'd forgotten all about it so we went inside I ordered takeout they told us to sit down while we waited, oh, water, thank you, isn't this water amazing, I ordered the mixed vegetable uttapam, and idli, and gobi masala, and why not chana masala too I should have some protein and then on our way back we decided to stop at Stuyvesant Park to relax and the air felt so good, doesn't the air feel good, we were holding hands on a bench and watching the park like a movie, did you see that, wait, did you see that, and then, oh, rain, I love the rain, and when we got back to the Sherbet Factory we held up the fabric, oh, it looks amazing, but maybe I need a shower, do you need anything, and TaraMielle asked if they could get in bed, yes, yes, of course, make yourselves comfortable.

There's really nothing like a shower on X, is there, the rain and all those lips on your skin, and soap, I love the smell of this soap, peppermint, and so many lips, but is it already getting cold, oh, these new towels so fresh and even a matching bathmat, and then I came out in my pink bathrobe and TaraMielle looked so cute with the paisley comforter, I was leaning over to look, this was so sweet and could I touch but actually they weren't sleeping, just closing their eyes, oh, those eyes, yes, Terry, get in with us, oh, bodies and breath the lips were in bed with us so much skin are you sleeping, no, how about you, no, but we closed our eyes we closed our eyes we closed our eyes and drifted, maybe we were asleep and maybe we were awake we were skin and bodies and organs and drifting and eventually we got up, and smoked more pot to bring back the X, oh this pot has something extra, yes.

TaraMielle still weren't hungry but I ate the uttapam, it was so good, are you sure you don't want any, okay, how about Red Zinger, there's plenty of Red Zinger, yes, vitamin C and there's orange juice in the refrigerator, does anyone want orange juice, yes, the colors, and then we did more coke and went over to their apartment with the sewing machines and the fabric so they could make the curtains, and I brought the chana masala because I knew I would get hungry, wouldn't I, and they couldn't believe I could still eat, I told them it was my magic trick but really the magic was the curtains, the way they measured and sewed, measured and sewed, and then I had butterflies everywhere, they were giving me butterflies, and paisley, and more butterflies, and more butterflies, and more butterflies I felt like I could fly away when we got back to the Sherbet Factory and put up the curtains and we were all hugging it looked so good and then TaraMielle said they should go home because Mielle had to work the next day, what day was it, oh, Tuesday, the costume designer. Uptown. They wanted me to know they were dealing X now. In case I needed anything.

Let's trade, they said, whenever you're ready, and I said yes, yes, and I realized this must have been something Sid did too, she gave them her X connection, right, and now we could trade, Sid was holding us together and then it was already Wednesday, right, I mean I took some pills and got in bed, and then I got out of bed, and took more pills, and then it was Wednesday, and I was crying again and I wanted to call my mothers and tell them why Sid was gone, why she wasn't coming back, maybe they thought it was a breakup but it was so much worse.

But I couldn't tell my mothers so I did more coke, and then I was ready. And then I smoked more pot, yes, that's much better and then I remembered I still had all that food in the refrigerator, so I heated up the gobi masala and sat down at my new table, with oats, yes, everything was just right but I was thinking about how maybe coke was my heroin, right, or even pot but everyone smoked pot, I mean everyone who wasn't a mess, and should I make a calendar like Sid's, to mark off the days, but what would I do instead of coke I mean Sid left a sheet of acid in the safe that she didn't tell me about, and I couldn't do acid that much but would today be a good day, Sid's memorial, maybe I needed a few bumps to make up my mind, and then okay, just a tiny piece of one hit, maybe a quarter, I cut it off with scissors and then I was ready to plan my outfit.

The acid was the right idea because I was starting to see the structure of things, not like the bricks coming out of the walls or the butterflies flying around the room but the sensation that this was possible and that was where my outfit came from, and also Sid's accessories bags, I'd inherited her accessories and wigs, yes, I'd never seen her in a wig but she had so many from before we met and my favorite was the fluorescent green one because there was so much hair so I pulled that up and clipped it together with the darker green one to make it even bigger and the theme was butterflies, and green—green glitter, green lips, green eyeshadow, with yellow and pink to set everything off, I had plenty of glitter, jars and jars from the craft store, don't waste your money on cosmetic glitter no way—and then I found the right dress, yes that green taffeta '80s gown with three tutus underneath to take it up, up, everything up to the sky, okay maybe two tutus were enough and I cut off the sleeves of the dress and made them into bracelets, covered my neck in so many necklaces you couldn't count, and then I realized I needed something for the wig, it wasn't blending, so I pulled my hair down and then twisted it up into the wig, and yes, this was perfect, it was like I was wearing three wigs and then Sid's green lashes, but I need to tell you about the memorial because it was a disaster, I mean it all went wrong even before we left the house, for example:

1. Cleo and Jaysun arrived first, and I could tell right away that Cleo was shocked about the apartment because she didn't say anything about my outfit, she just kept looking around and eventually she said so are you on acid now or what, and I said yeah, just a tiny bit, like a quarter of a hit, which wasn't the right answer.
2. I could tell Jaysun had already been crying, but when I asked if she wanted a hug she just asked for acid. So I gave her acid. Even Cleo asked for a hit, and Cleo didn't do acid.
3. Cleo got angry at TaraMielle because they were wearing Sid's clothes. But she gave them her clothes, I said, she wanted them to wear her clothes. And I shouldn't have said that, because Cleo was a drama queen, and it was Sid who kept us together.
4. TaraMielle looked amazing. They were taller than Sid, but the clothes fit they just stretched and when they added the platforms it was everything. After Cleo got angry I kept telling TaraMielle

how incredible they looked, because I felt bad for them. And maybe I should've just said that once, so Cleo wouldn't get too annoyed, but they really did look incredible, and wasn't that what they wanted to hear, we all wanted to hear that. Maybe I should have told Cleo that she looked incredible.

5. I should have felt bad for Cleo too, but I was upset at her for trying to ruin everything. Didn't she understand that Sid wanted us to go on? She wanted us to go on. She wanted us to go on.

6. Maybe everyone just kept thinking that Sid wasn't there, but that's not what she wanted us to think about. I didn't say that, but I should have.

7. Michael Alig was at the door when we got to the club, and he looked right over at me and said my, my, if Terry Dactyl doesn't have on extra wings tonight. He had never said anything to me before, so everyone must have been scandalized because Sid had a history with Michael Alig and it wasn't good. None of us knew the history because Sid wouldn't tell us, but she would totally freeze whenever Michael was around, although we went to all her parties anyway, but was Michael Alig ever at the door before, it almost seemed like she was waiting for us.

8. We shouldn't have done that acid. That was my fault. I should've stuck to that quarter of a hit, and kept it quiet, but we'd always shared before so I was sharing. Sharing was caring, but Jaysun's eyes were already rolling into her head when we got to the club and Cleo was making all these weird expressions, and I felt like I could fly away, so I did.

9. Jorge and Miguel were smashed. They looked incredible—total showgirls, Escuelita style—big boobs, sequins and feathers, rhinestones and pearls and stilettos, the whole thing, I didn't even recognize them at first. But they were falling-down drunk, and that was before the X.

10. Right, the X. That was supposed to be the highlight. But we were already spinning.

11. Sid invited her regulars to join us—not all of them, of course, but a few specific ones—a banker, a realtor, a Gaultier fashion victim,

and a few suburbanites, and of course they were all professional cokeheads, but they were amateurs about everything else. I don't mean to be snotty about it, but they didn't know how to handle the X.

12. Sid must have invited the regulars for me, so they would still feel connected, but we were already connected because I'd been the one answering the door ever since Sid extended her heroin vacation and the regulars all got to the Limelight early, because we were on club time, and they weren't, and maybe that's why they were all so drunk, not just Jorge and Miguel, who had started drinking before they left the house.

13. One of the regulars thought she was having a heart attack when the X kicked in. She kept saying should I go to the hospital.

14. I brought the acid, and I was giving it away upstairs when Michael Alig came over and I gave her a hit, and she said I'll take two, please. This was the second time we'd ever talked.

15. I shouldn't have liked it that Michael Alig was talking to me, but I liked it, I did, I'll admit it. Sid always said there were club kids and club trash, and obviously Michael Alig was club trash, so I guess this was the night I became club trash too.

16. I hadn't noticed at first, but TaraMielle were wearing the dress that Sid was wearing when I met her, I mean they stretched it out and they both got inside, and they were doing that dance, and it was like I was seeing double. I looked up at Cleo and Jaysun, and they were breathing smoke. Not literally, I mean none of us smoked because Sid hated smoking, I mean cigarettes, and I was always the one with the pot, but they were just sitting together and staring at TaraMielle like they wanted to kill them.

17. I went down and danced with TaraMielle and I could feel the pull of their hands through the fabric, and then their arms just kept going and going, fabric and hands we were back-and-forth like a yo-yo, salt water taffy, the sand when it meets the ocean, and breath, focus on the breath, yes, I was flying.

18. Someone stole TaraMielle's platforms. Because they took them off to dance. I was wondering about that, and then I wasn't wondering,

and somewhere between wondering and not wondering the platforms wandered off.

19. I tried to calm Cleo and Jaysun down by saying look at the lights, but that didn't work because then Cleo said she saw the devil in the lights and one of the regulars almost fell off the balcony trying to fly so then she went home.
20. If you haven't candy-flipped, let me tell you how it works. Your eyes go in and out, one moment you're here and the next moment you're somewhere else. You can't stay still or else you're stuck. So I was flying, but Cleo and Jaysun were staying still.
21. Sid loved lists but maybe not lists like this. I mean she wasn't a fan of drama. But let me just tell you the highlight—we lost the ashes. I'm serious. Jorge and Miguel couldn't find the box anywhere. First, they thought they left it in the van, but then they remembered they didn't bring the van, that's how smashed they were, and the X wasn't helping with clarity although they did like the lights.
22. So we didn't have any ashes—should we go to the piers anyway? We couldn't decide.
23. I remembered this was how we all met, right? It was JoJo's memorial but I didn't know it yet.
24. I shouldn't have said that, because then Cleo lost it—she told me I was using Sid, and now I was using JoJo. We were outside at this point, everyone, Cleo looked at me like she wanted me dead, and then pulled Jaysun who wasn't Jaysun anymore just a doll in a furry coat with eyelids that flipped up and down, she pulled the Jaysun doll into a cab and they were gone.
25. What was that, I said, did you see that? No one else saw it.
26. I tried to focus on the light. But we were outside a church. What were we doing outside a church. I focused on the architecture, I'd always liked the architecture of churches, but then all I could see was the skeleton of the church, like it had burned down and we were standing outside but obviously that was the acid so I turned around.
27. All the regulars had left. Or maybe we left them behind. I couldn't even remember how many there were, but luckily they remembered

my phone number later, except maybe that woman who went to the hospital, I can't even remember who that was, I just remember that panicked look in her eyes. Wait, wait, no, she called later and left a message saying that she loved me, so okay, I think the X kicked in before she got to the hospital.

28. Jorge was vomiting, and Miguel was massaging her back. Somehow this was kind of cute—I wanted to taste the vomit, that's how high I was.

29. TaraMielle, Jorge, Miguel, and I squeezed into a cab over to the Sherbet Factory, and then we all got in bed. I was worried it wouldn't be big enough, but then it was.

Sid always said don't buzz anyone in unless you're expecting them, you never know with these cokeheads, you have to have boundaries, but one night someone was pressing the buzzer over and over, and I wasn't answering but then I gave up and it was Mielle, so I buzzed her in, and when I opened the door she rushed in and said what do you do if you find a dead body.

On the street, I said, and she said no, in my apartment.

I was doing my makeup, getting ready for the Palladium, or Webster Hall, or maybe somewhere else, I'm not quite sure, and now there was a chill going through my body and it's true that I had the windows wide open in the cold but I always had the windows wide open in the cold because you couldn't turn off the heat, but what did Mielle just say. Something about a dead body?

In a movie, I said, they call the cops.

So Mielle picked up the phone and called the cops before I could say wait, this isn't a movie, or wait, what are you doing, I was just joking, or maybe just wait.

Mielle said I just found a body.

My girlfriend.

A noose.

In our apartment.

Yes it's still there.

No, I'm not there now. I don't know if I can go inside.

Okay, I'm right around the corner, I'll be right back.

And then Mielle ran out the door and down the stairs before I could say anything, and my first thought was I'm so glad the cops aren't coming here.

My second thought was wait, did she just say my girlfriend. I was definitely in shock. Because I was still getting ready for the Palladium, my eyelashes were ready but did Mielle just say Tara was dead, in a noose, I wasn't sure, so I did a few bumps, and I finished getting ready, and after a while Mielle came back, and she looked better.

Mielle, I said.

And she said I can't talk about it. Can I stay here. I can't go back.

Of course, I said. Do you need anything.

I made Red Zinger. We sat at the blue table in the purple chairs, with our red mugs, and we did a few lines. Mielle said she'd already taken a hit of X, did I want one. Not yet, I said.

No, that doesn't sound like me. I must have said yes. Why would I have said not yet?

At some point that night, wherever we went, I was still in shock, even with the X, sometimes shock pushes through. And Mielle said she was Meow now, not Mielle, and that made sense, I was petting her.

Meow came back to the Sherbet Factory, and the next day she asked if I could come with her to get some stuff, could she stay a few days—I didn't have to come in, it wouldn't take long.

After that, she basically moved in—we would cuddle in bed, and I would pet her, and she would pet me. She did X every day, and every night, so I did too. I didn't know how to ask what happened, and she didn't know how to say it. Before there was TaraMielle, and now there was just Meow. She started dressing as a cat, and everyone would pet her. She sold a lot of X, everyone knew where to get it now, just look for Meow, and every night she would leave piles of twenties on the kitchen table before stacking them neatly the next day. I was taking a break from coke, why not, with all this X coming my way, but that didn't mean I was taking a break from selling it so I had my own piles of twenties too, just not on the table.

When you do that much X for weeks on end, your head goes kind of blank and you're mumbling all the time but your body is humming and then you blast off into the sky again and it's all about extending that high—keep smoking pot, take a shower, deep breathing, warm liquids, another shower, orange juice, vitamin C, another shower, the colors to take you up and the lights yes the lights.

Meow said she was saving her money to move to Santa Fe, but why Santa Fe. She would talk about the desert, sunset in the clouds, magic, and joining a puppet troupe, and I didn't realize she was serious until one day she asked if I could go over to her place to help her pack. She was sending everything on Greyhound and taking the train on Saturday. I wasn't good at packing, so I called Jorge and Miguel. They came over on Friday, and we took Meow to the train station on Saturday. Everything happened so fast.

The first time I went over to Michael Alig's, she opened the door in a blond wig and Jackie Os, and said bitch, even your daywear—I was relieved because I was trying not to look too dressed up or too dressed down. Aside from the wig and sunglasses, her outfit was just a T-shirt and jeans, but that's not what mattered, what mattered was that she said bitch, even your daywear.

Her apartment wasn't what I'd expected, this hideous high-rise in Midtown where everything was new and ugly. We sat down on the sofa in front of the TV and she lowered her sunglasses and said: So, have you ever gone on a heroin vacation?

I thought I might vomit. Or shit. I mean I was scared. I wasn't shaking, but I felt like I was shaking. A heroin vacation. That was Sid's phrase. No one else said that.

Michael was testing me, but I didn't know what he wanted. I tried not to react. I looked her right in the eyes and I didn't move, I mean my eyelids were moving but nothing else.

Finally she said: Let's do some K. She poured it onto the mirror on the coffee table, handed me a long straw, and we each did a line, and then we sat back on the sofa, and she turned on the TV.

Meow was in Santa Fe, Tara was dead, and Michael Alig was suddenly paying attention to me. I knew it was about Sid, but I decided to play the game. What else did I have?

I would go over Michael's apartment, and we would do K, or coke, or usually both, and play, it was our little escape except there was always that moment when everything would change. Like when she looked at me and said: Sid was using you, you know that.

What do you mean, I said.

You were her drug mule. Things were getting dicey. And spicy. A tad bit lice-y. She needed an exit plan.

It was like Michael was trying to get back at Sid for something. But Sid was dead. So he was trying to get back at me for believing in her.

And even if Sid was using me, or I was using her, or we were both using one another the way Michael said she got you strung out and then turned you out, like I was just some windup toy, because that's how he would have done it, right? But even if Sid was using me, and I was using her, it's not like there wasn't anything else.

And now, when I went out, I was Michael Alig's best friend. Everyone who never paid attention to me before was paying attention. And it was good for business, I couldn't deny that. Michael Alig knew all about business.

One time she asked if she could do my makeup—her makeup was always something to look at so I said sure. But when she was done I looked way too much like a model—a space alien model, maybe, but still a model. So I kept the right side of my face, and then smeared the left, added my layers of glitter and my double lashes on that side, but not the right, and then extended my lipstick all the way over to my left ear, and then I told her I was ready, after I added the white glitter bumps under my nose that were becoming a trademark. And Michael covered her mouth like she was pretending to be shocked.

Shock was her thing. So when she said she killed Angel, chopped up his body and threw it in the river, I just said can I at least have her wings.

And she laughed, oh how she laughed.

You couldn't believe anything Michael Alig said, especially when it was about herself. I didn't even realize she had roommates. Until the murder made the news.

There was never anyone else there when I went over, that's what I said. Just the two of us. I didn't even know Angel.

You knew Angel, people would say.

I mean I knew her, but I didn't know her, that's what I said.

Michael had already told everyone. We thought she was bragging. And then. And then. And then I couldn't stop thinking about it. What if I was there? I could have been there on that day. I could have been there on that night.

Or afterward, I know I was there afterward. Do you realize how much of a mess I was at that point, I could have been anywhere. And what would I have done.

When I was in first grade, teachers were concerned that I might have a speech impediment. Or a learning disability. They wanted to do some testing.

Eileen asked what kind of testing, or where the concern originated. And it turned out the teachers were worried because I was calling boys she.

And I picture my mothers laughing so hard, oh how they must have laughed.

But they weren't laughing, they were strategizing. They told the teachers they would address this. I didn't need any testing, not yet.

So when we sat down for dinner, Eileen said as you know, sometimes children are much smarter than adults, but unfortunately schools have certain rules, and some of them don't make sense. It's a shame, I know, but it's part of the system. For example, they don't like you to take off your shoes in class, but at our house everyone takes off their shoes as soon as they arrive, and it's more comfortable that way, isn't it? But at school they believe this is a health concern.

And Paula said we don't have a problem when you put your feet up on the sofa, but at school they don't let you put your feet up, do they.

And Eileen said at school they have a boys' restroom and a girls' restroom, but at home of course we don't need that formality.

And Paula said we live in a world of the universal she, but your school doesn't understand that.

And Eileen said can you tell us the names of the other kids in your class.

And I told them the names.

And Paula said they want you to separate the boys from the girls. In their world, boys can only be he, and girls are she—Eileen's right, it's a stupid rule. I know you're not supposed to say that word at school, but we can say it here. Yes, some rules are stupid stupid stupid, but if you don't follow those rules then they punish you, and we don't want them to punish you, do we.

It's really just because of their lack of imagination, Eileen said, but you can't teach imagination, can you. And we want them to be impressed by your reading ability, your conversation skills, your vocabulary, your poise, and your imagination. We don't want them to get distracted.

And Paula said can you separate the boys from the girls, just for school?

And I said okay.

And Eileen said do you have any questions, do you have any questions for us.

I said can I wear dresses to school, and Eileen said no, that wouldn't be advisable.

And Paula said but you can wear anything you want when you get home.

Even makeup, I asked.

Even makeup, Paula said, at home.

So that was our deal, until high school when I started wearing makeup all the time, it was subtle at first and by the time it wasn't so subtle it was just the way it was.

At least my mothers never asked me to cut my hair, I always had those long curls to protect me. Everyone always thought I was a girl anyway, so when I was little I was the chubby girl who always knew the answers to all the questions at school and I smiled a lot to cover up my shyness but also so the boys wouldn't call me names. Then just before ninth grade I had this dramatic growth spurt so suddenly I was taller than everyone, even most of the boys, awkward in this new body, and when I smiled my face got all lopsided so I looked like I was in pain and the boys would call me Big Bird, which was better than faggot or pussy or fudgepacker or asscrack or It, hey It, what is It wearing today, or whatever else they would invent just for me, hey, hey, are you a girl or a boy, hey, hey, but I was getting better and better at my makeup, wasn't I, in high school all the girls were asking me for tips, I'd been studying Paula and all the queens since we would go over Jack and Rudy's when I was little, and everyone loved when I played dress-up, which was all the time, but then it got more complicated when I wasn't just a girl over Jack and Rudy's, and that was the thing about the clubs—I was just Terry Dactyl. No one tried to make me into anything else, so I could fly.

It's strange how I can remember every single detail of an outfit I wore twenty-five years ago, but then I can't remember where I went in that outfit. But I guess that's how memory works—there's more forgetting than remembering, and your body is the editing machine. And of course I rarely went out unless I was on at least two or three drugs, so I'm sure that doesn't help.

I'll always remember the DJ booth in the bathroom at the Tunnel, but then someone says there wasn't a DJ booth in the bathroom, it was a bar, and that's not possible, is it? There must have been a DJ booth in the bathroom because I'll always remember it.

And then there was the music, like the first time I heard Junior play "If Madonna Calls" and the whole room just stopped, I mean we were trying to figure out if that was really Madonna on the phone saying Junior, this is Madonna, call me in Miami, and then when Junior in the song says Actually if she calls disconnect her I couldn't help looking for Jaysun because this was exactly her type of track and when I found her she was looking me right in the eyes and finally we were in the sky together again I mean we still weren't talking but do you see what the music can do.

I guess that's when everyone started saying Madonna was done, but then there she was doing a special set at 2:00 a.m. for two hundred dollars at the Roxy, or whatever, and everyone was like how do I get tickets, how do I get tickets, and that was when Madonna moved on from Junior to Victor Calderone, so suddenly everyone was over Junior and into Victor, but I was never over Junior, no one could mix like Junior, no one, she would trick you every time you thought oh no the record just skipped or when she would just stop the sound, everything, not a fadeout everything would just stop and you were waiting waiting waiting and then boom Junior hit you over the head with the second half of something she played two hours ago.

But then there was what the music couldn't do. Sid always said that whenever it got overwhelming, you needed to take a break, you didn't need to go out all the time for business because you had the regulars. So when we took a break we'd do something low-key like cocktails at Wonder Bar or Crowbar or some new place we were curious about, we'd do some coke and smoke pot and maybe get something to eat, and get home before last call, I mean unless we got carried away and headed over to Save the Robots. But after a week or two of not getting carried away—or, who am I kidding, usually after a few days—we always needed the rush of walking into the club, I mean there's really nothing like it, the pounding of the sound system in your heart.

Most club kids don't like to walk anywhere except into the club, I swear some of these girls would take a cab just to get across the street, so I was relieved when I met these two dykes at Wonder Bar, and they said do you want to go to Meow Mix, and we started walking, I mean it was just six blocks, but still, I knew plenty of people who would have insisted on a cab.

Meow Mix was new but it didn't look new it just looked like someone put up a new sign on an old bar and the first thing I noticed when I got inside was that the music was awful. And then I realized I'd never been to a dyke bar before, and it had a totally different energy—I don't just mean because the music was guitars and drums and of course I recognized some of the songs, but not in a good way—the real difference was the sexual energy, I mean at the clubs there were hardly any dykes but at Meow Mix that was everyone, and I was into it but they weren't into me, that I could tell, everyone was looking at me like I didn't belong so I was drinking way too much, especially after the dykes who brought me there went home to fuck, I was hoping they'd invite me over I mean I could feel the sexual tension or maybe I was imagining it and I didn't want to make the first move unless I was sure—Sid was the one who approached me. Same with Claire. And even Meow. And everyone in between.

Sid didn't like dyke bars because she said everyone knew everyone and you would be dating your ex-girlfriend's ex within a few days, and maybe that's why the one time I went to the Clit Club I got nervous because I wasn't sure if I was supposed to walk right past the line like at any other club or if that would be snotty so I just turned around, but I did meet Marya at Meow Mix, she was working the punk professor look with rhinestone cat eye glasses and the cutest fluffy cardigan with embroidered flowers, bleached hair parted in the middle and I laughed when it turned out she actually went to Evergreen because that's what it looked like but now she was working at CBS and she asked me if I knew where to get coke.

Sid always said don't deal to dykes, it's too much drama, so I just said I had some at home, do you want to come over, and that's where it all started. We would do coke and talk talk talk she really liked to talk and she asked a lot of questions they kind of came out of nowhere like do you believe in voting?

I said I don't know.

What do you mean, do you vote or not.

I voted for Clinton when I was eighteen because everyone said we had to get Bush out but then it didn't really feel that different.

Yes, Clinton did everything the Republicans dreamed of—he gutted the welfare system, he passed NAFTA and that horrible racist crime bill, three strikes and mandatory life sentences, and don't even get me started on Don't Ask Don't Tell because why are we fighting to be in the military when we could be fighting against the military—so you haven't voted since then, are you an anarchist?

I don't know.

What do you mean—you either believe in the tyranny of the state or you don't, which one is it.

I guess I don't.

Then you're an anarchist.

So it would go on like that for hours and I was kind of in awe because I didn't know anyone who talked about politics that way, she would just get more and more wired and I would smoke pot to even everything out but she didn't like pot so eventually I started laughing at her and then we would make out until she got freaked out about the time because she had to work in the morning so then she'd go home.

One time she said she wanted to take me out for dinner so we went to Caravan of Dreams. I'd only gone once before, and I thought it was okay but not as good as Angelica's, it wasn't gross like Kate's Joint or anything but also it was double the price. Although it was a great place for a date the way it felt like you'd snuck into someone's hippy version of paradise right on Sixth Street, plus it was quiet and the lighting was dim and the food was better than I remembered or maybe it was just because I was with Marya.

Then we went to her place and she had a whole wall of dildos over her bed, she caught me looking and said which one do you want to try first, and then we were making out, I loved making out with her because she would stretch her tongue so far it was like a dare for you to swallow it, and then I would stretch my tongue out too, feeling all the textures between teeth and gums and cheeks and throat and it felt more intense that night, maybe because we hadn't been drinking or doing drugs, or because of dinner, I could still taste the sweetness of the roasted squash, and then she said so, have you decided, and I pointed to the double-headed pink one just because it was the most absurd, and we both started laughing.

She said you know I'm just kidding, right, I'm not bisexual.

I said me neither, and Marya laughed, and even though I wasn't sure if she knew what I meant it was a great laugh and sometimes that makes up for everything. But after that she wouldn't call me back and I didn't know what was going on but I just went back into my world and then eventually I ran into her at Wonder Bar, this was months later and I felt kind of sad seeing her, sad and nervous even though I'd already had three cocktails and she came right over and said I'm sorry I never called you back—there's something you should know—I have a girlfriend, we're not monogamous but we're not supposed to get emotionally attached, and I was getting emotionally attached, so.

I said: You could have just told me that, and then we were back at my place doing coke and she was talk talk talking and eventually we were making out again, but we never really had sex, I mean we would make out a lot, it was hot and connected so who's to say that's not sex but we never took off our clothes and she always called me when she was drunk and we did coke every time and then she felt guilty because she didn't really want to do coke, maybe that's what Sid meant about drama, but Marya taught me a lot about basic things like the best programs to listen to on WBAI, I mean I never really listened to the radio but eventually that became the place where I got all my news, or most of it, and after the murder of Matthew Shepard, Marya was part of a group organizing a political funeral, they were flyering at every gay bar in the city—I ran into her at Meow Mix, and she handed me the flyer, this tiny hot pink square saying Matthew Shepard was beaten, bludgeoned, and hung on a fence post to die in Wyoming.

He was twenty-two. I was twenty-five. The flyer said this was a community response. After Marya left, I thought about that word, community. I wasn't sure if I knew what it meant. Maybe I knew when I was eleven or twelve and after Pride I got on my balcony with Jack and Rudy, we were all in our pink dresses welcoming everyone to the party and people would say Rapunzel, Rapunzel, let down your golden hair because Jack and Rudy were both wearing these giant blond wigs and I was throwing confetti and we were blowing bubbles and everything was sparkling in the sun and was that community. Or when I went to memorials with my mothers and people were sobbing and laughing and we held the ashes in our hands we kissed our hands we kissed the ashes we kissed one another I wanted to know what the ashes tasted like and then I did. And now people were still dying but it was quieter, we weren't supposed to talk about it because the meds were working although they weren't working for Miguel, at home in bed while Jorge was running the moving business alone and I kept saying do you need anything, do you need anything, but they said no.

And here was this flyer making the connection between homophobia and AIDS deaths and a crackdown on queer visibility and the murder of Matthew Shepard, and I thought about going, I thought about my outfit, I thought about bringing one of those safety whistles that everyone was always giving out but I'd never used, not even at the clubs I was never a whistle girl I just wanted to fling my arms to Divas to the dance floor, please, di-divas to the dance floor, I mean that already felt like ages ago but there were some songs that would always live on in my heart, all the girls out there flinging it to Divas to the dance floor and maybe that was community.

But this was a community of protest—I wish I could say I went on that day when they were expecting a thousand people if they were lucky but then ten thousand showed up. How they had over a hundred marshals to guide the crowd but then the cops arrested all the marshals first, there were just a few left, how those last marshals took off their red armbands so the cops wouldn't recognize them, they weren't supposed to target the marshals but they did. How there were people in suits and ties, coming to the protest right from work, standing quietly on the sidewalk with their candles in hand, there were activists and weirdos and everyone who was angry but maybe not angry enough because no one would step into the street after all the marshals got arrested but then what did they get arrested for.

I wish I could say I was one of the people who stepped into the street, and then finally people followed, and then half the crowd was blocking Fifth Avenue, and then more than half, thousands of people blocking traffic while marching downtown but then the cops split the crowd into parts there was one group that got attacked on horseback, the cops were charging the crowd and yelling cocksuckers you fucking cocksuckers the cocksuckers were sitting down in the street to calm the horses but that didn't calm the cops trampling the crowd sending two dykes to the hospital, one with broken ribs, everyone was yelling Shame Shame Shame the cops were cutting people off into small groups one dyke fell to the ground trying to get through a police line and a cop leaned over with his baton and said I'm going to crack your head like a coconut, one cop was swinging his baton in every direction saying I'm going to kill you, I'm going to fucking kill you, they wanted to kill us because we were saying we deserved to live.

I wish I could say I was there when Martha Stewart got stuck while trying to drive home from work but was that really Martha Stewart I mean didn't she have a driver but people said it was her and I wish I could say I was there as we were trying to get back to Fifth Avenue to join up with the rest of the march but we were being attacked by the cops in every direction because one of us had been murdered so brutally in Wyoming it became national news and as punishment for our grief we were being beaten and bloodied on the streets of New York, I wish I could say I was there chanting the whole world is watching, the whole world is watching, I wish I could say I was yelling or crying or screaming or running for my life, I wish I could say I got to the end of the march at Madison Square Park, when there was someone with blood dripping down their face speaking to the media, I wish I could say I did jail support to get people out or that I went to meetings afterward to plan more political funerals, like when Lauryn Paige, an eighteen-year-old trans girl was stabbed to death and then thrown in a ditch in Austin, Texas, I wish I could say I was there at the political funeral for Billy Jack Gaither, beaten to death with an axe handle, burned on a pyre of tires, murdered for being gay in Alabama, I wish I could say I was there to make the connection between all these deaths, and the lynching of James Byrd Jr. in Texas, and the murder of Amadou Diallo by the NYPD in a hail of forty-one bullets and so many other police murders of unarmed people of color they just went on and on I wish I could say I was there to make the connection between the NYPD gunning down people of color, raping Abner Louima with a broomstick, arresting trans women and youth of color on the street for daring to exist, raping sex workers under threat of arrest, cracking down on public sex and protest and queer visibility while privatizing public space, shutting down the clubs and persecuting nightlife while making Times Square safe for Disney the whole city safe for corporate profit I wish I could say I made these connections on my own but I was doing lines with one of my regulars during the political funeral because I wasn't ready, I wasn't ready yet but then soon enough Marya and I were doing coke again and she was talk talk talking I was in awe again and maybe it didn't seem like I was listening but I was listening.

When Cara Canale showed up at her opening with blood dripping down her face, Sabine went right up to her and said Ana Mendieta, we are so honored to have you with us. Cara's show was called *Ana Mendieta Is Still Alive*, and that night she would only answer as Ana. And I'm glad Sabine caught on right when Cara stepped in the door, because it took me a little longer.

But here she was, Ana Mendieta, with her hair slicked back and parted in the middle, gold hoop earrings, eyebrows plucked to perfection, and blood dripping down her face and onto her red dress.

Cara Canale, dressed as Ana Mendieta, covered in blood, walking from the building where her husband, the artist Carl Andre, pushed her out their thirty-fourth floor window, and she fell to her death in 1985. But no one saw the murder, and Carl Andre was acquitted.

Before the show, Cara created a route of bloody footprints leading from 300 Mercer Street, where Ana Mendieta lived with Carl Andre, to the gallery. Cara wanted to use her own blood at first, that's the kind of performance artist she was, but there wouldn't have been enough to walk the whole way and survive, so she decided to use animal blood like Ana Mendieta would have, but then she realized the blood would wash away and she wanted something more permanent so she used red paint, which was a relief to me, that's for sure.

It really did look like blood, though, she got the color right. Bloody footprints leading all the way to the gallery, they lasted for months, and then once inside the gallery the footprints turned to glitter, glitter footprints leading to that back wall, and then the outline of Ana's body which was really Cara's body, in glitter on the wall, like one of Ana Mendieta's *Siluetas*. And then on the other walls too, a room full of glitter *Siluetas*. Two rooms. Some of the *Siluetas* were faint imprints, and some showed her whole body, remnants of a life beyond death. It was stunning if you knew Ana Mendieta's work, and it was stunning if you didn't.

I found Cara because of Emma Sulkowicz, who decided to carry a dorm room mattress everywhere at Columbia until Emma's rapist was expelled or Emma graduated. That was in 2014, and every time

I watched an interview of Emma speaking, or footage of other students helping to carry that mattress to class, I found myself sobbing. Sobbing.

Suddenly I remembered those mattresses. Suddenly I remembered Columbia. Suddenly I remembered what happened to me.

Of course I'd never forgotten. But now I really remembered.

I thought about everyone carrying that mattress around with Emma, this collective act of care, a demand for accountability.

Carry That Weight was a performance art piece that was part of Sulkowicz's senior thesis, but it was so much more than that. We were all carrying that weight. And if other people could carry it with us, maybe somehow we could release the trauma.

I kept watching the footage from a speak-out on campus, and especially one student, who says, "Hi, I'm Dorothy, I'm a freshman, I've been on this campus for two weeks, and I was sexually assaulted six days ago"—she gasps, and then she's crying, and her friend is crying with her hands over her face—and Dorothy says, "And no one tells you where to go from there, so . . ."

And that's all she can say.

You can see all the pain in her face, and then she can't speak anymore. She turns quickly toward her friend, and then quickly in the other direction, and then hands the bullhorn to someone else and walks off with her friend as they're both sobbing.

I kept rewinding that clip. Dorothy was a freshman who had just been sexually assaulted and she was already speaking out. It had been twenty-three years for me and I hadn't told anyone.

There was someone else at the speak-out, Jen, a former student at Barnard who was raped off-campus twenty-two years before, and she said after her rape she couldn't sleep at night, she could only sleep during the day, and that's what happened for me but I had never made that connection before.

I wanted to tell someone. I finally wanted to tell someone. Everyone. I thought of writing a Facebook post but was I just thinking about Facebook because it was distant. I hated that distance. And you could never predict what someone would want to argue about, or what kind of horrible advice they would give you when you weren't asking for advice.

So then I thought of making a video installation with that one loop of Dorothy, over and over again.

But that felt like exploiting her pain.

I thought of a second idea for a video installation, a loop of the other woman, Jen, saying, "That was twenty-two years ago, and what has changed."

And what has changed. And what has changed. And what has changed. I thought of hearing that over and over in the gallery, and including my story, and inviting Emma Sulkowicz to bring *Carry That Weight* to Sabine Roth, but wouldn't that depoliticize it?

So then I thought of making the gallery into a place where survivors could write their stories on the walls for a month, and the gallery would become a gathering space. I didn't know if Sabine would be interested, I knew she didn't consider herself a feminist even though she'd always shown mostly women artists. And maybe my idea was cheesy or dated, but every time I watched footage from that speak-out at Columbia I started crying again, and wasn't that a kind of power?

So I went to Sabine with the idea. She said tell me your inspiration. And I told her about *Carry That Weight*. Maybe she could tell I was about to cry, so she said what is your personal stake?

And I said I was raped. At Columbia. Twenty-three years ago. It's why I dropped out. And never went back.

I wasn't planning to tell Sabine, but then I told her, just like that, and it didn't faze her at all, she just said yes, I think this is a strong idea for a show. I assume you'll include your inspiration in the curatorial statement.

And that was it. She only focused on the specifics of the show. Somehow this was the best possible response. I already felt so much less afraid.

I rarely wrote anything for the curatorial statements, that was Sabine's territory. She knew the perfect way to say something about nothing, or nothing about something, or whatever they wanted you to do in those statements. But she assigned this one to me. Because she knew I needed to tell my story.

I called the show *The Writing on the Wall*. Within a week, the walls were entirely covered. Sabine came out and said it looks like we need more walls. So we added freestanding walls in front of the gallery walls, which looked stark at first, like we were creating a maze, but then people covered both sides of those walls too.

When I sent my mothers my artist's statement, I was worried they'd ask me why I hadn't told them before. But they just told me I was brave. They told me they were proud of me for breaking the silence. They said it reminded them of consciousness-raising groups they used to be in—that was before you were born, Eileen said. And Paula said thank you for continuing that work. And Eileen said let us know if there's any way we can help.

Saturdays at the gallery were for survivors only, we would sit in a circle at noon to share our stories. On the first Saturday, maybe a half-hour before the circle, Jaysun walked in the door carrying a bouquet of white roses and said surprise!

Jaysun hadn't lived in New York in over a decade.

What, am I early, she said, and she held up the roses.

Jaysun, I said, I can't believe you're here—we hugged hello, and then I went in the back to get a vase, and I arranged the roses on the table I'd set up for the circle.

Originally I thought we would sit on the floor, but then Sabine said some people might want chairs, and what about light refreshments, so we had a large circular table that doubled as a place for the art supplies, and then we added bottles of Apollinaris water, since Sabine thought the green glass would be an elegant touch, and some fresh fruit and roasted almonds.

Sabine wasn't coming in on Saturdays for the show because she said she wasn't sure if she qualified as a survivor. I might very well be, she said, and looked me right in the eyes.

But I don't want to be presumptuous, she said, and left it at that.

But now here was Jaysun with roses, saying girl did I scare you or something. She'd been living in Seattle ever since Brad got a job there, remember Brad? Turned out he wasn't straight, because he brought Jaysun with him, and they were living together in some high-rise in Belltown, of all places, first he had some job in the music industry but then he was recruited by Amazon, and he got Jaysun a job there too, an entry-level position in human resources, whatever that meant, and somehow this was working out until they both got strung out on crystal.

The highlight was when they both tested positive, and Brad blamed Jaysun, even though he was the one sleeping around the whole time. So he kicked Jaysun out of the apartment, changed the locks and everything.

Luckily Jaysun still had her job—she was in a different department from Brad, and she still had her credit cards, so she checked into the Moore Hotel because it was right around the corner, and it was probably the cheapest place besides the Green Tortoise, and she convinced Brad to drop off her clothes at the front desk. After that, she moved into a studio at the Olive Terrace because she thought maybe they wouldn't do a credit check, and then she loved living there because it was near all the bars.

Eventually she got off crystal, right around the same time I stopped doing drugs too, so we kind of became a cross-country support system, calling each other whenever we were breaking down. We called it the Club Kid Diaspora Helpline. Brad disappeared and Jaysun became a workaholic and bought a two-bedroom condo when the market crashed. It was in this hideous '60s building but when she sent me a picture of the view I couldn't argue with that. Instead of her old thrift store coats, now she was maxing out her credit cards to buy Burberry and Prada, and talking about all the boring things that bougie fags talk about, but also she hated bougie fags, so we would call each other up to rant. But neither of us had ever talked about rape.

But here she was now, hugging me, with flowers. I said did you come for the circle?

She said are you telling me I'm in the wrong place.

And then we were laughing, and the circle was about to start. The next person to arrive was an older woman with gray braids who said what a lovely centerpiece, and then she motioned me over.

I thought this was a safe space, she said.

What do you mean, I said.

She said I thought it was women-only.

And I said no, it's survivors-only. All survivors are welcome. And then she left.

The next person to arrive was Cara Canale, that's when I met her, and by the time we started the circle I think there were about ten people. I didn't know what I was doing, but people looked at me like I knew what I was doing, so then it felt like I knew what I was doing.

We were all telling our stories in whatever way we wanted to, some of us were shaking and some of us were crying and some of us were totally collected, and it felt joyful. Maybe joyful is the wrong word when you're talking about trauma, but I don't know what other word to use.

Cara told us about Ana Mendieta's *Rape Scene*, which she made in 1973 when she was a grad student at Iowa University, in response to the rape and murder of a nursing student there. People were invited to the show at Mendieta's apartment—it was a reenactment—Ana was bent over a table, ass and legs exposed, arms and head tied down, blood dripping down her body and onto the floor. She stayed still like that for an hour.

Cara said she wanted to bring Ana Mendieta into the gallery because it was Ana's work that helped Cara to get her body back after she was raped, when she was a grad student at NYU. It wasn't the same rape, she said, because I survived.

Ana had already been murdered then, Cara said, but if she were alive today, and living at 300 Mercer Street, she could walk right over to join us. Can we imagine that, she said, let's take a moment to imagine Ana with us.

One woman said she'd been raped by her boyfriend so many times that she forgot what consent was. Another said she'd been assaulted on the subway during rush hour the other day, some guy reached under her skirt and they were so close that she couldn't push him away without pushing everyone so she just stood there frozen until the next stop. Another woman said it was her mother who abused her and no one believed her when she said that, they wanted mothers to be nurturing and caring but it isn't always that way, she knew it wasn't always that way but still she felt so guilty even saying it.

When it was Jaysun's turn to speak, she said where do I begin—well, I guess with my father. Do I have to start with my father? I was fifteen. One night when I was sleeping he got in bed behind me, started kissing my neck . . . The hardest part, she said, the hardest part was that I enjoyed it. That cheap cologne he wore all the time, the smell of liquor on his breath when his lips were on my neck, the feeling of his hands grabbing my chest, he even brought lube, that's how prepared he was. He even brought lube. There wasn't any pain, not really, just a feeling like everything in the room was getting hot, and then, and then . . .

The next day he came into my room with a gun, Jaysun said. He said: I've killed the enemy before and I can kill the enemy again.

That was the only part of the story that I'd heard before, just the last part.

Then Jaysun said okay, so I got the hell out of there. But that was only the beginning, right, picture this clueless Jersey girl on the rough streets of Times Square at the tender age of fifteen in the '80s, you get the point, don't you? But it didn't stop there, did it. I wish I could say it stopped there. I used to wear these big old ratty coats, with nothing on underneath, or almost nothing. It was the only way I could feel my body.

And that's when she started crying. I'd never seen Jaysun cry before. In all the years I'd known her, I'd never seen her cry.

And she'd never seen me cry. Finally we were crying together.

Even if, when we went to dinner afterward, she said girl, let's just pretend I never said any of that, okay.

But I couldn't pretend any longer.

You know when you go to a doctor's office and they ask you to describe your pain on a scale of one to ten, and all you can think is why are you trying to make it worse. Then they want you to list every symptom—when it started, how long it's been going on, and by the time you're done with that you're ready to go to bed. Forever.

At least I could sleep, that was the one thing I could do after I stopped doing drugs. I could sleep forever, but I just felt worse and worse. People act like after you stop doing drugs you feel better, but that never happened for me.

I could say that it started with the headache, like a drill going through my head, or maybe it started with the sensitivity to smoke, and that caused the headache, even though I'd been smoking pot every day for almost two decades, and going to smoky bars until there weren't any more smoky bars but suddenly I couldn't even handle smoke close to me when I was outside or there would be that headache again. And don't even mention the fabric softener pouring in through my windows, that rancid cooking grease smell, all the car exhaust, someone's perfume in the stairwell, the smell of the rats in the walls, everything, I was sensitive to everything.

Or maybe it started when suddenly I couldn't digest anything, even my favorite foods would just go right through me I mean for years, but that was so much better than now, when everything gets stuck, the bloating waking me up in the middle of the night but if I get up it's worse, if I turn to the side it's worse, what do I do to make it better I guess I could stop eating but then how would I stay alive.

Or maybe it started with the jaw pain, I'd wake up with so much pain in my jaw it hurt to chew so I went to see the TMJ specialist and he said actually this might be systemic, so he tested all my pressure points, and diagnosed me with fibromyalgia. It's a syndrome, he said, and he gave me a list of symptoms, I had all the symptoms. And that was useful at first because it connected the pain to the exhaustion to everything else, but the problem with a syndrome is that it describes the symptoms but not the solutions because really they have no clue, and don't even make me list all the doctors I've gone to see.

So maybe it started with the pain, like when it became difficult to do even the smallest things like opening a door or carrying a bag, and then I started getting headaches triggered by the light, especially the sun, oh the sun, but really any light any uneven light, so this could happen on a cloudy day or even at night walking down the street and the car headlights suddenly got so bright or those horrible LED streetlights or even worse the convenience stores that were suddenly a hundred times brighter I mean you couldn't even call them bodegas anymore, they just looked like something on the side of the highway but this was First Avenue or wherever and who invented those horrible LEDs and luckily I already had blackout curtains at home and the gallery lighting was always even but then there was the rest of the world, and in that world there was the neurologist who diagnosed me with migraines, he said he could prescribe these pills that probably won't work, but honey if I wanted to try pills I already know the pills that work so let's not talk about pills, and, yes, sometimes I think it would be better if I never stopped the drugs but then there's that moment at dusk when everything gets soft or someone smiles at me in a particular way on the street or I notice a sudden burst of flavor and what is that, oh, it's the lemon, it's just lemon, and that's when I think I can get somewhere, maybe I can get somewhere without the drugs.

Of course I've gone to chiropractic acupuncture massage biofeedback meditation yoga Qigong craniosacral acupressure reflexology kinesiology herbal medicine homeopathy naturopathic medicine integrative medicine and whatever else and yes I take digestive enzymes nettles ginseng peony B12 folic acid multivitamins glutamine amino acids quercetin isoquercitrin rutin goldenseal lobelia mushroom tincture artichoke leaf peptides CBD oil licorice root echinacea probiotics magnesium vitamin C calcium NAC iron omega-3 fatty acids 5HTP d-ribose electrolytes trace minerals colloidal silver zinc garlic drops and who knows what else and yes if I stop the supplements then everything gets worse but that doesn't mean I'm getting better, and whenever I hear someone in their forties saying they feel like they're middle-aged I think there's no way I'm calling myself middle-aged until I feel good for at least a year and at this point I rarely even feel good for an hour so it looks like I'm staying young forever.

Before I stopped the drugs, I came home after work one day and I was so tired I got in bed without even taking any pills, and instead of sleeping for four hours like usual I slept twelve hours, and when I got up I just kept looking at the clock and I couldn't figure out what was going on because I'd gone to bed around eight, and the clock still said eight something, so I thought maybe I'd just slept for twenty minutes, that's how delirious I was, but then I looked out the window and sure enough it was eight in the morning. So I did some coke, got ready for work, and after work I went to Souen, like usual, and then when I got home I was so tired again that I got right in bed. And I slept for twelve hours that night too. This kept happening, all I wanted to do was sleep, I didn't even care about going out anymore—what was the point, everything was totally boring, it was just another routine, like getting up for work, and why was I doing coke just to get to work, I mean what could be more depressing.

I figured my body needed the rest—I hadn't really slept in fifteen years so maybe I was catching up. But after two weeks I figured it was time. It was time to get rid of the drugs, right? It was getting close to July 4, when the gallery closed for the summer, and Sabine always said that if I ever needed to get away, she had a place in Baltimore, and I always thought why the hell would I want to go to Baltimore. Yes, I'd become one of those New Yorkers.

But now I was ready to take Sabine up on her offer, and she said of course, just tell me what you need, Mary goes over every other week to tidy the place and check in on everything, so if you need groceries or any other amenities, kindly provide me with me a list.

Sabine was always ahead. Groceries—I hadn't even thought about groceries. Yes, I would give her a list, absolutely, thank you. Then she asked how long I'd like to stay, and I said how about until Labor Day, and she said I'll arrange everything with Mary.

I don't really need to tell you about those two months except to say that I got in a cab at the train station and we just kept driving and driving, at first it looked like a city but then it was like we were in the woods, and I said is this still Baltimore, and the driver said Mount Washington, right, and then we crossed a bridge and passed some old brick warehouses and I remembered Sabine did say something about a converted mill town and we went up the hill on a woodsy street that looked like the English countryside and I guess this was Mount Washington.

Sabine's place was this sprawling Victorian mansion with a huge fenced-in yard and all these enormous trees and of course everything was spotless but it was so different from Sabine's sleek modernist aesthetic that I knew it must have been a family home that she was preserving, filled with bulky antiques and turn-of-the-century landscape paintings that I couldn't have imagined her tolerating otherwise.

So I was in this mansion on a hill on the outskirts of a city I didn't know, and what could be a better way to get off drugs, I mean it actually worked, even when I was totally losing it on the phone with Jaysun and she said why don't you scream and I said I don't want to scare anyone, and she said all you can see is trees from your window, no one's going to hear you. And she was right. So then I was screaming all day, and it worked, all this screaming, I would go out naked in the sun and roll in the grass drenched in sweat and I felt like maybe this was a cleansing.

But I never got my energy back, that was the problem.

I didn't sleep for fifteen years, and then I slept for fifteen years, and then as soon as this pandemic started I couldn't sleep again, I mean I was just lying in bed with my brain racing in every direction, people were fleeing and everything was closing and what was left, were you left, why were you left, I mean why was I left, what was left for me, all the ambulances going by and then when there weren't any ambulances I still felt like I was hearing the sirens I mean my building was emptying out of the people paying $4,000 for the same apartment as mine, the ones who left their trash in the hall like someone was going to pick it up for them, as if the building wasn't already infested with rats, and then if someone stole their packages they'd put up signs saying YOU ASSHOLE STOP TAKING MY FUCKING PACKAGES I'M GOING TO CALL THE COPS, as if the cops would give a shit about their packages, they were going home to their parents or they were moving upstate or to Santa Fe or Mexico City to work remotely or whatever, but I felt no joy about this at all I just felt lost.

People were leaving but the rats were staying, they would always stay, they were out there looking for their next meal and I would lie in bed thinking about escape—I couldn't take a plane during the pandemic, people were still flying but what the hell were they thinking and I couldn't take a train either—I didn't have a car, and even if I did have a car I didn't have a license and I certainly couldn't drive cross-country on my own but I definitely couldn't be in a car with anyone else and even if I did drive cross-country on my own then where would I sleep unless I slept in the car—and, yes, I was fantasizing about driving to Seattle, even though the only time I went back, which was right after I stopped doing drugs, that last week before Labor Day in 2005, it was awful, and that was why I hadn't gone back in fifteen years.

But now all I could think about was more space, I needed more space on the sidewalk I needed air that I could actually breathe I needed trees that weren't fenced off in parks so you couldn't get too close I mean I had my favorite trees in New York like that one on my block that pushed the sidewalk away so you had to walk on a more narrow part of the sidewalk to get by I mean they made it more narrow for the tree how long would that last and suddenly even the Hare Krishna Tree in Tompkins started to look sick and anyway I needed a nighttime walk in the rain with no one else around.

No, Seattle didn't feel like home anymore in 2005, not when I walked up to the house and I knew my mothers had renovated but somehow I was still shocked that they'd painted it gray, why gray, who needed more gray in Seattle? Then I opened the door and nothing was the same except the chandeliers—no mirrors, no disco ball, no purple sofas, just some kind of streamlined emptiness with rustic touches, but the worst part was that over by the fireplace, which was where they'd kept photos of everyone who died, and then cards and artwork and knick-knacks and ashes in little urns and glass jars and I used to stand there and look through everything just to remember—none of that was there, and I was so shocked I couldn't even say anything.

At this point my mothers had moved into my room and converted the basement into a guest suite, so that's where I stayed but it was no longer the Den of Iniquity it looked like an ad for West Elm—everything was gray and tan and beige with hints of teal and burnt sienna but the mattress was comfortable and at least I could go to Volunteer Park and check in on my favorite trees. The first day I walked down to Broadway to go to the Gravity Bar, I mean I remembered it was gone but I didn't realize the whole Broadway Market was gone, I'd forgotten about that big snowstorm my mothers told me about, when the roof caved in and then after that somehow the whole Market became QFC—just a fucking supermarket, no Gravity Bar, no flower shop, no B&O Espresso, no Bulldog News, no Pink Zone or gay underwear store none of those little carts where people were selling socks or keychains or wearable art no atrium where you could sit for hours no queer kids hanging out meeting up looking for drugs or drama or a haircut or a tattoo or someone to walk back and forth on Broadway with, checking out the outfits.

The best moment was one night when we sat down for dinner and my mothers were talking about a friend of theirs who had a daughter who was trying to get into the art world, and they mentioned that their daughter worked at a gallery in New York, and I smiled when I realized they were finally calling me their daughter, it had taken a long time but here it was. But then they started talking about gay marriage. Of course it was all over the news because of the legal battles, and I was doing my best to ignore it because what could be worse than marriage, any kind of marriage, and it was my mothers who taught me this. But now they were going into all the intricacies of the court case in Washington State and I just stopped them right there and said wait, do you believe in marriage at all? And they looked at me like I was totally out of my mind. Eileen said this is about civil rights. And Paula said we deserve the same rights as heterosexuals, nothing more and nothing less.

My whole childhood they never said anything about marriage except that it was a backward institution based on the oppression of women and now they were telling me they deserved the same rights as heterosexuals. Honestly I don't know if I'll ever recover from the card they sent out after they got married in 2012, right when gay marriage became legal in Washington. It was a professional photo of the two of them in Volunteer Park by my favorite weeping cherry tree—Paula was wearing the top of a white gown, and black slacks, and Eileen was wearing the bottom of the gown, with a black tuxedo jacket, and they were framed by those flowing pink flowers from the tree, and sure I was annoyed that they were using the beauty of the cherry blossoms for this pointless posturing but I couldn't deny the symmetry of everything except then I opened up the card and it said FINALLY IT'S LEGITIMATE!!!

Yes, there were three exclamation marks and I wanted to think this was a joke, but if it was a joke then why were they celebrating? I just kept looking at that photo over and over again until eventually I threw it away so I wouldn't keep looking at it.

Fifteen years later, Jaysun was trying to convince me to move back to Seattle and buy a condo. I told her no way but she kept saying girl, listen, there's so much more space here, you would have your own laundry, you could control your environment, we would be neighbors, you would be with your favorite trees.

I said even if I wanted to move to Seattle I don't have the money to buy a condo and she said you don't have to have the money, you just need the down payment and a good job, and you've been working at Sabine Roth for eternity so you're the ideal candidate, I can lend you the down payment, don't even worry about it, I was planning on buying a place in Palm Springs but now everyone's buying a place in Palm Springs so the prices are insane, just think about it, you need to get out of New York, you tell me that every day.

Then one day I went out to do laundry—I'd always done laundry on Tuesdays in the middle of the day when it was least crowded but now you couldn't predict anything because everyone might be there trying the same thing, anyway I was excited because no one was there but then as soon as I threw all my laundry into the washer I heard this loud hacking cough, and it was the person working there, the son of the owners—luckily I hadn't started the machine so I squeezed everything back into my laundry bag and ran outside as fast as possible, I didn't bother trying to get my quarters out of the machine I just went up the street to Cosmo's, but right when I walked in I saw two people without masks on, so I took my dirty laundry back to my apartment and called Jaysun.

I said send me some listings, just for me to look at, and she said oh my God I'm calling Sandy right away, she'll be so excited.

Don't call Sandy yet, I'm not ready to talk to a realtor, I'm just curious.

Sandy loves curiosity, don't you worry about Sandy, she'll send us a list, I just need to know if you want a one bedroom or two.

I mean how much do you think a one bedroom would be.

Probably about 400,000, a little more a little less—somewhere like the Brix would be more, and that's a great building, or Press, they've got amazing units, or that one on Pine, what's that one called? The Braeburn. But then anything down by Melrose, all the converted midcentury buildings, those are cheaper. You could get a nice co-op in the 300s for sure. But you might want to think about a two-bedroom, it's a better investment. You could get a two-bedroom for under 600,000, I got mine for pocket change, but that was a short sale after the market crashed and I know you don't want a short sale, do you.

What's a short sale?

Oh, you know, girl, it's when you're saving someone from foreclosure, but I know you'd feel guilty, wouldn't you.

What do you mean saving someone?

Girl, let's not get technical here, I'll break it down for you. You're exploiting their misery, it's as simple as that. It just sounds better than saying you bought a foreclosure, which is really how I got my place, let me be honest for a sec. And then that gave me so much more money for renovations. But let's get back to business. I'll just tell Sandy to send us anything that looks promising to give us a sense of what's available, but let's get your needs clear. I know you need in-unit laundry, hardwood floors, and a lot of windows for air circulation, an upper floor so no one's smoke gets into your sensitive nostrils—I know you prefer those dusty old buildings so you can pretend you're still in New York, but is there anything else?

My credit is terrible, I don't know how I would get a mortgage.

Listen, we can worry about that later. If you want to get a place, I'm your girl—I just cashed in my stock options, so it's like I won the lottery. The lottery of indentured servitude, that is. I wasn't going to tell you this, but I was going to buy a place in Palm Springs with cash. So I could be your mortgage, I'm just saying. So I'll send Sandy a text, and then we'll take a look.

Just as long as she knows that I'm not really thinking about it right now, I'm just curious.

Trust me, my lips are sealed. Okay, now I have to get back to work, the Evil Empire is waiting.

One good thing about the lockdown was that at least the streets were quieter and the graffiti was back and there were all these discarded objects to look at on the street although these were the ruins of everyone's lives, right, but one day I was walking to work and I noticed all these mannequins inside a big glass display case, one was missing its head and a few had broken legs or missing arms and it felt like a metaphor, right, I wanted to take a picture but I didn't have my camera and I know Jaysun would say girl you need a cell phone, everyone has a cell phone, but I didn't want to be everyone I just wanted a photo, and then I realized the case was on wheels so I wheeled it right into the gallery.

I called Sabine and she said oh that is a good metaphor, and she started laughing, and I don't know if I'd ever heard Sabine laugh like that, I mean it sounded like her whole body was in on it, and Sabine didn't usually use her whole body but nowadays she was getting pretty loopy on the phone and I wondered if she was drinking, I mean she'd always liked a glass of champagne every now and then but now it seemed like maybe it was morning, noon, and night, but who wasn't loopy now, I know I was getting wacky in the gallery sitting around all day without much to do and Sabine said Terry, don't forget about all the art supplies in back.

And I had forgotten about the art supplies. So I went back to see what was there—tons of spray paint, tools, every kind of tape measure, boxes of nails and tacks and staples and safety pins and paperclips. So then I took the mannequins out of the case, and they all stood up on their own, even the one without a head. I got inspired and took them up on the roof and spray-painted them all silver, went back downstairs to check on everything, went back to the roof and the silver was too bright so I added black, and then gold, and that illuminated the ruin in just the right way so I left the mannequins on the roof to dry, it didn't look like it was going to rain.

 I dreamed that I met the mannequins at the Limelight and they came home with me, or maybe I wasn't dreaming I was still awake and I was thinking about their outfits. When you're a club kid for fifteen years you accumulate piles and piles of everything you love and you save it all because you might need it again six months later like surprise, I'm bringing out my googly eyes again so that's what I was thinking about now, yes, I would cover one of the mannequins in googly eyes, another in sequins, oh and then one of them could be wearing that flamingo stuffed animal that I used as a fake backpack by tying the arms around my chest, and the huge blue snake that I would wrap around my neck, and then the other stuffed animals, oh, and one of them I could drape in this weird gauze, and then I remembered that Armani suit that I found at Century 21 the one time Jaysun convinced me to go with her and she said honey, you have to get that suit because it fits so well, but then I never had a reason to wear an Armani suit, even if I did get it for forty dollars or something ridiculous. But now I realized it would be perfect on that headless mannequin, wouldn't it. And then the last one I could just hammer nails into until it cracked apart.

 So the next day I started with the hammer and nails, and it was great because chunks of the mannequin started breaking off so I did that with the others too and then I spray-painted the holes with red and magenta and green and added glitter I had plenty of glitter and when I got home that night I realized they needed wings, so I got out my wings and put on six pairs over my sweater, yes it was awkward and yes someone did yell fuck if it isn't Halloween already but it was worth it because those mannequins definitely needed those wings so then I told Sabine to take a look.

Sabine called me right at ten the next day and she was laughing again. Terry, she said, oh, Terry, forgive me, but I was just struck by a memory of the day we met, and you were wearing those wings, weren't you, you flew into the gallery painted head to toe in pink and I did not know what you were but I knew the gallery was Rethinking Pink and then I was rethinking everything. You arrived on that day to reimagine the gallery, and Terry, I want you to know that I am grateful, I am so grateful for the last twenty-three years, I want you to know that I truly appreciate everything you've brought to the gallery, and to my life, forgive me, I'm getting sentimental, I know it's not like me but at this point I have arrived at my ninth decade, now, shh, don't tell a soul, it will be in the papers any moment but hold on a second, hold on, I'm choking on something, excuse me, where was I?

Yes, your installation piece. It's marvelous. It speaks to our times with both humor and pathos, it is at once enigmatic and emblematic, you gesture toward and away from the trouble, evoking and provoking the long legacy of assemblage art and yes there are hints of Duchamp or Dubuffet and dare I say Martha Rosler meets Keith Haring on the way to dinner with Leigh Bowery in one of Nick Cave's *Soundsuits* and yet, and this is crucial, your installation is astonishingly current. You, Terry, have always been an original, truly an original, and I'm thrilled to chaperone this work to the broader public in the very near future, when do you think it will be ready?

Sabine, I said, first of all I just want to thank you . . .

Nonsense, Sabine said, nonsense. And she started laughing again. I loved her laugh. At least someone was laughing.

Now, Sabine said, let me offer two suggestions, take them or leave them. First of all, do the mannequins need masks? We have plenty of N95s.

Sabine.

Wonderful, Sabine said, and second, I noticed that the mannequins will not fit back into the display case with the wings, which are absolutely necessary to establish the positionality inside cataclysm hovering over existential dread, and yet this case, I think, could be crucial in enhancing the potent absurdity. So, I would suggest arranging the mannequins in front of the case, and then filling it to the brim with . . . And, bear with me, here's my idea—would you mind checking on something for me in the back? Now, on the very top shelf in the closet, you will notice a number of unmarked blue Mylar bags. I preserved a little remnant from our past, just in case, and I think it may be time for an unveiling.

And then she was laughing again, and I was laughing, even though I didn't know what I was laughing about.

And Sabine said would you mind taking a look and calling me once you have a chance to examine the contents and assess whether they might offer a sufficient way to bridge positive and negative space.

Sabine was a genius. In the back somehow she had preserved my wall decorations from Club Kid Diaspora, everything had been compacted into these blue bags, and when I opened them with a box cutter everything expanded and spilled out, so I started stuffing whatever would fit into the case, a glass container for all those dolls and dresses and broken toys wig heads stuffed animals children's clothing pacifiers necklaces and every kind of brightly colored unidentifiable metal plastic junk everything crushed and packed together in glass behind the mannequins, I mean it was like the whole world was squashed into the case and then in front was a parade of brokenness.

Then I remembered the masks. Of course they were exactly what the mannequins needed, so I took out the glue gun and sequined one so the sequins came out past the edges of the mask, then googly eyes for another, then I hid one under the gauze for the gauzy mannequin, and for the one with the nails I pushed one safety pin after another through until it was covered, and then extended a chain of safety pins all the way to the ground like chain mail, and for the stuffed animal model I put the mask on backward, but really the best one was the headless Armani, because for that one I just folded the mask carefully into the suit pocket. I still had more work to do—maybe more spray paint or glitter or googly eyes but other than that basically the piece was done.

Jaysun called when I was about to call Sabine, and she said okay, what did you think of the Vertigo? Yes, I know it's a '60s building, but it's a two-bedroom on the southwest corner with unobstructed Space Needle views and bamboo floors, and I think 565 is a steal for it, don't you? I happen to know that just a few years ago they redid the whole building envelope—all new windows and insulation and that's why it looks surprisingly contemporary, don't you think, and I know you don't need parking but that tandem parking spot does increase the resale value.

Jaysun, I didn't really look at that one because I can't imagine living in a '60s building. And why is it called the Vertigo?

Girl, don't pay attention to those details, every building in Seattle has a crazy name, remember? My building is called the Lamplighter, but does it have what you need or doesn't it. I did notice that carpet in the bedrooms, which may be required in the declaration so let me call Sandy and asked her to expand the search beyond what's available now, since it is a time of low inventory, especially when it comes to two-bedrooms and then we can take a look at any buildings that might be suitable so that if a unit becomes available we're ready to pounce.

Okay, as long as that isn't too much work.

Work, who said anything about work? This is the most fun I've had since lockdown started, I'll be in touch as soon as I hear from Sandy.

And then I called Sabine. Suddenly it felt like so much was going on, even though nothing was going on. But actually, something was going on.

1. Sabine said I'm closing the gallery.
2. Is that really what she said first? Maybe she said I'm starting a foundation. The Sabine Roth Foundation for the Arts. To support artists in times of trouble. Would you consider joining the board?
3. But she was closing the gallery.
4. She would continue paying me my full salary for two years.
5. She was already talking to potential buyers about my installation. Did we have a title yet?
6. I know I'm getting the order wrong, but sometimes the order is wrong.

7. I'm just going to forget about the order. When you write a list, it doesn't have to be in order. You can use a highlighter to mark what's important.
8. The *New York Times* was doing a profile on Sabine. A retrospective. Also the *New Yorker*. If we were lucky they would happen in the same week.
9. Sabine wanted to auction off my installation. What did I think? I would receive 10% of the proceeds. After all the press coverage, she was confident the auction would raise at least a million dollars. That meant $100,000 would go to me. Was I interested?
10. I told her I would donate the art.
11. Nonsense, she said, I will pay you 10% of the proceeds. You have to think about your future.
12. Here's the hardest part.
13. Why was it so hard?
14. She said I'm not going to be around much longer. You know that, right? Let me be direct. Stage IV brain cancer. I don't have much time. I already look like a ragdoll, but thanks to this pandemic no one has to see me. You are aware of Dr. Kevorkian, correct? You may know that he does not practice in New York. When I speak about Dr. Kevorkian, I'm using him as a metaphor. You understand what I'm saying, correct? There are ways of arranging things. I'm arranging things.
15. Sabine said don't mourn my loss.
16. When someone tells you not to mourn their loss, what do you do?
17. I bought a car. I walked outside one day and there it was for sale, a white Volvo station wagon like the one my mothers had when I learned to drive. All my friends would pile in, and we would drive to Golden Gardens in the summer, or Dykiki, any of Seattle's beaches. It was our beach getaway car.
18. This one had tinted windows. It was for sale for $2,000. I paid cash.
19. Of course I didn't have a driver's license. When you need to get away, you worry about these things, but at the same time, you don't worry too much. Because you need to get away.

20. Did I mention the auction made $7.25 million for the foundation. So I made $725,000, just like that. There it was in my account. Even though I'd worked in the art world for twenty-three years, this still didn't feel real. I kept looking at my account to make sure I wasn't reading the zeros wrong.
21. It felt like stolen money, like I needed to get rid of it fast.
22. "Fast Car," by Tracy Chapman, is still one of my favorite songs. Or not one of my favorite songs, but one of the songs that will always make me emotional. Drive drive drive drive away, she says.
23. A Volvo is not a fast car. But it is safe. That's what they say. I needed a way to get cross-country, and so I decided I was going to buy a bunch of crystal and stay up for as long as it took to get there. That was the safest way.
24. Everyone was dying. I'd survived this long, and I did not want to die of COVID-19.
25. If I had to stop, at least there were tinted windows. I could sleep in the car, but how safe was that.
26. I listened to "Fast Car" with Claire when we were fifteen, crashing from crystal. She was the one that needed to get away. That's why that song always makes me emotional.
27. I assume Claire never got away, but maybe she did, I mean it's possible.
28. Jaysun kept calling me with listings. This was before I had the money. She was going to lend it to me. I would pay her back. She even said: If you want to buy a place in New York instead, I could lend you the money for a studio. And I said no way. And she said I was just checking. I just wanted to make sure. I don't want to be selfish.
29. Sometimes the most selfish people are the most generous.
30. I don't need to tell you about all the listings, but one day Jaysun called and said I found the one. This wasn't the first time she said that, but it was the one. It was a gorgeous prewar building, corner unit, stained hardwood floors like the ones I grew up with, a huge walk-in closet, and everything had been updated—new pipes, stainless steel counters, new appliances, two bedrooms, fourth floor

facing the back of the building, with only a house directly behind it that was law offices, and a two-story '60s building, so there was a view of the Space Needle and the mountains.
31. Jaysun said they could build anywhere, so you can't count on anything, but for now that view could be yours.
32. The only downside was that to the south it faced another building that was only a few feet away, so you were looking right into someone else's windows and Jaysun said she did smell fabric softener when she opened the window. She really was thinking about me.
33. She said but it's not like you're not used to looking into other people's windows.
34. Jaysun arranged everything—the painters who only used no-voc paint, blackout curtains and shades, new laundry machines, hypoallergenic organic mattresses and simple platform bed frames, pine wood treated only with linseed oil, from a place called Soaring Heart, even the movers from New York, she had all these connections because she worked for the Evil Empire. She could do everything fast.
35. I decided on red curtains. Jaysun said are you sure?
36. Yes, I said, red curtains.
37. But not red walls, right, she said. Don't get carried away.
38. No, not red walls, let's keep the same colors as the Sherbet Factory, do you remember those colors?
39. Yes, Jaysun said, but I'll need pictures to match them.
40. Actually let's change it up a bit, I said. Orange in the living room. Mint green in the kitchen. Lavender in the bathroom. Bubblegum pink in my bedroom, whatever looks good in the other bedroom.
41. You can't say whatever looks good, Jaysun said.
42. Okay, I said, how about pale yellow.
43. And we'll keep all the trim white, Jaysun said. It wasn't a question, so I figured she was right.
44. Why do I always feel like there should be a second *r* in sherbet?
45. I want to say something about the *New York Times* article, but there's too much. Let me just tell you the sentence that shocked me the most. "Everything I've accomplished over the last two

decades has only been possible thanks to the extraordinary creative inspiration of Terry Dactyl, my muse and co-conspirator, everything, the gallery would have closed long ago if it wasn't for her perspicacity."

46. She called me her muse. Did she really feel this way, or was this for the auction?
47. I called Dominic for crystal. He was the only one I could rely on, but his number had been disconnected. I wondered if he'd gotten out of the business, or if the business had gotten him.
48. Is it strange to say that I was worried about Dominic, even though we hadn't talked in fifteen years?
49. I called the Club Kid Diaspora Helpline. Now it had expanded to the four of us, for special occasions—Cleo, in Paris; Mielle, in Santa Fe; Jaysun, in Seattle; and me, still in New York. Jaysun always arranged the calls. There were a lot of time zones to get right.
50. Jaysun wanted to switch this call to Zoom, but I said no way. No way was I ever going on Zoom.
51. Who's zooming who, she said.
52. When crystal started hitting New York, people acted like it was some kind of delicacy, but it was cut with something—in high school, I would do one tiny bump and I'd be racing for hours, but this crystal you could snort like coke and it just made you feel dead. Also it was more expensive than coke, talk about a reversal. Then one time I asked Dominic for crystal, just to see how good it could get, and when I did that first line it was like all the lights were on in my head and I was so wired it was scary. I was up for four days. That's the crystal I needed to drive cross-country.
53. I can't tell you why Cleo moved to Paris. Officially it was because of a job offer.
54. Okay, Cleo moved to Paris because of legal issues. The neon factory burned to the ground. It turned out she wasn't actually the legal owner, the deed had never been transferred, so everything was in limbo. She decided to leave the country in case they decided she was liable.

55. No one died in the fire, but there was a lot of damage. Millions of dollars. Cleo sold her condo and took the job offer at Dior.
56. Cleo gave me Sid's red velvet sofa before she left. She said she thought it should stay in the family.
57. So we were family again.
58. I'm just filling you in on a few details. Remember what I said about the highlighter, you can always use a highlighter.
59. The Club Kid Diaspora Helpline was divided about my crystal meth escape plan. Jaysun said: Catch me now I'm falling. Mielle said: It could damage your chakras. Cleo said: Don't you think this could make driving more dangerous.
60. Cleo was right.
61. Also, when Jaysun said aren't you already so wired you can't sleep? Just put that energy to good use.
62. Maybe I just wanted to do drugs. It had been fifteen years.
63. When I realized I wanted to do drugs, that's when I knew I couldn't do drugs.
64. I don't know what else to tell you.
65. It's not like I can't tell you later.
66. I got in the car.

In Seattle, I can finally breathe. Yes, I still have to dodge the dog walkers, the joggers, and the couples, but there's so much space—you can just walk into the street if there's someone up ahead, and drivers actually avoid you. When I get to Volunteer Park I can run through the grass and raise my arms to match the angles of the trees to try and move out of pain so much pain from all that driving I thought I was going to crack apart but the pain was keeping me going because I couldn't sleep I went into the headache I focused up ahead but on nothing and eventually through the nothing I arrived. And it was such a relief when Jaysun offered to drive to the co-op and bring me groceries once a week, she already had a spare key so now she leaves the groceries outside my door. I say are you sure that's okay, and she says girl I was worried that Volvo wasn't going to make it but now you're here you're here so it's the least I can do, and I'm pretty sure I already had COVID, right?

And I say what do you mean?

And she says remember in January, when I had that hacking cough that went on for weeks and then I couldn't breathe, and I went to the hospital where they gave me steroids and then I went home and felt like I was about to have a heart attack so I went back and they gave me a bunch of antibiotics which did nothing except make me shit all day and remember, you said antibiotics always make you sicker, but I was sick for like a month, remember, it was worse than when I first got the AIDS.

So you think it was COVID?

Girl, doesn't that seem most likely—but, don't worry, I'm still being cautious and everything, I'm just not as scared because I must have some immunity, I know we don't really know anything but I'm just saying.

Jaysun got me all these cloth masks from some local clothing store called Freeman—it sounds gay but it's not gay at all, she says, but it is next to the gay underwear store where I've been going for curbside because I need to check in on the new arrivals.

What are the new arrivals, I ask, and she says you yes you, and we hold out our arms like we're about to hug, but from ten feet away, and then we hug ourselves like we're hugging each other, it's all about the eye contact and blowing each other kisses.

Jaysun's working all the time because the world may be ending but the Evil Empire is expanding—did you see what they said about hiring 100,000 more workers, she says. Make that 200,000—and usually my whole job is about firing people, so let's just say there's a lot to do.

I spend my days sleeping, and walking to the park yes the park, there's a symphony out here by the duck pond, with the squeaks of newborn ducklings, the chirps of the ones that have been around a little while, the quacks of the older ducks, and the laughter of those of us on the sidelines.

And I guess I'm not the only person who counts the ducklings. This woman says: I was here the other day, and there were nine.

Ten, I say.

She says: I thought this was my respite from the coronavirus, and now they're getting eaten.

And some guy yells: Three days ago, there were ten!

And someone says: Aw!

And he says: Yeah, the crows like them.

The crows? I ask. I think I saw an eagle.

And he says: That'll do it, that'll do it in a second. They're very vulnerable.

And it feels good to be vulnerable with these people.

In the park there are all these signs that say KEEP IT MOVING, so I'm doing contact improv with the trees. I was going to start in my favorite cedar grove although there's someone over there with her kids playing on one of the trees that must have died because they chopped it down but they left this giant stump with broken arms in all directions and it looks spooky to me but now kids play on it like it's a jungle gym. I guess I could still roll around on the other cedars, the rest of them are there in all their glory but the squawking of the kids doesn't relax me like the squawking of the birds so I'm under the giant sequoia with the widest trunk ever, all on my own, and one branch fits so smoothly against my lower back I can lean right into it and rotate side to side and into my armpit and then my back up against the higher part sliding my arm along the bark kicking my back leg up to stretch out my hamstrings, and then the other leg, and then kissing the bark from rough to smooth, I guess this is the only kissing I'm going to get, and then there's a sun break through the branches I'm looking down at all the pine cones suddenly illuminated and then up at the branches covered in moss just a soft covering, not as much as that tree over there all green but this constellation of branches flowing over and down, eyes up to the sky a layer of clouds, a layer of blue, another layer of clouds the green of the grass connecting with the green of the sequoia not-leaves, what do you call them, needles, still pressing my back against the branch and into that tension along my spine and then down to my lower back cradled into this one spot that feels like it was made just for my body and then I can really let everything go, the tree as support as balance beam as tactile experiment as stable partner I crouch down under the branch now above my back pressing me down and then back and then down and then when I walk again there's so much lightness but also my feet rolling into the ground the ground rolling into my feet a bounce roll bounce almost like being on K but let's not get carried away.

Wait, those azaleas are taking magenta to another level. And then on the corner there's a flyer on a tree offering Quarantine Paintings, Nudes by Delivery. And then the sounds, my feet in the gravel the bus driving by, did the 10 always go down this alley, I don't remember ever going down this alley then I'm staring down the hill at this giant fir tree, I think it's a fir, rising into the puffy white clouds mixed in with gray and then suddenly all these patches of blue, and yes, that means sun and shadow, the shifting light—don't worry, I'm wearing my sun hat and sunglasses, I never leave the house without them, so I can look at the dark blues of the trees at the base of the Cascades beneath clouds in the distance, turn to face the sun, and then I'm at this scenic overlook and it's funny how some things in Seattle can be so familiar and some feel like I've never experienced them before, and this one can be both.

Maybe it's how the view is never the same, like today the water is sparkling and pale blue, the clouds hanging over everything, a gentle mist and yes I know there are mountains so many mountains behind those clouds stretching on and on but today if I didn't know then I wouldn't know.

And then there's the part where you turn, and you're walking on an elevated sidewalk next to the ravine, and up ahead are two tall pine trees growing straight up, or almost straight up, and then a spruce, sage and rosemary and lavender tumbling down the ravine and I've never been to Santa Fe but I think this might be what it looks like, and when I send a picture to Mielle she says yes, it is kind of like that, except the clouds are always at eye level so you're walking in the sky it's all sky and there wouldn't be that brick house on the left.

And then a kid with pink hair goes into that house, and I think wait, that might be me.

So if I stand in certain places I'm flooded by one memory after another, like in front of the Biltmore and my body becomes a slideshow I can barely move there's so much inside but then there are places that don't feel familiar at all, like even just walking down 13th, a block from where I grew up, because as a kid I always walked down 12th, or 15th, or Broadway, Pike or Pine, all the busiest streets, but now I'm trying to avoid as many people as possible so I walk down the alley between 11th and 12th, and it's like I'm looking at someplace I've never seen before, even if it's just the backs of the houses, or at night when I walk down 13th, all those giant trees with branches crossing the entire street and up above that leafy canopy and suddenly so many rabbits, everywhere there are rabbits running back and forth across the street, and as a kid maybe I saw a rabbit once in a while but now I see them every night, somehow the pandemic brought out the rabbits and I like to make the motion of their hopping with my arms so maybe we can hop together even though of course they're hopping away from me, and up ahead there's someone walking toward me so I pull aside because the sidewalk isn't very wide, I walk up the stairs toward someone's house, and this person looks up at me in the dark, and pauses, and thanks me, and she looks so grateful for such a small gesture, these little ways that we try to take care of one another.

Back at the park there's the giant holly tree behind the Asian Art Museum which I guess just expanded, I can see the extra glass in the back, Jaysun said it was closed for three years and she went right after it opened in March, when people were thinking should we be wearing masks or shouldn't we, there was a shiny coat made of dog tags from the Korean army, spreading out in a circle onto the floor, that's what she remembered the most, but also the museum was kind of crowded and that felt comforting like this coronavirus thing wouldn't be a big deal, and then a week later that's when everything closed.

So now I'm under the holly tree with all the trunks, a kind of shelter from the rain, just a drizzle at the moment, and there are all these nodes that I can use to press into the tension in my back, and also on the ground all these shiny condom wrappers, and then I see the condoms too, in the dirt among the crushed leaves, and as a kid I always liked watching the ways they would change form over time, they would wrinkle and mold into different shapes, and even when they decayed there was a kind of preservation in the way that the ring would stay intact, but these haven't started decaying yet, they look kind of fresh, still a bit shiny from the lube, a hint of shit or dirt and looking closer at the condom wrappers I see LifeStyles, one of them non-latex, one of them lubricated, I see a Trojan, another LifeStyles in a different colored wrapper, bronze instead of gray, and then one that's ultra-thin, a Durex, a Coke can, plus lots of wet tissues and is there all this sex still happening now, a blue medical mask crushed in the dirt by the trees, and one black fingerless glove like for yardwork or biking or just to keep warm, all these remnants of touch.

But I wanted to tell you about leaning against all these nodes to massage my back and then how each trunk is at a different angle so I can push my hips in and release and turn around to the side and lean my shoulders against the nodes too, and press the sore spots in my arms so really this is the massage tree, and if I take off my hat, and feel my head against the bark too, looking up at the white light filtered through the prickly leaves that go up so high, you don't think of a holly tree this way, not usually, or I haven't thought of one in this way for a while, the way that slowly moving my hips back and forth against the tree my shoulders can open up my spine with my head resting and rolling against the tree too and when I pull my head away

I feel a crack in my spine, yes, an adjustment, and then I feel the tension in my calves again so I stand up on one of the lower nodes to stretch.

And then I'm ready to twirl across the park to get back to the cedar grove, yes there are kids screaming in the background but I've decided to ignore them so I can lean into this outstretched trunk that sheltered so many of my first longings, the way the upper branches bounce up and down in the wind but the lower branches are gigantic, and I can still curl up on them, even now, anyone could, they're that big and this was where I first learned to climb, now I see how, all the stability where everything stretches out horizontally the giant arms of the tree opening up to hold you I sit up so I have one leg on each side and my legs barely stretch across, now I'm moving my butt and hips back and forth to unwind the tension in my inner thighs and this was where I learned to masturbate even before I knew what masturbation was, pressing against these trees, now I sit up against the tree and lean back and rest with my feet up above, looking at the way the tree stretches up, you forget about that direction when you're down here with branches so wide and then I roll onto my side, press my feet up against a different part—so I can turn and fall right onto my chest to feel my sternum, maybe too much pressure so I roll over and back, the tension in my calves again, what was I doing with my calves when I was driving, and eventually I kick my legs over and back so I fall across the branch, arms reaching down and out, body rounding over the tree I'm tempted to do a somersault onto the ground but I don't want to hurt myself, just notice breath, right, that's what this is about, and then how the ground is formed by the roots of the trees, the red and brown of the trunks, the needles and small branches piling up on top of one another and I've always thought of these trees as boats, how we're swimming through the air flowing from the ground.

And then I realize I need to piss, so I exit the cedar grove and head toward the bathroom, in the field up ahead there are kids running after one another, I'm not really paying attention to them until one of the boys points at me, and yells COVID. And then he says it again, CO-VID. And they all turn to stare.

Yes I'm not wearing a mask but I'm thirty or forty feet away from these kids and we're in a park where I don't need a mask, do I, I mean I've been so cautious this whole time—I drove cross-country just to make sure I wasn't in contact with anyone, I slept in the car or really I didn't sleep I would just pull over and close my eyes and drift away when I felt like I was going to drive off the road, and then before I drifted too far I would start driving again, it was the delirium that kept me going the windows open wide all that air and those moments between light and dark, dark and light when everything got huge I mean I'd never been up at dawn before except on drugs so this felt like drugs and I tried to keep myself there in the way the landscape would slowly expand, and I was going up, up, up, and away, or right at the moment in the evening when I noticed everything softening I could finally take off the sunglasses and throw them aside and welcome night glorious night before the car lights started up and inside the desperation keeping me going there was some kind of calm even though what if I didn't make it, what if I just fell off the road and no one ever found me what if I ended up in the hospital in who-knows-where but the car stereo thankfully had a CD player so I would blast Green Velvet, Ellen Allien, Carl Cox, Paul Johnson, Claude VonStroke, Chicks on Speed, Josh Wink, Soft Pink Truth, Carl Craig, Richie Hawtin and yes there were my old favorites like Junior, Danny, and even Peter Rauhofer I mean obviously this was drama but mostly I needed the knock-you-down of Frankie Bones, the relentless push and pull the rattle the boom into the tunnel and over the bridge with that distorted vocal in the background becoming part of the beat until just one sample or that laugh track like Josh Wink but someone else I mean Ms. Bones was taking me through the fields of desperation past the factories of devastation and I just kept going, going, going I was yelling yes, Ms. Bones, take me there, Ms. Bones was making the sun rise she was making the sun set she was everything in between even though she was really some straight guy from Brooklyn but maybe I was the straight guy on this trip I pissed in jars I shit behind bushes so I didn't have to go into any of those rest areas, I brought peanut butter and jelly sandwiches or okay I don't eat jelly too much sugar, or peanuts really, so I brought cashew butter on unleavened 100% rye bread, with snow peas for the crunch, and almond butter on kamut bread with radishes and scallions for a change of pace, and so many gallons of water and lemons to keep me hydrated I didn't stop except in the backs of parking lots when I couldn't stay awake or when I needed to stretch I tried to stretch as much as possible and now that I'm in Seattle I don't go inside anywhere except my building so now that I think about it why am I even heading toward this bathroom instead of into the bushes maybe because there aren't many bushes left in the park everything's been trimmed back or maybe because of the parents around and parents don't want their babies to see you shitting, they might call the cops but here I am in the park enjoying this beautiful day and why am I so upset by these obnoxious teenagers telling me I'm COVID, yes it's because I can't help thinking about how these are the kids who use Volunteer Park as their backyard and I was one of these kids when I was their age, and we had that AIDS awareness assembly where I came prepared because I wanted to talk about everyone I knew who had died, all these glorious queens who I missed, but then after that the teachers were worried and all the kids were pointing at me like these kids in the park.

I dream that I'm walking into a public square during a street festival, and there are a bunch of ragged styley weirdos who are excited to see me. Maybe this is what I'm always looking for, a sudden home in someone's eyes and now we're here together. The sky is orange and red and everyone is flailing their arms so I join them. Someone leans her back against mine and we start dancing like that, our bodies moving slowly around, arms up in the air and we're leaning against one another, movement rolling over movement so we can fly. The feeling of her neck against mine, looking up at the sky and everything in my body says yes, even though I know I'll smell like someone else's smoke and liquor and sweat I'm ready to make out as lips roll over neck except then I remember the coronavirus, so I pull myself awake in fear before our lips meet.

I'm a few minutes late to meet Jaysun in the park, and there she is, setting up the blankets. Girl, she says, you brought the sun, thank you for bringing the sun!

It's the least I could do.

Girl, those earrings, you've always been the best at earrings, but those dangly spiral ones are new, aren't they, and those big amber ones, yes, amber, yes, the asymmetrical look is great on you, and where did you get that dress?

I'm not sure, maybe Ragstock?

Ragstock? What—girl, you keep things that long?

Honey, you know I keep everything. You look beautiful too. I love that flower shirt.

Oh, girl, stop it, I'm fat. Don't even try to tell me anything else. The shirt's Todd Oldham. Pants are Prada. Sandals handmade in Italia. Sunglasses by Gucci. Have a seat, I made lunch.

You what?

Girl, I made lunch.

Stop it.

Girl, I made dahl.

You're joking.

No, I'm serious, it's my culture—okay, you want to know how this happened, I know you want to know. Listen, it was all these racist bitches asking me to cook for them, or one bitch in particular, I mean Brad was horrible in almost every way but he actually wasn't racist, he totally fetishized me but it was because I was so skinny. He would kiss me from head to toe, and he would trace my bones with his fingers. I'm serious, he would trace my bones. And you know I got even skinnier when we were twacked out, like you could see the bones in my face, it was scary, and he loved it. Anyway, let's not get stuck there, my point is that after Brad, after the Crystal Lite Diet, when I was actually eating again, and trying to date, or something, I mean what was I thinking trying to date but that's another story, anyway, I met this guy, on our first date he cooked me dinner—something fancy, like a flank steak with risotto, and we didn't even sleep together, and then the second time he had me over again, maybe he made salmon that time, and then the next time he made grilled tuna with noodles and you know that cliché about the fastest way to someone's heart is a good meal, I mean I'm probably disgusting you with all this meat but anyway it was working, and after we slept together he said why don't you cook next time, and I said yes but then I was totally nervous because I'd never cooked anything in my life. Nothing. I mean maybe microwave pizza or Cup-a-Soup or burnt toast, but that was about it. At first I thought I would just buy something at Whole Foods and pretend I'd cooked it, but their food isn't really that good, is it, so then I thought I would make broiled sole but just looking at that slimy fish in my kitchen it was so gross I threw it out. Then I decided to make lasagna, I got this recipe online, and I made it like three times beforehand—the first time it was burned to a crisp, the second time it was too chewy, and the third time it was kind of good, so I figured the fourth time was going to work out, and then I made a really yummy salad, I picked out the best radicchio and endive and frisée so it wouldn't look like I was cheap, and then shredded fennel and beets and a citrus vinaigrette, and I felt really fancy about it, served it with an expensive bottle of red, but I could tell something was wrong as soon as he got to my place, even though I was kind of proud of myself, I was using cloth napkins, I was still living at the Olive Terrace then so who was I kidding, but I was trying, that was the point, I was trying.

But he just kept saying lasagna, huh. And I thought it was pretty good, maybe it wasn't fancy enough but it was good, and I know my lasagna because I grew up in Jersey, right, and there's a lot of lasagna in Jersey. Anyway, we got to the end of the meal and we weren't making out yet like usual so I said is something wrong? And he said no, I just thought you were going to teach me about your culture.

No, he did not say that.

He did, girl, he did. And I just let it slip because the sex was great and then after he cooked dinner the next time, maybe it was rack of lamb, I told him I was going to make Sri Lankan food, and his eyes lit up and honey you know I bought Indian food right down the street and just mixed things up a bit, like I combined the vindaloo with the masala and added extra lemon and threw out the containers, and he was asking me all these questions about my cooking and I was making shit up and he loved it. But I felt so gross. It was worse than when I was turning tricks because at least they knew I wasn't going to cook. Anyway, long story short, that relationship didn't last but then there were all the other tacky bitches who wanted me to teach them about my culture and I knew they didn't mean Jersey so I figured a cooking class at Seattle Central wouldn't hurt anyone, and I did learn how to cook dahl, so that's what I made for you yes you, and don't even worry I know you can't eat ghee or coconut milk so I used olive oil instead, your favorite, and there are no chilies so it isn't too spicy, and I made brown rice for the first time, or actually it's red rice because doesn't that sound better, and I cooked it with vegetable stock to give us more flavor because brown rice can be kind of dull, right, I'm not usually a fan of brown rice but this is for you, girl, and I brought you some bottled water, Voss, because I thought you'd like the glass bottles, and kaffir limes to squeeze on the dahl or wherever you want, oh, and alcohol wipes in case you want to wipe anything off first, don't trust me, girl, just wipe it all off, wipe off those germs, we don't want any germs here. Okay, okay, I'm going to close my eyes while you taste it.

I can't believe you cooked for me.

Just tell me if it's awful, okay, tell me if it's awful.

Honey, it's amazing. But what you said about all those racist assholes.

Girl, let's forget about those racist assholes, I gave up on dating like a decade ago, I just go to the park and get fucked in the bushes.

Oh, that reminds me—did the cruising area move to the other side of the park?

Girl, have you been following me? Yes, I can't remember why, maybe because of the way they changed the lighting over here so it's kind of bright at night, I mean I remember you told me about those trees right over there but now it's over on the other side of the Asian Art Museum.

Are people still having sex in the park now?

Girl, "People Are Still Having Sex," oh my god I remember dancing to that, it was like one of my favorite songs, was that before we met?

Yes, I was still in Seattle then, that was my senior year of high school, but what did they mean when they said "This AIDS thing's not working," wasn't that kind of homophobic?

Oh, I don't know, I think they were just pretending to be straight. Like all these girls in the park, honey, you would not believe the levels they go to, I mean how long have I been in these places—since I was fifteen, right, when I was a street urchin in Times Square, but let's not go back to that, I don't want to get too depressed, I mean I used to be embarrassed but now everyone else is embarrassed, and I'm like girls, pull it together, let's just say hi, we see each other every day. And sometimes I don't even want sex, I just come to the park because I want a hug, and where else am I going to find a hug, especially now. But no one wants a hug, they just want cock or ass, it's like it's not even attached to your body and what if I want someone to compliment me on my Gucci loafers I mean my smile, don't worry, I don't wear Gucci when I'm cruising, it's all about something butch like REI, but can I tell you something? Promise you won't judge me.

Why would I judge you?

Girl, I haven't even told you yet, just promise.

Okay, whatever, just tell me.

Okay, you won't believe this, but the pandemic has turned me into a top. Yes, me, I'm a top now. I mean I should have done this fifteen or twenty years ago before that Brad bitch dumped me, but anyway.

He didn't dump you, he locked you out of the house.

Same thing, girl.

No, it's worse, he cheated on you and then he kicked you out of the house.

Girl, he did kick me out of the house, but he didn't cheat on me. You remember when we first met, right? He was still straight then, but he was obsessed. But it was really sweet, in a way, he just wanted to cuddle in bed and kiss me all over, and then we started jerking off, and then we would suck each other off, but it was sweet, I mean he wasn't sweet in general, but he was sweet to me.

Yeah he definitely wasn't sweet in general.

Anyway, it was the crystal, after the crystal he just wanted to get fucked. And obviously you can't get hard on crystal, so that was out of the question. So I said go ahead and find someone else, I'm not stopping you. And he did. Which was fine. I didn't want to have sex on crystal, not really, drugs were never sexual for me. Definitely not crystal. It's like you're grinding your teeth and you can't stop running around the room, that means it's time to go dancing, right?

I feel the same way. Drugs were never really sexual for me either. I just wanted to be high. I wanted to be way beyond that.

That's why you were always so fun to cuddle with—anyway, Brad started hooking up on Craigslist, and that was that. Then he would come home and fuck me. I guess he got horny again when he was crashing.

I thought you said drugs were never sexual.

Girl, you had sex on drugs.

Well obviously.

See, that's what I mean. Anyway, he didn't cheat on me. It's just that he lied. We weren't using condoms, but we were supposed to with everyone else.

What an asshole. I always hated him.

I know. But you hid it well. You're good at hiding things.

What's that supposed to mean?

I mean you're nice. That's all. What about Marya?

Marya, what do you mean?

You're still in love with her, aren't you.

What, I was never in love with Marya.

Stop. You were in love with her for—when did she dump you?

She did not dump me. We were never going out.

Okay, when did she get that job in Hollywood, and ditch you for her girlfriend?

Like fifteen years ago, but she did not ditch me. We weren't even having sex. We would just go on adventures.

Adventures.

Yes, like she would call me when she was at Meow Mix, or after Meow Mix closed she'd call from whatever bar she went to, and we would go out wheatpasting, or stenciling. It was hot.

Hot. You just said it was hot.

I mean it was fun. She taught me that hating the cops could be more than just hating the cops because they busted your favorite night.

Girl, she's not the only one who hated the cops.

Honey, I know, but I didn't even know what ACAB meant, did you?

I mean you won't believe how many times I've tried to get a cab.

Exactly, I had no clue. The first time she said we need to abolish the police abolish the prisons the whole damn thing has got to go or we'll never get anywhere I just thought she was coked out of her mind I mean she was coked out of her mind but when she said listen, do you really think there are good cops and bad cops, that was all I needed.

But I already knew that.

Honey, I'm not talking about you, I'm talking about me, and you might have known that but did you walk around stenciling Abolish the Police on the sidewalk by the precinct? I thought ATP was about science, and 1312 was just someone's lucky number.

It is my lucky number.

Mine too, but honestly before Marya I had no clue. I mean I had a clue, but I didn't realize it. I would never even have known about *Democracy Now!* without her.

So she's the one we have to thank for Amy Goodman. And Juan. And Nermeen. But do you think Juan had Botox?

Stop. He did not have Botox. It's just the lighting.

I don't know, I think it started before the lighting. But do you remember when they started hiring that makeup artist for Amy? At least the pandemic put an end to that. But do you think she had COVID?

What? She's never out of the office.

But that cough.

No, that started way before the pandemic, she totally has a lung issue, you're right, but she's never mentioned it.

She never mentions anything personal. That's the only problem. I wish she would get more personal. Anyway, don't get me distracted. Back to Marya.

Listen, we were never girlfriends, we didn't even fuck.

Girl, okay, don't look, but there's someone over there in a spacesuit telling people to KEEP IT MOVING, I'm serious, what are we going to do.

Should we just pretend we don't notice?

Look, people are leaving. There's not even anyone here. There's plenty of room for social distancing. What's going on. I'm so angry. Okay, let's just pretend we're packing up, so she doesn't come over here. I can't handle this. I might start screaming. Let's just fold up the blankets, okay, okay, she went over there. Do you think we should move?

I don't know. This is my favorite place to sit in the sun.

But I don't want that girl in the spacesuit to come back. I might just start going off on her, and that would not be cute. Did you really like the food?

Honey, I love it. I totally love it. And I love you.

I made extra. You want the rest? You can totally have the rest.

Yes, please, I get so bored of my own cooking.

Okay, let's just put everything in the car, and then walk around. It's such a nice day. It's so nice to be out in the sun.

I know.

Oh my god, she's coming back. Yes, we're keeping it moving, you fucking bitch, we're keeping it moving, stop following us. Sorry, girl, I'm getting carried away. It's my meds.

What are you taking?

Girl, you don't even want to know. Dexedrine.

What, they still prescribe that?

Yes, I was having trouble focusing at work, I mean who isn't having trouble when you're staring at a computer screen all day long in your apartment, after a few glasses of wine things start to blur but anyway they asked if I'd ever been diagnosed with ADHD, and I said yes I took Ritalin as a kid, because I couldn't focus at school. But I couldn't focus at school because my mother kept hitting me over the head. That's what I should have told those bitches when they asked about my culture. That's my culture. My father beating up my mother. My mother beating up the kids. We were American. We did not eat Indian food, or Sri Lankan food, that was way beneath my mother. She cooked spaghetti and meatballs. Meatloaf. Tuna casserole. Porkchops. American. My father beat her up, and then she beat my brother, she beat my sister, she beat me. My father would just laugh. My brother got it the worst, because he was the oldest, so guess what? He became a cop. Just like my father. And then my sister, she joined ROTC. Anyway, my mother would just slam me over the head anytime I was doing something wrong, like forgetting to tie my shoes. Or getting food on my shirt. She wouldn't even say anything. She would just slam me in the head. So I was dizzy. I was dizzy all the time. I couldn't focus at school, I just wanted to get up and run around. And they gave me Ritalin, so I could focus. After that I would watch the second hand on the clock at school and I could count how many times it was going around. I would count the drops of sweat that were dripping down my forehead. I would listen to the air conditioning. I would make this tapping sound with my tongue that no one else could hear, just so I could stay still. I can't say that made me a drug addict for life, but anyway, I told the doctor I cannot do Ritalin because I did that as a kid, and he said oh, you were diagnosed with ADD as a kid, and I didn't tell him about my mother slamming me in the head every day, so when he suggested Dexedrine I almost lost it, I mean wasn't that what Andy was doing at the Factory.

Something like that.

Don't worry, it's not like speed, I mean it is speed but it's not like crystal, because I'm fat. You can't get fat on crystal. But there was something I wanted to ask you about. Oh, Marya.

Honey, we don't even talk anymore. Her girlfriend was too jealous. They moved to LA and got married. I haven't heard from her in at least five years. She even unfriended me on Facebook.

See, you should have broken them up.

Stop.

Anyway, I was going to tell you how the pandemic made me into a top—I need touch, I need some kind of touch, or I'm going to go crazy. And when the pandemic started I thought maybe I would figure something else out, something besides the park, I even reactivated Grindr just to see, and I posted what I actually wanted, which was someone to hug, and no one even responded. No one. So I went back to the park. I figured it would be safer to top now, during the pandemic, because I can keep my mask on, right?

I mean I guess.

Don't guess, it's true. That's why we're here, because it's safer. Besides, no one wants my ass anymore because I'm fat. But when they see a hard dick they just want that load up their ass.

What about condoms?

Girl, no one uses condoms anymore.

Someone uses condoms, because I saw all these condoms under the tree.

Okay, someone uses condoms, but no one who has sex with me. I'm undetectable, what's the difference. No one cares anyway. They just want that load. You said you weren't going to judge me.

I'm not judging you, I'm just saying I saw condoms in the park.

Okay, you're right, some people use condoms, I'm being a bitch, anyway, my life is depressing. I work for the Evil Empire, I get smashed, and then I go to the park. So I got a prescription for Viagra, I take it before I go to the park and when it kicks in it's like my dick isn't part of my body. And I don't even like fucking. But here's the thing. Once my dick is in some guy's ass, I can rub his chest, I can hug him so tight, I can kiss his neck, okay, sometimes I take off my mask, but not usually, no one wants kissing anyway, they just want that dick and I can stay hard forever because of the Viagra and I don't want to come anyway, all I want is a hug, and I'm not going to get it any other way.

These are the days of crying for no apparent reason. I mean we all know the reason. Are we all crying?

Walking down the busiest streets on Capitol Hill, some of the busiest streets in the city, and they're almost totally abandoned. I feel like I'm lost on a movie set that isn't finished yet.

But can anything compare to this new building, S-O-L-I-S, which is obviously pronounced Soulless, I mean they're just asking for it. It's not open yet, but there's an ominous white gate maybe two stories high that I guess is supposed to be decorative, abstract art for the penal colony, with a banner advertising ULTRA SUSTAINABLE LUXURY APARTMENTS.

On the banner there's a woman in a yellow dress playing with beads and looking to the distance in a drugged-out stupor, and yes her harlequin makeup turns me on, yes I would cover half my face with that blue eyeshadow if she let me borrow it, and no I'm not against that yellow dress, it's totally something I would have worn in my high school Holly Hobbie phase, but how does this drugged-out model relate to the whitest of white buildings. Maybe she's Chloe?

No, Chloe is a dog, I saw a dog on the banner for the building called Chloe. Yes, a dog.

But at Soulless it says OUR AIR IS BETTER.

Yes it's 24/7 FILTERED AIR, does that mean your windows don't open, and you're locked inside the white gate forever? No, I don't want to tell you about Beryl, which gives mint green a bad name, or all the buildings with fake balconies attached to the side so you don't fall out when you open your oversized windows, or the Electric Sunset, with the prison yard aesthetic and an enormous black gate, although at least they have that lightning bolt, I just want to tell you that as I'm fleeing across the astroturf of the playfield and past the wall of new buildings next to Cal Anderson, the sun is starting to set, and so everything is changing.

My favorite moment of the day, yes, every day, is the eight o'clock noisemaking celebration—in New York it was at seven so at first I didn't think it was going on here but I figured it out fast enough. So now I always make sure I'm home at eight so I can lean out the window and scream for essential workers with my neighbors, then blow my whistle three times, and then scream again, this time for all of us, and there's always that awkward moment right before eight when you wonder who's going to make noise first, since mostly we can't see one another to coordinate and maybe no one wants to be first but also we don't want to miss it, do we, and tonight there's this huge crescendo of pots and pans and toy whistles and hooting and laughter, yes, I think I hear laughter, and after I'm done screaming some girl yells THAT'S NOT HOW YOU DO IT, BABY.

    I can't see her, so I don't know if she's talking to me, but I yell TELL ME HOW TO DO IT, BABY.

    She screams.
    I scream.
    She screams.
    I scream.
    She screams.
    Who says you can't have sex without touch?
    But then there's the next day in the park, and I can't help watching this straight couple blocking the sidewalk every twenty feet or so when they stop to make out. He lifts her in the air, all her blond hair blowing in the wind, she giggles and their lips meet, this really is my favorite horror movie.

    There should be a rule that if your perfume smells stronger than the park, you need to go home and take a shower. Or three showers. These are the people who really should KEEP IT MOVING.

    Then there are the ones who snap photos of you while simultaneously refusing to acknowledge your existence. But there's an intellectual conversation about polyamory over by the duck pond:

    "There was this really famous duck that had two long-term partners, and he lived for a really long time."

    "Really?? Would you do that?"
    "NOOOOOO!!"
    I haven't told my mothers I'm here yet. I think I'm nervous because how do I say hi without hugging them. Maybe that feels too sad. So I just keep walking by, and looking at the house.

There's the birch tree that leans away from the house, and the one that leans toward it. There's the way the ivy covers the ground on both sides of the staircase, it completely covers the ground so there's no grass at all and it's always been that way, the cherry tree on the right and the rhododendron and camelia bushes by the front porch. There's one of those IN THIS HOUSE, WE BELIEVE lawn signs coming out of the ivy, and I don't know what I think about those signs exactly, everyone has them here, but what do they really mean except we believe in this lawn sign.

In the park there's this queen riding her bike in circles while blasting a Beethoven concerto or something, and I don't generally like classical music but I love this. Then there's a crow holding up a shiny piece of foil to the ducks on the hill overlooking the reservoir, but the ducks are not interested. A father is teaching his son how to fly a drone, while the mother looks on and smiles. For some reason this makes me miss my mothers. I'm so glad they taught me deep breathing instead of teaching me how to fly a drone.

So I'm walking back toward the house, and just as I'm about to dodge this woman taking up the whole sidewalk with a baby carriage, she pulls aside and says I'm sorry, no one knows how to walk anymore. And we smile at one another, it's a good moment.

Then I look up and my mothers are on the balcony. No, it's Eileen, and someone else. They're both wearing masks. Eileen, I say, and she looks down. Oh my God, she says, am I seeing things?

Jenny, she says to her friend, is that my daughter Terry?

And Jenny says I haven't seen Terry since she was in high school, when was that?

And I say almost thirty years ago. And Eileen says thirty years, has it really been that long?

Terry, she says, oh my God. Pau-la, she yells, Pau-la. And Paula comes out on the balcony wearing a mask and looks down. Terry, she says, how the hell did you get there? And then she looks over at Eileen, and says what the hell are we doing up here? And Eileen says I'm kind of in disbelief—Terry, is that really you? And Paula says of course it's her, don't you recognize your own daughter, and she says Terry, we'll be right down.

When the door opens, Eileen comes running down the stairs first, but then she stops. Honey, do you have a mask, she says, we have N95s.

I say I have plenty of masks, it's just that I'm outside. And Paula says of course, it's good to get fresh air. And their friend says well I think I'll be on my way—Terry, it's so nice to see you after all these years, you look so striking. I hope to see you again while you're in town. And Paula says you remember Jenny, right?

And even though I don't remember Jenny, I nod my head, and Jenny says Paula, Eileen, it's been such a pleasure to reconnect. We should do this again sometime soon. And she heads over to her car.

Jenny drives off, and it's kind of surreal with my mothers in their duck masks, eyes so big and I know we're all thinking about the same thing, so I say I guess we shouldn't hug, just to be safe, right? But how about if we do what I do with Jaysun, and we open our arms really big, and then hug ourselves like we're hugging one another.

And Paula says that sounds wonderful, I suppose we can take off these masks—what do you think, Eileen. And Eileen says yes, we are outside. And then we give each other the air hug, it's fun to do it with three people, looking back and forth. But after that we just stand there and stare at one another like we don't know what to do. Or maybe we don't know what to feel? Or we don't know how to feel what we need to feel. With the distance.

I'm looking at Paula's blow-dried hair dyed her natural color and then subtly tinted a few shades lighter, and those teardrop pearl earrings, and is that really a gray-and-mauve pinstriped power suit? Her makeup is flawless as always but it's so subtle. Eileen's the quirkier one now, wearing a green embroidered Mexican dress and beaded earrings, green eyeglasses with a hint of silver that plays off her big gray curls. She's gained weight, and Paula's gotten skinnier.

What a marvelous day, Paula says, and Eileen says oh it's just wonderful. It's a terrible year, but the weather has been delightful. Terry, do you want to come in back, we have a lovely setup now.

We're walking back, and Eileen turns around, and says oh, honey, I just don't want to take my eyes off you. And suddenly she looks so fragile. I want to hug her but I can't, I know I can't, and I feel like I'm going to cry, are we all going to cry, shouldn't we be crying.

Now there's a metal canopy with a glass roof that extends from the house, slate tiles on the ground and all these comfortable outdoor sofas and a dining table with bottled water in the center, heat lamps on the sides and so many lush potted plants.

Help yourself to water, Paula says, we have plenty of water out here. And hand sanitizer. Are you hungry, Eileen says, should I get you something to eat?

I say I'm okay at the moment, I have nuts in my pocket, and Eileen says I just don't want to take my eyes off you. I know I said that already, but Paula, can you believe this, what a surprise.

And Paula says how long will you be in town?

And I say well, I guess I bought a place.

And Eileen says oh that's wonderful—I always love visiting your apartment, and I know it's rent-controlled, but a sixth-floor walk-up does get to be a little much after a while. Is your new place in the East Village?

No, I say, it's at Harvard and Harrison.

Harvard and Harrison, Eileen says, what neighborhood is that?

And Paula says Eileen, Harvard and Harrison, by the Broadway Market.

And Eileen says what, you bought a place in Seattle?

And I nod my head.

And Eileen says well I'll be damned. You're living here with us again. In the neighborhood.

And Paula says are you here, are you here . . .

And I say I guess I'm here . . . I mean unless something happens.

And Eileen says this might be the best surprise of my life. And then we just sit there like that, looking at one another again.

And Paula says well you must have brought the good weather.

And Eileen says sorry we've been out of touch, there's a lot that's been going on, for all of us, I'm sure, and I'm so relieved we have plenty of time to catch up. Paula, do you want to tell her?

And Paula says well a few months ago, we got a call, was it a few months ago?

And Eileen says maybe a month and a half, it's hard to tell these days. I answered the phone, and some old lady with a cranky voice says Paula—you might say that I'm an old lady now too, but, you know, someone, older. And I said who is this? And she said it's Norma Jodorofsy. I'm calling to speak to my daughter. Your daughter, I said. My daughter, she said. And Terry, as you know, Paula hadn't spoken to her mother in . . . How long, Paula.

Sixty years.

And Eileen says so I was dumbfounded. I said to Paula, there's someone on the phone that says she's your mother. And Paula looked—well, Paula, I'll let you tell this part of the story.

I was shocked, Paula says, let's put it that way, I was shocked.

And I say how did she get your number?

And Paula says 411? How many Paula Jodorofsys can there be in Seattle? But get this, as soon as I pick up the phone, she says Paula? And I didn't even recognize the voice, but I said Mom? I don't know why I said that, I just did. And she said Paula, they're trying to kill me. And I said who's trying to kill you? And she said you've got to get me out of here, they've locked me in a room and they're trying to kill me.

So it turns out she was in a home in Salem, Eileen says—memory care, a small place with just four residents.

Not in Salem, Paula says, but near Salem. Close to where I grew up. So I called my brother.

Your brother, I say—do you talk to your brother?

Once in a while, Paula says. Once in a while, he calls to ask for help. The last time was—when was that, Eileen?

2004.

His wife had cancer, Paula says. The treatment she needed wasn't covered. So he either had to mortgage the house, or . . .

Or ask Paula for money, Eileen says, so you can bet which option he chose.

And Paula says it was the right thing to do, I did it because it was the right thing to do.

And Eileen says oh I know, I'm just . . .

And Paula says you're right, he would never do the same thing for me. Never in a million years. But where were we? Long story short, my brother tells me that my mother is in a home where everyone is sick with COVID. All the other patients except her. So they locked her in her room. That part was true. She had late-stage dementia, but that part was true. I don't know how she was even getting her meals. Oh, Eileen, what happened next?

Eileen says we got her out, that's the important part.

And Paula says we got her out because everyone else died, or they had to be moved, I'm not sure, but she was the only one left, they had to close the facility.

And I say you went down to Salem?

And Eileen says yes, it was awful. It was like the dark ages. We stayed at a hotel where they gave us twin beds.

It was hardly a hotel, Paula says.

A motel, Eileen says, we went to our room and there were two twin beds.

On opposite sides of the room, Paula says.

Yes, Eileen says, with this bulky furniture between them. So we went down to the receptionist and said there's been a misunderstanding, we would like a queen or king, and they looked at us like we were robbing a bank.

If we wanted to rob a bank, we wouldn't have done it there, Paula says.

You're absolutely right about that, Eileen says. Can you imagine, if we were husband and wife? But should we spare all the gory details?

Okay, Paula says, there were legal issues. My brother was the one with power of attorney. But long story short, my mother came to live with us.

She came here, I say.

Yes, in this very house, Eileen says. Downstairs. You know it's practically a separate apartment already, she didn't need to come upstairs, so we could all be safe. We arranged twenty-four-hour care. Her nurse, Mariana, has been an angel. An absolute angel. Of course we paid her well.

So she's still here, I say.

Mariana is still here, Paula says. We're letting her stay as long as she needs. Eileen is right, she was an angel. Of course we couldn't have done it without her.

And Eileen says it all worked out pretty well, considering.

Considering it was a nightmare, Paula says.

And it's not over yet, Eileen says. We're going down to Oregon.

For the funeral, Paula says.

It's on Friday, Eileen says, do you want to come? I'm kidding, we would never subject you to that. I know I shouldn't joke about things like this.

And Paula says no, it helps, it helps to joke about things like this—it was a shock. When she called me on the phone that day, a total shock. We hadn't talked in sixty years. Sixty years. Since I was sixteen years old and I got the hell out of there. Sixty years. My whole life. When I first saw her, I didn't even recognize her.

Through the window, Eileen says, how would you recognize anyone.

That's right, Paula says, in Oregon we could only see her through the window. We left before she was released. We didn't know if it was going to happen.

But we arranged transportation, Eileen says.

So she came up here, Paula says, and Mariana opens up the door of the van, and this tiny old lady steps out.

No, she didn't step out, Eileen says, not on her own.

That's right, Paula says, Mariana was helping her to walk. But I came down the stairs, and this lady, my mother, this little old lady looks up at me and says Paula? And I said Norma? And I walked toward her, and she grabbed me in a hug. A hug. My mother. She was so tiny. All skin and bones. Her head barely went up to my breasts, and as you know I'm only 5' 5". It was like she was the child, and I was the mother. I knew I shouldn't be hugging her, not now, with all the risks, but we just stood there like that, mother and child, child and mother, and I felt all this moisture on my face, under the mask, before I realized I was crying, and my mother too, was she crying? We just stood there like that, mother and daughter, holding one another, it was so, I don't know how to say it, but it was, after all these years, there was something there.

Jaysun: Welcome, kids, to a special episode of the Club Kid Diaspora Helpline. Today we are crossing nine time zones, and who may I say is joining us?

TERRY: It's just me right now, I think.

JAYSUN: Girl, I can almost see you from here.

CLEO: Bienvenue, ladies.

JAYSUN: Oh, bienvenue! Bisous. Formidable. That's about all I can do.

MIELLE: Can everyone hear me?

JAYSUN: Loud and clear, honey, loud and clear. You're the driver, baby, we're all here for you, the helpline is yours, give us your damage.

MIELLE: Can I just hear everyone's voices first, I'm nervous.

TERRY: Mielle, I love you!

CLEO: We're here for you.

JAYSUN: Drinking a cocktail in your honor!

MIELLE: Okay, well, I don't want to take up too much space . . .

JAYSUN: Honey, take up all the space you want, the space is yours, take it to the runway.

MIELLE: Okay, well, it's about Tara. I just . . . Let me back up a bit. The pandemic. I know we're all feeling lonely, are we all feeling lonely?

CLEO: Lonely would be an understatement.

TERRY: Of course, honey, we're all feeling lonely.

JAYSUN: Speak for yourselves, bitches, I just mix myself a cosmo and I'm feeling flawless.

CLEO: And I'm sipping a glass of ouzo.

JAYSUN: So European!

TERRY: I'm toasting with a glass of filtered water, so don't feel alone, Mielle.

MIELLE: Okay, I'm drinking mint tea. So I just want to say, I just want to say, I've never talked about this before, so I'm nervous, but the pandemic, I feel really lucky to be here in Santa Fe, in my own casita, you know how the owner was going to shut everything down but now there's so much demand with all the people fleeing the big cities so she switched to monthly rentals instead of nightly because people will pay just as much, and everyone has a separate casita here so I think it's safe, I'm not nervous about that, I feel really lucky that I still have my job, I just make breakfasts and leave them outside people's doors instead of in the main house, which is still closed for safety, and then I bring fresh sheets and toiletries and do errands, that kind of thing. Oh, and I'm sewing masks now too, on the side, and they're selling really well, if anyone needs masks I can send you some. But that's not what I want to talk about, it's Tara. You know, when she, when she . . . Terry, do you remember?

TERRY: I remember.

MIELLE: So I found her . . . Let me back up. You know how we grew up together, we were sisters, but not really sisters, because I was adopted, and we escaped together, and we became twins, right, you all know this, we were inseparable, we were TaraMielle, right, we were just one being in the world.

CLEO: Of course we remember, that's how we met you, you were so fierce with that twins look.

JAYSUN: Say that again, girl. I love it when my French girlfriend says fierce.

CLEO: Fieeeeeerce.

TERRY: We all remember, Mielle, and we love you just as much now.

MIELLE: Thank you for saying that, Terry, you know I have all this time alone now, the last few months, here in the desert, and this place is magical, it's healed me in so many ways, just getting up and looking at the sky, even that, just the sky, but something about the last few months and the fear . . . In Santa Fe we have so much space for social distancing but some people care and some people don't and there's this whole notion of freedom that can be so healing but also toxic and I guess I've just been thinking about all of that, and remembering, I guess I just want to say, maybe you didn't know this, but Tara was really controlling. TaraMielle was really her, it was her idea and I was there, I was with her, but it was her—she decided on the outfits, the makeup, the shoes we'd wear so it looked like we were the exact same height, even the drugs we took, all of it, it was all her, and I loved it because she gave me a container, we were in that container together and we fit, we fit together and it helped me, it helped me to know that I was always a part of something, someone, we were in this symbiotic relationship, and it was sweet too, the way she would hold me I always felt held but you know, when she, when I found her, when I found her in our apartment, let me back up a bit and tell you she was always threatening to kill herself. Whenever we had a fight about anything. Anything. Like that night, was it even night, I can't remember, I just remember that I told her I needed space, that I was going on a walk, and she told me that when I got back she wouldn't be there, but I didn't realize, I didn't realize, I didn't realize what she meant.

TERRY: Mielle, it wasn't your fault.

MIELLE: I know, I know it wasn't my fault, but there's knowing and there's feeling and I guess what I've been feeling, I've been feeling so much guilt, it's been twenty-something years, and I thought I was over it, I thought I'd healed, but suddenly I feel like, I feel like it was my fault again.

JAYSUN: Girl, I just wish I could give you a hug.

MIELLE: I think that's what it is, I'm so used to being physical with everyone, really touchy, and now, and now there's nothing. I feel so lost. I feel so, so, so lost.

JAYSUN: Let it out, girl, just let it out, you can cry with us, it's okay.

MIELLE: Thank you, I've been crying a lot. A lot. I don't know what else to say, I don't want to take up too much space, it feels good to talk about it, I guess, I guess I just wanted to say that I've thought about, I mean I'm not going to do it but I've thought about, I don't think I'd ever thought about it before, but I've thought about . . .

CLEO: Trust me, I understand. The lockdown in Paris has been so intense, it's like we can't even leave our apartments. So intense. And I'm a foreigner here. It really makes me feel like a foreigner again. There are some days . . .

JAYSUN: Girls, we are not going to make any suicide pacts on this hotline, okay?

TERRY: It's okay to talk about it. We're here for you.

JAYSUN: Okay, this is getting intense, I'm going to pour myself another cocktail. Does anyone else need anything?

CLEO: A joint would be nice. Sorry. I know the rest of you don't do drugs.
MIELLE: I did go on that ayahuasca retreat.
CLEO: Ooh girl don't scare me. You know I can't handle being nauseous. I just want to say that you're not alone, Mielle, I've been working from home, but what is home, I have no idea. People here tell me I look like Josephine Baker, and I don't have a problem with that, sure we both have spit curls but other than that I'm not sure I see the similarity but when they say that, they're telling me I belong, because here was this Black woman from the States who became French, she was part of the Resistance during World War II, there's a square named after her, so when people say I look like her they're inviting me in, it's not like when they say RuPaul, or Michael, Michael Jackson, the French love Michael Jackson even more than Americans but listen, I'll stick with Josephine Baker, okay, but where was I going with this.
JAYSUN: Girl, you are taking us on a tour!
CLEO: Loneliness, that's what I meant to say. Who the hell would I be if I wasn't working for Dior? No one.
JAYSUN: That's not true, you were already a star.
CLEO: I was not a star. I made neon.
JAYSUN: Girl, that neon made you rich. That neon got you the job at Dior and that got you out of the country. You still light up my life.
CLEO: I guess that's it. I don't want to sound dramatic, but sometimes I just feel like the lights have gone out, and who am I kidding, I'm fifty-three years old now and trannies do not age well.
JAYSUN: Honey, you don't look a day over thirty.
MIELLE: We're all old now, I'm turning fifty-one this year.
CLEO: I get stuck too, I get stuck thinking about the past.
JAYSUN: Well let's not go there.
CLEO: Mielle, you've been thinking about Tara, and I've been thinking about Sid.
JAYSUN: Oh no.
TERRY: Sid brought us together, didn't she?
MIELLE: I still miss Sid.
JAYSUN: We all do, that's obvious, but let's not get stuck there.

CLEO: What are you afraid of, that I'm going to ask how she died?

JAYSUN: She died of AIDS, Cleo, she died of AIDS.

CLEO: Who appointed you the spokesperson?

JAYSUN: Girl, I think you need to lay off that ouzo, it's not making you nice.

CLEO: I want to know how Sid died. Terry?

TERRY: She didn't tell you?

CLEO: She told me she was going to go when she was ready. Was she ready?

JAYSUN: Cleo, what is this. Sid's dead, she's been dead for twenty-five years.

CLEO: Mielle brought up Tara, and she's been dead for almost as long. Can't I talk about what I want to talk about?

JAYSUN: Go ahead, Cleo, what do you want to say? That you're still upset about those ashes?

CLEO: Well?

JAYSUN: I'm sick of hearing about it. You're working my last nerve.

CLEO: Well. Does anyone else want to hear what I have to say?

JAYSUN: Cleo, I can't believe you're doing this again—I'm sick of hearing it. Sick sick sick. She died on her own terms. Her own terms. That's what she wanted. You've been such a bitch about this for twenty-five years, I'm just sick of it. I'm over it.

CLEO: I'm not accusing anyone of anything. I'm just saying that if Sid stayed alive a little longer . . .

JAYSUN: Then what? Sid did not want to be alive any longer. She was done. She told you that. She was done. Stop blaming Terry. I don't want to hear about this anymore, that's all there is to it, I'm done.

Sid hated birthdays, absolutely hated them, and holidays, anything that she was supposed to think was special she was against, and I loved that about her, I loved it so much that I guess I started feeling the same way. And Jaysun stopped celebrating her birthday when she turned forty because she said she couldn't just keep turning twenty-nine, could she. No one even knows it's my birthday anymore, it's just my mothers who call unless I accidentally mention it to someone. Sometimes Mielle will surprise me and remember, but usually a week or two later. But this year my mothers said can't we do something for you, just a little something, how about if we cook dinner?

So I get there and everything's already set up outside—the pomegranate tempeh, cauliflower and baked yams with tahini dressing in a rice casserole, they even made a pressed salad out of shredded beets and daikon radish with shiso leaves.

Oh, and in case you need to use the bathroom, Paula says, wait until you see this. And she hands me the garage remote.

Is this like a magic trick, I say.

Try it, Eileen says, I think you'll be pleasantly surprised.

So I go over to the garage, and I press the remote, and it's like a greenhouse in there, all the walls totally covered in plants, you can't even see where one plant begins and the other ends, everything looks so healthy and lush. There's a jacuzzi, a sauna, a glass shower, and a little room in the back with a toilet and sink and an antique mirror.

What do you think, Paula says. It's our little retreat.

I can't believe it, I say.

That key is yours, Eileen says, use it whenever you need to. Oh, and see that roof, if you just use the switch in the back, it opens up. Don't worry about the rain, there are drains in the floor, so if you want to see the stars sometime.

Paula says we came up with the idea when we were on vacation in Costa Rica, we stayed at this world-class resort.

Eileen says they had everything. Everything.

So it's our little Costa Rica, Paula says. We even ordered Costa Rican tiles for the floor, see how the leaves in the tiles match the plants?

They're concrete, Eileen says, so they last forever. It's our oasis. And now, let's eat.

So then we're all eating and smiling, eating and smiling, and Eileen says oh, let's not forget the cake, we made a cake for the birthday girl.

And Paula says don't worry, we know you don't eat sugar or gluten, so it's just cornbread really, no sweeteners or yeast just soymilk and kernels of corn cooked inside, should we bring it out?

Sure, I say, so they both go inside, and I'm looking at all the flowering plants they have out here, and thinking about how food is always better when other people cook for you, as long as they know what to cook, and then my mothers bring out this heart-shaped cornbread with a heart-shaped candle that says forty-seven, where'd you get that candle?

And Eileen says somewhere online, Paula?

And Paula says everything is just somewhere online now, isn't it? Don't worry, it wasn't Amazon.

Okay, make a wish, Eileen says.

So I close my eyes, and of course I wish for an end to the coronavirus, can we end it all now, just with this wish, so we can hug? And then I blow out the candle, and when I taste the cornbread I can't believe how chewy it is, still warm from the oven, this is the best birthday ever.

Then Eileen says Terry, there's something I've been meaning to ask you—who do you think Joe Biden should choose as his running mate?

And I say I don't want to think about that.

But if you had to choose, Paula says, who would it be.

And I say how about Margaret Thatcher.

She's taken, Eileen says. Thank Goddess.

Who's your second choice, Paula says.

Melania Trump, I say, and Eileen almost spits out her food. That would ruffle some feathers, she says. But I shouldn't have brought up politics, not on your birthday.

But then why did she, that's what I'm thinking when I'm walking home, and I'm totally losing it, I mean we're supposed to choose between two rapists, we're supposed to believe in someone who already says he'll veto Medicare-for-All, he says he'll invoke the Defense Production Act to make personal protective equipment but what about using it to move the White House to the bottom of the ocean, that would save lives, and what about Laura Bush as a running mate, she's got experience, maybe they can take some snorkeling lessons together and hang out with the sea creatures and my new health insurance that costs $650 a month wants to give me a step-by-step tutorial on the new payment system but I don't want a payment system I want universal healthcare so everyone can stay alive, not just me, everyone, no one should be dying of COVID-19 in slaughterhouses I mean isn't it obvious that now is the time to shut the whole industry down permanently and get people better jobs that don't involve killing killing killing it's all about killing in the slaughterhouses called assisted living where you have to pay thousands of dollars a month for your own death, people are still dying there, they're still dying, there are thousands and thousands of workers who are trapped on cruise ships, some of them have been trapped for months without pay, without pay, but everyone just wants to talk about who Joe Biden is going to choose for his running mate, so they can go on a cruise together in Costa Rica and pick out cement tiles, and why am I walking down 12th, this sidewalk is so tiny I'm practically falling into the street, they could definitely use new cement tiles here.

So then I turn down Mercer, this is better, there's grass on the side, I can lean against this hedge. I think about calling Jaysun, but she'll just tell me everything would be better if Hillary were president, and then we'll get stuck in some conversation about Hillary Hillary go Hillary with her pantsuit coup in Honduras and that's so close to Costa Rica, maybe she could help us pick out cement tiles, I'm with Her—Jaysun will say why didn't more people vote for Hillary but she won the fucking election by three million votes, it's just that we don't have direct elections and this happens every four years but everyone just wants to tell you that if you don't vote for Hillary or Joe or whatever other monster then you're the problem, even though the problem is that we only have these monsters, and I'm just so sick of monsters, wasn't Hillary supposed to get us universal healthcare when her husband was president, and everyone says she didn't win because she was a woman, but she won, she won the fucking election, if you want to change something then get rid of the Electoral College and I'm walking by the boarded-up Wells Fargo and all I can think about is pulling off that plywood and smashing all the windows except I'm sure that would hurt my body and my body already hurts enough.

But now it's almost 8:00 p.m. and I'm back in my apartment and yes, I'm screaming until my voice is sore, I'm blowing my whistle, and then I'm screaming again, but it's over so fast. So fast. And I'm still angry, I'm angry and frantic and I can't believe my mothers asked me that question, I mean do we really need more rapists? And people who support rapists. That's what I should have said, but it was such a nice dinner, I didn't want to ruin dinner.

And then I'm thinking about Marya again, maybe Jaysun's right that I was in love with her, of course you don't have to have sex with someone to be in love, maybe I was always kind of waiting for her to call, and yes I did feel so lost when she unfriended me on Facebook because her girlfriend was jealous but jealous of what, we weren't even on the same coast anymore, at least after that I didn't have to look at photos of her wedding by the beach but I did, honey, I did, jealousy can be so exhausting but I guess I'm thinking about Marya because she'd understand everything I'm feeling now, all of it, we could go out and smash windows, she could show me how, and we could walk through the dark streets together, I miss those walks.

I guess I still have her number—it's a 917 number, no one gets rid of a 917 number. So I call her.

And she answers.

Marya, I say, and she says who's this?

Terry, I say. And she says Terry, it's so great to hear from you, is this your new number?

Yes, I say, and she says I can't talk now, Christina . . .

And I say that's okay, I just wanted to call, just in case.

And she says I'll call you back, I'll call you sometime, I'd love to catch up.

And I think of saying I love you, the way I say it to Jaysun or Mielle or my mothers or anyone I love, really, but then I think that'll just scare her so I say have a great night, and then I hang up, and I feel worse, because I know she's not going to call me back. To catch up. She'll probably just block my number.

The sun is down, and it's time for another walk, yes, a walk to the park, so I grab my purple coat, the one Sid gave me so many years ago, maybe it's too warm out for that coat but I don't care, I want something soft. No, wait, I should save that coat for the fall when I'll need it, and I haven't worn the plaid one yet, I just love how it's shaped like a motorcycle jacket but made of wool, and then I can wear those magenta and yellow plaid pants, and the clear plastic belt, all the contrasting plaids and the purple shirt with the big collar and maybe I should add some drama to my makeup, yes, silver eyeshadow spreading down from the blue and green, purple eyeliner, perfect, oh, and then I'll twist my hair around in the center so you can see the shaved parts underneath and yes, I even have a plaid hairclip, I don't know why I get dressed up just to walk to the park at night, but why not.

Yes, the walk clears my head, and when I get to the park it's dark but the sky is still a bright blue and everything isn't quite in silhouette yet. There's that tree that smells like bubble gum, I can't figure out which one it is and there are a lot of people out, actually, I guess because it was such a warm day. "If I was a duck," someone is saying, but I can't hear the rest.

There's a little party in the grass by the Asian Art Museum, this group of dykes, and oh there's one of those big puffy birthday balloons with your age, so someone has the same birthday as me, she's thirty-six, and these dykes look kind of interesting, one of them is staring at me and then they all turn to look so I smile and wave and I'm walking toward them but then they all turn away, just like that, so I turn around and pretend to look at the Space Needle as the blue of the sky gets darker and the lights around the reservoir start to reflect in the water, then I'm walking to the cedar grove and someone drives up in a red Mercedes convertible, I'm always shocked when I see a convertible in Seattle I mean could anything be tackier. Where do you park it for the ten months of the year when you can't possibly use it? So I'm watching to see what kind of mess gets out, baseball cap and a hoodie, black jeans, hiking shoes, nothing stands out until this girl starts to walk and I realize it's Jaysun.

Jaysun, I'm yelling, Jaysun, and she turns around and says oh my God what are you doing here, and I say what are you doing here, and she says you know what I'm doing here, and I say honey, I can't believe you have a convertible, and she says girl you know I'm the tackiest bitch in the Emerald City and I do have two parking spaces and oh my God, my next convertible should be emerald green, that would be so hideous, wouldn't it, but girl, speaking of emeralds, you look so so so good, let's do our fake hug right now, okay, yes, yes, save me from my degradation, you're the hottest piece I've seen in this park in years, how are you, girl, how are you?

And I say I'm better now, honey, definitely better now. And she says oh my God, have you seen it, have you seen it? And I say seen what? And she says my new jerk-off video, it's the best thing ever, wait, where's my phone, where's my phone, oh right, in my glove compartment, shh, I'll be right back.

Jaysun comes back, and she's holding up her phone, and there's someone throwing a shopping cart into a huge fire, where is this?

And Jaysun says Minneapolis, and then I hear the protestors yelling George Floyd, and Black Lives Matter, and Jaysun says isn't it the best, I could watch this over and over, I just hope my father, wherever he is, I hope he's watching this, I hope that piece of shit is watching this, I just wish he was in that station while it was burning down, I know he's in Jersey but that would be a fabulous early birthday gift, wouldn't it?

It is my birthday, I say, and Jaysun says are you serious? No fucking way. Well happy fucking birthday, girl, talk about the best birthday gift ever, happy fucking birthday.

It's dark on Pine except for the clouds of tear gas illuminated by streetlights, people are running and screaming as explosions are going off, and you can hear Omari choking on the tear gas.

"Shit he hit me," someone says.

"Oh man, are those rubber bullets," Omari says. "Rubber bullets deployed, rubber bullets deployed. Rubber bullets, tear gas, pepper spray."

The cops are shooting tear gas and flash bang grenades right into the crowd, and Omari yells "Why are they throwing at all these people, they're throwing at all these people. I see that, they threw that in the middle of all these people," and you see all the clouds of smoke in the dark, more explosions in the street.

And then he's screaming "Oh shit, oh shit, we got hit, we're getting hit, we're getting hit." He's choking, saying "Oh my God . . . this is Seattle. Guys, share the stream, I don't know how much battery I got. Share the stream, share the stream, share the stream. Oh shit, there goes the tear gas. Goddammit. Oh shit, rubber bullets. They shooting, they shooting, share the stream."

This is the *Morning Update Show* on Converge Media, a local podcast that Jaysun told me about, two Black reporters from the Central District, Omari Salisbury and Tre Holiday. Omari says he was heading home after a peaceful protest last night when the cops started attacking people because someone threw a water bottle at them. Tear gas, flash bang grenades, rubber bullets, because of a water bottle. He said he heard one of the state troopers say "Hit 'em hard, just don't kill 'em."

Another clip. "It's smoky here, y'all," Omari says, and you see the rainbow crosswalks at Broadway and Pine—the cops are shooting people with tear gas and rubber bullets on the rainbow crosswalks, how could you even make this up. There's the Egyptian Theatre where I saw so many of my favorite movies as a kid, and people are chanting "Hands Up, Don't Shoot," and then Omari's screaming "Oh, goddammit, goddammit, I got hit," and someone says "Are you alright?" He says "Yeah, I'm alright, y'all see this? Share the stream. Share the stream . . . Mom, I'm alright, I got hit though. I got hit, though . . . Two nights in a row."

"This is an opportunity for leadership in this city," Omari says, gasping for breath. "Every crisis creates an opportunity . . ."

Someone says it reminds them of the Gaza Strip.

"The first time they came with this, Omari says, they said that someone threw some water. The last two times here, they've now deployed tear gas on people who stood there with their hands up."

Then he pans the camera, which is his phone held vertically, to show some of the protesters, mostly young people who look dazed, eyes watering from the tear gas, standing still or walking forward, texting or running away. "Here's someone with some scrubs," Omari says, and this guy looks over. "I'm a nurse," this guy says, "just off my shift, came straight here."

How are these people so calm, I'm thinking. How can they handle all the tear gas.

"We need bridgebuilders, not gatekeepers," Omari says, and shows the nurse with his hands up, "these are the faces of the protesters."

I'm sobbing now. How could I not be. I'm just completely losing it.

George Floyd was murdered by the cops while gasping I can't breathe, I can't breathe, I can't breathe. So now the cops are using tear gas and pepper spray on protesters until no one can breathe.

I remember when Marya was in Fed Up Queers, and after the murder of Amadou Diallo by the NYPD in 1999 they chained themselves across Broadway to block rush-hour traffic on a freezing winter day. Reporters leaned down with their microphones to say why are you here, and Marya said: Because people of color are being gunned down on the streets of New York, and it's a state of emergency.

Twenty years later, and it's the same thing.

Or is it different now, because George Floyd was murdered in Minneapolis, Breonna Taylor was murdered in Louisville, but the protests are everywhere. Or is the tear gas the difference, now the tear gas is everywhere. And rubber bullets. Stun grenades. Blast balls. Sound cannons. Armored personnel carriers. New weapons that I don't even know the names of.

Every journalist is a war reporter now, dodging tear gas just to cover protests, and is this becoming routine? Everyone wants to talk about Trump, but this is Jenny Durkan, Seattle's lesbian mayor, tear-gassing protestors on the rainbow crosswalks of Capitol Hill. Tear-gassing the whole neighborhood, even all the tech workers in those shiny new apartments, the Electric Sunset is right at the police line.

The cops don't want anyone to get too close to the police station on 12th. I grew up on 12th, so I walked by that police station all the time. I don't remember ever not hating it. Doesn't every kid who drinks or does drugs hate the cops? Why do so many grow up to trust them?

Carmen Best, Seattle's Black police chief, tear-gassing people chanting Black Lives Matter. Across the country, we have lesbian mayors, gay mayors, Black mayors, progressive mayors, and all their favorite police chiefs, united in their love of tear gas.

What would it look like if these mayors just sent the cops home? Permanently. How could they possibly think the damage would be greater?

I need to know what's going on. It's making me too frantic just to watch all the footage Jaysun sends me. Cal Anderson is only five blocks away, the protests are right on the other side of the park, the helicopters are flying overhead at night, every night, I want to scream Black Lives Matter at 8:00 p.m. when I make noise with my neighbors but I don't know if anyone will do it with me.

So I head over to Cal Anderson the next day. The tear gas starts at night, and I can't risk the tear gas, but I can risk going over during the day. Crossing John, I see the windows on the ground level of one of the new buildings have been smashed, and on the boards covering the windows someone spray-painted George Floyd MATTERS.

The walk signal says Fuck 12 PUSH for ACAB Motivation. So I'm feeling motivated.

A block from Cal Anderson, and people have chalked their driveways with BLACK LIVES MATTER, cases of bottled water with a sign that says FREE, and then I get to the park and everything is covered in graffiti, ACAB and Black Lives Matter and Abolish the Police and George Floyd, Breonna Taylor, other names I don't know, Fuck the Police, anarchy signs everywhere, there are tables where people are giving out masks and water and first-aid supplies.

Cal Anderson is a strange place for me because when I was a kid it was just the reservoir, and a playfield, but then they moved the reservoir underground and made this weird park with a fake hill and a playground and the playfield got covered in astroturf and it was all named after Cal Anderson, Seattle's first out gay elected official, who died of AIDS in 1995. My mothers told me about the park when it was just an idea, and then they gave me updates until it was finished around when I visited in 2005. They said you remember Cal, right? But I didn't remember him.

Now that the park is covered in graffiti, it finally feels like it isn't fake. And then I get to the protest at Pine and 11th, which is as close as you can get to the police station. People are chanting Black Lives Matter and George Floyd and yelling at the cops, it's a little scary that everyone's so close together so I'm standing at the back, making sure to keep ten feet away from anyone but I can feel all the tension and possibility.

My eyes are burning from the residue of the tear gas, that's how much they've used, it still smells like it everywhere—tear gas, and pepper spray, even with my N95, maybe I'm not wearing it right because I know it's supposed to block smells but I feel like it's trapping everything in so I take it off, and use two bandannas instead and at least that doesn't hurt my neck as much. Too many people smoking, maybe that's what's activating the tear gas, so I decide to walk around the block.

There's a shrine for George Floyd. Signs with organizers' demands to Defund the Seattle Police Department, Fund Community-Based Health and Safety, and Drop all Charges Against Protesters. The boarded-up windows of all the businesses are covered in graffiti, so they finally have a purpose. Flyers with information about local people murdered by the cops—John T. Williams, a Native woodcarver who was shot dead by a Seattle police officer while crossing the street in 2010. Charleena Lyles, a thirty-year-old pregnant Black mother who called the cops for help in 2017, and they shot her dead in her own home. Manuel Ellis, a thirty-three-year-old Black man who was killed by Tacoma cops just a few months ago, choked to death while saying I can't breathe, just like George Floyd.

It never ends, I'm thinking. It never ends.

But then on my way home I see people on their porches with water, masks, baking soda to wash off tear gas, and first aid supplies to offer protesters. We're in this together, that's what it feels like.

So when eight o'clock comes around, I yell Black Lives Matter, Abolish the Police. And then I yell it again. Three times before blowing my whistle. No one yells it with me, but they wait until I'm done, and then there's more noise than usual, I mean it goes on for longer and I feel such a relief. Like I can do this every night now. I feel like I'm a part of something.

But I need more than just yelling out my window at 8:00 p.m. so I start going to the protests every day. Maybe it's different for me, because I'm still staying ten feet away from people, and I don't stay too long because I can't risk the tear gas but shouldn't protest be about difference—in small towns, people are holding up Black Lives Matter signs alone on street corners, right, and the call is to join in whatever way you can.

One day I get to the park and it's more crowded than usual, maybe it's Saturday? I can never remember the days anymore. By the fake hill, there's a speak-out where someone's talking about community alternatives to the police, and in the center of the park there's a sound system and music and tables set up, but this turns out to be for a Black self-empowerment speaker, and then I see these two muscular white guys with an enormous boombox—they go under a tree and start attaching ropes and I realize they're doing CrossFit. I'm exhausted already, but I like the way I can hear the music from both sound systems so I decide to dance.

The Parks Department has drawn these ten-foot circles in the grass so I guess you can stay in your circle and keep your social distancing so I pick a circle and take off my shoes to feel the grass to ground me, then I'm spinning and bouncing with the sun on my face and four kids come running up to ask if they can dance with me, I saw them looking at me before, kind of like tourists, but now I realize it's a little group of queers of color who've come into town to see what's going on, and they're excited to see me because there aren't many visible queers here, so then we dance in the grass together for a few minutes, arms in the air all our smiles our feet into the beat and eyes yes eyes.

And then sometime that night, after I'm gone, the cops show up and tear gas everyone. There is a threat—dancing, CrossFit, speakout, thousands of people calling for justice, so what could be a better response than tear gas, have you tried tear gas today? It's great for the complexion. It's great for spreading COVID-19. It's great for the economy.

I was thinking that my allergies were suddenly getting dramatically worse, but now I realize this must be from all the tear gas in the air, right, night after night. When it was just my eyes and nose and ears, that felt like allergies, but now my lips are burning too, and that's not an allergy I've ever experienced.

The cops attack protesters every day right around 8:00 p.m., when people across the city are making a joyful noise to support healthcare workers. Maybe cops think they're supporting healthcare workers by sending more people to the emergency room.

Yes, it feels like the 8:00 p.m. screaming in my neighborhood is starting to merge with chants of BLACK LIVES MATTER, even if that's only me and a few people around the corner, but I'll assume the crescendo of sound afterward is in our favor. I'm getting pretty good at blowing extremely loudly on my whistle to the tune of BLACK LIVES MAT-TERRRRRRRRRR, ABOLISH THE POLICE, BLACK LIVES MAT-TERRRRRRRRRR, ABOLISH THE POLICE. Also I found these cute butterfly barrettes to keep my hair out of my face while I'm swaying side to side and sticking my head out the window, and you can't really argue with cute barrettes. Sure, one night someone yells SHUT THE FUCK UP, but I'm four floors up so I can pretend not to hear that.

Apparently there are thousands of complaints against the police department. There's even a handmade ACAB banner flying proudly from the window of one of those luxury loft condos on Pike. But wait, the bars are reopening already? Fags standing outside the Cuff, right next to the metal gates the cops installed in the middle of the street to protect the police station from the protests.

A wheatpaste that says Breonna Should Be Celebrating Her 27th Birthday above Black Trans Lives Matter and Hong Kong Solidarity. A stencil of some guy with a blue face wearing a green mask, pink background, which says YOU HAVE THE RIGHT TO REMAIN HEARD. A stencil that says END $PD. A banner that says Amnesty for All—No Bad Protesters, No Good Cops. And the memorial to George Floyd is getting bigger, candles crowding the sidewalk, flowers and photos of so many of the people who have been murdered by the cops.

A whiteboard that counts documented police killings in 2019 in various countries—

Japan 2
UK 3
Australia 4
Germany 11
France 26
Canada 36
US 1004.

Another night I go outside at 10:00 p.m. to hear some amazing steel drumming on Broadway, yes, I'm dancing in the street, my own nightclub at last, and someone walks by with a giant pink neon BLM sign around their neck, heading toward Cal Anderson and I'm shrieking with the drums going into the ground, the ground into my feet and it's like I actually have a body again.

The next day in the protest zone, I see the WRONG SIDE OF HISTORY on a dumpster. A NO PARKING sign covered by stickers that say I Can't Breathe. Justice for Ahmaud Arbery. Philando Castile. Sandra Bland. Walter Scott. Terence Crutcher. Breonna Taylor. A sticker of the police station burning down, and up high it says DEFUND SPD. Down low, it says Burn it down/ To Start Again.

Let's Riot, spray-painted on a wall, in beautiful script. And KILL THE COP INSIDE YOU. I love that one, I really love that one.

I get to the police station, and it looks like it's actually true that the cops have left. The whole building is boarded up and fenced off. Someone painted over the sign at the front entrance, so it says Seattle People's Department. COP FREE ZONE, spray-painted in pink, directly on the building, with a gold heart underneath. CHARLEENA LYLES, spray-painted along the bottom. BLM ACAB FUCK 12 on the boards. Barricades that now protect the area from the cops, instead of for the cops—I mean don't forget the guy who drove right into the protest, Terry, you're already forgetting things. What would have happened if a protester didn't stop him from going further? Daniel Gregory, that's the protester's name, a twenty-seven-year-old Black guy who somehow managed to reach into the car while it was moving, hold onto the steering wheel and that's when he got shot by the driver.

Then the shooter got out of the car and waved his gun at the protesters, before running toward the police line like the cops were his friends. I mean they probably are his friends, because it turns out his brother works at the police station.

And was there even more tear gas after that, Terry, how long did it go on? How can we remember anything, with all this tear gas, I mean how can we forget.

But now it's a COP FREE ZONE. People are camped out in tents in front of the police station. Bloody handprints and Black Power fists stenciled in the entrance to the driveway. I'm taking in all the excitement, and some guy comes up to me, and says: Were those sunglasses expensive?

Yes, I say, but they're the only sunglasses that kind of prevent me from getting a migraine.

And then he takes the exact same sunglasses out of his pocket, holds them up, and says I've bought at least fifteen pairs of these, do you know where to get a good deal?

No, I say, where do I get a good deal?

You become an Oakley member, he says, and he tells me how to register. I can't tell if he's flirting with me, or just trying to be friendly. But he's the only person who says anything to me.

Then he points to the police station, and says: Do you think we should be in there? We have locksmiths, if we wanted to get inside, we'd be inside, right?"

And I think about what Marya said once about undercover cops—they target the people who look out of place, they bond with you about something you have in common, and then they try to get you to say something incendiary. So I just smile, and shrug my shoulders, and say well it's nice to meet you, and walk away.

All these boarded-up windows with signs that say WE ARE OPEN. A high-end sneaker store that's evacuated, but there's a cute dog staring at me from inside, begging for attention.

Meanwhile, the state of Washington says it's on course to test all nursing home residents and staff for COVID by the end of the week. What? How was this not done three months ago? Through the windows of a restaurant, I'm watching people eating together, and I feel like I'm witnessing something completely bizarre and frightening.

Jaysun says she was waiting for her gas mask to arrive, but now that the cops have left she wants to go down with me. So we meet outside my building the next day. She's wearing a shimmery silk trench coat and long lashes, bright red lipstick. And, her platforms.

Honey, I say, you look amazing, and she says girl, I'm just trying to compete with you—silk, for summer 2020. It's Versace. Lashes and lipstick by MAC. I know you don't like RuPaul, but she does know her lashes. Your makeup is still better than mine, no one can compete with those eyes—I could spot that neon pink from down the block, even with your sunglasses. And that hat, honey, it bends all around your face like some movie star, and are those birds in your hat with all the flowers, where did you get those birds?

Remember when I used to wear them in my wigs?

Girl, I had no idea birds could survive that long. And that lipstick, how did you get so many colors at once, I'm jealous. Plus, your earrings are getting better and better, if that's even possible. All that glitter on the left, and then dangle, dangle, dangle, like some lovely wind ornaments on the right. You always take it to the next level.

Honey, your platforms.

Oh, these old things, I guess you're not the only one who likes to keep stuff around. I couldn't decide on the right mask, so then I figured I'd do it your way, and just stay ten feet away from these bitches, and you know they'll be staying ten feet away from me anyway.

With Jaysun in her platforms, I'm really feeling the runway, it's almost like we're back together at the clubs, and I guess I'm not the only one thinking that because then she says wait, wait, I'm having a flashback, remember when Girlina had that room in the back at the Roxy?

Was that at the Roxy? Are you sure that wasn't Life?

Oh, Life, I forgot about Life—wherever it was, she would play the hits and the girls would walk, and you know I was never that good but I would walk and walk until I was in a trance and remember that night when you just fell on the floor, you slid into it, and the whole room stopped just for that moment as you curled around and twisted up into a spiral it was like you were the ghost of Sid, you were her, for that moment you were her, and everyone knew it.

Honey, I don't remember that at all.

Well, remember it now. Is that water really free? Just when I was getting thirsty.

We get to the park, and Jaysun throws her arms up to the sky, and yells Black Lives Mat-ter!

And I throw up my arms, and yell Abolish the Police.

And she's screaming yes, girl, yes, girl, this is what I was waiting for. But your voice, let me hear the whole thing.

And I yell Black Lives Mat-ter, Abolish the Police.

And she says oh, you get it deep into your chest, it's so big, you're like one of those opera divas, contralto, girl, you might be a contralto. And she yells Black Lives Mat-ter.

And I yell Abolish the Police.

Two guys give us the Black Power salute, a white guy and a Black guy. So we keep it going. Another white guy gives us the Black Power salute, and I look at my hand to make sure I'm doing it right—the fingers go forward, right? And Jaysun says oh my God, oh my God, she works for the Evil Empire.

Which one, I say, and she says the last one, I know I've seen her, I just have to remember where. Maybe not everyone I work with is totally evil.

Honey, of course not, I mean not if you work there.

Girl, don't flatter me, you know I'm as evil as it gets—if I told you everything I do for my paycheck, all the lives I've ruined, you would drop me like a rag and then someone would have to call poison control just to take care of the fumes. And girl I would totally deserve it, but anyway, let's get to the party. I need to see this thing in action.

We walk by a group of people having some sort of meeting, we stop for a moment and someone says "Not all cops are the enemy," so Jaysun grabs my hand and we keep walking. There's someone painting a mural on the old pump station for the reservoir, in the middle of the day. Even since yesterday, there's more graffiti.

We get to Pine, and there are sofas in the street over by 11th, a hot dog vendor, and then across the street is the No Cop Co-op. They're giving out pizza and bunches of wilted kale.

Okay, it is getting a little crowded here, Jaysun says, and she pulls up her bandana, red, to match the coat, and I pull up my bandanas, which are pink. And Jaysun says I'm so glad those bandannas finally came, but you're right, honey, it does smell like tear gas here. Are you okay, she said, take off your sunglasses a sec—that's what I thought, your eyes look red. Your makeup still looks flawless, but your eyes look red.

Really, you can tell?

I can tell, girl.

I guess I'm getting used to it.

Girl, you're not getting used to it, you're just blocking it out. But let's get to the main attraction.

We get to the police station, and now it's covered in protest signs, there's a new mural on the side, people are painting in the street.

Burn it DOWN, Jaysun yells, burn it fucking DOWN!

I'm laughing, and someone comes over to Jaysun, and says hey man, keep it down. Jaysun looks over at him and says what are you, my mother. And the guy says I'm just saying. And Jaysun says well I'm just saying BURN IT DOWN.

And then I have to walk fast to catch up with her, she's heading up Pine toward 13th, past the stencil that says Capitol Hill Autonomous Zone, the barricades with a stop sign that says STOP COPS, and she says did you see that?

What, I say, and she says: That was my mother.

What do you mean?

That bitch was always telling me to keep it down, keep it down. The only thing that guy didn't do was smack me in the head.

I think he was just worried about the cops.

Did you see the cops, Jaysun says, I thought the cops were gone.

Well they're probably still here, just undercover.

I don't care if they're undercover, we should burn it down. Like in Minneapolis. Minneapolis didn't wait. Did you see how they were looking at us? That place was homophobic. They did not like us at all. You saw the way they were looking at my lashes. These are MAC. The coat is Versace. Stop looking at me like that.

Are you sure?

Honey, I'm sure. You noticed too, you're just blocking it out. I'm glad you're going, it's just not the place for me. Let's take 13th, okay, I made food for you. Let me go home, and change out of this, and I'll meet you at the park, I can't believe I used to wear these platforms all the time, my ankles are hurting, ouch, my ankles. It's because I'm fat.

You look amazing.

That's the important thing, girl, sorry I'm getting emotional. But it just makes me angry. Why can't we burn it down. I'm ready to burn it down. They can arrest me, and I'll show up in that courtroom in Gucci.

But you can't wear Gucci in prison.

Don't worry, honey, I would never do it when someone was looking, would I? Wait, wait, let me get a picture of you in front of those flowers, oh my God, it's like you're another flower, yes, yes, that pink looks so good with you, sorry, I didn't even notice that outfit before, did you sew that houndstooth jacket together with that ruffle skirt, oh my God those layers? With the floral leggings, it's everything. You're the best.

Okay, listen, Jaysun says, I'll go home and change out of this, and I'll meet you back at the park—are the KEEP IT MOVING spacesuit robot people gone?

I'm not sure, we should probably meet at the Union graveyard.

Girl, I am going to scream, I mean the bars are opening, and they're still telling people to keep it out of the park.

I know, it's scary.

Don't judge me, but you know I'll be in those bars soon, I miss those messy bitches. I'm buying rounds for everyone as soon as I get there, and if that isn't love then I don't know what is. Today I was looking into the windows of La Cocina and my lips were watering even though you know that food is nothing to miss. But I do miss Artusi. And Spinasse. Stateside. Terra Plata. Via Tribunali. La Spiga. Cook Weaver, oh my God that's so close. Okay, don't get me started—I haven't gone anywhere yet, but wait, today I made chana masala, yes, I'll just go back and heat it up and make sure it isn't awful and then I'll be at the graveyard in my WonderMobile before you even click your heels. Don't worry, I'll bring alcohol wipes so you can make sure everything is safe, don't even trust me for a second. Okay, let's do our fake hug—yes, yes, yes, I love you, see you in a flash.

Jaysun leaves and then I realize I'm so tired I can barely stand up, so I figure I'll stop at my mothers' to get some water and maybe a snack since they've been leaving things for me in the garage oasis, there's a little refrigerator and a microwave, and I can't pretend that bathroom isn't an amazing treat after being at the protests—I almost want to get into the jacuzzi but I'm meeting Jaysun so I just freshen up a bit and then open the door and there's someone sitting outside at the table.

Oh, it must be Mariana. My mothers didn't tell me she was trans. Long hair, kind of punked out in a low-key way with those rockabilly bangs and smokey eyes and crimson lipstick.

Hi, I say, and she looks up, and says you must be Terry, it's so nice to finally meet you . . .

She's looking me right in the eyes like she's taking it all in and oh, those eyes. I feel like we're in a movie, but we can't be in that movie because of the pandemic. So then I'm walking to the park and looking up at all the flowers and how are there so many birds in that one tree, all chirping together.

It takes me a while to get to the graveyard and of course Jaysun's there before me, everything is already set up and I haven't had chana masala in years, ever since I realized that restaurant oil makes me sick, and Jaysun even added carrots and cauliflower and that lime again, this time it's just a regular lime but it really brings everything out.

This is incredible, I say, and Jaysun says girl, you're just flattering me, but I'm glad you're eating it anyway and are you okay, you look a little spacey.

Oh I'm okay, I'm just thinking.

Girl, don't keep it a secret.

Well I ran into Mariana at my mothers' place, she's the person they hired to take care of . . .

Mariana, and Marya, I'm getting goosebumps already. Tell me everything.

Well she's a trans girl, and I think she's a dyke.

Girl, I knew you were going to say that. Did you fuck?

Stop, it was just the way she looked at me.

That's so lesbionic. You should have jumped in the jacuzzi with her—girl, I know, you're keeping it safe, I agree, but Marya and Mariana, think about it, it's like an omen. Speaking of Marya, I poured myself some red when I got home, just a smidge, and then I got this idea, listen, okay, let me have another sip, I brought some in this Minnie Mouse thermos, isn't she cute, shh, don't tell, but I have this idea, I can be your Marya, and we can go stenciling together, it'll be our own little protest. If we can't burn it down, at least we can go stenciling, what do you think?

I mean sure, but Marya was the one that always came up with the ideas.

Girl, I know you have ideas. Let's just figure it out right now, something about Jenny Durkan, right, I know you hate that bitch.

You know I can't do the spray-painting because of my hands.

Girl, don't even worry, I know all about your pain, I've got that covered. I'll do the spraying, you just guide me. I can cut out the stencils once you do the outline, it'll be fun, I'm ready. We can be Dykes Against Durkan.

Wait, that's perfect—Dykes Against Durkan. That can be our stencil. Then we can do Fags Against Durkan. DAD and FAD. And then TAD, Trannies Against Durkan.

Oh my fucking juicy cunt yes.

And what about Queers Against Durkan? But that doesn't have a good acronym. Or maybe QUAD—Queers United Against Durkan? Girl, what about Merkins Against Durkan. That would be MAD. Oh my God this is going to be fun fun fun, we can wear merkins together while we're stenciling.

Do people even know what a merkin is?

Girl, who cares, we know, that's the point, this is about us. DAD, FAD, MAD, TAD, I'm ready, let's do it, I'm so excited, okay, now I need a nap. I just wish we could cuddle.

So then we lie in the sun, and I actually pass out, it's much more comfortable on the blanket Jaysun brought for me, usually I try to pass out in the grass because I can't carry anything but then all the bugs in the grass start biting me.

But the strangest part is that a few days later Marya actually calls, what is it they say about your ears burning, not that I believe in that, but anyway she calls.

How are you doing, she says, it's been so long.

And I'm thinking it's been so long because you cut me off, but I just say I'm okay, there's a lot going on here right now, what's it like in LA?

And she says oh, you know, quarantine has been difficult for me and Christina, it's a challenge, you know how she can get kind of jealous.

She's jealous of you while you're in quarantine together?

No, no, it's just that we spend so much time together now, so much time. It's putting a strain on our relationship. We have a separate apartment downstairs, we were AirBnbing it before but obviously not now, and I've actually thought about moving in temporarily but I know Christina would take it the wrong way so I just started going for walks around the neighborhood, that's what I'm doing now.

Where do you live?

Silver Lake. It's so scenic here. I've never walked around before.

Never?

Not really. We drive everywhere. The Hollywood lifestyle. I know it's tragic. We both have our careers, but I don't want to bore you with that bougie crap. Tell me about the Autonomous Zone, do you live nearby?

Like five blocks.

Wow, I would love to be there. I've actually thought of driving up and camping out for a few days, just to get away. Christina and I are really strict about social distancing, though, we don't go in anywhere. So I thought of going on a camping trip.

A camping trip in Seattle?

Well it was just an idea. I hear people are camping out in the park there, what's it called?

Cal Anderson. There are people camping out. But it's not quiet.

I don't need quiet, I just would need somewhere to take a shower.

I can ask my mothers, they have a separate place that might work. But the park is really chaotic. The cops aren't technically there now, but they were shooting tear gas at everyone every day, you can still smell it, it's everywhere, so basically you'd be camping out in tear gas, it's even worse when it rains, you'd think it would get better but it gets worse because it comes off the buildings, or something.

Does it feel like Occupy?

I don't know, not really, it's not organized like that. You really have no idea what's going on, I mean sometimes I go over and there's a march so I join in, sometimes there are signs for meetings, but then you show up and there's no meeting, and people aren't friendly, they don't come up to you like at Occupy, they're not asking for volunteers, there aren't any committees except security, as far as I can tell, and that's all these white survivalist types.

White survivalists?

With guns. Some of them have guns.

Are there a lot of white people?

It's mostly white people. This is Seattle. The people leading things are Black, but then almost everyone else is white. Not everyone, but at least eighty percent. Probably more.

So I guess I wouldn't stand out then?

No, you wouldn't stand out. But what would Christina think?

I was just going to say I was camping in the LA mountains.

And you think she wouldn't notice?

The mountains are out of cell phone range.

Well I can ask my mothers about the shower, but you know it's a really long drive.

I get off the phone with Marya, and I feel kind of gross. Like she was just using me to find out about the protests. I call my mothers anyway, since I said I would ask about the shower. Eileen picks up the phone and says Terry, we were just talking about you.

What were you saying?

Well we just said goodbye to Mariana.

Where'd she go?

She got a new job in Portland, so she's on her way down. I think it'll be better for her there, she doesn't know anyone in Seattle. She said she enjoyed meeting you.

I was going to ask her if she wanted to go on a walk.

She would have loved that, I know. Did she tell you about her family? Her brother, he was murdered by Duterte, for smoking a joint. Smoking a joint, can you imagine? Duterte is like Trump on steroids. It's so sad, Mariana had to flee the country, she's been here a few years, but I don't think she has papers. We didn't talk about that directly, but how are you, Terry—Paula and I were just watching the news about the protests, we know you've been going down and does it still feel safe?

Well it's better now that the cops are gone.

Oh really?

Of course, I mean they were tear-gassing everyone every day. Every day. It was awful.

But is it still safe at night?

What do you mean? Jenny Durkan's been tear-gassing people every night, shooting rubber bullets at reporters, sending people to the hospital. Did you hear about the woman who got hit in the chest by a blast ball, and she died three times, that's what they said when she went to the hospital, they said she died three times. She's still alive, but she died three times.

Oh yes, that was just unbelievable. No one would condone that kind of violence.

But it's Jenny Durkan. She's the one. She's condoning it.

Oh I wouldn't say that, Jenny's stuck between a rock and a hard place, you have to admit that.

What? She declared a ban on tear gas, and then used it hours later.

Terry, she's in a tough place. She faces a lot of pressure as a woman, and a lesbian. She can't appear to be weak. She's had to overcome so many barriers. You have to think about it from her side of the fence.

What, I can't believe this, what are you saying. I don't want to be on her side of the fence. I'm embarrassed that she's a lesbian.

Terry, listen, it's not a black-and-white issue, Paula and I have known Jenny for years. Believe you me, we know she has everyone's best interests in mind.

What, you know her?

Of course we know her. Paula has been instrumental to the careers of every gay and lesbian elected official in Washington state. And beyond. Instrumental. Even when she hasn't worked on their campaigns directly. Everyone since Tina Podlodowski. Even before Tina, remember Hands Off Washington? Paula doesn't like to take credit, but I say give credit where credit is due. Come to think of it, you met Jenny when you were a kid. And she was here at the house when you surprised us, I still remember when we were on that balcony together and there you were, it was the best surprise of my life.

That was Jenny Durkan?

Of course, who did you think it was? Listen, I don't want to upset you, I just think you have to consider all sides.

I get off the phone because I have to scream, I completely forgot about asking about the bathroom but whatever, it's almost 8:00 p.m. anyway, and luckily two people join in for Abolish the Police, and I feel a little better afterward but I wish we could scream for longer, three minutes just isn't enough, I mean my voice gets hoarse but I could blow the whistle for a long time, and then there's the person with the cowbell, and someone playing all these toy instruments, and the person who always goes MEOW, and then there's someone who blasts "We Will Rock You," and someone else in the distance playing some disco song, I can't quite place it, and I wish we could add in that steel drumming I heard the other night, wouldn't that be great, every night at 8:00 p.m., steel drumming in the streets, I can already hear it in my head but wait, what is that, it actually does sound like drumming, is there a protest?

I put on a mask and rush outside to see what's going on, and there's a march going right down Broadway, people are drumming and yelling and clapping and then there's the call-and-response chant that starts with Whose lives matter?

Black Lives Matter.
Whose lives matter?
Black Lives Matter.
I could do this every night.

I know I said I would never go on Zoom, but it's the first meeting of the Sabine Roth Foundation, and I have an agenda. Jaysun gave me a Zoom tutorial ahead of time, and we practiced together, and figured out the lighting. That was the hardest part, because at first she gave me her extra ring light but when I tried it I could feel a migraine coming on right away so instead I figured out this elaborate setup where my computer is balanced on a table on top of a table, so that way I can stand the whole time because sitting still and staring at the computer always hurts my whole body. And then I have a lamp behind the computer, and lamps on both sides of me, so I think the light stays even that way.

It's weird to see everyone in their little rectangles, but I can tell they all have a ring light or some other kind of tricky setup except for Brenda, who's looking down at the screen while sitting at her desk. She's the only one of Sabine's artists on the board, so Sabine must have requested her, and Veronica made the rest of the decisions so there are five artists from her gallery, all straight guys, I think, but racially diverse, and then her husband Henri, who's an investment banker from Switzerland, and me.

I almost never went to openings because it wasn't part of my job, except for Veronica's openings. Sabine and I didn't talk about the shows, she would just grab my wrist if something was particularly terrible, and we would stare at it, and that's when Veronica would come over and say oh, isn't this impressive, and we would nod our heads. Sabine always knew what to say, so I would just keep quiet.

Sabine once said to me: Veronica knows how to make money, and you know how to have fun. And that was that. Sabine funded Veronica's gallery, so I'm sure she had a financial stake, and I'm sure Veronica was the one who got Sabine all that press right before her death, and of course that helped the foundation, and me, so here we are now, the nine of us, staring at our computer screens to talk about how we're going to distribute the money. The foundation has a thirty-two million dollar endowment, and we're required to give away four to six percent of that per year, so that means we have a million or two to give away to artists, right?

The meeting starts, and we're all either fixing our hair or adjusting the angle of the camera or looking at what's visible in other people's apartments. Veronica begins by saying I think we all know one another, don't we, so why don't we keep this informal and leave our microphones on, like a virtual cocktail party, we're all friends here. Should we do a quick go-around?

It looks like everyone except Brenda has their own art on display in the background, and Veronica and her husband have Warhol's *Mao*. I wonder how much that cost.

When it's my turn to introduce myself, Veronica notices I have Cleo's *Art Is Not Dead* in the background, which Sabine gave to me, and she says Terry, whatever happened to CleoPatrick, she was in ascendance, and then . . .

She works at Dior now.

Oh, I'm wearing Dior, Veronica says, and she and Henri turn to smile at one another.

Veronica goes through all the details about the endowment, and our responsibilities on the board, and mentions that Henri will be the financial planner for the foundation, which he will be doing . . . and she looks over at him.

And he says: I'm donating my services for this worthwhile cause.

And everyone applauds.

So, Veronica says, since we are obligated to give away four to six percent per calendar year to artists . . .

Henri starts applauding right there, and then everyone applauds again, and Veronica smiles, takes a sip of her wine, and says: Let's start spending.

And then Henri says I propose we distribute 5 percent this year, which would give us a budget of 1.5 million plus change.

And everyone claps again.

And Veronica says I would like to propose that we give $100,000 to fifteen qualified artists, or $150,000 to ten artists. None of that 10,000 or 20,000 at a time crap. Meaningful stipends that could make an impact in someone's life. Does anyone have a preference?

Everyone smiles quietly.

Then why don't we wait to see who is nominated, Veronica says. Any questions?

What's the process for consideration, Rajneesh asks. He's the one who made a porcelain miniature of the Taj Mahal, with life-size replicas of Queen Elizabeth's corgis standing in front, almost blocking out the palace. It was a sensation. The critics hailed it as a postcolonial masterpiece. A collector bought it for the Tate. Rajneesh became a star overnight. That was the first time Sabine grabbed my wrist at the gallery, when we were looking at those corgis.

Let's keep it informal, Veronica says. We don't want to get bogged down in process. Sabine never got bogged down in process, did she.

And everyone applauds.

Why don't we each come up with a name or two, Veronica says, and then discuss at the next meeting.

Brenda asks if these are need-based scholarships, or . . .

Well of course every artist is in need, Veronica says. The Sabine Roth Foundation is here to provide a crucial source of funding in challenging times.

How will we be making our decisions, Edwin asks. He's the one who paints something that looks like a Mondrian or a Rothko, and then adds little creatures with googly eyes.

Veronica says talent is what matters, we will be deciding based on talent, and everyone smiles smugly while no doubt thinking about which close friend of theirs to pick, who will do the most for their career.

Am I correct that we can only consider New York artists, Roland asks. He's the one I offended once by saying that his art reminded me of Basquiat. Wasn't that a compliment? But no, we weren't supposed to say that aloud.

Absolutely, Veronica says, that is in the articles of incorporation. The five boroughs only.

Is this open to artists in every medium, asks Paulo, who recreates Frida Kahlo's work, but to depict himself, a straight guy descended from Italian royalty. When asked to describe his inspiration, he likes to say: Frida and I have the same eyebrows.

Every medium of visual art, Veronica says.

I guess now is my chance.

This is so exciting, I say, thank you for all your work, Veronica.

Everyone applauds.

I'm thrilled to collaborate with so many artists whose work I admire, I say, and I look around the room at each rectangle, although can people tell when I'm looking at them? I have no idea, but then everyone starts clapping again, so I'm on a roll.

And I love how smooth this process already feels, I say, I know Sabine wanted us to focus on distributing the resources.

Another round of applause.

I just have one suggestion, I say. I wonder if, given the times we're living in, with protests across the country for Black Lives Matter, I wonder if we could give one of the grants to an artist, or a group of artists, to make a creative intervention in the streetscape of New York.

What do you have in mind, Veronica says.

I was thinking of an immediate grant to fund graffiti or public art, some kind of interruption in the city to support the protests.

Dead silence.

Okay, here I go—if all else fails, make something up.

Sabine loved graffiti, I say, she was always pointing it out to me.

Veronica looks confused. Everyone freezes in their pensive poses, until Brenda says Terry, you are absolutely correct. Ever since the 1970s, when Sabine and I first met, we would go on walks around the neighborhood, and marvel.

Now everyone looks surprised.

And what would you marvel at, Veronica asks.

Oh I can't say for sure, Brenda says, but Keith Haring was one example. And remember René, with those murals that said "I Am the Best Artist," right there in Soho, those were a hoot. SAMO was another early example. There was a lot to decode there. When it was Basquiat, and . . . Before Basquiat became . . .

Famous, I think we can say famous, Roland says. When I was coming up as a youngster in the '80s, he says, that's what got me started. His commitment. The ritual. That visual language. The immediacy.

And I like Terry's idea. To give support directly to the street, where it's needed most. I know some wildly talented and extremely crafty fellows from my old hood in the Bronx who have yet to be recognized, and I believe they could put together an immediate intervention in our current moment, as Terry suggests.

An intervention, Rajneesh says, I like the concept.

It's important to be on the right side of history, says Manuel, the artist known for hiring undocumented workers to make his sculptures. This is supposed to be a critique of the art world, but it's unclear how much he pays people. When asked this in interviews, he just says: I like to preserve the ambiguity.

But when Manuel says it's important to be on the right side of history, Veronica raises her glass for a toast. So then we all raise our glasses and water bottles and coffee mugs.

Veronica says: For Sabine. And we all take a sip of whatever we're drinking.

Then Roland says: I have one suggestion.

And we all look over.

And he says I think this grant should be anonymous. For the safety of the street artists. As you know, street art is not quite . . .

I'm all for keeping it real, says Paulo.

A magnificent idea, Veronica says—Roland, Terry, would you like to discuss this amongst yourselves.

And I say I would be happy to offer suggestions, but Roland, since you're in New York, and it sounds like you already have an idea, why don't you go ahead with your plans, and feel free to give me a call at any point if you need advice.

If someone can give you a knowing look over Zoom, that's what Roland gives me.

It sounds like we are all in agreement, Veronica says. And, rest assured that there is no stipulation in our articles of incorporation as to attribution, am I correct? And she looks over at Henri, who nods his head, and says absolutely, the only stipulation is that we distribute the funds in a timely manner to artists of quality.

And everyone applauds.

Magnificent, Veronica says. Roland, let me know when you've made a decision, and I will disburse the funds posthaste. Anything else?

No one responds

Until July then, Veronica says. A profound thank-you to each and every one of you for being a part of Sabine's legacy. On behalf of all artists in New York City, I thank you. And she blows the screen a kiss.

So we all blow kisses, or wave, or nod our heads, until the screen says This meeting has been ended by the host.

Jaysun says girl, I know I told you the pandemic made me into a top but I gave up, it wasn't working, the Viagra was giving me a headache and making my heart race when I was trying to sleep, and no one fell for it, so anyway the other night I was getting fucked by some guy in the park and then he pulled out and ran away because he saw someone better, that's what they all do, so then when I was pulling up my pants this Asian guy who was watching us came over for a hug and you know I'm usually racist against Asians but I'm trying to get over that because guess what bitch look in the mirror but anyway we were hugging and it felt nice I mean he was wearing that gross cologne but I closed my eyes and started drifting away like I could fall asleep standing up so I said I think I have to go to bed.

And he said me too.

And I said well it's nice meeting you.

And he said do you live nearby?

Not far, I said, and he said I'd like to go to bed with you.

And I said I'm not having anyone over.

And he said I understand.

But then he said it again—I'd like to go to bed with you. And we were both wearing masks so I know he wasn't totally clueless but I was starting to think he didn't really get what I was saying so I said I can't sleep with anyone in bed with me.

And he said me neither.

And I said okay, well it was nice meeting you, and I gave him another hug, but this time I had to pull away when he was still holding on, and you know I'm the one who always likes hugs. So that's when it got weird because he was following me and telling me it was so hard for him to meet people and I said me too, but I have to go home, and he said me too, but then he just kept following me, and repeating whatever I said so I said listen, I'm going home by myself, and I walked right past my car because I didn't want him to see me getting in, I just kept walking until he wasn't behind me anymore and then I had to go back and get my car, and by that time I was really tired—I don't know, he wasn't scary or anything, I don't think, but you never know, right? Should we do our fake hug now? I need a fake hug.

So then we do our fake hug, and get ready for our stencils. We're practicing right across the street from my building, because there's this boarded-up house that's always covered in graffiti until it gets painted over, right now there's this giant tag of a toaster, so DYKES AGAINST DURKAN can go right on the ground by the toaster. Jaysun ordered me some hilarious gray-and-black or maybe it's charcoal-and-steel athletic wear, she said you should have something discreet, don't you think—and trust me when I say I've never worn athletic wear, it almost feels like I'm naked but that doesn't make sense because I have this giant hood on the windbreaker that covers my whole face, so maybe I feel naked because I'm not wearing makeup, or I'm wearing makeup but just something subtle, and then there's my mask, and when do I ever leave the house like this, I mean never ever ever ever, and the first thing Jaysun says is oh my, you should totally try cruising the park in that outfit, no one would even know you're a girl.

But I look like a dead raver.

Oh my God you're right, you're right, next time I have to bring music.

Now everyone's calling the protest area the Capitol Hill Autonomous Zone, or CHAZ, You Are Now Entering Free Capitol Hill it says on the barricades and it does feel kind of autonomous with the cops staying away, and all the people camping out in tents in the park and even building little structures, someone's planting a community garden and the tornado fountain is covered from top to bottom in graffiti, no water just a cascade of Black Lives Matter and Antifa and I Can't Breathe and Fuck the Police and BLM is spray-painted literally everywhere in the neighborhood, on garage doors and on the cement and brick walls and windows and in the street and the CHAZ is graffiti 24/7, no one even stops to look at us for a second, with Jaysun giving baseball cap realness and me in my North Face dead raver look, it's like a magic trick, we could probably stand right outside City Hall like this, spray-painting in our REI shopping bags, and would anyone even stop us.

We get several of each of the stencils done, and then Jaysun says she has to get ready for bed so she can get up and work for the Evil Empire, and on our way back we see that someone spray-painted FAGS AGAINST COPS on the rainbow crosswalk, so then we're fantasizing that we're going to find this queen, no luck on that but we do find this incredible installation by the George Floyd memorial, with mannequin hands attached to the wall and "8 minutes 46 seconds" for all the time that cop had his knees on George Floyd's neck and we all know the name of that cop but I don't even want to say it, now there are protests every day at 8:00 p.m., I try to catch them after screaming with my neighbors, and for a few days in a row the protest starts at Pine and Broadway, where everyone goes silent for George Floyd at 8:46 p.m. and then the march leaves after that, I join for five or six blocks but I turn around before it goes downtown so I don't get stuck in some police nightmare, but then after a few nights I can't find the protest anymore. Everything changes every day, and it's hard to keep track.

One day I get to the CHAZ, and it looks like a group of white people are carrying some white guy who looks like he's Jesus away on their shoulders, while a Black guy directs them. I can't tell if it's because Jesus is high or if he did something wrong but they're carrying him out of the CHAZ, which I guess now people are calling the CHOP, for Capitol Hill Organized Protest because they say it really isn't autonomous, but isn't autonomy always a dream—I'm trying to be a part of something but still from the distance, and honestly it's always a little awkward when I start talking to someone because it feels like they're testing me and I don't know how to pass the test so then it's like the conversation is already over.

Sometimes I have to watch the news to understand what I just witnessed. Like after I went to the protest where Kshama Sawant spoke on the playfield and there were a lot of people there, way more queers than usual but I was standing across the street, leaning on the railing by the Richmark building and that's when Kshama called on Jenny Durkan to resign and of course I was screaming, and then she said we need to tax Amazon, sure, but the best part was when she called for abolishing the police, abolishing ICE, abolishing borders, and that's pretty radical for a city councilmember, isn't it.

I went home when people started marching downtown to City Hall, but then when they got there Kshama let everyone in with her key and hundreds of people were protesting inside and I was glad I wasn't there because obviously there wasn't room for social distancing but also I was hoping that people were going to occupy City Hall and refuse to leave. They were only inside for a few hours, but they got all this attention and then the pressure was on Jenny from both sides when Trump said she was too soft on protesters so Jenny said Go Back to Your Bunker and then all the liberals across the country were like go Jenny go Jenny go and suddenly she was some national hero even though everyone in Seattle knew she should be in that bunker with Trump.

But I need to tell you about the GEORGE FLOYD graffiti that covers the old pump station in Cal Anderson, it must be thirty feet across in such gorgeous bubbly '80s lettering, blue and purple letters alternating with orange and green, on a bright pink background, and then it reflects in the water so everything is doubled, with the blue sky in both directions. And now BLACK LIVES MATTER is projected in huge letters on the Richmark building, and WE CAN'T BREATHE. On the corner, someone's giving out free coffee, with Free Capitol Hill stenciled on the ground.

But did I tell you about the girl who was looking up at me from the sidewalk in front of the law offices behind my building the other night when I leaned out my window. I always look down at those law offices because they're in an old Victorian house on its own little hill, and I like looking at that house. This woman yelled are you the one with the whistle—I get so much joy hearing you from my place that I decided to come down to meet you.

So I said let's do it together. She was a little shy about Abolish the Police but she danced when I blew the whistle and it was a beautiful moment. I said maybe we should go on a walk and chat sometime, but I couldn't tell what she thought of that idea.

Then one day I'm at the CHOP and there's some argument going on in the street because city employees with a truck are putting up barriers by the police station, this guy's screaming at the city workers and there are a bunch of people gathered around so I step into the street to support them. Then I realize that activists from the CHOP are arguing with one another too, and that's when some guy steps behind me and kind of lifts me up and pushes me away so he can get into the argument, and I'm kind of shocked because that's the first person who's touched me in three months.

These are Black guys arguing with one another and maybe I'm just some white girl who doesn't belong. But what about all the other white people here. Move the tranny out of the way, it's time to get down to business. Suddenly I feel so lost—is it better or worse that he said EXCUSE ME while shoving me out of the way?

I go home to try to figure out what was going on, it takes a while but eventually I realize some of the organizers made a deal with the city to install barriers in the middle of the street to allow cars to go through in one direction, and when I go back people are painting the barriers and it feels like some bad city-sponsored art installation. Maybe it doesn't help that on the way I see a handmade sign that says BLACK QUEER LIVES MATTER, just a piece of paper attached to a utility pole with a few pieces of duct tape, but I guess someone was so threatened by the word QUEER that they took off most of the duct tape just to cover up that word, and maybe that's why DYKES and FAGS and TRANNIES keep getting covered up on the stencils I did with Jaysun and then I think about how whenever someone puts up BLACK TRANS LIVES MATTER it gets taken down or covered up so quickly, I mean a lot of things get covered up fast but the queer things go faster.

I'm out with Jaysun to do more stenciling—our backup singers are police helicopters, surveillance drones, and spy planes. We're reading the Tax Amazon flyers, and Jaysun says 1.7%—is this a joke, don't you think we should tax them 100%?

And she's the expert.

Things that make me feel less lonely tonight: graffiti, trees, the moon, hydrangeas, the breeze, the coolness of my fingers.

Things that make me feel less lonely tonight: rabbits, diagonal tree trunks, the light between the clouds, how the pattern of the leaves against the sky looks like lace.

Things that make me feel less lonely tonight: one tiny cloud floating past the half-moon, the way the trees are reaching up, the way the sky is still so blue after the sun goes down.

Things that make me feel less lonely tonight: the way the ground gives way under my feet, the sound of the wind blowing through the leaves, the way the trees are dancing whenever I look up, the way this small shrub supports all my weight when I lean against it.

But someone on my block actually has an ALL LIVES MATTER sign displayed on their back windshield. How is there still glass there?

Also there's a rainbow teddy bear on the dashboard. I call Jaysun. She says girl, the gays are the worst, we need to smash those windows. I bet he goes to the Cuff. The other night I was there—don't worry, just on the patio, and you know that patio is huge, but these faggots were out there complaining about the protests, one girl with her biker cap and chains said can't they shut up already it's hurting my ears. And then some muscle bear said first we had the pandemic, and now this— and I almost smashed my glass over her head, but it wasn't a glass it was just a plastic cup. I totally bet that was the rainbow ALL LIVES MATTER bitch, some of these bears, you would not believe.

I wake up and the helicopters are flying over again. Every time I hear the helicopters, I think about the cops shooting tear gas at everyone, night after night. Tear gas, rubber bullets, stun grenades, pepper spray. You can still smell the residue, even though that was several weeks ago, wasn't it.

Speaking of trauma, I'm at the CHOP one day and I see that same guy who told me where to get a deal on my Oakley sunglasses, the one I was pretty sure was an undercover cop, and now he's in charge of one of the armed security stations to prevent the cops from coming in. I kind of freeze when I notice him, and he kind of freezes too. Or am I just imagining that?

Back at home, I'm not intending to look at anything on social media, but then I see a livestream of bike cops surrounding two people on Pine, I think it's Pine, tackling them to the ground to arrest them. People are yelling GET YOUR KNEE OFF HIS NECK, GET YOUR KNEE OFF HIS NECK. Sure enough, you can see the cop's knee on this person's neck, until he pulls it away because of the protesters screaming. Is this what it takes—a whole crowd needs to be right there, in the middle of mass protests. All these people need to be right there, to yell GET YOUR KNEE OFF HIS NECK.

Someone calls from an unavailable number, usually that means telemarketing but I pick it up anyway and it's Cleo. I don't know if she's ever called me before, what time is it in Paris, it must be late.

She says I'm sorry I've been such a bitch for the last twenty-five years, it's just that I was always jealous of you and Sid—JoJo taught me how to walk, and after she was gone I wanted Sid to take over but then she had you. So I've always been jealous, I'm a jealous bitch. I get it now—you weren't responsible for her death, I'm not angry at you for that, except when I get irrational and think you could've saved her, but, like Jaysun says, you can't save someone from AIDS and I have my own struggles with that, maybe you don't know this but I'm positive, it's been a decade now and I haven't told anyone except Jaysun and I know I'm supposed to be grateful for the meds that make this into a manageable condition or whatever, but it doesn't feel so manageable to me. Jaysun says she doesn't even notice the meds but girl I get these horrible side effects, like everything in the book, and everything out of the book, it's like the book is just closing in on my face and I might not die of AIDS but I'm not so sure I won't die of the side effects. And I know you're a delicate flower too, so you know what I'm saying. I told Jaysun I need a break, I can't talk to her right now, she's trying to control my life, I want to go back and visit my mother, and take care of her, now that my father's gone, he needed an operation but there was a backlog at the hospital, and he ended up dying in his sleep. And I don't want to miss my mother like that. She took care of me as a kid, even if she wasn't so great later on but now she at least calls me Cleo some of the time thanks to Oprah or whatever and she says she wants to see me and I miss her, I really do, I know I'm just going on and on, sorry to spew all this at you, but there's one thing I've always wondered, and you don't have to answer if you don't want to, I just don't get why you became friends with Michael Alig after Sid died, what was that about?

I don't know what that was about.

That's not an answer, do you want to answer or not?

I don't know how to answer. I lost Sid, and then I lost you and Jaysun, and then I lost Tara and Mielle, so what was I supposed to do.

You know what he did to Sid, right.

No, I don't know, and I don't know if I want to know.

They shot up together, and she OD'ed, and he just left her there, he left her there to die. They were inseparable before that, they were like sisters, this was before he was anyone. She was the star. And he just left her there like that. He probably wanted to watch someone OD— no wonder he killed Angel, that's what he was like, Sid couldn't even look at him, you know that.

As soon as I get off the phone with Cleo, Jaysun calls. Actually, maybe she was calling before, I could hear my call waiting but I wasn't looking. She says Cleo didn't call you, did she?

And I say I just got off the phone with her.

Jaysun says what, I told that bitch not to call you, why was she calling you, I don't understand.

I guess she wanted to talk about Michael Alig?

Michael who, I cannot believe it, why is that bitch still thinking about Michael Alig, I told her not to call you about that, I knew it would upset you, how are you doing, are you okay?

I don't know, maybe I'm kind of dissociated.

Girl, don't think about Michael Alig, that bitch is not worth it, why did Cleo ask you that, she's just up in the middle of the night taking it out on you and you don't deserve that. She told me I was too controlling—I'm not controlling, she's in Paris, that's 5,000 miles away, and I can't control her. I just said I'm not going to let you throw your life away by trying to save someone who treated you like trash. Terry, maybe you don't know this, but she went back to visit her parents one time, when we were still living together, and they wouldn't even let her in the door. I saw her outfit before she got on that train, and you know Cleo can be kind of messy, but that day she looked flawless. Everything was in place. And her parents wouldn't even let her in the door, that's how ashamed they were. The only reason I'd go back to see my parents is to burn their house down. My brother tried to get in touch with me recently, he found me on Facebook, I don't even know how he knew it was me it's not like I have the same last name but he sent me a message saying I know we haven't been in touch in a while, and I'm like bitch what do you mean we haven't been in touch, did you even try to find me until now. Now? Bitch I'm forty-seven, not fifteen. Get the fuck out.

Anyway, he says I just want to let you know that Mom's sick, and it isn't looking good. So I blocked him as fast as I could—what was he trying to do, make me feel guilty? You make me go back to that house, and I will burn it down, I will burn that house to the ground.

I get off the phone with Jaysun and I have this feeling like where am I, oh, way up in the sky there's my head rolling back my eyes where are my eyes and I'm craving really craving drugs for the first time in a while I just want to stay up in the sky my head rolling back my head rolling back my eyes where are my eyes and what's going on. Terry, what's going on.

So I look in the mirror, but no, wrong choice. Too much trauma, who is this.

Michael Alig, why. I don't know why. We had fun together, until we didn't. And then we were still together, it's true. She chose me, she complimented my look, I felt something. There was something there. The clubs were full of people like that, she's just the one that got the attention. She was gross, and then she was worse than gross.

Maybe I was worse than gross too.

After Sid died, I was lost. Totally lost. If I didn't have the drugs then I would've been gone. That routine. Taking care of people—a baggie, a gram, five grams, ten grams, just tell me what you need, honey. I needed that routine.

Some of Sid's regulars had known her longer than me, much longer. This one girl, she asked me how Sid died, and when I said AIDS her head fell into her hands her whole body was shaking everything was sobs and I was lost. Days went by, and I went by, and I wasn't even there, but I was there, I was there in the clubs, they were there for me. Just getting dressed up, and going out, it was everything. That moment when you arrive, and I don't just mean the moment when you get there but when you're up in the sky looking down or even better when you're so high you're above the sky, there's nothing there except that floating up, up, up, and away, you are so far away hello stars you just keep going up, up, up and away until pop, everything opens up the colors that smile the lights the beat you're up, up, up, and away and that's where I wanted to stay.

People say trauma freezes you in the past, and of course I know all about that. But also there's the way trauma freezes you in the present, you can't move from that traumatized place, it's everywhere, how long will this last.

And then there's hope, which is trauma in the future.

Yes, I'm watching city employees remove all the graffiti on the streets in the CHOP with pressure washers while protected by heavily armed cops. In the middle of the night, the cops pulled people out of their tents to arrest them, threw everyone's belongings into dumpsters, and then right away city workers were painting over all the graffiti on the police station.

Now Cal Anderson is closed. No one can enter the park. They've evicted everyone, mowed the grass, and painted everything beige. The cops have driven their patrol cars inside to protect the beige.

Even that gorgeous George Floyd graffiti on the pump station, they painted it over. Why? Where is the threat? The city of Seattle removed this beauty. This statement. This remembrance. This resistance. They replaced it with beige.

They want us to know they're keeping protest signs in storage, they call this preserving the art. They will be maintaining the Black Lives Matter mural in the middle of Pine because it's in all the photos captured by drone footage for national media. In a few years some museum will announce a triumphant show about the protests—everyone feels good about a memorial, right? But the art is all over the streets, spray-painted on buildings that are now being whitewashed to return the neighborhood to its gentrified blandness.

Art is just art, and yet. When it is such a beautiful tribute to someone's life. To George Floyd's life. And then the city paints it over, just in time for July 4th. At least the city canceled the fireworks because of the pandemic. But then I'm walking through the neighborhood as everyone lights off their own fireworks, firecrackers, fire-whatever, and it feels extra-surreal because of all the explosions over the last month.

But some people just want more explosions. These jocks are screaming in the dark like they've accomplished something, but what, what do jocks ever accomplish?

My walk continues when I'm asleep, I'm walking past the explosions with Sid and do they ever end? Then, finally, silence in the dark streets, it's just the two of us and the trees, but what's that up ahead, more fireworks but silent this time, and when I get closer I realize no, these are snowflakes falling in the night light, just in this one area between trees. But snowflakes like the ones you cut with paper when you were a kid, except here they're sheets of glittery ice and I pick some up and slip them over my wrists like bracelets. They're heavy, but not too heavy. I know they're going to melt soon, but still I want to touch this surprising beauty, I want to hold onto it.

8:00 p.m. is still my favorite time, screaming with my neighbors—if you told me a few months ago that white people in Seattle would be giving each other the Black Power salute, I would have thought you were joking. But then someone on the street raises their fist to me, and I raise my fist back.

Things that make me feel less lonely tonight: the cat that runs down a flight of stairs to join me on the sidewalk, the flashing yellow lights of the new walk signal, a friendly person who says hello on the corner, the smile her boyfriend gives me, the coolness of my lips.

But how do I talk about Summer Taylor without crying? Summer was dancing in the middle of I-5 while it was blocked off by the cops for the nightly protest, late at night on July 4. I guess that's why all the helicopters were flying over. Protesters were dancing in the middle of the highway when a driver entered through an exit ramp, gunned his engine, and sped right into the protest, killing Summer and sending another protester to the hospital in critical condition. Both of them nonbinary white people dedicated to protesting for Black lives, dancing on the highway at 1:00 a.m., murdered by a Black guy in a white Jaguar. Nothing makes sense anymore.

So many people have died at these protests, and is this being normalized too? First it was nineteen-year-old Lorenzo Anderson, a Black high school student who wasn't involved with the protests, he was just in the CHOP with friends one night. I saw the candles for him on Pine the next day, and I was hoping I would learn more about him but the only people there were reporters, and a few of his friends, and I didn't want to bother them.

Lorenzo was shot in the CHOP by someone who knew him, that's what it sounds like. The protest medics were trying to help him, they begged the Fire Department to send an ambulance. The fire station is just two blocks up the street, but they wouldn't come without the cops. They wouldn't even meet activists at the edge of the CHOP. Could Lorenzo have lived if the Fire Department sent an ambulance?

And then there was sixteen-year-old Rico, who ran away from home in San Diego to join the protests, that's what he told people. In Seattle he stole a white Jeep and drove it through Cal Anderson in the middle of the night, the people sleeping in tents thought they were under attack, they heard gunfire, but was there gunfire? Rico was on some deranged joyride through the park with a fourteen-year-old in the passenger seat, they sped through the CHOP until the CHOP security opened fire on the car and killed him in a hail of bullets, sending the other kid to the hospital.

Two Black teenagers doing something dangerous and scary, but what was their intent? Rico came to join the protests, didn't he? He and the other teenager mugged some guy using a pickaxe, that guy was hurt and scared and gave them the keys to his Jeep, but it's still so hard to understand what happened next. That hail of bullets until the Jeep crashed into the CHOP security barrier, and then there's this horrible footage of white activists scrubbing blood off the streets, I can't get it out of my head.

So then the city shut down the CHOP. They blamed these murders, but of course they were planning to do it the whole time, they were just waiting for the right excuse. But what was going on with these kids, and why were they killed? So much paranoia in the CHOP every night, you could feel it building, but who were the people working security that night? I just keep thinking about that guy with the sunglasses, wasn't he an undercover cop? So maybe I'm paranoid too. But obviously there were undercover cops the whole time, everyone knew this. There was speculation about many of the central organizers right from the beginning. These were Black activists, but I always wondered about the white guys with guns. Who were they, and why were they there?

But now I'm watching a march for Summer Taylor in Minneapolis, where protesters are carrying a banner that says SUMMER FOREVER, in letters stretching across the entire street. Summer forever. And I'm crying again.

Things that make me feel less lonely tonight: picking rosemary from a sidewalk garden, the smell of lavender but without the bees that are there during the day, suddenly noticing the stars above this giant pine tree when I'm pissing in the park.

But is that a coyote, staring right at me in the dark? I don't know whether I should be scared but it seems more scared of me so I say hi, twice, in a friendly voice, like maybe how I would talk to a dog, and then it runs away as soon as I move.

I'm stretching on the railing of the stairway by the little park on Federal, and this guy is telling his friends about the union organizing he does, and then they're getting ready to say goodbye, and he says: I haven't hugged anyone since March, so it'll be weird. He puts his mask on, and they hug goodbye, and I'm crying again. So much crying. I haven't hugged anyone since March either.

How the sadness hits you all the sudden, suddenly you're lost. You're feeling the loss. How a hug is no longer just a hug. How a hug is no longer.

One day I'd like to live in a country that I don't hate as much as this one, and is it strange to think that I want that to be this country?

So much hope, and so much hopelessness, they are so close together, have they ever been this close.

I'm on my way to Lake View Cemetery to look at the toppled Confederate monument—it's the most gorgeous day in the history of the world and I'm wearing my short-shorts. Just kidding—if I managed not to wear shorts for twenty years in New York I'm not going to start now, but it's the most gorgeous day in the history of the world so I'm wearing my purple dress with the white lace stripes and pointy shoulders. With lime green tights, and my biggest magenta hat, the one with so much underwire that I can shape it into these crazy positions, today it's a capsized boat. Jaysun's working her Hawaiian ensemble.

Maybe you're wondering about the Confederate monument in Seattle, when was Seattle part of the Confederacy? Apparently in 1926, when the Daughters of the Confederacy built this lovely ten-ton granite archway to hell. And now the whole monstrosity is in pieces on the ground, covered in red paint and BLM and anarchy signs. Jaysun and I are jumping up and down on the remnants and someone drives over. Turns out it's one of the main activists from the CHOP, I recognize him but I don't know his name, and he asks if we want a picture. Sure, we say, and Jaysun hands him her phone while we model our wackiest poses, and then we all talk about how isn't this so great, this should happen every day.

My second time visiting the toppled Confederate monument doesn't go as well. The weather is still amazing, though—I'm sitting on the ruins, hoping to meet other people celebrating. Cars are driving by, stopping, staring over, but no one gets out, so it's a little eerie.

Then someone stops his car, and gets out, but he doesn't look happy. He just keeps saying why? Why?

Because it was a Confederate monument, I say.

But why would they do this to it, he says.

Because it was a monument to slavery.

But why would they do this?

This time I just ignore him, because doesn't it seem pretty obvious?

It was the Democrats who owned slaves, he says, and that's when I realize he tricked me into this conversation, he drove by just to see the toppled Confederate monument, and to argue with someone about it.

His wife, or girlfriend, or whoever that is who's still in the car, says do you know who was buried there?

No one was buried there, I say, it was a monument to the Confederacy.

At least it wasn't a grave, she says.

Why would it matter, I say, it's just a piece of stone.

It's terrible, she says, just terrible.

And then the guy says why would they do this? And that's when I say I can't talk to you, this is ridiculous, and I walk away.

Back in Volunteer Park, some guy is using a football as a pillow while he's sunbathing—this might be the first time I've found anything even remotely interesting about a football. It's one of those days when it's so nice out that you never want to go inside again. Summer in Seattle is such a relief, after all those unbearable summers in New York, how did I survive? As soon as spring started I was always panicking. But every day in Seattle the summer gets better, and now the Parks Department isn't telling us to KEEP IT MOVING, I mean the signs are still up but no one's harassing us, so I can actually pass out with my hat over my face, hoping the bugs in the grass don't bite me too much.

Still crying about Summer Taylor. Is it okay to say that I miss them, even if I didn't know them? I feel like I knew them, just reading all the messages at the memorial in front of the animal shelter where Summer used to work, it's just a few blocks from my building so I keep visiting. SUMMER EVERY DAY, it says, with a Black Power fist between EVERY and DAY, a garland of fake red sunflowers around the stencil, and then so many arrangements of real sunflowers and chalk hearts and SUMMER ALL YEAR on the sidewalk.

So many notes for Summer taped to the outside of the windows, one of them says: "Summer, you were one of the first people I met in Seattle you greeted me dancing I love to dance it was exactly what I needed you were exactly what we all needed."

I'm thinking about one night in the CHOP when I got dressed up and I was dancing on the playfield, and there were a lot of people dressed up. It was Juneteenth, so people were celebrating, it was actually the first time I'd been in the CHOP when the majority of people there were Black, and is it strange to say that's when I felt the most welcome?

An older man came up to me and complimented me on my outfit, and he said you knew Charleena, right?

He was pretty drunk, at first I wasn't sure what he said, but he was waiting for an answer so I said Charleena Lyles?

He said yeah, Charleena liked to dance, I seen you with her.

It wasn't really a question, so I smiled, and he said Charleena liked to party, that's for sure. Then a younger woman, maybe his daughter, came over and said is he giving you trouble?

And I said no, and then we each danced to our own rhythm from ten feet away, I didn't recognize the songs but the bass was hard and I was feeling it.

Charleena was already dead when I got back to Seattle, the cops had already killed her. But now I felt like maybe I could have known her, if she lived. Maybe we could have danced together in the park.

And then yesterday, two years after her murder, the head of the Seattle police union said her death was "suicide by cop." On the *Morning Show*, the Black news program made famous for covering the protests. How is this allowed.

I do not want to give the cops the right to do anything but leave the police force. They should not be allowed to do anything until then. Why would we want to hear from them? They don't deserve to speak to us.

I just keep thinking: How many more people need to die. How many more will the cops kill. The cops, and the people who think like the cops. How many more. The surveillance helicopter is circling the area, so there must be a protest nearby, but where. It's so hard to figure anything out.

Let the grief bloom. Do you know what I mean? So we won't only have more grief.

I'm on the way home from my nighttime walk, finally relaxed, and there it is again, the ALL LIVES MATTER car. All I can think about is smashing the windows—there's no one around and there are all these pebbles right in front of my building, some of them might be large enough but also they might just bounce off the windshield and hit me. And I don't want anyone to see me.

But Jaysun bought me that dead raver outfit for a reason, right? So I go upstairs, wash off my makeup, take off all my earrings, and change into my disguise. The hood covers my face, but I remember Marya said the bridge of the nose is how they recognize you from a security camera, it's a good thing we can wear masks now and that's just normal but I can't tell if my mask completely blocks the bridge of my nose so I add character glasses, thick black frames. I have a whole purse full of glasses—Jaysun's right, I save everything. And there's no way anyone would recognize me now.

I look out my window—no one's around, and the car is still there. Okay, now what do I use? I have this cute little hammer with a floral pattern covering the metal that used to be Sid's, and it would easily fit in my pocket, but is it heavy enough, I'm not sure so I take the regular hammer instead, it looks awkward in my pocket but I know it will work. Am I really doing this?

I kind of want to call Jaysun to be a lookout, but I'm ready now—that car, it can't stay there, not like that, so I walk out the back door, go right up to the back windshield where it says ALL LIVES MATTER, and hit it as hard as I can with the hammer and it shatters just like that. It's not even that loud, I could duck right back into my building but just in case anyone saw me I walk to the corner instead, and turn left, my heart racing, and I'm thinking stay calm, Terry, walk slowly, you didn't see anything.

Marya always said if you smash a window never look back or they'll know it's you, so I don't look back but I feel like everyone's looking at the hammer sticking out of my pocket even though no one's looking at me at all, and when I turn on Thomas I see that towering cedar, I step up on the roots and think yes, we're in this together, touching the bark as I'm walking up the hill but my heart is still racing when I turn onto Harvard, get to my building and rush up the stairs and when I'm finally back in my apartment I'm laughing, yes, I'm laughing, Terry, yes, we did it.

I'll admit it—I always look forward to the food my mothers cook for me because I barely know how to cook anymore, and does that make me some awful stereotype? I mean I became one of those New Yorkers who basically didn't cook for twenty years except oats in the morning, and then the pandemic started and I had to go back to cooking everything. But I just cook the simplest things—a grain, a bean, and a vegetable every morning—and then I eat the same thing all day unless I'm eating with my mothers or Jaysun. I mean my food is fine, it's healthy, it's just boring.

But when I'm with my mothers, we always end up arguing about something and that never used to happen, just once in a while, and I realize it's because of the pandemic. Usually we'd be hugging, sitting on the sofa together, laughing, touching one another, there would be so much physical intimacy and now I haven't even been inside the house. Yes, they always cook the best food and I love sitting outside but then we get in an argument and I leave feeling lost.

So here we are again, looking at one another across the table, and today they made a lentil loaf with shiitake mushrooms and roasted carrots and turnips, all these chewy textures, and then a millet-quinoa-teff blend that tastes like polenta, and pickled beets with an orange-thyme zest, and grilled asparagus in a raspberry vinaigrette, it's all so delicious and we're looking at one another and talking about the weather, and the food, and then Paula says oh, Terry, you won't believe it, the other night we saw a protest go right by the house.

And Eileen says it was completely unexpected.

And Paula says you can say that again.

And Eileen says it was exactly like you described it, so well-organized, all these young kids, they spent quite a bit of time right here on our block.

So we came out on our balcony to join in with our pots and pans, Paula says, and everyone was cheering for us, they were so appreciative.

It was quite a week, Eileen says, quite a week.

What do you mean, I say, and Paula says oh, the next night, we heard some noise again, there was chanting, right, was that the next night, Eileen?

Two nights later, Eileen says. If you can call that chanting. I think they were saying fuck the pigs.

But we didn't realize that until we went onto the balcony, and it was an entirely different crowd, wouldn't you say so, Eileen?

You can say that again—an entirely different crowd, an entirely different attitude. Everyone was wearing all-black, hoods and ski masks covering their faces, some people were wearing goggles and gas masks and other costumes, it was a small crowd but it was frightening, to be quite candid.

What were you afraid of, I say.

Oh, you never know, Eileen says, it looked like it was getting out of hand.

We were thinking about what happened over at Cal Anderson, Paula says, how it became violent. We were worried about violence.

But it was the cops who created the violence, I say.

Yes, Eileen says, we are in agreement about that, but don't you think it got out of hand?

People were traumatized, I say, they were there to protest against police brutality and then every night the cops were attacking them. Every night. You saw the news, right? You could hear if from here—you didn't need the news, it was right around the corner. Every night. Just that alone. Tear gas, pepper spray, rubber bullets, flash bang grenades. Every night. Wouldn't that make you lose it? No one could trust anyone, they were living in that tear gas. Pepper spray. Flash bang grenades. Helicopters. Surveillance planes. Drones. National Guard troops. Everyone was living in a state of trauma. Because of the cops. Because of Jenny Durkan. Because of Carmen Best. Because of this city. They wanted autonomy, but how can you be autonomous if you can't breathe. That's what George Floyd said, right, I can't breathe. I can't breathe. I can't breathe. That knee on his neck. For how long? Eight minutes and forty-six seconds. You've seen the footage. Everyone's seen the footage. They shot Breonna Taylor in her own home, for no reason. No reason at all. There's never a reason. It's just, it's all they can do. They refuse to do anything else. They strangled Eric Garner, choked him to death, people were watching, what was he saying? I can't breathe. Remember his daughter? Erica Garner, she became an activist in her father's name until she died three years later of a heart attack, at age twenty-seven. Who dies of a heart attack at twenty-seven? How old was Breonna Taylor when the cops came into her house in the middle of the night for no reason. No reason. And shot her dead. Twenty-six, right? She was twenty-six. They shot her in her own apartment. She was asleep. The cops were looking for drugs, they didn't find any drugs. Do you know who has drugs when they're twenty-six? Wait, let me rephrase that. Did you know anyone who didn't have drugs when you were twenty-six? Were they shot and killed by the cops in their own home? I mean she didn't have drugs, but no one should die for having drugs anyway, that's not a reason to die. Sandra Bland didn't kill herself in that jail cell, everyone knows that. And even if she did it was because of the cops. A traffic stop. Who dies because of a traffic stop? Have you survived a traffic stop? What did the cops say when you told them you weren't driving that fast, or you didn't know your plates were expired, did they haul you out of the car or did they say something polite while handing you a ticket? Who gets killed for a traffic stop? Tamir Rice, on the playground. The playground. They shot him on the playground, two seconds after they arrived. Two seconds. Why do you think that happened? Did anyone call the cops on me when I was on the playground? Twelve years old, climbing the trees, did anyone call the cops on me? Atatania Jefferson, why was she killed? Because her front door was open. Have you ever left your front door open? Charleena Lyles, she called the cops for help. She wanted help. They came to her house and shot her dead. Where was that? Magnuson Park, right, we've all been there. They shot her dead, and we're responsible. The list goes on, it goes on and on and on and we are responsible, you know that, we all know that, and the list goes on, it goes on and on and on . . .

And then I hear something, and I look over, and there's Paula, she's crying, and I didn't even notice those purple flowers on that vine behind her head, Paula's crying and Eileen's nodding her head, is she nodding her head or nodding off no she's about to cry too, I'm making my mothers cry and I almost want to say sorry, I'm sorry for making you cry.

Roland says Terry, have you been getting my texts?
Roland, this is a landline, remember?
Oh shit, I forgot you were keeping it real. Do you have a sec, can I email you the images? I wanted you to check them out before the meeting.
Sure, should I call you back, or do you want to hold on?
I can hold on.
So I go in the other room and check my email. The first photo is a pile of cars in a vacant lot, on fire. Then the charred remains of the cars. The cars flipped onto their sides, cracking apart. And then a series of photos that show the wreckage covered in paint and transformed into a giant three-dimensional mural, each burned-out car a letter spelling out I CAN'T BREATHE.
Roland says so what do you think?
It's incredible. Where did they do this?
I can't say for sure.
Oh, of course, but where did they find all the cars?
Look close, some of them are police cruisers.
No way.
Look close.
I mean I believe you, but . . .
So I need your advice. How do I pitch it to Veronica?
Well you know her better than I do.
That may be true, but she's my dealer, right, so I know how she sees me. But I don't know how she sees . . . Let me put it this way, I went to some of your first shows back in the day, I was still in college, I knew nothing about the art world but this girl I was dating at the time, she basically grew up in it, so she was showing me around, we were going to openings in Soho and Chelsea and I was into the art, some of it, but the scene, it was a total clusterfuck. Everyone had their head up their ass, or someone else's ass, and then we walked into your Club Kid Diaspora show, and I was like whoa, hold on, what the fuck is this. You had that naked DJ playing the same song over and over in the dark, the walls were totally

covered in stuffed animals and Rubix Cubes and doll arms like the toy store closed and you put it all up and everyone looked like they'd stepped out of the funhouse, glowing in the neon of the words on the walls saying the art world was dead, Giuliani was dead, everyone was dead, and my girlfriend was explaining the inside jokes, and I was like how the fuck do you get away with that, you know what I'm saying?

I had no idea you were there.

I was there, Terry, and I went back. I went to all your shows for those first few years until I left New York to get my MFA at Yale and that was a whole other mindfuck.

Roland, I had no idea what I was doing.

But you did, that's my point—you fucked shit up, and that's what I was looking for, I didn't know it but I knew it when I saw it. It was everything at once, you didn't know what hit you, and NO MORE WHITE CUBE right at the entrance, that was balls-out.

Well that was Cleo's piece, and Sabine's idea to put it on the outside of the gallery, but here's the thing about Veronica. You should talk to her before the meeting, get her excited, and then let her run the show. Like it's her idea. She likes to run the show, right?

That's for sure.

So all you need to do is say what people would have said in your MFA program.

I didn't learn anything in that program, it was all theory, I hate that shit.

But Veronica will love it.

That's the only thing I learned—how to get a show. You talk to the people you know. That's really all I learned. So I called my ex, and she introduced me to Veronica. Did I need grad school for that, what the fuck. Without that introduction who knows where I'd be, I'd be nowhere. Once you're in, you're in, but if you're not already in then you'll never get in, you know what I'm saying?

I know what you're saying, but don't tell Veronica that, just talk about site-specific installation or time-based performance, something ridiculous like that. Say it's Dadaesque.

Okay, you've got something there . . . Like Duchamp's readymades?
Yes.
Translated through Rauschenberg in a dystopian J.G. Ballard hellscape . . .
Yes.
Riding Gordon Matta-Clark's car through the unseen cuts in the Bronx landscape, the inner-city vernacular of hip-hop braggadocio meets . . .
Yes, yes, yes . . .
Meets . . . Surveillance capitalism. The risky business of political engagement rearranging the terms of urban life.
Yes. You don't need me. Veronica is going to love it.

Today must be a day for art, because I get to the park to lie in the sun, and I notice something in the Volunteer Park Amphitheater. I walk down the hill to look closer, and it's Chilean poster art on the graffiti-covered brick walls, everything arranged like it would be in a gallery, so you step up onto the cement stage and here's the show, it's open to the world.

You can tell it was planned for a gallery because it's all mounted perfectly. But then the show was canceled due to the pandemic, so now we have it here in the park and it's the perfect place since these are political posters and photos from mass protests in Chile at the end of last year, there's even a free zine to go along with it, and you can almost hear the helicopters flying overhead.

There's this one poster in particular—a woman with gray hair and glasses, a green bandanna covering her mouth and nose, and the heading, "Hasta que valga la pena vivir"—"Until life is worth living."

This is from before COVID, so she's wearing the bandanna to protect from tear gas, to protest the ongoing impact of the Chilean dictatorship, but it's also like she's speaking to us about the pandemic right now—I mean when will life be worth living.

She looks a little like Eileen, actually.

I get home, and I'm still thinking about that show—and then I'm actually enjoying my food, especially the buckwheat—I added chopped parsnips at the beginning, so it tastes like candy. The phone rings, it's a 917 number so I figure it's Roland again but I pick it up and it turns out it's Marya.

I'm here, she says, I'm here.

You're in Seattle?

Yes, I finally made it, I'm right here in your town. In Fremont, by the Lenin statue, how did that get here?

How did you get here?

I drove.

How'd you end up in Fremont?

Oh I met this girl on Tinder.

What?

Yeah, Christina and I are taking a break.

A break, what kind of break?

Like a break from being together all the time, it was too much.

So she knows about this girl?

Not exactly.

Are you serious?

Since when are you so concerned about Christina?

I'm not concerned about Christina, I'm concerned about you. What are you doing?

Oh don't worry, we both got tested.

You both got tested? Did you quarantine for two weeks?

Terry, relax, we're just having fun.

Marya, what are you doing, I'm not going to relax. What do you want from me, what do you fucking want from me?

Dead silence. I guess she hung up on me.

I hate this world so much, why am I living in this world?

At least I get to scream at 8:00 p.m., and honey, I'm really letting it out tonight, I mean I'm shrieking and blowing that whistle for as long as possible because I need this, I need this.

But it's weird now because everyone waits until I start the chant, three rounds of Black Lives Matter, Abolish the Police and that's just me until there's the person with the cowbell, and a few other people screaming, and I need to keep this going because it's the one moment of my day when I feel the most connected, right?

So after it's done for the night I make a little flyer that says:

Hey neighbors!
DON'T FORGET OUR NIGHTLY NOISEMAKING AT 8 PM
TO SUPPORT ESSENTIAL WORKERS & BLACK LIVES MATTER
LET'S SHOW SEATTLE WE CARE!
FROM YOUR WINDOWS, FROM YOUR CAR, IN YOUR YARD, ON THE STREET OR ROOF OR ON YOUR BALCONY . . .
8 PM EVERY DAY!!

It's not like I have any graphic design skills but there are some nice fonts on Word now, and even these shadowing effects, but then I remember I don't have a printer so I call Jaysun and she says girl, no one has a printer anymore but send it over, I'll take it to FedEx first thing in the morning, and then these posters will be up before you go to bed, don't even think of joining me, I've got my staple gun so I'll cover the neighborhood, it'll be my treat. Besides, I might as well get a walk in that isn't just the walk of shame.

Speaking of walks, just leaning against these little round bushes on 13th trimmed so meticulously really relaxes my calves and thighs and butt, looking up at that sprawling contemporary mansion built on top of an old carriage house, all the lights are always on and as far as I can tell there's nothing on the walls, just this one guy who's always sitting at his computer and then behind the house a giant cedar all plush, and then when I turn in the other direction I can see the moon rising over the arbor vitae that have grown to their full height and width instead of trimmed to make a hedge, I love the way they spread out and point up at the same time, somehow this calms me.

And then it's time for who's Zooming who at the Sabine Roth Foundation. We're all sitting in the exact same spots as before, with slight adjustments, except for Brenda, who must have gotten some advice since now she's in front of her art too, and I like that collage, foil peeling off a grid with all these textures that look like burlap and tissue and I can tell right away that Roland figured out exactly what to say to Veronica because she starts off the meeting by saying thank you all for coming this evening, it's a momentous occasion indeed, because, thanks to Terry's magnificent idea and Roland's visionary initiative, we already have images from our first commissioned site-specific installation. I expect you will be blown away, as I was, by the uncommon bravery and explosive intimacy of this series of images that document a site of conflict and contiguity limning the boundaries of our urban landscape in this crucial time of renewed urban uprising against the stark realities of political amnesia camouflaged by vague notions of equality hailed as progress and yet, and yet . . .

But, don't let me get carried away, take a sip of your drinks as I share these images, and I cannot wait to hear your responses, please do keep your microphones on since we are an intimate group of friends here, and I do want to hear everything. Can we have a round of applause.

Everyone applauds as Veronica shares the slides, and it is pretty dramatic to hear a few gasps, a few cheers, and then we're back to seeing one another, and Veronica says: So, what did you think, should we have a quick go-around.

A tour de force, Brenda says, an absolute tour de force.

Magnifico, says Paulo, while holding up his glass of wine.

And we all toast.

I'll admit I was a bit taken aback at first, Rajneesh says, but as the images progressed I found myself transported. Shaken. Elevated. Transformed.

I CAN'T BREATHE like that at the end, Manuel says. The melting of the colors. It literally took my breath away. Diasporic vocality. Thanatos and veritas. The life-giving explosion of social change.

And the lettering alone, Edwin says. All I can say is fuck yeah. Fuck yeah. Black Lives Matter.

I'll second that, Roland says.

Abolish the police, I say, and everyone looks over.

Let's make another toast, Veronica says. To the Sabine Roth Foundation, forging space in the world for artists to cross boundaries, shift the terms of engagement, and renew the creative potential for us all.

Everyone raises their glasses, mugs, and water bottles.

Now, Veronica says, I assume we've all had a chance to familiarize ourselves with the work of the artists under consideration. Everyone offered at least one suggestion, except for you, Terry. Did I miss anything?

Oh, I say, I was wondering if, given the success of our first commission, we could award another anonymous commission for a public art piece as an intervention in our current political moment.

Excellent idea, Veronica says. And can I make another observation? Everyone proposed one artist except Brenda and I, who made two suggestions—I chose one for Henri—and that leaves us with nine total. If we add on Terry's idea, that leaves us with ten, and, if we have approximately $1.4 million left to give away this year, we could easily award $140,000 to each of these worthy candidates, and leave it at that. No need for unnecessary chitchat.

Everyone applauds.

Fantastic, Veronica says, then we are essentially done for the year. I will draw up these checks ASAP, put together a press release, and, since it doesn't look like we'll be able to meet in person, perhaps we could save the public celebration until next year, what do you think?

Everyone applauds.

Veronica holds up her glass, and says: It has been an honor and a pleasure to work with all of you—I want to thank you from the bottom of my heart for playing such a crucial role in fulfilling Sabine's legacy, and for giving so generously of your time and energy to support a thriving artistic community in New York—it's at times like these when artists need our support more than ever.

Jaysun says girl, I don't want to scare you but I just got a COVID test—my doctor was so sweet he came over after work with a swab and did it outside my building, I almost wanted to make out with him and he is gay but anyway I have to wait for my results before we get together, just in case.

Did something happen at the park?

Girl, worse. Club Z.

Club Z is open?

Girl, I didn't believe it either, but people were posting from there on Sniffies . . .

What's Sniffies?

Some terrible cruising app, but anyway I was like what, are you sure, I mean what loophole could they possibly be using? So I went over there just to see, like a detective, and sure enough there was this little paper sign next to the door that said Masks Required, and I couldn't believe it, so I opened the door.

Were people really wearing masks?

No, girl, I mean not for more than five seconds, especially not in that steam room.

What, you went in the steam room?

Girl, don't judge me. It was raining hard that night, I was desperate. I mean I'm always desperate—Sandy and I used to cuddle all the time but then she got married and her husband was jealous, can you believe he was jealous of me—married people are the worst. I used to cuddle with everyone and I miss that so much and I don't even know if I'm horny I just need something, right, so, no, I didn't actually go in the steam room but I was waiting outside when everyone was in there, and some guy came out with a hard-on so I was sucking his dick, even once he started coughing, he had this horrible hacking cough but now I was the center of attention I mean he was the center of attention but everyone was right there I could feel all those bodies someone had his hands on the back of my neck I mean it was hot even though he was practically coughing right on me, and you know I was doing so well avoiding the respiratory droplets, but anyway he didn't come, he was too tweaked out, everyone was tweaked out and now I might have COVID I mean I hope I'm at least partially immune from getting it before but who knows, right, I could be in the hospital on a ventilator in a week or maybe they won't even have a ventilator and what was I even doing at Club Z I've never gone there before it's just tweakers and bears and the messiest messes and what is wrong with me, I'm so stupid.

Do you have any symptoms?

I had a sore throat for a few days, and that's gone now, it was probably just from sucking his dick, it was too big for my throat but I was trying, girl, I was trying even after I heard that hacking cough and maybe this sounds even stupider but I was thinking I should stay on my knees for as long as possible because that way I was further from the cough but there's no air in that place, everything smell like poppers and feet and chlorine and rotting smelly bodies and why did I go there now of all times I'm such a mess, girl, and I wasn't even drunk, I mean sure I had a few cocktails but I don't drive if I've had more than three or four so I was just tipsy but I went inside anyway, I was so desperate, I mean I was curious but mostly because I was so desperate and that was five days ago, I just got tested so it'll take a few days before I get the results, but even if I'm all clear I definitely don't want to hang out with you for the full two weeks, just to make sure, right, I mean I know we need two weeks just to be sure.

Things that make me feel less lonely tonight: the curve of the moon, rubbing my chest to remind myself what's inside, the ACAB chant on repeat in my head, "A, C, A, B, all cops are bastards."

Things that make me feel less lonely tonight: the blue of the nighttime sky and how it softens at the horizon, all the different *V*s of tree trunks into branches, looking up and seeing the way the leaves pulse so gently with the wind and can I do that too.

Things that make me feel less lonely tonight: the shape of this tree that looks like it's dancing, a stained-glass rose in someone's bay window, the sound of a fountain that competes with the highway noise if I listen carefully enough.

Are people in your neighborhood still making noise at 8:00 p.m.? It's quieting down over here, and I'm worried, because this is my most reliable moment of the day, and what would I do without it.

Things that make me feel less lonely tonight: moving my hands in the shape of the flatter side of the moon, looking up at the top parts of the trees to see how the leaves meet the sky, the light of the fake candles in someone's wide-open windows.

Things that make me feel less lonely tonight: the rock that juts off a stairwell on a hill but somehow doesn't move, the fern growing out of the tree stump just behind this rock, leaning against the rock to soften my lower back, how a rock can soften.

Things that make me feel less lonely tonight: how a wall can be cracked and still stable, a striped corduroy sofa sitting outside in someone's entryway, realizing that strange bird sound is actually my right shoe, how a street can be so quiet in the middle of a city.

Things that make me feel less lonely tonight: leaning against the trunk of a holly tree on the sidewalk, running my hands along the surprising roughness of the bark, how the air can be warm and cool at the same time.

Things that make me feel less lonely tonight: the strange oblong shape of the giant cloud that's suddenly floating just above the moon and all of its textures, how it makes the moon look so much brighter, knowing that even when I don't see the rabbits they're here.

Things that make me feel less lonely tonight: how a tree can reach out in so many directions, how the bright light behind this fence means you can see through it, how the sound of the highway can somehow feel comforting when it's not too close.

Yes, I'm delighted to receive an email from my health insurance company with the subject line, "Learn about your mental health options," and a link that doesn't work.

But someone yelled LOVE YOU to me today from the building across the street after our 8:00 p.m. noisemaking—yes, this is what keeps me going. I think it's the same person who was yelling MEOW for a while, but I haven't heard that in a while.

Love as a public force, not a private impulse. Why is this so rare?

Things that make me feel less lonely tonight: the smell of rosemary on my fingers after I pick it from a sidewalk planter, the way a cat has eight legs when it runs across the street, everything growing on top of this old cement garage.

Things that make me feel less lonely tonight: the sound of the breeze, the trees that grow across the street like there's no street, the feeling of dry moss on a tree trunk, the way the best meditation is the one you don't expect.

Seattle, I don't know if I've ever seen the moon so crisp and clear in the sky, it's like a model for a full moon, a full moon model.

Things that make me feel less lonely tonight: a tiny rabbit hopping across the street, a gaudy homemade chandelier against a red wall, looking up into someone's '60s apartment filled with books and file boxes and cat art, the full moon in the crisp clear sky.

This queen on the sidewalk by Volunteer Park says can I tell you something, and I'm kind of excited because no one talks to me on the street here. But it turns out she wants to tell me there's a cure for COVID-19 and it's hydroxychloroquine, I give her a look but then she tells me Facebook is blocking the evidence, scientists have known since February that it's all a hoax and we don't have to worry. Then she says you look worried—you're not worried, are you worried, it's all a hoax.

Back at home I'm watching footage of white vigilantes blocking the street to prevent Black protesters from reaching the suburban home of Seattle's Black police chief—yes, I hate this world, but I hate this country even more.

But then there it is again, that big beautiful moon so clear in the sky, it surprised me because it moved over.

Things that make me feel less lonely tonight: the way one block can be totally still and one block can be windy, how stopping by the same trees every night gives me different feelings, how a square can become a diamond can become a square inside a window frame.

Things that make me feel less lonely tonight: finding a neighborhood cat in the park and sitting together, touching the ferns growing out of a retaining wall and sensing their strength, noticing that someone changed their lighting from fluorescents to something softer.

On Converge Media, Sadé Smith says, "It's not Black lives in the future, it's Black lives now."

And that's why I'm keeping my nightly protest going—this is what I can do on my own. It's not just Black Lives Matter at a protest, it's Black Lives Matter everywhere.

Things that make me feel less lonely tonight: the conversation between the rustling of metal streamers blowing on a balcony and the whitening of the horizon at twilight, leaning on a hedge and waving to people walking by, who actually say hello.

When you think you're having a really horrible day, but then you wake up the next day and you realize that was the good day, why does this happen so often. It's 9:30 p.m., and I'm relaxing on the sofa, trying to get enough energy to go out on my nighttime walk, when someone starts knocking on my door. I don't know anyone in the building, so I figure I'll just ignore it, but then it keeps going, so I go over to the door and I say hello?

It's Sally and Peter, someone says, we want to talk about the screaming.

The screaming.

Do you want to call me on the phone, I say.

We want to talk in-person, Sally says.

You're not asking me to come out and talk to you in the hallway in the middle of a pandemic, I say, right? Obviously there's not enough space for social distancing.

A pause. We'd like to talk to you in person.

Okay, I say, why don't I meet you outside in fifteen minutes.

Okay, Sally says.

What the fuck is going on? Sally was the first person in the building to actually introduce herself, she said it's so nice to see someone who knows how to wear color, you're brightening up the neighborhood, and at first I thought she was flirting with me, but then I met her husband. They're an older couple but younger than my mothers, so probably in their sixties, and they've always been friendly until now.

I can't believe they wanted me to come out in the hallway and talk to them—two feet away, with no ventilation, what the fuck. Why don't they just call me?

I look for something to wear—why did I say fifteen minutes, I need more than fifteen minutes.

This must be the time for the purple coat—it's probably too warm out, but whatever. It's a good look.

I walk downstairs, open the front door, and there they are, waiting for me. Let's go across the street, I say, and I cross the street without waiting for them to respond. I walk up the stairs by the boarded-up house, so we can be further apart and I'm not in anyone's way. I take off my mask, and make sure I'm at least ten feet away. What do you want to talk about, I say.

Sally says we want to talk about the screaming.

Do you mean me yelling Black Lives Matter, Abolish the Police every day?

Sally says it's not about the message, it's about the screaming.

But there's no message without the screaming.

I want you to realize that when you are screaming, it is insensitive, unkind, and you are disturbing the peace. Think about your neighbors. This is serving no one in a productive way.

Peter says Sally grew up in a household with a father who was always enraged, she was terrorized as a child, it was totally unpredictable, and still, whenever she hears yelling it brings her back to that place, she can't help it. She's done a lot of work on this over the years, but still she will start shaking, she can't sleep, she suffers from migraines, it gets in the way . . .

I grew up with the same father, I say, I know all about that.

Peter says okay. That calm voice—I hate people like that, that fake calm. I don't know why I just made up my father, I just know they were expecting to shut me up with Sally's trauma. But I'm through.

As someone who works with abuse survivors, Peter says, and I cut him off.

We're not talking about abuse, I say, we're talking about me yelling Black Lives Matter, Abolish the Police every day at 8:00 p.m. Every day at 8:00 p.m. It's predictable. You can plan for it.

It's an assault on our senses, Sally says. It's a disruption in service of one. I am surprised at your selfishness. Like you, we are just trying to hang on until the usurper is out of the White House and we regain some sanity in this country.

I'm not interested in sanity, I say. Who is this for, Sally says, you are fraying our already shredded nerves—screaming Black Lives Matter and Abolish the Police is serving no one in a productive way. Frontline workers have gone on the record to say that this nightly ritual does not help them. Period.

Just then, some random guy walks by—that's you, he says to me, and I smile. And he gives me a thumbs-up.

Nice coat, someone else says.

This is what it means to have neighbors. Why can't they all be like this?

Suddenly Sally switches to a different voice, it's like she's talking to a child, and she says: Do you need us?

What, I say.

And she says Terry, you don't seem like yourself.

I just stare at her, but I'm thinking honey, this is more myself than you've ever seen.

We just want you to think about the ramifications of your actions, Peter says.

What about the ramifications of your actions, I say.

And Sally yells YOU FUCKING CUNT, YOU FUCKING SELFISH CUNT.

And I say I love the word cunt, call me cunt any time!

I'm thinking about Kevin Aviance's song "Cunty." Cun-ty, cun-ty, cun-ty, cun-ty, cun-ty, cun-ty, cun-ty, cun-ty . . . Whatever happened to Ms. Aviance?

Peter and Sally go back into the building, and I'm so angry I'm shaking.

It means so much to me to scream with my neighbors. Even just a few minutes of collective joy, collective rage, collective struggle, isn't this why we live in cities?

When I was a kid and I would climb every tree, I remember the feeling of getting up there and leaning back and I wasn't looking down I was looking out at the world. And now when I lean against a hedge there's something similar in that weightlessness that relaxes my back, opens up my spine, lets in breath, allows my body to move more freely.

There's that cedar hedge at 11th and Aloha, it smells so fresh when you lean back and that really helps you to breathe deep. Start in front of the house on 11th, and then the hedge wraps all the way around on Aloha, and the best part is on the left side of the driveway because it's so thick and dense so you can really fall into it. And then as Aloha slopes downhill there's an arbor vitae hedge that's looser, it doesn't look like it will take your weight, but actually you can bounce and twist down the hill so you're dizzy when you get to Federal, and if you want to keep going then you can cross the street and take a look at the rosebushes with their names printed on white placards, and then maybe rest against the cement retaining wall before another strand of arbor vitae that you can roll through. Roll and bounce, roll and bounce, all the way to 10th. And, since we're going in that direction, I might as well mention the cedar hedge in front of that black house with a sign for Capitol Hill Wealth Management, right next to Quest Bookshop and how is that still there, after all these years, but we're not here for wealth management or New Age books, we're here to lean against that cedar hedge. It's always trimmed tight so it's not as relaxing but the branches press up against your shoulders and if you lean all the way into them then your lower back lets go.

Don't let me forget this one bouncy round shrub on Harvard—I don't know what it is, but you can really sink into it, almost like you're going to fall, and maybe you do, a little, but into the bush and around in a circle, and because you fall so far back there's an even deeper release, a freedom in the hips, so when you get to that low hedge over by Republican that doesn't look like much at all, but wait, lean your calves into it, try it from the front and back, roll through it in circles, and then when you start walking again your legs swing wider.

Then there's that tall hedge around the corner from the scenic overlook on 15th, you can let your whole body weight fall into it and then roll down the hill while looking across the street at that house with palm trees that should be in LA. But, don't roll too far, because just across the street toward the Union graveyard is that boxwood hedge that's one of the bounciest. I like to lean into that one from all different angles and bounce, bounce, catching the sun on my face.

Then there's the short hedge in the graveyard that's perfect for letting your lower back go, it doesn't look like it will hold you, but it does, it really does, from any direction. And then back on Federal by the biggest mansions, someone has very thick ivy falling down their wall, and that's fun to lean into. Oh—and that giant hedge next to the church over by Prospect, that one doesn't feel as stable at first but you can really fall back, and it still catches you. Then there's the skinny but deep cedar hedge up a block, and next door there's an architecture firm in a house with a really strong hedge, sometimes too strong because it pokes into you, but speaking of poking into you, there's that hedge that they just trimmed way back on Mercer near 11th—they cut it so far back that there aren't any leaves, it kind of looks dead but it's still great as an acupressure massage tool, you can really get into those pressure points. Try it on your back, shoulders, chest, just don't fall on it too fast or you might hurt yourself.

Oh—up the hill on Republican and Malden there's a laurel hedge that you can lean on in two directions—from Malden, and from Republican. Speaking of sinking in, across 15th on Harrison there are these giant shrubs trimmed into big round shapes, and maybe they're laurel too, but so lush you can fall all the way inside. Just don't do it when it's raining, or you'll get really wet, no matter how many layers you're wearing the water will get between them.

Don't let me forget that juniper hedge on Melrose overlooking the highway—between Harrison and Thomas. That one is so fun to fall into, it really gives you such a supportive back massage like some sort of memory foam but it's juniper not memory so it smells amazing, even with the highway right there. Oh, and that reminds me of the rounded tall juniper bushes on Bellevue and Harrison, those can be fun because you can get lots of different angles, and maybe it's not as much of a commitment, just one tall bush at a time. Then walk to the dead-end overlooking the highway and the skyline, stretch your legs on that wooden barrier while looking at the Space Needle, and across the street there are those short juniper bushes that help to even out your calves. Which reminds me of another juniper hedge just up the hill on Boylston and Thomas, that one works best if you find a spot that will support your lower back, and then you can kind of sit right there facing the brick apartment building across the street with the bamboo that they're always cutting back, the three trees growing in a circle on the little traffic island and there's that pale blue craftsman house across the street that's subdivided into apartments and if you look to the left you can let your eyes soften into the neon signs on Olive Way, and then scan the lights in the windows of the apartment buildings, all the tones of white and yellow but also magenta and red and that's one of my favorite ways to relax, letting my eyes blur.

Speaking of relaxing, don't let me forget that enormous cedar tree that towers above all the buildings that's just down the hill, the bark is so soft you can lean against it and look up at the moon when the moon is out, or just feel the rain falling softly on your face if you're angled in the right direction.

And, I just discovered an incredible dense hedge with orange berries on Olive Street and Summit—it's on the downhill slope, so you can relax your body at every height, it's the perfect relaxation partner although I'm not sure the gawkers who cross the street to avoid me are thinking the same thing.

Maybe you guessed that I'm talking about hedges because I don't want to talk about Sally and Peter pounding on my door so hard that something falls off the wall and shatters on the floor. Oh, it's that vintage glass stoplight cover that was hanging on a nail in the corner, but the sound is so loud that at first I thought it was outside.

No, I don't want to talk about the harassing notes on my door or the emails Sally and Peter send to the condo association, starting with the one where Sally describes me as "he/she"—yes, he/she. What year is this? No, I don't want to talk about conversations with board members or the property management company, everyone telling me they agree with me, but.

Between you and me, these people say, but how the hell does that help me. No, I don't want to talk about that I'll just tell you that yes, I'm still screaming with my neighbors, every night at 8:00 p.m., yes, Black Lives Matter, Abolish the Police, Black Lives Matter, Abolish the Police, Black Lives Matter, Abolish the Police, join me.

Jaysun says do you want me to smash their windows, and it's true that Sally and Peter live on the second floor, which is just a few steps above ground level in the front, so their windows would be really easy to smash but anyway, that's not where we're going with this, I mean it wouldn't help me, not for more than a few minutes of elation but the high wouldn't be worth the crash so no, honey, I don't want you to smash their windows because they would know it was me.

But it wouldn't be you, Jaysun says, it would be me.

Trust me, honey, they would know.

So I don't want to talk about the nuisance complaint they made when obviously they're the nuisance, and, yes, I'll just keep screaming and making noise and there's that cowbell again, I love that cowbell, did I tell you that Sally and Peter thought I was using the cowbell and the whistle at the same time, even though they're coming from two different directions? That's because their apartment is on the opposite side of the building. For a few days I was thinking okay, I can think of a different noisemaker, something that isn't as loud as the safety whistle, I even started ordering things online but then I realized wait, they don't care about the whistle it's that I'm yelling Black Lives Matter, that's what they can't handle.

So let me tell you about Facebook—yes, I post about this on Facebook, and ask people to show up and join me from downstairs if anyone's nearby, and I get so many supportive comments I can hardly believe it because Facebook never works for me and of course this doesn't last, but let's not talk about that, let's talk about Tia, the livestreamer who found me when I was posting pictures of Dykes Against Durkan. Now she says: If that lady in your building needs a copy of *White Fragility*, I can deliver it to her door.

And when I respond with a bunch of hearts, and say she might need several copies, Tia says: If you need someone to come on over, I'm just around the corner on Belmont.

And then here she is, joining me from downstairs with the chant they always do at the evening march, and I'm laughing because I can never remember all the parts, but then there are other people across the street joining in and afterward I yell down and ask Tia if she wants to go on a walk—yes, she says, I'm going to the co-op, do you want to walk me there?

Tia's wearing this headwrap that looks like a bow at the front, green and pink and yellow with black stripes and the funny thing is that it almost matches the skirt I'm wearing although mine's more of a geometric pattern. She's wearing cobalt blue eyeliner with her Black Lives Matter mask and I love her DECOLONIZE BLACKNESS T-shirt, she says: I made it because it's the work I need to do—I was not a woke child, I was like the good Negro neighbor for all the white families in the Central District because my dad was a lawyer and my white mom worked for Microsoft, and I went to the same private schools as the white kids so this made their parents feel less guilty about how they were gentrifying the fuck out of everything with their leaf blowers and SUVs and designer dogs. And don't even get me started on landscaping crews and Teslas and designer babies. My parents were gentrifiers too—they bought that old mansion for nothing and fixed it up and now it's worth millions but at least they did it because they wanted me to grow up around Black people. Have you been over to 23rd and Union lately?

No, I say.

What's happening to Capitol Hill is bad, but that's worse. It's like a spaceship landed and the gentrifiers got out and swept everything away. Union was already white hipster territory, but that block between 22nd and 23rd—you know there's like the gentrification where suddenly the houses are renovated and the new owners bring in drought-tolerant plants and pollinators and fences and babies and that's how I grew up, but then there's the gentrification where you can't even figure out what used to be there. That Uncle Ike's on the corner, it's like the biggest fuck-you to the neighborhood, or what used to be the neighborhood, when he opened his first pot shop he called the cops on Black kids selling pot across the street so he could have a monopoly—capitalism has no shame. And people still shop there, how many stores does he have now, he makes millions off the school-to-prison pipeline, sorry, I'm sure you already know all this, it's just that whenever I go over to see my parents I have to walk through that disaster zone and yes I have a route where I can kind of avoid it and just look at the houses and get angry at all the new cracker boxes but then sometimes you really need to feel the damage, don't you—sorry, I have a tendency to talk too much—where did you grow up?

12th and Aloha, I say.

Same thing, without the Black people, she says. I went to school over there, white guilt central.

I think I went to the same school, I say, and we laugh, but neither of us mentions which school we went to.

We get to the co-op, and Tia suggests an elbow bump but I've been avoiding that the whole time so I say how about a fake hug, and then we're both smiling under our masks and it feels nice to make a new friend.

Then as I'm walking home I hear something that sounds like a protest, but where is it, I rush down the hill and there it is on Broadway, a small Black Bloc march, everyone all masked up, and it sounds larger than it is because they have a bullhorn, maybe a few dozen people, someone's spray-painting all the parking meters, why the parking meters, I'm not sure, but I join at the back so I can look casual, not like anyone would confuse me for being part of this march, someone's drumming and everyone's yelling and I'm yelling too and I am a part of this march, we pass the gas station and wind onto 10th, and just like that there's the sound of shattering glass, it's that new building that's going up, they just put in the windows and I love that sound, the lights are flashing in the building but there's no sound to the alarm and I turn back up 10th so I'm not there when the cops arrive, now I'm filled with all this adrenaline I want to keep going but I don't want to get arrested so I march home.

My mothers show up the next day at 8:00 p.m. with flowers, yes, flowers, a huge bouquet of dahlias and when I come down they say they're so proud of me—for staying true to your values, Eileen says. And Paula nods her head.

I ask if they want me to walk them home after I put the flowers in a vase, and when I come back down Paula says oh, your hair, we haven't seen your lovely hair in so long, and I guess she's right because I'm always wearing a hat when we get together because I need to protect my eyes from the light, and Eileen says of course we love all your hats too, everything, you are quite the fashion plate—Paula, we know where she got her sense of style, don't we.

Paula says I wish I could take credit for that.

We walk past some of those new box condos and Eileen stops, and says they all look the same, don't they.

And Paula says couldn't they at least have put some landscaping in.

You mean something that isn't already dead, Eileen says.

What a shame, Paula says.

And we're all in agreement about that.

Eileen says Terry, we want you to know that we are in full support of your First Amendment rights—isn't that right, Paula?

And Paula says 150 percent. Tell that woman to spend some time with a decent therapist. It's harassment what she's doing, pure and simple. It just makes me furious, the injustice of it all.

If I were her therapist, Eileen says, I would suggest that she join you. Get out there and scream, let it loose, shake off the trauma. Don't let your body freeze. Every evening at 8:00 p.m., you are giving her an opportunity to release her trauma and support an important political cause at the same time.

Who doesn't need a little catharsis, Paula says. Every night at eight, we will be on our balcony with our pots and pans.

If you need any legal advice, Eileen says, Paula is connected to every lawyer in town—aren't you, Paula?

Not property lawyers, Paula says, but I'm sure I could get a referral. Speaking of property, Eileen, remember when all the houses in the neighborhood looked like this?

We look over at the old house that always has a giant stack of rotting newspapers outside, blackberry vines surrounding one of the cars in the driveway, ferns growing from the roof of the house. And Eileen says oh, I didn't even realize, Paula, look over there, Andre's place, what a shame.

Paula says Terry, you remember Andre, right?

I'm not sure, I say.

Andrea? Got you dressed up in his fake fur coat and you went to the Broadway Grill.

Oh Andrea, I say. I remember her. She chain-smoked Virginia Slims, and always had that flask of gin in her purse.

I forgot about that flask of gin, Eileen says. Sometimes I regret that we didn't provide better role models.

Don't say that—they were perfect. Those were the girls who taught me how to live.

But they didn't live, Paula says, what a shame.

And here we are, Eileen says, going down memory lane.

I'm okay with memory lane, I say.

Let me tell you something then, Paula says. Sometimes, Terry, when we get together, I end up thinking of all our old friends, the ones we lost, and you know what it is? You still talk a bit like them, the cadence in your voice.

Is it the universal she?

I forgot about the universal she, Paula says. That's what we called it, wasn't it. When your school thought you had a speech impediment, that was a hoot.

Or a learning disability, Eileen says. That was ridiculous. Let's go back down to 12th, oh, the hill is steep here, but look at that view, Paula.

I never get tired of that view, Paula says.

Back on 12th, Eileen says well at least this block still feels the same, although it wouldn't hurt if they'd fix the sidewalk, would it. I want to show you something, do you see that house up ahead on the corner, how long do you think they'll spend renovating? At least a year. Terry, can you believe the houses on our block are going for two million now? Over two million, on 12th. We bought our place for $72,000, and the owners were thrilled to get out. Just thrilled.

Terry, this has been such a pleasure, Paula says.
And Eileen says yes, we must do this again soon.

We give each other our fake hugs, and then I'm on my way to check in with my favorite trees in the park. The thing about loneliness is that it's always there, and yet, sometimes, suddenly, it isn't.

But now there's a nuisance complaint against me, and when I call Paula for legal advice, and she calls her friend, her friend says of course it should be a First Amendment matter, but condo law isn't the same as US law—if they find you guilty of an infraction as stated in the declaration then you can fight it, but it could get costly.

How costly, I ask.

Very costly, she says, if this gets dragged on.

Now Sally says that whenever I yell Black Lives Matter, it causes "shouting-related PTSD," even though she and Peter both admitted that if they put on noise canceling headphones and turn on the TV then they don't actually hear me, but, here's the catch, just the anticipation is what causes the PTSD. Just the anticipation.

Sally says: Instead of Black Lives Matter, Abolish the Police, Terry could yell "PB&J, that's all that I will eat," and the resulting emotional and mental damage I experience would be the same.

She put this in writing. This is what she put in writing.

Now she says that because of "Terry's cruelty," she suffers sleep loss and nightmares, loss of appetite, 24/7 anxiety, headaches and stomach pain, difficulty concentrating on work, and income loss. "Terry has long since crossed the line from bad neighbor to one who is intentionally inflicting emotional distress. I will not apologize to anyone for complaining about this, and I will not stop advocating for my well-being. There is no excuse for what she is doing."

She says she's been hospitalized, and medicated, and her quality of life has been destroyed by me yes me. Whenever I yell Black Lives Matter, she thinks it's an attack on her. But the only way it could relate to her is if it relates to her racism.

America, you gotta get it right, this guy is yelling as he throws his boomerang in the park. Needless to say, the boomerang is not coming back.

This woman is cheering her dog on as it drinks directly from the water fountain, even though there's a dog bowl with its own faucet. If only the dog could cheer her on while she gets on her knees and laps up that water.

Things that make me feel less lonely tonight: singing nothing nothing nothing NOTHING in my head until I notice the yellow-orange of the headlights on this old bus, the red-pink-orange of the horizon, and the way window panes can turn almost the same color as the sky.

Things that make me feel less lonely tonight: feeling the cool wind on my calves, kicking a discarded dog ball down the street, imagining I'm dancing with the leaves of the trees blowing in the wind until I am dancing with the leaves of the trees blowing in the wind.

Yes, I'm the one who crossed the street to watch these people make out in their fifth floor window, but now I can't find them. Everywhere a missing cat sign—are there more missing cats lately, or are there just more people missing their cats?

Things that make me feel less lonely tonight: the way the lights on the umbrella on the roof of this building make it look like a spaceship up there, shaking in the wind, everyone who has their doors open to let in the cool air, the way music from far away can still sound like music.

Things that make me feel less lonely tonight: standing on a pile of gravel in front of a construction site and looking up at the stars, finding the people who sit on the two chairs behind a house overlooking a parking lot and waving hello while yelling I like your little sitting area.

Things that make me feel less lonely tonight: looking up at the silhouette of a pine tree against the sky, and then all the trees, the sound of rabbits in the bushes, or are they squirrels, red geraniums at the entrance to a house with a red door.

Okay, I don't want to keep you in suspense anymore. I mean I don't want to keep me in suspense. I mean this is getting too stressful. So I agree to go outside for the noisemaking. Once I'm outside, Sally and Peter don't have any control over what I do, right?

Here I am, running down the stairs to get outside in time, and there's Jaysun, of course she arrived before me. She says girl, that glitter, where did you get that glitter.

Honey, you know I always have glitter.

And I love what you've done with your hair, she says, so many butterflies, and that shaved part underneath. The drama of it all.

Your hair looks cute too, I say, I like how you're growing it out.

My Indi-fro? I was styling it down with pomade and mousse, girl, remember mousse, I was trying to keep it under control without my usual salon styling but now I'm just going to let her loose, okay? It's not like I have to go into the office, or anything.

Oh, I brought a whistle for you.

Oh my God, with a pink lanyard, I love it. Okay, one minute to go.

We're across the street by the boarded-up house, and now I can do call and response with Jaysun.

Black Lives Mat-ter.

Abolish the Police.

Black Lives Mat-ter.

Abolish the Police.

Black Lives Mat-ter.

Abolish the Police.

Then when we're blowing our whistles I can hear the people joining in from the balconies at the Roni Lee so we move in that direction and now we can wave and cheer each other on, Jaysun's jumping up and down and she says this is fun, girl, this is fun.

Someone yells YOU GO GIRL from my building, and for a moment I'm excited but when I look over I see that it's Sally, waving from her window.

What?

Jaysun, I say, did you see that? No, wait, don't look, let's walk around the block, okay?

Girl, that's perfect because I have gifts for you.

More gifts?

Girl, don't even try to tell me no gifts, I have to get a rush somehow. Let's walk over to that little park on Boylston.

Tashkent?

Oh my God, it's called Tashkent, how exotic, like we're going on a trip. Okay, I have two gifts, one of them I know you'll like because it'll make it easy to smash windows. Just in case. I'm not suggesting anything,

I mean just in case. That was fun, though, I like yelling Abolish the Police, girl, you're really good with the whistle, I have to catch up with your whistle skills. Let's make this our daily plan, okay, it will be good for me, I need to get some exercise and did you see those people cheering, you're famous.

At the Roni Lee?

And in the other one with the rocks. Even the Broadway Market. And in the other direction there was someone with a cowbell. I think it was the building on the other side, I'll look over there next time. But there was someone in your building too.

Honey, that was Sally.

Who's Sally. Wait, girl, that racist bitch who called you a he/she?

Yes.

Girl, the shade. She says you're driving her to suicide but then she's there watching you and cheering you on, I thought she was so traumatized she had to go to the hospital. I thought she couldn't handle the noise. I thought it reminded her of her father. Girl, I don't even know what to say. People act like Seattleites are friendly on the outside but cold underneath, but actually they're cold on the outside and vicious monsters underneath. Okay, well I'll be your bodyguard, in case she starts throwing things. Girl, speaking of throwing things, I just lost it in the park the other night. I totally lost it.

What happened?

Girl, now that my COVID scare is over, I decided I'm only going after what I want, no more just settling, it's what I want or nothing.

What do you want?

Hugs, girl, hugs. Intimacy. I don't just want body parts, I want connection.

That makes sense.

Well, that's easy for you to say, but how do I make it happen?

I have no idea, I mean I'm so shut down I don't even think about sex. I think about hugs, but I know they can't happen, so I hug the trees. I really miss ecstatic dance, that's what I miss the most. The other day I woke up from this dream where I was about to come, and I realized I'd shoved the body pillow almost up my cunt.

Girl, that's hot, maybe I need a body pillow.

It was hot, but then I woke up, and I wanted to stay in that place, right, all that energy when you're about to come, but I couldn't get back there, I was already too tired.

What about that girl who came over the other day, she was hot.

Honey, she's like twenty-something—twenty-five, at most.

There's nothing wrong with twenty-something, you don't look a day over thirty.

But I feel like three hundred.

Well there's nothing wrong with three hundred either, I know that's how I felt by the time I turned twenty-one—girl, how did we survive?

Honey, I have no idea. Anyway, it was fun hanging out with Tia because she's so smart, and she knows everything about the protests, but I'm not dating a twenty-five-year-old. Or anyone, I'm fine with that. I just miss dancing. And I know what you're saying about hugs.

Yes, hugs. But these bitches at the park are so fucked up, if you touch anything that isn't their dick they like freak out and run away.

Where's the consent?

Girl, there's no consent, that's for dykes, you know that, these fags are incapable—if you say as much as hello then you've already lost your chance but it's even worse on the apps because then they just lie about everything. Everything. The last time I went on Grindr someone told me he was looking for a long-term relationship and asked if he could text me so I said sure, even though I knew that wasn't going anywhere and at first when he said the pandemic was devastating I thought okay, here's someone who's laying his emotions out right away so I said it was devastating for me too and then he said he was coping by learning about cryptocurrency.

Cryptocurrency?

Yes, girl, it was a total scam. I knew he was out of my league but I thought maybe he had an Asian fetish but it wasn't even that it was just some scam to steal money from lonely faggots and leave me alone, I already work for the Evil Empire. At least at the park it's just bend over and take my load, but wait, I'm getting distracted, so the other night there was this whole group gathered under the tree and I got excited at first because I like groups but then I realized it was a circle jerk where no one was even touching anyone it was like they were dead inside I mean I'm glad people were wearing masks but the energy was so gross because there was this Abercrombie model couple there, total A-list, and we don't usually get A-list at the park I mean even B-list is unusual but anyway, there they were, slumming with us, so all these girls were acting extra-masculine to prove they were worthy of being in the company of the Aberzombies so it was like a bunch of straight guys jerking off even though I'm sure they just wanted that Aberzombie cock up their ass but the Aberzombies weren't letting anyone touch them, nothing at all, they were too good for us and I just wanted them gone from this world, gone gone gone gone GONE—but anyway, here we are, in Tashkent, and I got you some gifts. Let's go in a dark corner, just for kicks. Not by the tents, that other corner down there. Okay, close your eyes and hold out your hands.

Jaysun puts something in my hands, cold metal, heavy and compact.

Okay, now you can look, she says, it has a spring and a spike, open it up.

I open it up, and it's a little hammer with a lot of weight at the end, but instead of a hammer it's sharp. And you can fold it up so the spike is totally out of the way. The handle even has an ergonomic grip on it. Jaysun's right, it does seem perfect for smashing windows.

Where'd you get this, I say.

Girl, I did my research. Now, the next gift I know you don't want, but listen, remember what you said about dancing, this is about dancing. I know it's been extra-stressful with those racists in your building, even though now we have our party time every night at eight, but, listen, I got you something so you can play music on your walks, in case you want to ignore everyone and dance, yes, it's a cell phone, I won't tell anyone, it's just so you can play music, tune everyone out, you don't have to use it, but just in case. No one has the number, it'll be our little secret. It's just a burner phone, I paid for the first six months, I knew you wouldn't want an iPhone so I got you this fossil and all you need is SoundCloud to play music, I already installed it. Just choose a few DJs and then SoundCloud will start making suggestions, and if you don't like it then throw the phone away but just in case, girl, just in case, oh, and I was going to get you these cute magenta noise-canceling headphones but then I realized you couldn't wear them with your hat so I got you Sony earbuds, they're the best earbuds and maybe just try it out sometime when you're bored and lonely, don't even think about the phone part, it's just about the music, and I know you like music, so you can dance with the trees. Okay, just slip the goods into the pockets in those cute purple pants, where did you get those pants, no, don't tell me, I know it's going to be somewhere in New York that isn't even open anymore but okay, kisses, don't forget to wipe everything off with alcohol when you get home and I'll see you tomorrow, girl, I'll be there waiting.

Things that make me feel less lonely tonight: looking up into someone's house and seeing a beautiful jade plant that's almost the same shape as the fir tree outside, an orange door next to a yellow light, hearing the water running underneath the street.

Things that make me feel less lonely tonight: leaning against the ivy and how it takes over, noticing how red a stop sign can be, looking up at the sculpture of the tree branches with the sky peeking through.

Things that make me feel less lonely tonight: the sound of someone sawing on their front stoop, which at first I thought was part of the music upstairs, the way even the ugliest light can create beautiful shadows, the way the moon can be lopsided like us.

And then I see a car for sale on the street, a Volvo station wagon not that different from the one I bought in New York, and it's like I'm remembering another world. Getting in that car and trying to remember how to drive, holding onto that steering wheel on the highway like I could fly.

I made it. Somehow, I made it. And then I ditched the car as soon as I got here, I didn't want to see that thing ever again.

That was only four months ago—how is this possible?

I'm leaning on one of my favorite hedges in the dark, and some woman comes over with her shaggy dog that's jumping all around. She's staring at me so I say hi.

She says excuse me, but I'd appreciate it if you didn't lean on my hedge. There are these brown parts, it's not healthy.

That's not because of me, I say.

I planted this new section, she says, and it's taking so long to grow in.

That's not my fault, I say. I lean on this hedge every day.

She says well I'd appreciate it if you didn't.

She leaves, and I'm thinking about burning the hedge down, I could go over to that smoke shop on Broadway that's been open the entire pandemic because it's an essential service, isn't it, I could buy lighter fluid and matches, roll up some newspapers and stuff them inside the hedge and then burn baby burn.

I'm trying to decide whether to go over there now, or wait until tomorrow, but then suddenly I'm struck by the sadness that's everything—I'm trying not to fall on the ground and just lie there, but would it feel good, okay let me try it. So I lie down right in the grass on Broadway and Aloha. And actually it does feel good, the dry grass and the stars, the way my body can relax into the ground, my breath going back, maybe I should do this more often.

I sit up, and someone walks by with some designer dog, pulling the leash tight like I'm a threat. I say hi, but this person says nothing, so I decide to sit here for a little longer, it's kind of comfortable, actually, I'm smelling the juniper and looking at the houses from the ground, there's a new fence over there with flat slats, more geometric than usual so the light comes through in a dramatic way and I wonder if they realize we can see through the slats. Oh, and that brick building across the street with the Murphy beds, there was this girl I met at a party after high school in the Summer of Love, that's what I called the summer before I went away to college, and I guess it wasn't too long before or was it after Rudy's death when I met this girl at a party in the U District, I can't remember how I got to the party or even who was there, but that's how that summer was, you ran into someone on the street and they were going somewhere and then you went too. And late that night I met this girl with a shaved head and tons of tattoos and plugs in her ears who said do you want to walk over the University Bridge? To see the sunrise.

She said it to everyone, but no one else wanted to go. And it was the best idea ever, standing on that bridge and the way it shook with the cars, all that pink in the sky and the water, the way the sky was the water yes we were on X we were in the sky and when we kissed everything was pulsing, I could feel that current going from lips into mouth down throat and into my pelvic floor, yes, there it was, the pelvic floor, just like my mothers taught me, I remember thinking about the wind on my legs, the wind blowing our hair all over the place, or my hair because she had a shaved head, and then we were holding hands in that way that meant forever so of course you know I never saw her again. Not after dropping her off at her apartment in that building right there, I remember thinking about the Murphy bed, how we were going to pull it out of the wall but at some point she asked me how old I was and even on ecstasy I could feel her surprise. But still all that air, I remember the air on that walk more than anything because I felt like, I felt like I was really living.

And then there was Rudy's memorial—I never saw my mothers argue because they would go in their Den of Iniquity but I could feel it when they were talking to me afterward, when we were looking at the invitations, Paula was the one sending them out. In Rudy's dementia she'd forgotten that Paula and Eileen were sober, or maybe she hadn't forgotten, but it said very specifically that everyone at the memorial had to do acid, those were her wishes, it was an acid memorial, dust to dust, acid to acid. I remember Paula saying of course we can't go, it would be disrespectful.

And I said what do you mean?

And Eileen said we thought of going, and not doing acid, but those weren't Rudy's wishes.

And Paula said we'll have our own memorial, and you'll be part of it.

And then there was a pause, and Eileen said we know you're an adult now, and we want you to make your own choices so naturally you are welcome to attend both memorials.

So of course I went. The memorial was called FAIRY DUST, and our job was to sprinkle Rudy's ashes all over the city in designated areas—Northgate Mall, Dilettante Chocolates, the Jade Pagoda, the urinal at the Brass Connection, the Swish Alps, Volunteer Park, Sodomy Point, inside the shoes at Nordstrom downtown, I can't remember where else—oh, the Cloud Room, that was supposed to be the finale.

Everyone had to dress up as one of Charlie's Angels.

NO BOSLEY, the invitation said.

ONLY GIRLS, I WANT YOU TO TAKE ME TO HEAVEN, GIRLS.

JUST KIDDING, NONE OF US ARE GETTING INTO HEAVEN BUT WE MIGHT AS WELL PRETEND.

And then at the bottom it said LEAVE MY FAIRY DUST WHERE IT BELONGS, IF THERE'S ANYWHERE I FORGOT I TRUST YOUR VISION, GIRLS. DUST TO DUST, MY DUSTY TRUSTY ACID ANGELS.

I went as Kelly because I looked more like her than the others, and I knew there would be a lot of Jills. I found this chartreuse pantsuit at Chicken Soup, and Paula had the perfect wig for me, she'd saved it from that trip to visit Eileen's mother when I was how old. Three or four, we were trying to remember. Paula styled the wig and did my makeup too—there was something in the way she was looking at me, I don't know how to describe it exactly, but it was like we were together again like when I was a kid, girls doing our hair, and it was okay for me to stay that way. I mean it was another decade or more before they really got it, but I guess they slowly stopped trying not to get it, that's what I mean. And when we were done I really did kind of look like Kelly, or at least enough for people to know who I was right away.

The memorial started at Rudy's apartment at the Biltmore, that's where we took the acid. Someone said a prayer, or something like a prayer, I don't remember what it was, I just remember that Carmen, this straight girl who used to work with Paula at the salon, who might have been the only Sabrina at the memorial, but she was a Sabrina porn star, she looked at me in surprise, and said where's Paula, is she too good for us now.

I felt like she was saying I didn't belong, but once the acid kicked in I forgot and I was just one of the girls, that's how everyone was treating me, not like a kid but like one of them.

Wait, there was another Sabrina, who was that? Someone made a rule that we could only call each other by who we were dressed as, and once we were all tripping it was hard to keep track of who was who, all these queens with their wigs and makeup and fake tits and everyone was at their weirdest and wildest and I was one of them, we were on an adventure together, scaring everyone in the ladies' room at the Northgate Mall, and someone called the cops.

The cops didn't know what to do.

Fifteen or twenty queens in the ladies' room at Northgate Mall, no one had seen this before.

Maybe it was the acid, but I swear it turned out Carmen knew one of the cops, they'd grown up together in Lynnwood, she gave him a hug and then everything was okay.

We had a procession of cars making our way across the city with Rudy's fairy dust, I remember I was in some big old '50s car with a burgundy velvet interior and someone kept calling it Rudy's Velvet Cunt and we were in it, we were in that cunt and I was feeling it.

I remember thinking, at a certain point, that the Velvet Cunt was our superpower, we could turn anything into velvet, and every time someone said cunt I could feel it, that velvet cunt and I don't know if I'd ever said cunt that much before but after that journey it was mine.

We were driving across the city, I don't remember the order except that we started at Northgate Mall because that was the furthest away, but I have no idea what came next. Someone made pot brownies, mint chocolate chip, and even though I knew they weren't vegan I couldn't resist and then there were snacks in the trunk of the Velvet Cunt, yes, open up the cunt, someone would say, get her open, and in the trunk there were all these pastries and croissants and I couldn't eat any of that even though I ate the pot brownie—that was special—but then there was this bread with nuts in it—walnuts, sunflower seeds, pecans, and cashews, and no one else was eating the bread because they had all the pastries and where did all this come from—oh, it was Big Teddy, who owned a bakery, I thought she was Kelly too but it turned out she was Julie, I was thinking Julie from *Love Boat* but that didn't make sense, do you see how it was getting confusing.

At a certain point I started to see our wings, they weren't like the way people thought of wings they were like little trails of stars, I was seeing all these stars I mean we were sparkling we were all made of fairy dust, right, I kept looking at the ashes we were ashes made of stars, fairy dust we were dust we were angels in the sky.

But also we were at Nordstrom, and our job was to slip Rudy's ashes into the shoes, so here we were, fifteen or twenty angels flying into the shoe department I saw our wings and someone said ruby slippers, I need ruby slippers, and everyone knew everyone in that shoe department, it was our department, the department of angels, and someone asked what size, and then this salesperson brought out a pair of ruby slippers, they were real, everyone could see, those were real rubies, slip them on, we were sprinkling fairy dust into the shoes on display but then we had the rubies too, those ruby slippers, when we got back into the Velvet Cunt with those rubies I asked if they were heavy, it was one of the Jills, she said heavy as stars, and I saw the wings coming out of her eyes we were staring into the wings we were flying, in the car we kept saying Jill is wearing Rudy's ruby slippers, we kept saying it, Rudy's ruby slippers, Rudy's ruby slippers, Rudy's ruby slippers and did I have another pot brownie, lemon water with mint, to balance our electrolytes, that velvet cunt, I could feel it, we were Rudy's ruby slippers in that velvet cunt, balancing our electrolytes we were at Sodomy Point with the water lilies and the geese no the geese were at Madison Beach, we were sprinkling the fairy dust for the geese they could fly we could fly and water, but where was it, near the end, yes, it was Volunteer Park, on the main lawn, I think it was dark at that point and I could really see the stars, we were drinking mushroom tea with sage and some queen came out of the bushes and said I want to join your party. And I was startled because I didn't realize, wait, what didn't I realize? I didn't realize there were humans here, that's what I remember thinking. Were angels human, that's what I was wondering.

And someone said ashes to ashes, dust to dust.

And this queen said who died. She didn't say it like she cared. She said it like death was getting in the way of her party.

And someone said Rudy Tuesday.

And this queen gasped and said: Rudy used to cut my hair. And she started sobbing, just like that, it was like she flipped the switch and then we were all sobbing, all of Rudy's ruby angels, we were sobbing together in the grass in the sky with our wings but now we were falling.

Yes, I'm out in the poisonous hellscape, burning eyes and wind blowing the ash in all directions, air we're not supposed to breathe and yet still the coolness on my skin. The yellow-gray light of the sooty sky—Seattle, if you need to cry today, I recommend crying inside. If you cry outside, it will really burn your eyes.

But I do appreciate that the crows have a lot to say. Even today, they have a lot to say.

I make it to the park and there's no one out, no one at all, and I'm so tired that I just fall down in the grass and try to pass out. It kind of works, but when I sit up my nostrils are so dry they feel sealed shut, and my neck hurts so much from keeping the mask on that I take it off—oh, it smells like I'm in the Holland Tunnel, put that mask back on.

Stumbling back home, I'm trying to focus on the flowers—the world is dying, but there are still so many flowers.

The air is better in my apartment now, but it's hard for me to keep the windows closed because it feels so stuffy. I never close the windows, not all the way. I call Jaysun. She says girl, I can't believe you went out there, are you okay?

No, I'm not okay, I'm sitting here trying to decide which is worse—the headache from staying inside, the headache from going outside, or the headache from trying to decide.

Girl, is your air purifier not working?

Not enough.

I should've warned you, after the last few years of forest fires I bought six air purifiers—two for the living room, one for each bedroom, one in the bathroom, one in the kitchen, and one in the hallway, Blueair, because they're not as ugly—I know they're still ugly, but not that ugly, and you know I'm a tacky bitch anyway. Wait, is that seven—I guess I have seven air purifiers, maybe one day I'll learn how to count.

Honey, where do you keep seven air purifiers?

In my storage unit, of course, girl, don't you have one?

After I get off the phone, I realize I'm totally dehydrated even though I already drank three glasses of water when I got home, but I drink another four and then the bloating kicks in but I need to eat anyway so I heat up some millet with steamed vegetables and black-eyed peas and it tastes pretty good but then my whole body hurts so I lie on the floor until I realize that makes my body hurt more so I get out my stretching mat but here's the headache again, that pounding in my temples, and then the sinus headache from the poison outside, and then the headache behind my eyes from everything, do I need more water, why do I still feel thirsty.

Then I realize it's almost 8:00 p.m., so I rush outside and it's dark out already, I pull off my mask and scream Black Lives Matter, Abolish the Police, three times like usual, and my throat hurts, but then I blow the whistle to the same tune, the crescendo into the blow out, I mean I'm blowing as hard as possible to make as much noise as I can until the whistle blows out of my mouth and it's just me out here tonight, just me with the burning eyes and the scratchy throat, the streets are abandoned.

I go back inside, and take a quick shower to rinse off the smoke, and in the shower I realize this is my opportunity—it's dark out, no one's outside, I have a little hammer, let's play.

So I get out the dead raver outfit, but then I figure I should wear a dress underneath, so I can pull off the jacket and the hood, flip the dress over the pants, tie the jacket around my waist, and then I'll be a totally different person, right?

Maybe that long dress Sid made for me, the one she sewed from all these different squares of polyester fabric, contrasting patterns tight around my chest and then flaring way out at the bottom, all the way down to my ankles, oh it's so gorgeous even if it is much tighter now, but no, I don't want to wear this out in the doomsday hellscape, let's save it for later.

Tonight it's just dead raver, let's try it out and see how it goes. With those black glasses and the N95, dead raver on doomsday, how could I go wrong.

Music, I need music, don't I?

I haven't taken the phone yet, should I do it? I mean I found some good mixes on SoundCloud, Jaysun was right about SoundCloud, I just haven't tried it out in the world.

Let's dance, Terry, let's dance.

But wait, let's make a plan first. Somewhere to try out this little hammer. Maybe those new box condos on Harrison, why not?

But first let's go over on 13th, past Union, there are whole alleys filled with those cracker boxes, as Tia calls them, nothing else but cracker boxes.

But Terry, that's too far, isn't it? Let's start with Harrison.

But is that too close?

I turn on the music, yes, beat beat beat my house, that's what it's saying, how can you argue with beat beat beat my house, any house song that says house is my favorite house.

Okay, here we are in the hazy streets, beat beat beat my house—yes, Terry, this music is so good, why didn't I try this before. Yes, that build with the beats spinning out behind me, spinning me out, yes, Terry, I'm ready, the burning eyes behind the glasses, use those burning eyes.

Wait, Capitol Hill Wealth Management.

This beat, we're here in the smoke, they've definitely turned up that fog machine. Where is everyone? The music is fantastic, we should do this more often.

Oh, too many lights at Capitol Hill Wealth Management, and I would have to walk past the hedge and onto their property. Not a good idea, let's just dance against this hedge, yes, loosen your back, honey, let it go, use that headache, let it glow.

But is this song talking about my fine ass, how did they know?

Terry, what's next?

Okay, Harrison.

Wait, wait, Mercer. No, those windows are way too small. They aren't even worth shattering.

Back to Harrison, where the landscaping is already dead. The one my mothers pointed out. Yes, this is it, honey, this is it.

Take the hammer, take the hammer, wait, wait for the beat, use that wrist, oh, yes, add that shattered glass to the soundtrack, another window, please, another window, another window.

No alarms, I don't hear any alarms. Alarms, alarms—even if I love that sound, and it would go great with the music, we don't need alarms, Terry, do we.

My heart is pounding, but Terry, this is the best I've felt in a while.

Still no one around. We'll just saunter down Federal, slip across Broadway, take the back route behind QFC and then over to home, sweet home. Pick up my mail, yes, my mail. Use it to fan my face. Honey, where did you get that fan?

Back in the shower to wash everything off, Terry, that was fun. Your hair looks pretty good for the apocalypse. So I guess those movies were right about something.

But why did I keep all my windows closed when I went to bed, why? Because that's what everyone recommends, with the poison air, and yes my face hurt so much when I got inside, but this is worse, now I feel like I'll never breathe again so I get up and open all the windows, I need air, even if it smells like someone's smoking in my bed, why is there so much poison in this world.

They told us the air quality would be better tomorrow. Tomorrow is taking a long time to get here. Apparently, when you obsessively refresh the air quality report, this doesn't improve the air quality.

Didn't they say that our dear president is scheduled to visit the forest fires? And I think it might really really help, if he just stays there, by the fire, don't you think.

Fighting fire with fire, thoughts and prayers?

But today I wipe the dust off the tops of the doors, put the bathmat in the dryer to freshen it up, open and close the windows to see if maybe, just maybe, is there any air out there, no. So I check the air quality again to find out it's the worst it's been yet. I'm doing great, really, I'm great.

Today I'm crying before I leave the house, which is a good thing because maybe my eyes won't burn as much when I'm outside.

But I have a plan, I have a plan tonight, and it's lucky thirteen, Jaysun was right, this hammer, it's hammer time, join me. I've saved my place in the music, all we have to do is press play.

Okay, okay, a dark alley filled with particleboard-and-plastic boxes under construction, no one around, let's work the magic, this music needs a little bit of "Warm Leatherette." You know—that shattering glass sound. Take us there, Terry, take us there.

Oh, honey, this isn't just Grace Jones's "Warm Leatherette," this is the Peter Rauhofer remix, yes, Ms. Rauhofer, just when we need her—Vienna calling. But this isn't Falco, it's New York.

This is New York, and Seattle. Smash that glass, honey, smash that glass. Redecorate.

Oh, that sound, honey, it's everything.

It's me, Lula, I'm in the speaker.

Did I mention these ones have flashing lights? Yes, light show, it's a light show.

But no sound, not yet, I've got that on my headphones.

Oh, someone over there, a dog walker, focus on the music. It's all about the music, Terry, the runway, let's go.

Honey, this is making me edgy, you didn't tell me about all the edges. Go slow. Don't look back. Is this real, this is the reel. Am I real?

Okay, we made it to the other side, past the Cuff, still those rainbow lights in the sidewalk, are they open?

Terry, let's not check.

Okay, we made it, my whole body is shaking, Terry, you didn't tell me about the shaking, and I need to shit, Terry, I really need to shit, okay, can we make it to that garden down the street, oh, it's so much further than I thought, I'm sweating so much, take off the jacket, take off the mask, take off the glasses, throw your hair up, let them see you, you're someone else, yes, finally, we're finally there, behind Andrea's house, or what used to be Andrea's house, the corner of the beautiful garden between buildings, not quite a public garden but not quite not a public garden, down this way, along this new cement wall, yes, don't fall, yes, down here, it's a little hard to balance but let's pull down those pants and let it out, yes, that feels better. Cover it up with dirt and leaves, okay, check in with the trees—that old pear tree in the back, oh I love her so much. Now, back to dead raver realness, let's get ourselves home.

Seattle, even the rain is letting us down, what is wrong with this rain? It's not improving the air quality, it's just bringing the pollution closer. But the music has been great, we've been having so much fun at the club, haven't we, the club of broken glass, now for the music of

8:00 p.m., that's just us, Terry, get ready to yell yes my voice is getting hoarse but that's nothing that a thousand throat lozenges can't fix for at least a few minutes. Black Lives Mat-ter, Abolish the Police. Black Lives Mat-ter, Abolish the Police. Black Lives Mat-ter, Abolish the Police. And now, for the whistle.

Seattle, we're watching that air quality report go from HAZARDOUS to VERY UNHEALTHY to UNHEALTHY, but we're still hovering at the border of VERY UNHEALTHY—no, I'm not obsessively checking the readings, not at all. Can we make it down to UNHEALTHY FOR SENSITIVE GROUPS, or MODERATE, or even, one day, GOOD?

In the meantime, I'm making it over to take care of some more windows, yes, let's hear it for the broken glass soundtrack, and don't worry, it's not just any windows Terry Dactyl takes care of, just the ones in uninhabited, better-left-unfinished trash heaps of new construction, and yes, they're just going to replace the windows, but we might as well have some fun before then, don't you think? So many opportunities—Harrison or 10th or, well, no need to list them, just listen to this song saying party from the East to the West Coast, yes, Terry, we are that bridge from east to west, hammering to those tinny beats fading out—can we get some more bass, Terry, turn up the bass.

Oh, those snaky snares, freaky flares, brakey blares, move those hips yes the hips and a little tap to get that subtle explosion, just checking to see if we have double pane windows, no more pain we're leaving it here in the broken glass, yes, I'm leaning against the railing on the stairway leading into this tiny park at night, and a woman living in the park comes up to ask me if I'm okay, do I need any water, and how this gesture of kindness makes me feel so present and so sad at once. How the world destroys the people who will offer you water, pushes them aside.

Then she goes over to give water to the giant tree in the traffic island, before saying a prayer for it, and then going back to dismantling shopping carts to place them upside-down on the stairway. I'm saying this is someone we need, even if this country tells us to discard her.

I keep thinking about the twelve million dollar settlement for Breonna Taylor's murder, how this is described as historic. When I say I keep thinking about it, I mean I keep sobbing.

Historic. I can't get this out of my head. Breonna Taylor's dead body is worth twelve million dollars.

But Seattle, there's big news. The air quality has slipped into UNHEALTHY FOR SENSITIVE GROUPS—I am sensitive groups, but let's keep this rain going so we can get to MODERATE or even GOOD or what about VERY GOOD I know that isn't on the chart because I guess we never get there, but what about EXCELLENT or DELIGHTFUL or FABULOUS or PHENOMENAL or SPECTACULAR, yes, I want SPECTACULAR air, don't you? But did I tell you about my headache, my burning eyes, my broken body, a history of shattered glass?

What is mourning, and what is rage? What is silence, and what is a cage? I'm screaming Black Lives Matter, Abolish the Police until my voice is hoarse I need to rest so I'm on my way up the hill to the oasis, yes, the garage oasis, tonight we are finally going to try out that jacuzzi, yes, Terry, it's time for the jacuzzi. Let's just keep that garage door closed and take the side door, oh it smells awful in here, how did all the smoke get inside, maybe if I open the skylight and let the night in but wait, there's an air filtration system, isn't there, yes, turn it on, Terry, turn that filter on. Oh, do we need music, no, water, wait, I need to shit again, it's all coming out now, Terry, let it out and yes, let's wash off all the ash in the shower before the jacuzzi, such great water pressure, it feels so good on my neck, watching the plants through the glass door and then there's the moonlight up above, soft towels, yes, my makeup got wet but now it looks even better, Terry, what did you put in your hair, all that bounce, are you using Pantene for the apocalypse?

I think the air is starting to smell like air, maybe I should sleep here, this air filter is better than mine, and all these vines, let's climb the vines, oh, the jacuzzi, let's fill it up, watch the plants growing while we wait, all these psychedelic pink and purple leaves with green at the edges, what are those called? Coleus, yes, coleus for color. And colon, is this what my colon looks like, all the shit finally coming out, Terry, we can only hope for the softness of these leaves. Those plants like peace lilies but with the bright red leaves that feel like plastic, the ridges on the stamen, we all know what that looks like, Georgia

O'Keefe, that spongy feeling, how the leaves stay cool in the heat, all these pothos vines and spider plants and ferns, so many textures of leaves and all the plants with names I don't know, climbing the walls, we're climbing up to the sky and yes, the jacuzzi is ready, I think it's ready. Let's just drink a few more bottles of water, so glad there's bottled water here.

Terry, this was the best idea ever, there's so much space I can stretch all the way out so much room turn on the jets, yes, feel that back massage, shoulders and ribs, tits and sternum and legs, hands and thighs and feet I can feel my body relaxing, all that tension going into the water and sinking down, yes, down and sure I can still smell the smoke but it must not be as bad because now I'm actually breathing, yes, I think I'm breathing, let's feel those jets massaging my ass and I'm leaning back to take it all in until a sudden shaking of the garage door or is that my heart, someone says back door is open and I think of running but where would I go I'm naked in the jacuzzi with all the shimmering plants the door opens someone yells police a gun pointing right at my face two guns this isn't happening, Terry, is this happening I'm trying to say something I don't know what to say how do you speak to a gun and suddenly the gun goes down there's a face, it's a cop saying I think we made a mistake.

And the other, behind him, he puts down his gun too.

Do you live here, the first cop says.

I'm trying to say something but I can't so I nod my head, he says do you live here?

And I say my mothers.

You're visiting, he says.

And I nod my head.

I'm just sitting there naked in the tub in the moonlight I don't know how to hide until he says ma'am, sir, my apologies, and he takes off his hat to salute me, is that what he's doing, and then he turns to leave, the other cop is already out the door.

He closes the door and then I hear them walking up the stairs I hear them talking to my mothers, I hear them walking down the stairs, I hear them leaving and then someone's knocking, Paula's knocking at the door, she says Terry, we are so sorry. I hear her saying Terry, we had no idea, I hear her saying Terry, we panicked, we haven't gone outside in days, because of the smoke, we weren't thinking rationally, we thought how could anyone be out there, who would be out there, Terry, we are so sorry.

I'm sobbing and I'm shaking, I'm sobbing and I'm shaking, I'm sobbing and I'm shaking I can't stop sobbing and shaking and Terry, is the water getting cold.

Yes, I'm dancing in the Union graveyard, the music keeping me here among the living with the trees and the plush grass tilted at just the right angle to stay dry enough to fall into without any muddy messes yes I need my earthly caresses, see the way the sway turns the world and then the twirling into dizziness opens the gate between ground and sky.

There's a fine line between embodiment and dissociation, and I've crossed it. The trick is finding the switch to bring you back, but why, keep me here in these beats, yes, the other trick is making sure there's something worth coming back to.

There are two kinds of sleep—the kind that feels terrible the whole time, and the kind that feels terrible as soon as I wake up. Last night, though, in my dreams, I was offered the opportunity to dance at the opening reception for a new sleep supplement that promised it MUTILATES THE BROKEN RAIN WITH DANCE MUSICAL—talk about a dream job.

But I didn't even have a chance to respond, because then I woke up.

Terry, turn up the beat. Are they staring so intently at the graves to avoid looking at me, the living, dancing in the sun to the build and the bounce, the pounce and flounce and stretch out the arms to the sky and beyond baby I'm beyond or was there a special report on this Civil War graveyard that brought them here today, while I'm dancing to the song that says LEAVE MY BODY AND FLOAT AWAY yes Terry let's float away into the air raid siren damaging our eardrums who needs eardrums when you can float into that siren, yes.

Falling down a stairway in the darkness with maybe the moon as my witness, yes, there's a DJ in the park—I'm the DJ, I'm the DJ, I'm the DJ—thank you, Jaysun, for giving me this magic DJ but why are people staring at me when they could just join in but staring is caring so that means I'm dancing really dancing, yes, we're all here together in the park this is everything I needed this whole goddamn terrifying year.

How is it that I haven't done drugs in seven hundred million years, but whenever I hear BUMPS in a dance song I'm like yes girl here I come, the weaving back and forth across the street to avoid human contact, yes, make it bigger, Terry, take the distance and live in those

253

BUMPS, yes, one way to get enough energy to dance is to give up, try anyway, give up while trying, give in on the giving up, keep trying anyway, and somewhere past the giving up there's the glide, the flow, the softness, and maybe, sometimes, flight.

This song says SHALL WE DANCE, SHALL WE DANCE, and you know when the song says SHALL WE DANCE there's only one answer.

Just slipping under this one layer of dehydration, into the sweat that feels like salvation, and somewhere, on the other side of movement through sun and sweat, yes, please, more water. If only that water could feel like salvation too, for more than a few seconds.

If only anything could feel like salvation, for more than a few seconds. Invincibility, by which I mean opening up into the space, by which I mean vulnerability, by which I mean transcendence, by which I mean experiencing every sensation at once, by which I mean dancing, by which I mean breath.

To live in a body that isn't only a body of loss. To live in a body that isn't only a body of loss. To live in a body that isn't only a body. To live, in a body.

Imagining an entire world in the swinging of the vertical blinds in the wind, the spaces between, the light peeking through, the way they lean into one another, flip in and out, rotate back and forth, this could go on forever, the repetition and variation, on and on, this dance. Yes, I'm outside looking up, up, up with the noise of the highway my muse in the dark the wind blowing those blinds how there can be so much life in dreaming, a whole other world that feels like the world, everything, but then you wake up and feel like what the hell is this, how can I even get out of bed, no, I'm not going to stop dancing with this tree just because you're staring at me, okay? I want to feel all the moss, honey, you would be staring at me anyway. Stare all you want.

Okay, he went back into his house between graveyards, yes, he lives between graveyards, and don't we all. I know people like to invoke the power of the imagination, but sometimes it feels like there's so little imagination left in this world that it's scary.

But wait, here he is again, right behind me. Yes, he just came back out of the house with his leaf blower to get me to stop dancing with this tree. Keep dancing, Terry, don't even acknowledge that noise, he's not even there, fall gently to the side and twirl around into runway, yes, runway, walk, Terry, walk away and don't even look back.

So I'm dancing on a muddy hill in a vacant lot across the street from a building called DECIBEL. I'm out in that coat that looks like it was made from someone's '70s sofa, big fake fur collar and it's wool, honey, it repels the moisture, you can just brush the mud off, yes, here comes someone to take a video to show to his friends. Dancing is fun when no one's watching, but isn't it better when they are.

So I've become one of those people who walks around with headphones in her ears, listening to, what is she listening to?

Yes, end-of-the-world songs are always better than love-the-world songs, just like end-of-the-relationship songs are always better than relationship songs. Oh, Terry, the looks people give you just for doing a little dancing in a sun spot in the fresh mulch between the sidewalk and street, I mean the looks people give you just for trying to survive.

Give me something else, honey, give me something else.

When you're enjoying the sparkling lights on a downtown construction site in the distance, you know something must have changed, the light suddenly inside, let's keep it sparkling. So you're looking at the shiny condom wrappers under this tree, but it turns out they're hearts, yes, little shiny hearts in the dirt, just waiting.

And then more dog walkers in the graveyard looking at me like I'm completely incomprehensible when they are the ones turning the graveyard into an obstacle course with all that dogshit.

To dream of a world without this world in it.

To dream of this world without this world in it.

To dream of this world.

Yes, the best way to dance is with a broken heart. A dead leaf flying through the air like a butterfly. Music that tightrope between expansion and dislocation, renovation and retaliation, which way to cross.

To fall by the wayside. Whose side? To fall. To fall by. Falling.

That particular type of energy that consists of no energy plus less energy plus trying to figure out a way to figure out a way to have energy.

Yes, I'm sitting on a bike rack on the street, tears and the darkness, stay with the feeling, stay.

Yes, I'm lying on my back in the middle of the Cal Anderson playfield, looking up except I'm not looking, tears pouring to the sides, both sides, and when I open my eyes I'm looking out at the super bright stadium lights but it's just me and the sky and the astroturf. I like going to movies alone but sometimes you need to talk to someone after the movie, right? But when does this movie end.

Yes, the gold dress, Terry, get out there in the gold sequined dress, sequins of all sizes falling onto the ground, expand the action with all those tutus underneath, it's a golden day for feeling or frozen, feeling frozen it's all at once how I need that place where my body lives inside touch, where my body lives in motion I mean skin touching skin I need that so badly, Terry, we're all dressed up and nowhere to go but an empty astroturf drizzle field, feel the purple glitter silver makeup, the metallic lashes, back splashes. So so badly. How I'm crying again, almost, even with all these bright lights of the stadium playfield. Someone's kicking a soccer ball against the wall, and someone's walking a dog, and people are on the tennis court with their skateboards and a plane is flying over and there are cars driving by but still it's quiet, inside, with all this feeling. The possibility of trauma melting, the possibility for trauma to slide off, to slip away, the possibility for skin to skin in the dream of lips, bodies in motion without fear. How a movie is only a movie until we breathe. That sudden feeling of what drugs gave me, a place to exist in the pain, a way to take everything up a notch, up, up, up and away, right, that's what this movie is, those chills and sweats the pulsing in all directions wait look at your eyes. It's all there, in the eyes taking off.

I want in, and I want out.

Trauma as a place you can live in, right? We live there. We live there we live there we live there. How to feel it. How to move on.

Or just how to move. How to move, anyway. Body as an opening. I want this. I want. This. Sink into the astroturf, Terry, we've got the purple coat, dreaming of Sid. Everything that grows in an alley. It would be so much easier with touch, this I know, and yet.

How a tree can be so full of leaves and yet so tentatively. Yes, a pureed carrot-fennel-parsnip soup is the perfect treat to make at this time of year. Just throw three carrots, one parsnip, and one fennel bulb into a pot with water barely covering the vegetables, bring to boil then simmer for ten minutes and puree in the blender. The hardest part is not licking the blade at the end because you want to eat all the remnants. I can't believe I've been trying to digest food for this long—all my life, right? And yet.

Is there an award for the most throat lozenges consumed in a day, a month, a year, because, if so, I think I might be eligible.

The sound of the rain hitting the wet leaves on the ground but also the way the leaves reflect the lights in Volunteer Park, the pale cloudy sky and the silhouettes of the trees, so much sensation. How a tree can provide shade even at night and is this about the persistence of sky.

I will never understand the dream where you wake up because the light is so bright, but then you're awake and you think how is the light so bright when my eyes are closed and there's no light in the room. But also maybe this is what all dreams are like.

To be trapped in a state of expectation that feels like mourning, to be trapped in a state of mourning that feels like grief, to be trapped in a state of grief that becomes an expectation.

But there's finally good news—Donald Trump has COVID, and the whole world is celebrating, doesn't it feel different, Terry?

Yes, suddenly it feels different.

DO YOU THINK IT'S CUTE THAT I'M SO STUPID, this graffiti says—and, yes, it's cute, it's cute. FTP on the Parks Department lawn sign. BREAK THIS on the windows of Wells Fargo. ACAB on the entry gate to some mansion. PEEPSHOW on the sewer grate. But the newest addition is a graffiti gravestone that says.

TRUMP

COVID DENIER

1946–2020

R.I.P. BITCH

Everything written in red and outlined in black, with red flowers growing out of the black grass, and this is everything, isn't it.

MDMA up above, is that the graffiti artist's name—who is this girl, we might be speaking the same language.

Tonight more people join me at 8:00 p.m. for Black Lives Matter, Abolish the Police, yes, there's more noise tonight, isn't there? Everyone is celebrating. Then I'm back inside, and thinking that finally my apartment smells like clear crisp fresh fall air, yes, it's all blowing into my apartment I'm enjoying the air, and what is that, wait, do you hear something, Terry, is that a protest, I lean out my window, and yes, there it is, coming toward me on Harvard, so I throw on a mask and the purple coat, and I rush outside, yes, it's a Black Bloc protest, and I'm in purple, I'm at the back, at least a hundred people, which is large for the Black Bloc marches, masks and goggles and helmets and some gas masks and shields, graffiti along the way but why does it smell so much like smoke, oh, people are carrying incense, gross, why are they carrying incense, maybe so people don't notice the smell of spray paint so I move to the front, yes, now I'm at the front, more goggles and gas masks and another colorful girl my height or actually she's taller, probably a trans girl, she's got the goggles and the helmet but she's also got the color and we're jumping up and down as everyone's chanting DIE, TRUMP, DIE, yes this is the best thing ever and I yell AND BIDEN TOO, and then people are yelling DIE, TRUMP, DIE, AND BIDEN TOO, DIE, TRUMP, DIE, AND BIDEN TOO, DIE, TRUMP, DIE, AND BIDEN TOO, DIE, TRUMP, DIE, AND BIDEN TOO, DIE, TRUMP, DIE, AND BIDEN TOO, WHOSE LIVES MATTER, BLACK LIVES MATTER, WHOSE LIVES MATTER, BLACK LIVES MATTER, WHOSE LIVES MATTER, BLACK LIVES MATTER, WHOSE LIVES MATTER, BLACK LIVES MATTER, some guy in a gas mask leans over to give me the elbow bump, and then this guy says Terry, that coat, we should all be in purple, wait, it's Tia, no wonder I've never seen her at the protests, she's in disguise, is someone drumming or is that just the feeling of the best dance party ever, yes I'm jumping up and down and when we turn on Olive Way, going down the hill, I look back to see TRANNIES FOR ABOLITION spray painted in pink on the boards covering cc's, finally something to brighten up all that gray and gay, gay and gray, and we're going downhill are we going downtown but then suddenly people rush toward the Starbucks, don't look at them just listen, yes, metal hitting glass it takes several hits that glass is strong but when it shatters it's the Peter Rauhofer remix of Grace Jones's "Warm Leatherette" TIMES TEN yes it's that good, yes, listen to that shattering glass, it's everything, Terry, it's everything, and then suddenly the cops are there, probably they were just waiting because there's already a cop on a megaphone in the distance saying YOU ARE ORDERED TO DISPERSE, and the funny thing is that now I feel safer in purple, safer without a gas mask, safer because I can just walk away and say who, me, I don't even know what you're talking about, so I continue down the hill past Starbucks as everyone else rushes in the other direction and the police sirens are going off but I've always loved this corner, ever since I was a kid, walking out of the Biltmore and its own little enclave, but then we would get to Summit, turn toward Olive and there it was, the city, and that's when I first started dreaming of New York, looking downtown at the lights even though this was much more like New York, right here, outside the Biltmore in our own little world and now I'm walking downtown, there's that fancy pot shop on the corner with the sea creature murals, next door to the Olive Terrace, where Jaysun lived after Brad kicked her out—I hear the police sirens behind me, and Terry, I do like the way the wind blows the coat out, the glamour of the wind and which way, which way should we go, Terry, let's try Bellevue to Pine, but oh, Terry, suddenly I need to shit, not again, yes again, but where, Terry, where, okay, Freeway Park, it's been a while, yes, Freeway Park, let's get there as fast as possible, oh, this wind, I do like this wind, but all these new buildings, every one as ugly as the last but nothing as ugly as the new convention center they're building in that ditch, but why can't we ditch convention, I guess this new one on the right is going to be called Pivot, will the whole building pivot, Terry, pivot, Terry, pivot, Terry, pivot, but Terry, we need to get to Freeway Park, that's the way, the way for freedom, the freedom to shit, let's take the shortcut, the shortcut is still here but oh, downtown Seattle really is hideous, isn't it, but let's stay focused, we need to shit, and not in your pants, Terry, okay, not in your pants, at least we made the light. And, yes, it still says ACAB on these pillars, one letter for each pillar, and in between you can see the Camlin Hotel but it's not alone anymore, it's just this little old building in between towers, I wonder what the Cloud Room is like now, can you still see the clouds? Rudy, can you still see the clouds?

Okay, run, Terry, run downtown toward that glass tower under construction with those annihilating white lights but instead let's go left up the stairs so many stairs you didn't tell me there were so many stairs, Terry, around the cement wall, Terry, there's so much cement, you didn't tell me about all the cement for whose convention, no more conventions, Terry, where, okay, jump up past the rose garden, around this corner, okay, it already smells, pull up your coat and pull down your pants, I'm suddenly covered in sweat and there it goes, all of it, let it all out, okay, why is there burning, more piss, try to get it all out, Terry, we need to start carrying toilet paper around, don't we.

Wait, alcohol prep pads, yes, at least I have these in my pockets to keep my hands clean—thank you, COVID-19, for the alcohol prep pads.

Okay, stand up, push these leaves over to cover it all up, walk away from this smelly corner, at least we have this corner, thank you.

Honey, if I lose it entirely, you'll be here to witness, right? Maybe if we witness together, we can avoid losing it entirely.

But how is the highway so loud, there aren't that many cars but it's still so loud, no one in the park, I thought there would be people camped out but the cops must be coming through all the time there's always time for more cops but still I love this park, isn't it a miracle, how there can be all these trees growing on top of the highway.

But were the trees here always this big?

Of course not, Terry, we've all grown up, we've grown up together, but Terry, should we turn on the music.

ACKNOWLEDGMENTS

As always, I want to thank the brilliant and generous writers and friends, friends and writers who gave me crucial feedback on the manuscript—Jennifer Natalya Fink, Corinne Manning, Cara Hoffman, Emmy Smith-Stewart, Sarah Schulman, a million thanks to all of you for such deep engagement!

While I was writing this book, I read every chapter over the phone to Joey Carducci, and this deeply enriched every aspect of the process.

This book emerged sometime in the early part of the COVID-19 pandemic, I think it was in 2021 when I was going on long walks at every chance, and the character of Terry Dactyl emerged in my head, and everywhere I was walking I was thinking about her in minute detail—the house where she grew up, her formative years in Seattle, her relationship with her mothers—I thought this might be a short story, since I couldn't stop thinking about it. Even though I was finishing *Touching the Art* so I couldn't work on it yet, I just kept ruminating on every detail, and I shared some of my ideas with Adrian Lambert, who said absolutely, that would make a great book, and I thought what, I just meant a story. But of course Adrian was right, and here she is, *Terry Dactyl*. So even though Adrian and I are not friends anymore, maybe this book exists as part of the legacy of our friendship.

For tangibles and intangibles: Kevin Darling, Andy Slaght, Jessica Lawless, Todd Bohannon, Tony Radovich, Jed Walsh, Alex Neff, Morgan Owens, Dana Middleton, Jacob Olson, Dana Garza, Yasmin Nair, Alyssa Harad, Matthew Schnirmann, Kristen Millares Young, Katie Ellison, Lauren Goldstein, Jason Sellards, Karen Maeda Allman, Zee Boudreaux, Steve Zeeland, Keidy Merida, Devyn Mañibo, Madeline ffitch, David Naimon, Jory Mickelson, Karin Goldstein, Jack Curtis Dubowsky, Jeannie Vanasco, Christina Sharpe, Catherine Lacey, McKenzie Wark, Lisa Ko, Isabel Waidner, and anyone else I may have inadvertently forgotten—in spite of the length of this list, I'm sure there are many.

To Jason Porter and Heaven Quiban at the Seattle Art Museum for getting this party started in the ideal space.

To my editor at Coffee House, Jeremy M. Davies, for taking on this manuscript, yes, what a delight and an honor to work with you! Can't wait for more . . .

And, to the entire staff at Coffee House for going that extra level to make this a truly intimate and collaborative relationship, from the start. In particular, working with Laura Graveline and Mark Haber on publicity and marketing was truly a pleasure and a joy, and working with Robyn Earhart on production was always streamlined and connected. Thanks, also, to Sarah Schulte for the stunning book cover, it couldn't be more perfect! And, to everyone else at Coffee House who I may not have worked with as directly, thank you for all your work to create this gorgeous book.

To my agent, Rebecca Friedman, for accompanying me on this journey, always a thrill to work with you—to more magic and mayhem, please. And, to my speaking agent, Leslie Shipman, for all your support.

An early excerpt from a draft of this book appeared in the Nonbinary Issue of *Women's Studies Quarterly*, Fall/Winter 2023, thanks to editors Red Washburn and JV Fuqua.

As *Terry Dactyl* is about to come out, I'm emerging from a health crisis that I never could have imagined, after an emergency appendectomy and a frightening month-long hospital stay, so I want to thank everyone who has supported me during this crisis—visiting me in the hospital, bringing me things I need, sending me flowers, going on walks with me. Honestly I couldn't do it without you, so thank you all for everything, I'm so touched by this communal response.

And, last, no writer is a writer without other writers—I'm thankful for all of you, really. Let's do this together.

Coffee House Press began as a small letterpress operation in 1972 and has grown into an internationally renowned nonprofit publisher of literary fiction, essay, poetry, and other work that doesn't fit neatly into genre categories.

LITERATURE
is not the same thing as
PUBLISHING

FUNDER ACKNOWLEDGMENTS

Coffee House Press is an internationally renowned independent book publisher and arts nonprofit based in Minneapolis, MN; through its literary publications, Coffee House acts as a catalyst and connector—between authors and readers, ideas and resources, creativity and community, inspiration and action.

Coffee House Press books are made possible through the generous support of grants and donations from corporations, state and federal grant programs, family foundations, and the many individuals who believe in the transformational power of literature. This activity is made possible by the voters of Minnesota through a Minnesota State Arts Board Operating Support grant, thanks to the legislative appropriation from the Arts and Cultural Heritage Fund. Coffee House also receives major operating support from the Amazon Literary Partnership, McKnight Foundation, and the National Endowment for the Arts (NEA). To find out more about how NEA grants impact individuals and communities, visit www.arts.gov.

Coffee House Press receives additional support from Bookmobile; the Buckley Charitable Fund; Dorsey & Whitney LLP; and the Schwab Charitable Fund.

THE PUBLISHER'S CIRCLE OF COFFEE HOUSE PRESS

Publisher's Circle members make significant contributions to Coffee House Press's annual giving campaign. Understanding that a strong financial base is necessary for the press to meet the challenges and opportunities that arise each year, this group plays a crucial part in the success of Coffee House's mission.

Recent Publisher's Circle members include many anonymous donors, Patricia A. Beithon, Robin Chemers Neustein, Kelli Cloutier, Theodore Cornwell, Jane Dalrymple-Hollo, Jeremy M. Davies, Mary Ebert and Paul Stembler, Kamilah Foreman, Eva Galiber, Bryan Garrett, Roger Hale and Nor Hall, William Hardacker, Randy Hartten and Ron Lotz, Carl and Heidi Horsch, Amy L. Hubbard and Geoffrey J. Kehoe Fund of the St. Paul & Minnesota Foundation, Hyde Family Charitable Fund, Kenneth & Susan Kahn, the Kenneth Koch Literary Estate, Cinda Kornblum, the Lenfestey Family Foundation, Carol and Aaron Mack, Gillian McCain, Mary and Malcolm McDermid, Daniel N. Smith III and Maureen Millea Smith, Vance Opperman, Mr. Pancks' Fund in memory of Graham Kimpton, Alan Polsky, Robin Preble, Ronald Restrepo and Candace S. Baggett, Elizabeth Schnieders, Steve Smith, Jeffrey Sugerman and Sarah Schultz, Paul Thissen, Allyson Tucker, Grant Wood, Margaret Wurtele, Aptara Inc., The Buckley Charitable Fund, Dorsey and Whitney Foundation.

For more information about the Publisher's Circle and other ways to support Coffee House Press books, authors, and activities, please visit www.coffeehousepress.org/pages/donate or contact us at info@coffeehousepress.org.

Mattilda Bernstein Sycamore is the Lambda Literary Award-winning author of seven books, and the editor of six anthologies. Her most recent title, *Touching the Art*, was a finalist for a Washington State Book Award and a Pacific Northwest Book Award. Her previous title, *The Freezer Door*, was a *New York Times* Editors' Choice and a finalist for the PEN/Jean Stein Book Award.

Terry Dactyl was designed by Bookmobile Design & Digital Publisher Services. Text is set in Adobe Caslon Pro.